I0772313

THE HOLLIS TIMEWIRE SERIES
BOOK 3

THE PURE ONES

DANIELLE HARRINGTON

FROM THE TINY ACORN . . .
GROWS THE MIGHTY OAK

www.AcornPublishingLLC.com

For information, address:
Acorn Publishing, LLC
3943 Irvine Blvd. Ste. 218
Irvine, CA 92602

ISBN-13: 979-8-88528-047-1 (hardcover)
ISBN-13: 979-8-88528-046-4 (paperback)
Library of Congress Control Number: 2023901335

"After all of this is over,

all that will really matter is

how we treated each other."

—Unknown

I

I'VE NEVER CONSIDERED HOW I WOULD DIE. EVER SINCE the Test, death has been stalking me like a shadow, but I keep getting away . . .

Two strangers watch me with innocent eyes, but that doesn't ease the panic I feel. I was just on the platform with President Camille moments from being shot in the back of the head. Now, I'm standing with my friends in a large aircraft hangar with a ginger-haired man and a dark-skinned girl—and they've told me there are more of us.

There are more people with abilities? It seems too good to be true. It must be a trick. Power plays along my fingertips, and I seal my hold over them. They stiffen under my command.

My eyes rake over the concrete hangar, darting from the high steel arches to the stone balcony against the back wall. I'm searching for someone hiding in the dark, waiting to attack, but I don't see anyone else. With a flick, I pull the pair closer. They hold curious looks, like they're expecting something from me, but I can't guess what.

"You're not going to hurt us?" I ask.

"We're not going to hurt you," the girl affirms. She bites her lower lip and says, "I'm Olivia Turrick, and this is Terrace DuPont. I used my ability to rescue you."

The air in the giant room turns stale in my nostrils. I have a thousand questions, but I don't have time to ask. Keeping the two strangers bound under my power, I quickly take stock of who's with me. To my relief, I count five people. Everyone made it out.

Keith, Candice, and Ben are unscathed from the encounter with the President, but Rosalie is bleeding out on the floor from being stabbed. And Jonah is still bound and gagged. I have to help them. Rosalie needs medical attention, and I don't know the extent of Jonah's injuries, but I can't let my guard down. I can't fail my friends. *I* am their protection.

I channel tingling into the pair under my control. "If you hurt us . . . If you're lying to me, I swear on my ability—"

"We're not," Terrace says gently. "Please, let us help. We saw the President's broadcast. We saw what happened. Olivia teleported you out."

I search his amber eyes for deceit, but they hold a look I've come to know well: empathy. Jonah taught me that. Why would these people rescue us moments before our execution if they meant to harm us?

"Please," Terrace continues. "What do you need?"

My reservations dissolve. He's telling the truth, and Rosalie doesn't have time for my hesitation. She's losing too much blood.

"Help us," I plead. "Rosalie's been stabbed."

My grip on them vanishes, and with it, my strength. I turn to face our ragged group, sinking to my knees, overwhelmed. My face is tingling, but it's not from my ability. I suck in rattling breaths, trying my best not to pass out.

Olivia jumps into action, striding over to Rosalie. "Terrace, let's get the girl to Beezee. And tell Arthur we've got them. They're safe."

Footsteps scrape across the floor, and a metal door clangs against something hard, but I block it out. I have eyes for only one person.

"Jonah."

Saying his name aloud feels like shards of glass. I crawl over to him. He's crumpled on the concrete, half conscious. My heartbeat thunders in my ears as my hands fumble with the ropes binding him. I'm crying, attempting in vain to keep what's left of my composure. What did Camille do to him?

I wrestle with the knots, and Jonah's breathing turns shallow from the leather gag cutting into his cheekbone. He groans, so I abandon the ropes for a moment, gently loosening the gag. I pull it down under his chin, and he sputters, coughing up bile.

"Help is here," I whimper, cradling him. "You're going to be okay, Jonah."

I attack the knots binding him again. Tears roll down my face without mercy. I left him behind. At the Testing Center, Jonah got stuck behind the glass door when we rescued Maddy. I left him there, and he was tortured for it . . .

I try not to stare at his injuries, but they glare at me with venom, impossible to ignore. Above his right eye, a deep gash oozes blood. Bruising extends along his jawline, broken blood vessels streak across the whites of his eyes, and so much blood is caked into his hair that it's crusted over.

I untie the last of his bindings, and he winces.

"I'm sorry," I whisper, bowing my head over his. "I'm so sorry, Jonah. This is—"

Bang.

I spin around on my knees, and my hands spring up, ready for a fight. Half a dozen people enter the aircraft hangar, and voices echo off the high walls.

"Over here!" Olivia calls, hoarse. "The girl's been stabbed. And that man there." She points to Jonah. "He's injured as well."

Before I can say a word, two burly, clean-shaven men in white uniforms are standing over me. They lower a woven stretcher, and I look up, overcome.

Emotion chokes out any helpful information I could offer. All I manage to say is, "Help him."

They move quickly, both murmuring to one another. The man nearest me asks me a question, but I just stare at him. I have no idea what he's said. My brain is blocked in a fog I can't escape. I feel like a child, unable to do anything for myself, and for a moment, it's an incredible relief to know that adults are here. Help has come. We're not going to die.

The two men lift Jonah onto the stretcher, and his sharp groan of pain sends agony down to my bones. The government beat him—tortured him—because of me. And they were going to kill him.

Hot tears mix with the snot running down my nose, and I sniffle into my sleeve.

A few yards away, I watch as Rosalie is hoisted onto a second stretcher. Candice is clinging to her, refusing to let go. She staggers, as if drunk, and through her sobs she mutters, "Sh-she's been stabbed."

"It's going to be alright." Olivia pulls Candice's hands off of Rosalie. "Beezee is very good. I promise."

Candice stumbles, and her knees buckle. In a swift motion, Olivia catches her, lowering her down to the concrete.

I track the stretchers until Jonah and Rosalie vanish past the doors. The cacophony of metal sets my teeth on edge. Every part of my body is vibrating. I'm coming down from a fight-or-flight panic, and the ache of being man-handled by Camille's puppetry burns across my skin. He controlled my friends flawlessly, holding me down with their hands, and cursing at me with their words. He forced Ben to stab Rosalie, and I was too weak to stop him. And he was going to kill us all . . .

We're alive. How are we alive?

I'm so overwhelmed that I'm having a hard time breathing. I glance around, noting my friends once more.

Candice is weeping in Olivia's arms, Ben is cradling himself on the floor, and Keith is standing as still as a statue. They're all shell-shocked but alive. Everyone is alive.

My gaze lingers on Keith. His handsome features are frozen with angst, and his brow is knit together as if he were on the verge of a breakdown. I let out a whimper, burying my face in my hands. I don't know how much time passes, but when I look up, Olivia is crouched in front of me.

"Hollis?"

I blink several times, swallowing a knot that keeps resurfacing to choke me.

"They're going to be okay. Beezee will take care of Jonah and Rosalie. She's our healer."

I nod because words keep failing me. I have so many questions, but all I can do is sit here, staring blankly ahead. My arms and legs grow heavy as the tingling in my face extends down my limbs.

"Let me help you up."

Olivia offers me a hand, and I take it. She pulls me to my feet, but I can't keep myself upright. Black splotches crowd my vision, and I sink to the floor again.

"Woah." Olivia grimaces under my weight and falls with me. "Let's get you some food. And a place to rest. We have accommodations on the next floor up. For all of you. You're safe now."

We're safe now . . .

Can that possibly be true? Is the nightmare over? From the deepest part of me, I hope so. I don't know anything about these people, but they saved us from the government—from Camille. And Jonah and Rosalie have access to a healer. That's something our camp in the forest doesn't have because Liz Engel died in the bombing. Maybe, despite everything, things are going to turn out for the better.

My heartbeat is starting to slow. I clutch my jacket, taking a deep breath and centering myself on the feel of the rough fabric under my fingertips.

Yet again, the metal doors smash open, and my adrenaline

piques. I'm on my feet faster than I thought possible, and my brain runs wild with dread. Is someone here to announce the death of Jonah or Rosalie? What possible reason could these people have for throwing open the doors so violently? I tense, ready for the worst.

Two men approach, and I retreat, my palms raw with power out of instinct.

The first, and shorter of the two, looks like a bodyguard—muscly, bald, and ready for a fight. He wears all black. And slung over his beefy shoulder is a standard-issue, Testing Center machine gun. But it's the second man who chills me to the bone, stealing my voice away and plunging me into an unease I haven't felt since failing the Test.

The man's pale skin blends in with his shocking white hair, and his outfit is fitted to perfection. It's tailored with cornered edges—the same cornered edges of a Testing Center employee. He looks like he's been plucked directly from society. Everything about him commands respect, even fear, except for his brown eyes. They're soft, like he holds a secret.

I hold my palm out, on the brink of freezing him in his tracks.

"Hollis Timewire," he says. I stiffen at his proper tone. "It's a pleasure to finally meet you. May I shake your hand?"

Before I can reply, he grasps my right hand between icy fingers. I'm not familiar with this kind of introduction, and even though I've experienced touch for six months now, this feels off.

"My name is Arthur Evandrum." He bows low. "Would you please follow me?"

"Arthur, she needs to rest," Olivia says, walking up to him. Her arms weave together. "Surely this can wait. She was almost executed. *Publicly.* They're all in a bit of shock."

I glance between Arthur and Olivia. What can wait? What are they talking about?

"Then by all means, Miss Turrick, you may take the other three to the East Rooms, but I must insist on speaking with Miss Timewire. Immediately."

Arthur's tone is as icy as his demeanor, and Olivia shrinks back. But this doesn't stop her from pushing the issue further.

"They need to rest," she repeats with a defiant edge. "Didn't you see the President's broadcast? He—"

"I saw the broadcast, Miss Turrick," Arthur says, waving a spindly hand at her. "I saw it live, as you did. There will be no more discussion. Miss Timewire may rest later." He turns back to me, and his societal appearance knots my stomach. "Now, if you would kindly follow me."

I glance at my friends, unease zipping through me. Candice is peering at me behind Ben's shoulder. But it's Keith who catches my attention. He's not looking at me. In fact, he hasn't moved since the blue orb brought us here. He's still standing with a strange look on his face, and his expression is mixed with something else.

Arthur Evandrum clears his throat, but I ignore him.

"Keith?" I find my voice at last, and it cracks with a fresh wave of emotion. I feel like I'm going to pass out. I turn away from Arthur Evandrum and walk toward him. "Are you okay?"

He doesn't respond. I can only make out part of his face, but he's shivering, as if he were freezing.

"Keith?" I repeat, raising my voice, but still, he doesn't acknowledge me.

Candice untangles herself from Ben, trailing behind me and peering at her brother. "Keith? What's wrong?"

Keith's shivering intensifies, and I place a hand on his shoulder. But the moment I do, I understand, and horror fills me. The statuesque pose, the shivering, the forced look . . . and Keith's mouth is pressed shut.

I gasp. President Camille is *still* controlling him.

In a bolt of movement, Keith's strong hands grab me, and I'm lifted off my feet. He throws me backward, knocking the air from my lungs. I don't even have time to shield myself before he's on top of me, striking me with wild, uncontrolled blows.

People are screaming, and blurred voices cry out.

I pull as much of my ability into my hands as I can, trying to force my will over Keith as he continues to strike me. Pain burns across my skin like fire, and I shriek, unable to push him back.

Someone's calling my name . . .

My hands flail, filled to the brim with tingling. I attempt once more to force Keith away, but just as in the President's office, a power more potent than my own rips him from me. President Camille is stronger than I am, and I'm an empty vessel, helpless to do anything but watch as Keith's fists strike me over and over again.

Cold.

Spots of black and blue.

Stars.

So many stars . . .

My legs sprawl, and my hand slips on Keith's arm as the crack of fist against flesh persists. I'm slipping away, like the stream from the forest feeding itself into the churning rapids beyond.

$$\overline{}$$

2

$$\overline{}$$

I'M LYING IN A SOFT BED. THE FLORAL SCENT OF FRESH sheets mixes with another smell: sterile chemicals. Unpleasant warmth prickles across my skin, and as I come to, pain like daggers stabs throughout my body, throbbing with each heartbeat.

Harsh lighting burns my retinas, and I squint. Blinking through the watery fog of my vision, I attempt to sit up, but gentle hands hold me down.

A shock travels up the side of my face, and I wince.

"Good, you're awake," a honeyed voice says. "Lie back now."

A tall black woman smiles down at me. Her long gray hair is tied back in a braid, and her dark eyes glint in the brightness of the room. She's dressed in white scrubs pressed firm against her slender frame. She's perfect—nothing about her appearance is out of place. My pulse quickens, making my head hazy. Why is she dressed like that? She looks like a Testing Center nurse. I try to say something, but a strangled noise comes out instead, and pain thunders across my jaw.

"Don't speak, child," the woman says, placing a delicate hand on my arm. "You need to rest. In a few days, the swelling in your jaw will go down."

My hands move to my face, and my tongue runs along the inside of my teeth. Metal wire weaves my bottom teeth to my top ones.

"Broken jaw. I had to wire your mouth shut. Normally, you'd need six to eight weeks to heal, but I'll help it along. You won't be wired shut for long. Don't you fret."

She turns and begins rummaging in a large medical bag. I glance around, and my stomach drops. This looks like the room where I took my Test. White walls. Clean, barren, and cold. The only other thing in here besides my bed is a metal table on wheels with a bowl of water on its surface.

The woman pulls out a cloth. After wetting it in the bowl, she begins to dab my forehead. The cold of the cloth feels amazing, like the river from the forest. It's crisp with a hint of lemon.

"I'm Beezee-day Jones," she says in a soothing tone. "You may call me Beezee."

She moves the cloth across my forehead, patting softly, and I scoot myself up in the bed.

Immediately, I regret it. My ribs ache, and my breathing turns heavy. I moan, and even that hurts. My vocal cords feel like they've been scalded. I want to ask what's going on, but the metal wiring my teeth shut won't let me.

"Please lie back," Beezee chides, attempting to scoot me down again.

She places a hand on my shoulder, but I push it away, shaking my head.

Pain . . .

My vision turns dark, and I let my head fall back onto the pillow as I wait for my sight to return. When it does, I motion for a pen and paper by scrawling across mid-air. My stomach squirms. Every small movement is excruciating, and it takes all of my self-control not to cry.

Beezee stares at me, but when I motion again, she goes back to her medical bag and rustles through it. She extracts a scrap of prescription paper and hands it to me with a blue-tipped pen. I take it and scribble fervently.

Keith?

"That boy almost killed you." She brushes her long braid over her shoulder. "He broke your jaw and three of your ribs. You don't need to worry about him. He can't hurt you anymore."

My eyes widen, and my heart pounds so hard it hurts. An icy sensation curdles my blood. What did they do to him? I write on the paper again.

What do you mean?

"He's in one of our holding cells. It was all anyone could do to pry him off you. He went mad."

I shake my head, whimpering. They don't understand. Keith didn't mean to hurt me. The President was controlling him. I have to tell them, but Beezee pushes me back against the pillow.

"You need to lie still and rest!" she quips, folding her arms across her chest.

I continue writing.

Where is he?

"Hollis, you almost died. *Twice!*" Beezee tries to grab the pen and paper from me, but I keep an iron grip on it. "Please. Lie back. He's fine, child. I promise you. There's nothing that can be done about it right now."

I'm lightheaded, but my mind is on high alert. Where are they holding Keith? Are they going to hurt him? Why is this woman dressed like a Testing Center employee? Why does this room look like the Area 19 Testing Center? I don't know what to do.

I swallow, my tongue dry as sand. President Camille was controlling Keith the whole time. I should have seen it sooner. I should have sensed it . . . but how is it possible that Camille had control over him from so far away? This wasn't Keith's fault, but how could anyone here possibly know that?

Sweat creeps across my brow as another thought occurs to me. Could the President *still* have Keith under his ability? Is Keith fighting with Camille's power, locked in a cell somewhere, alone and terrified, thinking I'm dead by his hand? I need to let him know I'm okay—that I'm alive. He was trying to warn me. He was shivering in place, fighting Camille's hold.

I'm back to the paper.

I want to see Keith.

"Absolutely not! You're in no state." Beezee's tone is as sharp as her words. "You need rest."

My brain is buzzing. I can't rest. Where are my friends? Where is Jonah? I need to see him too. I have to tell him I'm sorry I wasn't strong enough to beat Camille. I have to make sure he's alright. He got trapped in the Testing Center when we rescued Maddy, but Pierce Bodegard meant that for me. That traitor wanted *me* to get left behind. I was supposed to get stuck behind the door. Not Jonah.

And Rosalie. Is this going to be Tiffany all over again? Have I lost her too?

My chest is heaving, and I'm trembling. Black spots flicker around me, and the more my mind races, the worse it gets.

"My goodness, you're in a state," Beezee says, her thin brow crinkling. "I think one more healing session should do the trick. Take a deep breath. This will make you feel better."

Beezee pulls back the soft covers, and I close my eyes to ease them from the strain of the lighting. I don't want to sleep, but exhaustion sweeps in.

"That's it," she says. "Now, I need you to hold still while I work. This will only take a minute, but you must be still. Do you understand me?"

I blink before nodding.

"Good."

She raises her hands above my rib cage, holding her palms down. With eyes closed, she moves her hands back and forth in a uniform manner until, "Ah, here we are."

She pushes on the right side of my chest, and intense heat seeps into my skin. I groan.

"I'm helping your body mend itself," Beezee explains. "Your cells seem to be responding nicely."

The heat increases to an uncomfortable level as the heel of Beezee's palm digs deeper.

"My ability speeds up the natural healing process by encouraging your body to work a little overtime," she adds.

She continues to press on my side.

"I can't fix everything right away, mind you. I'll have to work on your ribs for a few sessions. But you'll be patched up soon enough. And tomorrow I'll start healing your jaw. You're too swollen now."

After another minute of painful heat, Beezee finishes. She begins to tuck the covers around me, but I continue writing, now free of my promise to 'be still.'

Beezee scowls, her hand moving toward the pen. In response, I push her away, and the pain in my ribs sharpens. I grip the pen, refusing to back down. I can't speak because of the wiring, and I'm not done with my questions. I won't sleep if I don't know what's happened to Jonah and Rosalie.

She resigns herself with a sigh, allowing me to finish my message on the prescription paper. I scribble two names.

Jonah? Rosalie?

"I've attended to Rosalie and stitched up her wound," Beezee says. "She lost a lot of blood, but she's alright. She's on antibiotics and bedrest. And I'll be attending to Jonah when I'm done with you. He's okay, child. You don't need to worry. He's in good hands. I can promise you that."

My eyes burn with fatigue, and tears collect there. I grip the paper, crumpling it in my fist, overcome by an onslaught of too many emotions to process.

"Please rest." She tucks a strand of my blonde hair behind my ear. "I can't imagine what you've been through, but you're safe now. And all you have to do is sleep. I'll be back to check on you later."

I look down at the crinkled paper. Pressing it flat, I tear off a piece and write another message, handing it to Beezee. She reads it, then meets my gaze for a beat.

"I'll give Jonah your message. Time to sleep."

She grabs the medical bag and walks to the door. With a click, the room turns dark, and Beezee hovers in the doorway, looking at me with a smile.

"I'm glad we finally found you."

And without another word, she slips out, casting the room into pitch black.

My eyes wander through the darkness. They finally found me? They've been looking for me? For how long? What do these people want with me? I gulp, feeling panicked.

The blue orb . . .

That day by the river, I swore I saw someone dart behind a tree. That was the first time I saw it. The flash of blue I described to Jonah seemed to match Rachel's ability. Rachel was the girl who held up the crumbling compound with a force field so everyone could escape during the bombing. But it wasn't Rachel I saw. It was Olivia. Olivia Turrick was in the forest.

But if she already found me, then why didn't she reveal herself? Why did she wait until I was about to die on the President's platform?

I ponder the room, half expecting the answer to come to me, but it doesn't. Something isn't right. And what frightens me more than the convenience of our timely rescue is the fact that I've seen hints of society's influence here, and I'm in a room that looks remarkably like the Testing Center.

They've finally found me . . .

Do they know what I've done? I'm a traitor in the eyes of my people. I'm responsible for the deaths of over a hundred individuals. I'm the reason the government knows there are more of us. I'm Hollis Timewire, the most infamous person in the world.

Dread collects in me like a poison, and my head swims. I'm fighting exhaustion as my mind spirals down a path of questions with no answers.

Maybe these people know everything, and now that they have me, they can keep me from doing anything else destructive. A darkness deeper than the lack of light lurks about. It surrounds me, sweeping over every inch of my skin.

Pain shoots up the side of my face, and I whimper. Beezee's right. I need to sleep. My friends are okay. No one died. By some miracle, I've escaped with my life yet again. I stare into the blackness, and for the first time since rescuing Maddy from the Area 19 Testing Center, I close my eyes and fall into oblivion.

$$\text{—}\ 3\ \text{—}$$

IT'S BEEN SIX DAYS SINCE KEITH'S ATTACK, AND I'VE DE-manded to see Jonah. Beezee has staunchly protested this venture, however, now that the metal wiring is gone and I can speak freely, I've refused to take no for an answer.

I've had several more healing sessions, and although my recovery has been nothing short of miraculous by society's medical standards, the pain isn't gone. But I'll bear the discomfort if it means I get to see my teacher.

"Through here," Beezee says.

She escorts me down a long stone corridor, keeping a hand on my shoulder to steady my gait. We emerge into a chamber that's solid stone to the left but sheer and unobstructed to the right. It opens into a rocky chasm below. I peer over the metal railing. We must be on the third or fourth floor of . . . wherever we are.

I inhale sharply, leaning on a crutch to better fight the dull ache that persists in my ribcage and jaw. My feet scuff against the stone, the crutch echoing in step. I pause as a dizzy spell claims me.

"Are you alright, child?" Beezee peers at me with motherly concern.

"Yes," I lie, gritting my teeth.

"Mmm hmm." She gives me a look that says she knows I'm full of it. "I still think you ought to be in bed so you can—"

"No. I need to see Jonah."

"You're not well."

"I don't care."

I take a deep breath, trying not to sound so labored.

"Are you sure you're alright?"

"Yes."

We continue, moving past the chamber area through a set of metal doors. They open up into another hallway, but this time, everything's enclosed. The stone swallows us up, pressing in from all sides, and it magnifies the tapping of the crutch tenfold.

"Nearly there," Beezee says, pointing ahead. "Jonah's room is at the end."

I nod, attempting to calm my heaving chest. Sweat beads on my brow, my legs shake, and my pulse pounds into my ears. I never knew walking could be this much work, and the closer we get, the more I tremble.

I'm going to see Jonah. I'm going to speak to him for the first time since Maddy's rescue, and I don't know what to say. I keep reliving the moment on a loop—the pane of glass descends to the floor, trapping Jonah in. I stole the government's secret weapon, and they tortured him because of it.

"He's just in here," Beezee says, approaching the last door on the left.

Beezee removes her hand from my shoulder and steps ahead of me, grabbing the knob of the door and pushing it inward.

I stand in the hallway, frozen. I can't breathe. With watering eyes, I reach for the wall to feel the cold stone beneath my fingertips.

Beezee grabs my hand. "Come here, child."

With a delicate touch, she helps me through the doorway of the dimly lit room.

Jonah is lying in a bed, tucked under white sheets, and I hold my hand up to stifle a gasp. His chest and right arm are bandaged, dark bruising covers his face and neck, and his right eye is swollen shut.

He stirs. "Beezee, is that you?" The moment Jonah catches my eye, my throat closes. He stares at me. "Oh . . . Hollis."

Beezee moves to the corner of the room, grabs a metal folding chair, and places it in front of Jonah's bed. Supporting my arm, she helps me sit.

"I'll give you two some privacy."

She slips back through the door, closing it with a soft click.

My lips part, but no words come. I gaze at the broken man in front of me with weakened resolve. I'm so happy he's alive, but my belly burns hot with shame. Jonah's the reason the Council didn't execute me for my betrayal after the bombing. Jonah saved me, fought for me, and gave me a reason to work through my grief and find purpose again. I owe him everything, and when he needed me most, I failed. Camille was going to kill him because of me. *My* rescue plan. Maddy. The boy with the golden light; the government's prize.

My eyes brim with tears. I tried to beat Camille, but I couldn't save Jonah, and if Olivia hadn't intervened when she did, we'd all be dead.

Jonah's wearied face looks at mine. Without breaking eye-contact, he extends a loose fist, opening up his palm to reveal the prescription paper I'd asked Beezee to give him six days ago.

My handwriting glares back: *It should have been me behind the glass.*

"No, it shouldn't have," he says.

He drops the paper onto my lap. I hang my head, fighting back a mix of emotions. Memories from the rescue mission assault me: the alarms, the descending pane of glass, and Pierce forcing Maddy to stop running with his ability. Pierce was hoping that in the panic of the escape, I would get trapped. And in the thick of it all, Jonah came back for me. Jonah got stuck behind the door in my place, and we left him. *I* left him.

It's as if Jonah can read my mind.

"You had to leave me. They would have killed you."

There's a moment of deep silence, and the strangling sensation in my throat sharpens.

"Camille was going to execute you," I say. "I had to come back. I had to."

"I know."

Jonah pauses, closing his eyes and breathing deep. We sit without words for a few minutes, and the quiet between us burns. Then, Jonah clears his throat and stares at me with unease.

"Camille wanted information," he says.

My brain immediately leaps to the worst thing I can imagine: the people in the forest. Camille's a puppet master. Did he force Jonah to reveal the location of the camp?

"Everyone in the forest?" I say, an icy sensation thundering through me. "Does Camille know where they are?"

Jonah shakes his head. "No. He wanted information on you. Only you."

"Because I'm a puppet master too?"

"Yes."

My lower lip trembles. "What did he want to know?"

"How much you've learned. How strong you are. What you can do." Jonah pauses, resting his head in his hands. "And what would make you come to the Capitol."

A tear slips down my face. In the hours between Maddy's rescue and me returning to the Capitol, Camille did horrible things to him. I feel sick. Just looking at Jonah's injuries makes my skin crawl with pain.

"What did you tell him?" I ask.

"I told him . . . if you knew I was still alive, you would come," he says, his voice thick with grief. "He used me to get to you."

I choke back a sob. "Am I a fool for going to the Capitol?"

Jonah's face lights with compassion under the heavy bruising. "No."

I hang my head, gazing at white tile beneath my feet. The dull pain in my chest is growing more severe. I clutch at it and shiver. It's taking everything in me to remain calm.

"Jonah, I couldn't stop him. I couldn't break his control. I tried! But I couldn't take his power off of Ben, and then he stabbed Rosalie, and then—"

"Hollis, you couldn't have known," Jonah says, cutting me off gently. "No one could have known he had an ability. He played you."

"Then I *am* a fool!" I say bitterly, salty tears falling down into my mouth. "And I nearly got us killed because I was too weak to fight him. I failed you. I'm so sorry, Jonah. This is my fault. If I just grabbed Maddy when he stopped running—if you hadn't come back for me—then none of this would have happened."

Jonah sits up, grimacing. He places a hand on my shoulder. "Hollis, how long have you been a puppet master?"

"S-six months."

"This man has been one for decades. You can't blame yourself for what he did to Rosalie, or to me. His power is immense. You were not too weak, you were too inexperienced, and he knew that. This isn't your fault. Camille wanted you, and I was a convenient means to get to you."

I rub my chest to ease the growing pain. Every part of my body is throbbing, and I'm beginning to feel lightheaded.

"Hollis, look at me." I lift my head to meet my teacher's gaze, and his voice catches in his throat. "What you did at the Capitol was incredibly brave. Thank you for coming back for me."

My eyes sting and my vision blurs. I nod, sucking in uneven breaths. Jonah hugs me, and I hug him back, crying bitter tears. The shooting pain in my bones is becoming harder to bear, but I sink into his chest, completely overcome.

After a minute, the embrace ends, and I wipe my face on the sleeve of my jacket.

Jonah, now noting my appearance, asks, "What happened to you?"

"Keith, he—" My throat closes, and I swallow painfully. "When the blue orb took us here, the President still had Keith under his power. Camille used Keith to attack me."

Jonah's concern changes to shock. "He was still controlling Keith?"

"Yes. And I tried to take Keith back with my ability, but . . ." My fingertips sear at the thought. "I could feel Camille's power tearing Keith away from me. Then I woke up to Beezee."

"Where is he?"

"I don't know. I haven't seen him. Beezee said he's in a holding cell somewhere." I check over my shoulder and lower my voice. "Jonah, something's off about this place. They look like society members. Beezee's wearing Testing Center scrubs, and—"

A shout issues from beyond the door, and I jump, nearly falling out of the chair. Aggravated voices echo down the hall. Someone's coming, and they don't sound friendly.

I speak in a rapid whisper, and my voice dips through wild inflections. "Jonah, these people have been looking for me. Beezee said they've finally found me. Do you remember the blue light I saw in the forest by the river that day? It was Olivia Turrick, not Rachel. Olivia found me before we even went to rescue Maddy."

The shouting continues, the door creaks, and adrenaline spikes to the beat of my throbbing ribs.

"Jonah, where are we?"

"I don't know," he replies.

The door smacks open with a crash that makes my heart skip. The stout bodyguard I'd met before Keith's attack enters along with Terrace DuPont. They're both shouting at each other, but Beezee's voice overpowers theirs.

"ABSURD!" she exclaims, hands on her hips. Her gray braid swings around her shoulder like a whip. "The girl can barely walk! This can wait."

"No, it can't, Beezee-day!" the stout man snaps. His burly mustache ripples, and a speck of spit lands on his fat lip. He narrows his beady eyes and scratches his balding head. "Arthur said to bring the girl up as soon as she can walk." He looks past Beezee, pointing a thick finger at me. "Miss Timewire, Arthur Evandrum needs to speak with you. I am to escort you to him."

"HUGO!" Beezee shouts. "No. Absolutely not! She needs a few more days to rest. She's healing from a broken jaw and three broken ribs!"

"Beezee," he says, his words sharp. "You know Arthur wouldn't speak to the girl now if it weren't *necessary*. You know that. I'm sorry, but she needs to come with me."

"Hugo's right, Beezee-day," Terrace says. "Hollis can walk. We can't waste any more time."

I glance between the three of them. "Can't waste any more time for what? What's going on?"

Beezee sighs, knotting her arms together and glaring at him. "Hugo, I swear, if Arthur isn't quick about this—"

"He'll be quick," Terrace adds, swiping a hand through his ginger hair.

I turn to Jonah. To anyone who didn't know him, he'd appear stoic, but I know better. He's just as alarmed as I am. A pitter-patter settles in me, and I grab Jonah's hand. I don't want to leave him, but it looks like these people have other plans.

"Fine," Beezee says, coming to my side. "Let me help you up, child." She turns to Hugo with a fiery look. "Don't think Arthur won't have hell to pay for this! She's *my* patient."

"I'll be back," I say to Jonah. "I promise."

Beezee lifts me to my feet and hands me the crutch. I put it under my arm and walk nimbly over to Hugo's side. The dull pain in my ribs intensifies, and for a moment, stars twinkle around me.

Terrace and Hugo exit the room, and as I leave, I turn over my shoulder to see Jonah's nod of encouragement. The door shuts, and I'm left alone with three strangers.

Bracing myself against the rough stone wall, I take a calming breath. I channel what's left of my energy and push a confidence I don't feel into my tone. "What's this about?"

"Arthur will speak to you," is all Hugo says.

He marches forward like a soldier, and I follow him with Beezee's assistance.

I count each door I pass to settle my nerves. Something tells me that I'm about to find out why these people have been looking for me, and I'm not sure if I'm relieved or terrified.

"I like to count things too when I get nervous," Terrace mutters, stuffing his hands into his jacket pockets.

I stare at him, mouth askew. "What did you just say?"

"I like to count things too." He shrugs. "It keeps me calm."

How does he know I count things? I stumble, and Beezee catches me, holding me steady.

"Careful, child."

"Sorry, I—I'm just," I stutter, gaping at Terrace. I've never told anyone that before. No one knows I count things—not even Keith.

"Are you alright?" Terrace asks.

"Yes, fine," I lie.

"Hugo, slow down!" Beezee scolds. "Hollis can't keep this pace."

"My apologies, Beezee," Hugo states, and he slows. "We're going to the left, Miss Timewire."

Hugo moves toward the chamber I'd passed on my way to Jonah's room. My arms shake as I trudge along. The beating I took is wearing on me, and although Beezee's mantra of 'rest' is annoying, I wish I'd heeded her. Walking is exhausting all of my efforts.

I follow Hugo down the next corridor.

As we continue, I notice that Terrace is staring at me with alarming intensity. It's unnerving, so I stare back and ask, "Where are we?"

"We're in a mountain."

"A mountain?" I repeat loudly.

Hugo glares back at Terrace but says nothing. He marches on until we've passed through so many halls I lose count. Ahead, a set of double metal doors gleams under the fluorescents, and white walls extend beyond.

Hugo slams his beefy hand against a silver panel, and the doors open.

"Miss Timewire," he says in a monotone, gesturing me through.

The second I enter the white hall, the stench of chemicals causes me to gag. I crunch my nose, holding back a cough. What is this place?

I strain to keep the stitch in my chest at bay as my breathing turns shallow. I have half a mind to turn around and run back to Jonah's room, but that would accomplish nothing. I trudge on, a sinister thought snaking its way through my mind. If I ran, would they chase me? Would they hurt me? In all honesty, I don't know. The only reason I haven't completely panicked is that I know my ability is stronger than all three of theirs.

"Nearly there," Beezee says. "Then you can sit down."

I nod, forgetting about my wounded jaw, and attempt to smile. Pain slaps me across the face, and I yelp.

"Here we are," Hugo says, placing his palm against a scanner situated on the second to last door on the right. It flashes, and the door slides into the wall. "Terrace will help you to your seat. Beezee, you can come get Miss Timewire when we're done."

Beezee turns her nose up at Hugo. "If Arthur's not finished in half an hour, then I'm coming to get her. The poor girl needs *sleep*—a concept he's not familiar with." She crosses her arms and turns to walk back the way we came.

Terrace takes my arm and helps me into the large stone room. Nine screens line the far wall, and dozens of people are seated around a massive oval table. My heart drops. They're all dressed in white scrubs with slicked back hair styles and muted faces. Everyone turns toward me in unison, and my hands itch with the tingling of my ability. There's no doubt in my mind now. I'm in a room full of Testing Center employees. These people are society members.

——————
4
——————

"HOLLIS TIMEWIRE."

Arthur Evandrum stands from his seat at the end of the table. He's wearing a crisp white suit, and his thick white hair is gelled back, resting at the nape of his neck. He presses his hands together, fingertip to fingertip, and tilts his head to the side.

"I'm glad to see you're able to walk after what that boy did to you."

I lean on the crutch with my right hand but keep my left at the ready. Power collects in my fingertips.

"It wasn't his fault," I say.

Every eye in the room is on me, and I'm battling the urge to freeze everyone. Instinct is kick-starting my survival response, but I steady myself, elevating my posture so as to appear bold.

"The boy attacked you," Arthur states. "I saw it with my own eyes."

"But he didn't mean to. He . . . There was . . ."

I'm struggling with what to say and getting lightheaded. I grip the back of the chair in front of me.

"Terrace, help Miss Timewire to her seat." Arthur gestures to a black leather chair on his right-hand side. "We have much to discuss."

Terrace leads me to the end of the oval table and pulls out the chair. Without taking my eyes off Arthur, I sit, leaning back against the leather with stiff shoulders. Terrace then moves around Arthur, taking the seat to his left.

"I need to ask you some questions, Miss Timewire," Arthur begins, his deep brown eyes boring into mine. "And they regard a matter of great importance. I want you to know that we are here to help you. I understand this may seem a bit disconcerting—finding out there are so many more of us—but I assure you, we are on your side, and we mean you no harm." He pauses, and then his lips curl upward. "Where are the rest of your people? The ones from the compound that was destroyed?"

Immediately, alarms go off in my mind. This doesn't feel right. I don't know these people, and I can't blindly take them at their word. I am my people's protection, and I won't make the same mistake I did before.

"She's not sure if she can trust us," Terrace says, raising an eyebrow. "You can, Hollis. We just want to find everyone and bring them here safely. Vianne is still out there, right?"

At this, I snap.

"How do you know that name? Why are you all dressed as Testing Center employees? What's going on?"

"Terrace, you're making her nervous," Arthur chides. "It's

alright, Miss Timewire. Terrace has the ability to know things about a person just by looking at them. All he needs is to be present with someone to start learning, and the more powerful someone's ability, the more he can learn. Like your favorite hobby, for example. Or perhaps, your favorite color. Or other *deeper* things."

"Teal," Terrace says, giving me an encouraging smile. He scratches the red stubble growing on his chin. "Your favorite color is teal, right?"

I twist my fingers together under the table. So that's how he knows I count things when I get nervous.

"This really is of the utmost importance," Arthur continues. "Where are the rest of your people?"

At this, an unsettling thought occurs to me. Olivia Turrick and the blue orb. Something about this doesn't add up. Olivia found me back in the forest. Arthur should already know where my people are. If Olivia works for him, why hasn't she said anything?

"Why did you want to speak with me?" I ask.

It's clear Arthur wants something more than the location of my people. He was so insistent on speaking with me when I arrived. But I'm not going to give him anything until I know what's going on. Right now, I hold all the cards, which means I have all the power, and I'm going to keep it that way.

"What do you mean?" Arthur's inquisitive look sets my teeth on edge.

"I mean, why did you want to speak with *me* specifically?"

Arthur smiles, and his whole countenance is so off-putting

that my stomach whirls. "You're Hollis Timewire, the most famous person in the world. Or else . . . *infamous*."

"It would seem so. But that doesn't answer my question."

"Look, I'll level with you," he says, business-like. He folds his hands and places them on the table. "There are a few hundred people with abilities out there right now. I want to offer them a place of protection. And judging from what I witnessed on the President's broadcast, I know you understand how dangerous the world is. Especially now that we're out in the *open* again."

So they do know what I've done—or at least some of what I've done. So much has happened in the six months since my sixteenth birthday. I swallow a knot, and my jaw thunders with sharp jabs.

"How do I know I can trust you?" I glance around the table, speaking with venom. "Forgive me if I'm skeptical, but the last time I was in a room full of society members, I almost died. So, here's what's going to happen. You will answer *all* of my questions, and if I'm satisfied, I'll answer *some* of yours, because I will *die* before I betray my people."

The quiet of the room grows deeper, and sweat drenches my armpits. Right now, it seems it's one against thirty, but I've taken on thirty people before. I took on a thousand at the steps of the Capitol when I went to rescue Jonah. My ability purrs down my arm, vibrating to my fingertips.

"Do we have a deal?" I cock my head to challenge Arthur's steely gaze.

He purses his lips and says, "That seems fair to me. What do you want to know, Miss Timewire?"

I take a deep breath, my eyes never leaving Arthur Evandrum's.

"Beezee said you finally found me. What do you want with me?"

His smile is charming, and his voice is slippery. "My dear girl, you're going to help us change the world."

Power itches in my hands, and it takes a moment to rein it back in.

"I've already changed the world," I say. "And unfortunately, I've made it a worse place for people with powers. Do you know who I am? What I've done?"

Arthur's mouth twitches, and he begins to speak as if reciting something dull. His eyes wander the room. "Hollis Timewire . . . the girl who betrayed her people to help the government, the girl who exposed anew the existence of the Diseased Ones, the girl who stole the secret weapon of a hundred years ago, the girl the President wants dead."

I'm momentarily dumbfounded. Whoever he is, this man knows a lot more than I thought.

Arthur pulls on the collar of his suit jacket. "Yes, I know who you are, and what you've done."

"How?" I manage, after a few moments. "How do you know?"

"I'm the Chief Overseer of the Area 7 Testing Center, Miss Timewire," he replies, pristine in his societal composure. He draws himself up, towering over me. "It's part of my job to know about you."

My mouth turns to ash. He's a Chief Overseer? What is this? I almost bind him under my ability on the spot. He's my enemy.

He's one of the highest-ranking officials in society. Besides the head of the military and the President himself, no other position holds as much power.

"Then why would I *ever* tell you where my people are?" I stare him down, hoping my defiant attitude disguises my horror. I have to stay calm and in control. My friends' lives depend on it.

"Simple. Your people have powers. I'd like to bring them here," he says. "I can assure you I only want them alive and well. I have no interest in depleting our *stock*. The world has done enough of that."

"Depleting our stock?" I repeat. I don't like the sound of that. "Are you one of us?"

Arthur leans back in his seat. "You mean, a Diseased One?"

My skin crawls. I don't know anyone with a power who uses that term to refer to themselves. "I mean, do you have an ability?"

"I do. Would you like to see?"

I clench my hands into fists. "Yes."

Immediately, my brain slips into a fog. It feels like I'm caught in a limbo between being awake and falling asleep. I'm trying to maintain focus on Arthur, but everything is hazy.

"Miss Timewire, you seem gravely injured," Arthur says, his voice lazy. "Perhaps I'll call Beezee back and have her escort you to your room. I'll answer your questions at a later time. You don't look strong enough to stand."

"No!" The word tumbles from me faster than I have time to think. I grab the edge of the table and pull myself up, grimacing. "We had a deal. Answer my questions!"

"My apologies. Don't you think you'd rather sit?"

"Yes." I take my seat with uncanny speed, and my head pounds with the effort of fighting the strange, cloudy sensation that's come over me.

"Where are your manners? It's polite to say 'thank you' when someone offers you a seat. You know that, right?"

"Yes, thank you," I say.

Arthur leans forward. "Do you think it's a worthy cause to change the world?"

"Yes, I do."

He smiles, and it's disturbing. "I thought so."

Abruptly, my head clears, and I blink in the bright lighting. The fuzzy feeling in my mind is gone, and I glare at him. "What did you do to me?"

Arthur's fingertips press together. "I have a silver tongue. My *words* are my power, Miss Timewire. And you'll find I can be *very* convincing."

"How like a politician," I shoot back.

"But I have my limits. I can't get anyone to agree to anything they are strongly opposed to. For example . . ." His unnerving smile deepens, and the haze returns. "We should give Jonah to the government. What do you think?"

"NO!" I launch from my seat again, and a wave of sickening pain spills over me. I clutch the table with both hands, feeling like I might vomit. Sweat is pouring from my brow, and my arms shake.

The foggy feeling dissipates.

"See? I can't get you to agree to something I know you're

against," Arthur muses. "My ability doesn't quite reach that far. But it seems, Miss Timewire, that you're as ready to change the world as we are."

I scowl at him, lowering myself into the chair. "That's why you've been looking for me? You need me to help you change the world?" I scoff. "Why me? Why am I so special?"

Arthur's hands slide over the surface of the table and slip below its edge. He readjusts himself in his chair, and eagerness creeps across his face, as if he's hungry for something entirely out of his grasp.

"You are an incredibly powerful young woman. I want to know what you can do, puppet master," he replies. "*All* that you can do."

"Why?"

"Jonah is your trainer, correct?" Arthur asks, disregarding my question.

"Yes. He is."

"I want both of you to work together to explore your power. I'll give you and Jonah anything you need. Say the word, and whatever it is will be yours."

"Why?"

"Miss Timewire, you possess one of the most powerful abilities known to the Diseased Ones."

"Don't call us that!" I snap. "We're not diseased."

"My apologies." Arthur tips his head down. "It's a habit from my line of work, as you can imagine. The Area 7 Testing Center is a rather unfortunate Testing Center for President Alvaro Camille."

Arthur gestures around the table to the other Board members watching us. I'd almost forgotten they were there. They peer at me with curious eyes, but their societal attire pushes fear deeper into me.

"You all work at the Area 7 Testing Center?" I ask. "Is that why you're dressed like society members?"

Terrace answers in Arthur's place. "Yes. In fact, Area 7 is our base of operations, fully staffed with people who have abilities."

My mouth hangs open. These people have infiltrated and taken over an entire Testing Center and Camille hasn't noticed? How is that possible?

Arthur, reading my expression, continues, a growing excitement budding in his voice. "We have big plans for the future, Miss Timewire, and we'd like you to be a part of it. You are the most valuable asset to our kind, and if we don't explore that asset, we are putting ourselves at risk."

I shake my head, trying to process what he's just disclosed. He wants me for my ability. That much is clear. And he's apparently willing to give me anything I need to train, but to what end? That's what I need to find out.

My sweaty hands curl in my lap, and I bite the inside of my cheek. My jaw is throbbing from all the talking I've done, but I won't stop until I have answers.

"What do you need me to train for?"

"Can I ask you something, Miss Timewire?"

I stiffen. "I'm not done with my questions. What do you need me to train for?"

Arthur's look is hard to read, but something behind his dark eyes tells me that his brain is working fast. He rests a hand on his chin. "Why did you and your friends go to the Capitol Building?"

I stare at him, puzzled. I know he saw the broadcast. He said so himself. He knows why I went, so what game is he playing? I haven't told him anything, but if it's a game he wants to play, fine. I still hold all the power. Choosing my next words carefully, I challenge him. "The government was going to execute Jonah. I had to go."

"Yes, I saw the President's broadcast," Arthur says.

"Then why did you ask me that question?"

Arthur's mouth presses into a line, and he and Terrace exchange quick glances.

"We'd like to know how you were caught," Terrace says, and my attention turns to him. He's wearing a strange expression and studying me intently. He runs his fingers through his stringy, ginger hair.

Arthur clears his throat. "With an ability as powerful as yours, Miss Timewire, I didn't expect you to end up on the President's platform with a gun to your head—especially after you brought a thousand men to their knees."

Arthur clicks something on the sleeve of his suit jacket. Behind his head on the back wall, one of the nine wall screens flickers on, playing the Capitol City's street cam footage. There I am, standing halfway down the block leading up to the President's mansion. A sea of military men have their machine guns pointed at me, and in a torrent of power, all of them are forced to their knees as my hands fly from me. The scene loops over and over again behind Arthur's inquisitive eyes.

If these people have access to street cam footage, I wonder what else they have access to. I look down, collecting myself. Arthur's question tells me something critical about President Alvaro Camille. If the Chief Overseer of the Area 7 Testing Center doesn't know Camille is a puppet master, *no one* does. And the military at Camille's right hand are just puppets. *This* is my bartering chip. He won't get anything from me until I know why he wants me to train.

I grit my teeth, infusing force into my words. "That's a puzzle, isn't it?"

Arthur's pose elevates ever so slightly, and a vein against his pale neck ticks.

"Miss Timewire—"

"Mr. Evandrum, *why* do you want me to train?"

Arthur and Terrace look at each other as if gearing up for something. The silence that extends between them increases my unease. My heartbeat thuds with a sickening rhythm, and my injuries aren't helping.

Arthur's hands creep over the top of the table, and he stares directly into my face, fierce passion written into his strong features. "We want you to help us take the Area 19 Testing Center."

5

MY ABILITY ROARS THROUGH MY CHEST LIKE A LION SNARLING over a kill. "You want me to *what*?"

Arthur Evandrum's smirk is triumphant. "Like I said, we have big plans for the future—plans *you* can help us accomplish." He swivels in his chair to face the back wall where the street cam footage is still on loop. "I'd like to show you something, and perhaps after this we can discuss the location of your people?"

Arthur taps on a digital panel and then clicks the cuff of his sleeve. All nine screens light up, and live security cam footage plays. Each of the nine screens displays a grid that houses dozens of different videos. It's easily two hundred feeds. I scan over them quickly.

"Read the fine print, Miss Timewire," Arthur says, pointing up.

In the corner of every box in each grid, bold text stares back at me.

```
Testing Center, Area 6
Testing Center, Area 7
Testing Center, Area 8
```

My eyes fly over the screens, surveying every number as adrenaline overdoses my system. The numbers count up in order, with occasional gaps.

```
Testing Center, Area 52
Testing Center, Area 54
Testing Center, Area 57
```

I grip the edge of the table, and tingling travels down to my toes. It keeps going and going . . .

```
Testing Center, Area 137
Testing Center, Area 139
Testing Center, Area 141
```

And the last feed on the final screen reads:

```
Testing Center, Area 243
```

My cracked lips part, and for a second, I'm speechless. There are 263 Testing Centers in the world—one for each major country of the old world, with some larger geographical areas having multiple.

A dry sensation paves over my tongue and creeps down the back of my throat. What kind of plans do these people have? I pull myself away from the screens and back to Arthur Evandrum, finding my voice at last.

"What is all of this?"

"We have successfully infiltrated 83% of the world's Testing Centers," he replies, drumming his knuckles on the table. The noise reverberates through the stone room. "Each Testing

Center has several of our most powerful undercover informants, with Area 7 fully staffed."

"In fact," Terrace adds, "we even have one informant at the Area 19 Testing Center."

"Indeed." Arthur runs a thumb over his chin. "It's unfortunate we didn't reach you in time."

"Reach me in time? You mean the morning I failed my Test?"

"Yes," Arthur says. "Our informant at the Area 19 Testing Center was too late. You vanished. *Literally.*"

My eyes bounce between Terrace and Arthur. They're giving me so much information I'm struggling to keep up. "You've been looking for me since I failed my Test? How . . . what have you . . ." I'm stumbling over my words like a child, wide-eyed and weak in the knees. "How is this even possible?"

"It has taken vision, dedication, and time." Arthur nods to several people in the room. "And if you agree to join us, Miss Timewire, we can accomplish what we've set out to do in record time."

"And what is it you've set out to do?"

I'm trembling now, looking around the room in awe. All of the faces that stare back at me are filled with determination. They look like society members, but as I take them in, their eyes soften like they're inviting me into the fold.

I place my gaze back on Arthur Evandrum, and he draws himself up, speaking with boldness. "We plan to end the Test and take down the government, Miss Timewire."

At this, my blood runs cold, and the tingling in my body intensifies. This is beyond anything I thought possible. They're going to take down the government? The only way that could happen is if these people have the numbers. And if they're in 83% of the world's Testing Centers, it seems they do. In the span of one conversation, my understanding of the world has shattered, and hope for a better future blooms in my heart.

"You've already taken care of Maddy," Terrace says. "We were planning to extract the secret weapon at the opportune time, but it seems you've beat us to it."

"You know about Maddy?" I ask, my voice failing. "You know he's like us?"

Arthur laughs, drumming his fingers again. "I'm a Chief Overseer, Miss Timewire. Of course I know about the secret weapon. I've never seen him, but I've been briefed." He pauses, and then raises an eyebrow. "I'm truly impressed with you. You managed to steal a resource the government's protected for a hundred years."

I curl my nose at this. Maddy's not a resource, he's a person.

"Which brings me back to my question," he continues, locking eyes with me. "How did you get caught, Miss Timewire? If Miss Turrick hadn't acted when she did, you and your friends would be dead. How is that possible when you're so powerful?"

I bite my lower lip, pondering if I should reveal what I know about the President now that I've seen the Testing Center feeds. I rub the bridge of my nose and close my eyes. My body is still riddled with pain, and I'm desperate for sleep, but this conversation is far from over.

"Let me get this straight," I say, struggling with my words. "You want me to train so I can help you take the Area 19 Testing

Center so that you can take down the government?"

"Yes." Arthur's tone verges on icy, but his face holds no aggression. "Area 19 is the linchpin—the tipping point if you will. If we can secure the Capitol City's Testing Center, we can end the blood Test worldwide and pave a way to a brighter future. One in which we don't have to hide in the shadows of this world. We can rejoin society, abolish the old system built on the lies of history, and create a new one."

His chest rises with the passion of his conviction.

"Society holds the Testing Center at its heart. It's a noble institution that seeks to provide safety from an imaginary threat. And everyone blindly worships this illusion of security. You were raised on society's lies, Miss Timewire. You know the golden rule."

"The path to a perfect society is perfect obedience," I recite.

"Precisely." He claps his hands, making me jump. "But what if we could create a world where this institution no longer exists? What if we could end the Test in one striking blow, all across the world? If the institution were to fall, we'd have a chance to reach people."

My mind flashes to the tender moment between me and Keith up in the ceiling of the old compound, and his words come back to me: "I just wish I could do something, like my parents did. I wish that . . . I wish that the world could change. Maybe one day things will be different. Who knows? Maybe we won't have to hide forever."

Maybe we won't have to hide forever . . .

My heart swells at the idea. Is it possible? Could our people rejoin society? Could the genocide stop? Could we set the record of history straight and tell people the truth behind the Terror War?

"Securing the Area 19 Testing Center will be our greatest victory," Arthur says. "The Test is a construct meant to destroy those with the biomarker, and it has no place in the world we want to build—one where having an ability isn't evil. It's *right*. Good. Cherished."

Arthur puts his hand over his heart.

"I've dedicated my life's work to this vision of the future. I hope that you will consider our cause, and if it is a worthy one, join us. With your power, we can end the Test."

Something about this moment seals my decision. If Arthur can really accomplish this, I'm on board. I hate what I've done to my people. I hate that I've exposed them to the dangers of the government's tyranny because of my blind and naïve beliefs. But I've grown up. Now I can see past society's lies, and if I can help put an end to the Test and reintegrate our people into society, then I have to try. I owe them that.

I take a deep breath. What I'm about to say is going to throw a wrench into all of this, but maybe these people will have the answer.

I square my shoulders, preparing to deal the death blow. "Taking the Area 19 Testing Center isn't going to be as easy as you've imagined. President Alvaro Camille is a puppet master. He's like me."

The thunderous cascade of shocked looks pulls the room into such a ferocious silence that my ears rumble. Arthur sits, bracing himself against the back of his chair, looking at me wide-eyed. His mouth is askew, and I take the opportunity to forge ahead.

"And that's why I was on the platform with a gun to my head. Camille was controlling my friends and all the military, and I wasn't strong enough to stop him."

I'm sweating so much that it stings my eyes. Fatigue is choking me, but I continue, pushing through the discomfort.

"He's a man of great power—powerful enough to maintain control over someone from a great distance. Keith didn't hurt me on purpose. He would *never* hurt me. The President had control over him, and he attacked me because he was forced to."

My lungs heave, and the pain in my ribs sharpens like an axe.

"But the President couldn't use his ability on me, and I couldn't use mine on him. Somehow . . . we're immune to each other. And he didn't see that coming."

Arthur's eyebrows turn upward, and he speaks in a whisper. "You remarkable girl."

His tone is unsettling. Perhaps it's the trauma of the last six months, but I can't help but feel it's something deeper. He wants to take down the Test, and that's a good thing. I want to take down the Test too. But I still feel like he's not telling me something. It's lingering behind his eyes. He has a hunger I've come to know well, and in time, perhaps it will come to light.

I bite my lower lip, pondering what I should do next. Though he appears as frightening as any other Chief Overseer, he views people with abilities as precious, and that's something I can hold on to.

I'm not going to play my last card just yet. Before I tell him where my people are, there's something I need. I can't explain why, but I don't fully trust him.

"I will help you," I say.

The room bristles as a murmur sweeps across the Board members. People whisper things I can't catch, and Arthur and Terrace look relieved.

"You said Jonah and I can have anything we need to train?" I ask.

"Anything," Arthur says.

"Swear it. In front of all of them." I point to the people around the room. "Swear to me you'll give me anything I need."

He bows his head. "I swear to you. I will give you anything you need."

"Okay," I say, calculated. "These will be *private* lessons. Anything Jonah and I do while training will be exclusive. No one is allowed to watch us or listen to us. No cameras. No bugs. No unnecessary people unless we specifically request someone. And no interruptions."

The vein on Arthur's neck pulses, but he forces a charming smile, pressing his palms flat against one another. "Of course, Miss Timewire. Anything you need."

"Good. And Keith. I need to see him. Where are you holding him?"

Arthur clicks his tongue in displeasure. "If President Camille had that boy under his power, then I'm afraid he must remain where he is. We don't know what he can do, or to what extent the President has maintained control over him."

"Trust me, I have a similar concern," I say tersely. "Where are you holding him?"

No response.

"You said I can have whatever I need. You gave me your word. I need to see Keith, so where is he?"

Arthur and Terrace look to one another, and then Arthur nods.

Terrace clears his throat. "Mr. Keaton is in a holding cell on the first floor of our facility, Sector 2, cell B-9."

"Thank you."

"Now, Miss Timewire, your people?" Arthur leans forward and his mouth twitches, like he's trying to suppress appearing too eager.

I take a second to survey the room. When Hugo interrupted my conversation with Jonah, I thought I was being led into the worst kind of nightmare, but what I've learned is beyond anything I could have imagined. This could be a fresh start for us. My people are out in the elements, exposed to danger that could claim them at any time. It's honestly a miracle the government hasn't found us. We could be safe here. Arthur has resources and numbers. He's offering protection. And the forest was never a permanent solution . . .

Still, something holds me back. I need to ask him one more question.

"What if I don't tell you where they are? What will you do?"

Arthur pauses, and his look tempers. He appears somber, even defeated, but he addresses me with a quiet and respectful posture.

"I may have a silver tongue, but I will never be able to convince you to do anything you don't want to do. This is *your* decision, and I will respect it. And you, Jonah, and your friends may stay here even if you don't tell me their location. But if you do, and I send Olivia to them, please know that I will not force them to come here. It will be their decision as well. I have no intention of hurting them. They have powers, and I *must* offer to protect that."

He pauses, and his voice implores me to listen.

"I understand you don't know me, and trust takes time, but let me prove myself to you. When I give my word, I mean it. Everyone will be safe here. No more hiding, no more running, no more dying. Please."

I rise from my seat slowly, channeling the fierceness of my ability through my body. It vibrates down my arm, and I stretch out my hand, palm pointed directly over Arthur Evandrum's heart.

"If you do *anything* to hurt my people," I snarl, "you'll regret ever meeting me. I promise you that."

Arthur recoils and then his gaze softens. "Miss Timewire, your people *are* my people."

I exhale through tight lips, shaking from the intensity of power coursing through my blood. This is the moment I make the decision to reveal our camp or keep us hidden. Silence extends between us for nearly a minute . . .

"They're in a forest 300 miles south of the Area 19 Testing Center."

I drop my arm, lowering it from Arthur's chest, and his

shoulders relax. "Thank you, Miss Timewire, from the bottom of my heart. This is the start of a beautiful partnership."

I sit back in the leather chair, exhausted. "I agree."

"Assuming they consent, we will bring your people here. Miss Turrick will see to it. We have more than enough space and resources for everyone."

"Thank you. When should I expect to see them?"

"As soon as possible," Arthur replies, adjusting his white tie.

A sharp knock sounds from the hallway, and before anyone can answer it, the door slides into the wall. Beezee bursts in, nearly tripping. She collects herself quickly and pulls her long braid through her fingertips.

"Arthur, your time is up! I'm taking Hollis back to her room. If she doesn't rest, then there's no point to any of this, so I'm sorry, but this meeting is over."

Arthur looks amused. He clicks the cuff of his sleeve, and the nine wall screens turn off. "Your timing is impeccable, Beezee-day. We were just finishing." He turns to me once more and says, "Miss Timewire, please get some rest. We will discuss what can be done about President Camille later."

"Come with me, child," Beezee says. "I'm sure you're quite exhausted from all of this."

She frowns at Arthur, hands me the crutch, then helps me to my feet. No one says anything more, and the two of us make our way out of the room and into the white hallway.

I lean against the crutch, my mind buzzing.

"Don't let that man scare you," Beezee says, waving a hand through the air. "He can be quite intimidating, but he's a good man with a good heart. I can promise you that."

"Beezee?"

"Yes, child?"

"Do you work at the Area 7 Testing Center?"

Her hand rests on my shoulder as we continue down the corridor. "Yes, I do. Arthur showed you the security footage?"

"Yes."

"And did he show you his ability?"

I nod, fighting another dizzy spell.

Beezee gives me a knowing look. "Yes, his power has been quite helpful. It's one of the reasons we've been able to slowly worm our way back into society. That man's silver tongue! Truly a marvel. We have four hundred and sixty-three people working at the Area 7 Testing Center now, and with Arthur as the Chief Overseer, we have eyes and ears everywhere. He's quite high up in society, you know."

"Beezee?"

"Yes, child?"

"What do your people do at the Area 7 Testing Center?"

"We take stock of those who pass their Test, we keep tabs on the population of Area 7 . . . things like that," she answers. "We must keep up appearances or people will get suspicious. No one knows Area 7 is fully compromised. Has Arthur explained why we need your help?"

"He said he needs me to train so I can help you take the Area 19 Testing Center."

"And have you agreed to help us?" Beezee's posture straightens, nearly imperceptibly, but the society member in me recognizes this immediately. My brain hums on high alert, and my jaw tenses.

"Yes, I have."

Beezee smiles, rubbing my shoulder. "Wonderful! That's wonderful."

My nerves tingle. I haven't had time to process the information I've learned, let alone process what I've agreed to help them do. I don't know what to think, and all I want to do is sleep.

A pit settles in my stomach as I keep in step with Beezee. We continue toward my room. During the rest of the walk, I choose not to say anything further. I'll wait until I can see Jonah. Alone. With everything I've seen and heard, this could be the best possible twist of fate. These people have plans to destroy the Test for good, and they've enlisted my help. I could change the world for the better.

The only thing standing in my way is President Alvaro Camille. Unfortunately, Arthur Evandrum didn't account for two puppet masters.

—————

6

—————

It's been nine days since Olivia teleported us to the mountain, and today my people are coming. Before I join Arthur to greet them, I've insisted on seeing Keith. Beezee's performed several more healing sessions on my ribs and jaw, and now the pain is more of a dull ache—an incredible improvement from before.

I can walk without a crutch, but it's difficult. The bruising on my face, arms, and chest looks more severe than before, but Beezee says that's normal because it means I'm healing.

"I still don't think this is a good idea," Beezee states, escorting me down a flight of dimly lit stone steps. "You don't have much time either. Arthur wants you to be in the aircraft hangar early so that—"

"Beezee, I'll be fine," I say, snapping at her. "I need to see Keith. And anyway, Arthur has allowed it."

I add the second half as a defense. I need to see him so I can determine if Camille still has control over him. I have a theory. It's possible that Camille only maintained control over Keith because he grabbed him *prior* to Olivia teleporting us. In which case, his connection held strong over a vast distance. But if Camille relinquished his hold over Keith after these people detained him, he'd have no way of grabbing him again. And if that's true, Keith should be freed from his confinement immediately.

"Hollis, it doesn't matter what Arthur has or hasn't allowed. That boy almost beat you to death. This is not a good—"

"But he didn't!" I say, frustrated. "You don't understand."

Beezee sighs, shaking her head. Keith doesn't deserve for anyone to think he would intentionally hurt me, but I don't have the energy to explain that he was being controlled. I just want to see him.

After another minute, the two of us reach the landing of Sector 2. The lighting is horrible here, and I strain my eyes to keep from tripping. She leads me past a few stone alcoves and into another hall. The end of it expands into a small, circular, cave-like room with three doors.

"The middle door," Beezee says, and I grab the handle. The metal screeches open, and past it, my pupils are assaulted by bright lighting. The holding facility is quite large, and it houses rows of cells that are sealed off with thick panes of glass.

A guard in a beige uniform steps forward, blocking the entrance. He says something to Beezee, and she hands him a piece of paper. My eyes wander to the gun slung over the man's shoulder. It's a standard issue military machine gun. I understand why these people have weapons, but it still doesn't make it any less unpleasant.

The guard lets us pass with a low grunt, and I scan the rows of cells. I find Keith sitting on the floor in the cell labeled 'B-9.'

"Keith!" I exclaim, running to him and placing my hands on the glass.

"Hollis?" He jumps to his feet, runs over, and holds his hands across from mine. Two inches separate our palms. "You're alive?"

"Of course I'm alive! You didn't know? No one told you?" I shoot a disgruntled look at Beezee.

"No. No one's told me anything," he says, his eyebrows knitting together. "I thought you were dead."

"No!" I say, shaking my head. "I'm alright. And so is Rosalie and Jonah. We're okay! These people have powers. They're like us. And they're bringing everyone from the forest here."

Keith looks around. "Where are we?"

"In a mountain near the Area 7 Testing Center."

"What?"

"Yeah."

I'm breathless. I gaze into Keith's blue eyes, and all I want to do is hug him. The attack wasn't his fault. He would never hurt me. I smile, but he doesn't return the gesture. His hand slips down a few inches, and his head falls in shame.

"I tried to stop myself. I tried to warn you, but I couldn't speak. I couldn't move. Camille. He was in my head. He forced me to . . ."

Keith stops speaking and presses his fist against the glass in frustration.

"I know," I say, dropping my hand to match his. My soft voice carries across the large room. "It's alright, Keith. I know, but I'm okay. He didn't kill me. I'm alive! We're all alive, and everyone is coming here."

Keith's face fills with deep anguish, and I want to grab his hand, but the cold pane separates us. I turn to the man guarding the cells. Time to test my theory.

"Open his door," I say.

The guard doesn't look over, but he addresses me in a respectful tone. "I'm sorry, ma'am. I can't do that."

"Why?"

"I'm under strict orders from Arthur Evandrum," he says. "I have been informed of Mr. Keaton's situation, and his cell will remain closed until he can be deemed safe."

I turn to Keith, my eyes stinging.

"Hollis, no." He shakes his head and backs away. "I don't want to hurt you again. I don't know if he can still control me."

"Have you felt anything since you attacked me?"

"No, I haven't felt anything."

A jolt dances through my chest. Maybe my theory is right. "Can I try something?"

Keith gives me a puzzled look.

"Do you trust me?" I ask.

"With my life."

"Okay."

I back away from the glass and hold my hand out, twitching it. Keith freezes within his cell, and I sigh in relief. He's under *my* control. I close my eyes and move my hand forward, feeling my ability course through Keith's body. I flick, freeing him from my grasp with a huge smile.

"I can control you," I say. "I couldn't do that when Camille had you."

Keith nods, approaching the glass again. "That's good."

"That means we can get you out of here," I say, beaming. "There's no reason to keep you locked up."

"You're sure? You don't think Camille can control me anymore?"

"I'm sure. I think the only reason he was able to control you was because he grabbed you right before Olivia brought us here."

We put our hands together opposite one another, taking in the moment. Right now, no one else exists but him. This only lasts a few seconds before Beezee calls from across the room.

"Hollis, we'll be late!"

"Yes, nearly done," I say, waving her off.

Beezee and the guard turn to each other, muttering in low voices.

I turn my back to them, reach inside my pocket, and pull out two scraps of paper. I lean against the glass, locking eyes with Keith. I hold the first paper up to the thick pane, and Keith reads it quickly.

These people have been looking for me.

I push the second scrap to the glass.

I'll get you out of here. I promise.

I stuff the scraps back in my pocket, glancing sideways. Beezee and the guard haven't noticed. I hold Keith's gaze, and our hands meet across the barrier one last time. Right now, I'd like nothing more than to feel his arms around me.

"Hollis!" Beezee chimes. "We have to go. Now."

My stomach churns. I don't want to leave him. I could stay here all day, but I know our people are set to come any minute, and Arthur has insisted that I be present for their arrival.

"I'll come back," I say, attempting a smile.

Keith nods. "I'm glad you're okay. I thought I'd never see you again."

"Hollis, we really must go," Beezee scolds, beckoning me. "Arthur won't be happy if you're late."

I look at Beezee then turn back to Keith. "You can't get rid of me that easily," I tease. "I'm Hollis Timewire."

Keith chuckles, shaking his head. "You certainly are."

Hurrying over to Beezee's side, I stuff my hand into my right pocket. The scraps of paper brush against my fingertips, calming me. I wish I could tell Keith everything I've learned about these people, but it will have to wait.

The guard lets us pass then resumes his post, the machine gun clutched in his grasp. And even though I want to, I don't look back. I follow in Beezee's wake, and we move quickly up the flight of stairs leading to Sector 3. The giant concrete aircraft hangar resides there, and that's where everyone will come.

"Beezee?"

"Yes?"

"I have a question."

"What is it?"

"I know we're in a mountain, but . . . what is this place?" The high stone walls tower around us. From what I've seen so far, this compound is easily ten times the size of the old one, possibly larger.

"It's an abandoned nuclear weapons lab," she replies. "There was a nasty radioactive meltdown about fifty years ago, and the government had the mountain sealed off. Hundreds of workers were killed in the breach. It was an incredible amount of radiation—a seven on the International Nuclear Event Scale. But I suppose that's fortunate for us."

"A seven? What does that mean?"

"The INES is a scale from zero to seven that measures the severity of a nuclear accident. Seven is the worst because there's a major release of radioactive material with widespread health and environmental effects. No one comes near this mountain, and I suspect no one will for a long time. It's even a no-fly zone."

I stare at Beezee, perplexed.

"But how are we here? If there was that much radiation, how—"

"Mr. Kurt Canterbury!" she exclaims without missing a beat. She cracks a huge smile, walking with a swing in her step. "That incredible, incredible man! He dried the place right up— leached all the radioactivity out! He sucked it all into his palms. What a sweet, dear man! We wouldn't be here if it weren't for him."

I stifle a snort by pressing my hand over my mouth. If I didn't know any better, I'd say Beezee-day Jones has a crush on Mr. Kurt Canterbury.

"Incredible," I manage through a giggle.

Beezee looks back over her shoulder reproachfully. Color has cropped up in her face. "Nearly there. Are you alright, dear? How's your ribs?" she chirps.

"Fine," I say, panting.

We continue up the last flight of steps to Sector 3.

"Good. Very good," Beezee hums, looking straight ahead.

We round the corner, moving at a rapid pace, and I grimace. It seems that Beezee feels that if I'm late, it will be her fault. After a minute, we walk up to the double doors leading to the upper balcony of the hangar. Beezee grabs the handle and pulls, gesturing me through.

Arthur Evandrum stands with the rest of the Board members at the edge of the metal railing overlooking the room. Everyone turns in unison, and all eyes find me, but I'm not paying attention to them. I only care about one person. Jonah. He's standing next to Arthur, leaning on a cane.

"Jonah!" I smile, feeling more at ease than I did a moment ago.

"Miss Timewire." Arthur strides forward with a smirk that accentuates his shocking white hair. His societal look is nauseating. "You're just in time."

I nod, my shoulders stiffening.

Arthur looks past me. "Beezee-day, if you could join the others down below as we wait for our new guests. Terrace has informed me that one of the young ladies coming has a broken ankle. And there are a few others who will need medical attention."

"Of course." She vanishes back through the double doors.

"Come and join us at the railing, Miss Timewire." Arthur puts a hand on my back and steers me forward. His touch is cold and unwelcome, but I don't pull away. I stand next to Jonah facing the chasm.

"You look like you're doing better," I say.

"I am," he says, his tone more formal than usual. "I'm glad to see you're doing better as well."

"I thought you two would like to be here for the grand arrival," Arthur muses, his spindly hands gripping the metal.

I peer over the edge. Candice and Ben are waiting below, but Rosalie isn't present. She's still in the hospital. According to Beezee, being stabbed isn't the same as mending bones. Her ability can command the healing process, but she can't create more blood. Apparently, Rosalie got lucky. She lost a lot of blood, but not enough to kill her. Fortunately, Beezee was able to give her a blood transfusion from their blood bank, but she's still on strict bed rest.

Jonah's voice snaps me out of my thoughts.

"The broken ankle," he says, addressing Arthur, "were you referring to Vianne?"

"Yes. Beezee can mend her ankle, and we can provide Audrey with crutches. Such an unfortunate circumstance. It's a shame Audrey had to lose her leg."

I bite my tongue to hold it. Audrey lost her leg because it got crushed by the falling debris of the old compound when the government bombed us. Arthur seems to know so much already, but only because of Terrace DuPont's ability. How much does Terrace know about me? What other extraneous details were brought to light after I left that meeting? And the things that are private to me . . . how long until Arthur knows those too?

I shake myself, taking a deep breath. I should ask about Keith's release. He's been locked up for nine days, and now that

I'm certain the President doesn't have control of him, he should be released. I open my mouth, but Arthur's next words steal my attention away.

"I'd very much like to meet young Maddy," he murmurs.

A rush of protective instinct surges through me, and tingling trails down my fingers.

Arthur stands, shoulders faced squarely ahead, as if commanding an army. "What a fascinating ability. So powerful for one so small. Don't you think?"

"Indeed," Jonah says, leaning on his cane. He's matching Arthur's posture. "And I can say the same of your ability, Mr. Evandrum. It's quite captivating."

Arthur chuckles. "That's the word, isn't it? 'Captivating.'"

"Truly."

"And your ability, Jonah—well, I've not encountered anything like it. To be able to take on another person's power? Incredible. What a pair. You and Miss Timewire will discover much in your time here. I'm sure of it."

"As am I."

"I've prepared a room for your training sessions," Arthur continues. "Private, as Miss Timewire requested. I hope it will be to your liking."

Jonah doesn't respond. I watch him out of the corner of my eye. Since the meeting with Arthur, I haven't had a chance to speak with him alone. I've been with Beezee nonstop. The only thing I've been able to tell him is that Arthur wants us to train together, and he said we could have whatever we need.

Again, my gaze falls over the edge of the balcony. Ben and

Candice are huddled together, waiting patiently. Candice clutches Ben's hand, resting her head on his shoulder. I can just make out the look on Ben's face—sobered and nearly blank. I haven't talked with them since Keith's attack.

"Ah, Miss Turrick is right on time," Arthur says.

In the center of the room, the blue orb flashes into existence. It expands, larger and larger, filling the space to capacity and forcing the people standing below to step out of view under the balcony. I shield my eyes from the fierce glow.

With a pop, the orb bursts, and three hundred people appear. Chatter fills the high walls, echoing all around, and I breathe a sigh of relief. My people are here just as Arthur promised, and the small piece of uncertainty I've held since telling Arthur their location vanishes. So far, he's a man of his word.

Candice darts from under the balcony, rushing toward someone in the crowd. I follow her with my eyes as she tackles Darren Mitchell, the boy who denounced me after I betrayed everyone. Back in the forest, he wanted nothing to do with me. I don't blame him either. We weren't close. The only interaction I had with him prior to the bombing was playing games with him and the rest of my friends. Same with Audrey Rye—the mousy, competitive girl who floated the glittering marbles during the marble game. I never got to know her well, but she lost her leg because of me. And Darren will never forgive me for it.

I search the crowd, scouring it for Vianne Evolet. She went on the rescue mission with me to help save Maddy and snapped her ankle during our escape. I spot her quickly because of her hair. It flickers through several shades of pink, landing on a deep fuchsia. That girl is always morphing . . .

To my surprise, she's leaning on Ashton Teel, the boy I attacked with my ability. I did something to his power that day and it stopped working, but that didn't stop him from being a horrific bully toward me in the forest. He made it his mission to target me, even going as far as assaulting me by the wood stack until Jonah forbade him to go near me.

Ashton's hands are around Vianne's waist as she holds her broken ankle off the ground. And between them is Maddy. He clings to Ashton's leg, peering around the massive room in awe.

My stomach squirms. Why is Ashton holding Vianne like that? It looks like he's doing more than just supporting her weight.

"Greetings everyone!" Arthur says, and his voice booms ten times louder than normal. I jump, noticing a small, black, pea-sized microphone clipped to his white suit jacket. The chatter ceases, and everyone turns their attention to the balcony. "I'd like to welcome each and every one of you to your new home. I'm overjoyed to discover the gift of more of our kind. You make us, as a people, stronger. And I want you to know you will always have a place here."

As Arthur speaks, more and more people spot me. I feel sick to my stomach. A murmur bristles through the gathering.

"We have rooms, food, and clothing for all," Arthur continues. "I assure you that you are safe now. We are sheltered in a mountain outside the Area 7 Testing Center—well hidden from society's prying eyes."

The hushed voices below grow a little louder.

"Please, feel free to integrate yourself here." He points down over the edge. "If you would follow the group of volunteers I have below, we will show you to your living quarters. And if anyone needs medical attention, Beezee-Day Jones, our head physician, has a team waiting to help. Welcome home."

At this, voices rise back to full volume, and people move toward the group of volunteers. I turn from the railing, keen to find Vianne and Maddy, but Arthur's hand stops me.

"Not yet, Miss Timewire. I'd like you to stay."

"But I need—"

"Miss Turrick will only take a moment," he says.

The blue orb appears on the balcony in a flash of light that blinds us. Olivia tumbles out of the orb, and so does Ashton Teel, Vianne Evolet, and Maddy. They stumble a bit, disoriented. Ashton's strong features sour at the sight of me, and his pointed nose turns upward. He runs a hand through his dirty blond hair and looks away.

"Sorry about that," Olivia says. She twists a finger through her tight, black curls. "I probably should have warned you."

"Vianne!" I run to her, and her porcelain complexion lights up.

"Hollis!"

I hug her, and Ashton moves out of the way.

"Thank goodness you're alright," I say.

"Thank goodness *I'm* alright?" Vianne takes my shoulders in hand, hobbling on one foot and nearly falling over. Ashton catches her around the waist. "We saw the footage on Libbie's tablet. We thought you were . . ." Her eyes find Jonah, and her hair flickers from lavender to green to teal all in one burst of color. "Jonah!" she shrieks. "You're alive!"

But before anyone else can speak, Arthur Evandrum steps forward, stooping down to the floor. His composure shifts, his tongue runs along the top of his lip, and his attention cleaves to Maddy so ferociously it's like they're the only two in the room.

"So," he begins, his tone silky, "this is the secret weapon of a hundred years ago." His eyes grow hungry behind an enthusiastic smile, and he bares his teeth. "Well, young man, I'm pleased to make your acquaintance."

He holds his hand out to Maddy as if inviting him to sit on his lap.

"Come here, little one."

———
7
———

"Hɪ Mᴀᴅᴅʏ." I ꜱᴛᴇᴘ ᴅɪʀᴇᴄᴛʟʏ ɪɴ ꜰʀᴏɴᴛ ᴏꜰ Aʀᴛʜᴜʀ ᴀɴᴅ scoop Maddy into my arms. I hold him on my hip and put some distance between us.

Arthur's lips purse, but he's not lost his charming composure. "Young man, I'm very glad you're here."

My body tenses, and power rears in my palms.

"Are you one of the special people?" Maddy asks, staring at him with big blue eyes. His blond curls fall unkempt across his forehead. He leans sideways, and my grip on him slips, so I readjust, interlocking my fingers.

"I am."

"Vianne needs medical attention, Mr. Evandrum," I say. "Her ankle is broken."

Arthur disregards me. "Maddy, you have a very special power, don't you? Can you tell me about it?"

I clear my throat way louder than I need to. He's looking at

Maddy like I'm not here, and I don't like it. And he already knows what Maddy can do.

"I can use the golden light!" Maddy beams. He raises his hands above his head.

"Vianne needs medical attention," I say again, this time more aggressively.

Arthur steps back and plasters on an agreeable smile, bowing his head. "Of course. We shouldn't waste another moment." He turns to Olivia, hands pressed fingertip to fingertip. "Miss Turrick, can you take this young lady and her friend to Beezee-day?"

Olivia nods, and before I can say another word, the blue orb encases Vianne and Ashton, and they vanish with a pop. I stare at the spot they've vacated, my mouth askew. That's not what I meant. I wanted to go with Vianne and take Maddy along. The hungry look shrouded in Arthur's features is scaring me, so I say the next thing that comes to mind.

"Jonah and I will start our training now."

Arthur's mouth parts, and so does Jonah's. I press ahead, clutching Maddy to my hip and angling him away from Arthur.

"And I need to speak with Olivia," I add. "Privately."

"I . . . Now? Miss Timewire, don't you think—"

"You said you've prepared a room? I assume it's ready?"

"Well, yes. But—"

"Good. Can you show us?" Maddy is growing heavy in my arms, and my bones ache, but I don't slacken my grasp. "Well?"

Arthur fiddles with his suit jacket by tugging on the collar, and the lower line of his lip fights a frown. "Very well. Let me show you to your training quarters."

"Thank you."

"Right this way." Arthur gestures Jonah and me through the double doors exiting the balcony.

I sigh, relieved. Good. My escape plan worked. I'm not letting Arthur anywhere near Maddy. Now that we've freed this little boy from the government, I'm not letting anyone hurt him ever again.

I'm not sure why Arthur's so interested in him, but Terrace's words at the Board meeting come back to me: "We were planning to extract the secret weapon at the opportune time, but it seems you've beat us to it."

He clearly views Maddy as more of an ability than a person. And I can't help but feel that's how he sees me too. We both have powerful type two abilities. Arthur is a type two himself. Abilities like ours are rarer because they require other people to work, whereas type one abilities work regardless of the presence of others. People with type two abilities tend to be more powerful than type ones in many ways.

With all I've been through, I've learned to trust my gut, and my gut says to keep Maddy close.

I fall in step behind Jonah as Arthur leads us down a stone corridor and up several flights of stairs. I lose track of how many turns we make. Jonah and I are both panting from the injuries we've sustained, but neither of us say a word. There will be plenty of time for that in private.

"Just this way, Miss Timewire," Arthur says, pointing ahead.

The corridor splits into two more. We take the one on the right and continue for another minute until we come to a heavy metal door. Arthur takes hold of the handle and yanks it open. The metal slinks into the stone.

"I hope it is to your liking."

My jaw drops. The room is massive. It's half the size of the aircraft hangar. Couches line the far wall, tables and chairs are sectioned off to the right, and several cots are set up on the left, creating an open living room area furnished with cabinets, dressers, lamps, curtains, a coffee table, and mirrors. And in the center, there is a large, foamy mat—a perfect training platform.

"Does this suffice?" Arthur asks, turning to me.

"I . . . Y-yes, thank you," I stammer.

"You should have everything you need, and if there is anything else you require, don't hesitate to ask."

"Thank you. This is very generous."

"Anything you need," he says. "As promised."

"Yes," I say, tearing my gaze away from the room and fixing it back on Arthur. "Please send Olivia over as soon as she's available. Jonah and I need to . . . to practice now."

I end my sentence in a lame attempt to sound business-like. Arthur doesn't look convinced.

Nonetheless, he gives me a stiff nod. "Of course." His eyes linger on Maddy, and his mouth curls.

"As soon as possible!" I quip, hoping this will hurry him away.

"Miss Turrick is busy at the moment, but I'll send her down when she's free."

"Thank you."

And with that, Arthur exits the room, sliding the door shut

behind him. It clangs, scratching against the stone. The instant the door closes, I drop Maddy from my hip.

"Hollis," Jonah says, finally speaking up. "Why did you insist on—"

I shake my head furiously, holding my hand up, and Jonah stops talking.

I set about the room, overturning everything I can. For a moment, Jonah looks puzzled, but as soon as he realizes what I'm doing, he limps over to a plush armchair and waits for me to finish.

I feel under every surface—tables, chairs, cots, and couches. I check the hem of the training mat, the air vents, the light fixtures, and behind all of the outlets. I even turn over the bedding, throwing it on the floor to check the lining. Maddy has joined in now, thinking it's a game. He tosses blankets onto the concrete and plays with the pillows. His sweet laugh echoes off the stone.

It takes me fifteen minutes before I'm satisfied.

I'm sticky with sweat, panting and exhausted. I rub the stitch in my chest tenderly, approaching Jonah. "Okay. No bugs. Arthur's kept his word."

"That's good," he says. He leans against his cane, pale and tired.

Finally, after nine days in the mountain, I'm alone with my teacher, and there's so much I want to say, I feel like I'm going to burst.

"How much do you know?" I ask. "What has Arthur told you?"

He grimaces, shifting himself in the chair. "He told me you've promised to help them secure the Area 19 Testing Center."

I breathe through tight lips. "Did he show you the live feeds from the other Testing Centers? Did he explain that they have undercover informants with abilities at 83% of the world's Testing Centers?"

"Yes." Jonah pauses, his brows knitting together. His right hand grips the cane until his knuckles turn white. "He also told me about Area 7, and that he's a Chief Overseer."

"So, you experienced the same shock I did."

He exhales sharply. "That's an understatement."

My stomach churns. I'm physically spent and emotionally overwhelmed. It feels like a weight crushing me from within. I sit at my teacher's feet and speak with a heavy heart.

"Jonah, did I make the right decision? Telling Arthur about the camp in the forest?"

I can't bring myself to lift my head. I will never be able to take back betraying my people to the government, but everything I've done since that moment has been for them. And to think I may have put them in danger once more . . .

"Hollis, look at me." Jonah's soft voice encourages my gaze upward. "You made the right decision. We were scraping by in the forest. Food was running low. It was cold. And even with the protection of Libbie's tree dome, there was no guarantee the government wasn't going to find us. It was never a permanent solution."

I blow air out between trembling lips, and comfort washes over me. The fact that Jonah's voiced aloud the exact phrase I thought to myself at the Board meeting puts my spirit at ease.

Maddy joins my side and pulls on my arm, giggling, so I scoop him into a hug. I stare up at the vaulted ceiling. "What do you think about all of this?"

"It's impressive," Jonah says.

I shake my head. "I just . . . I have a bad feeling about Arthur. I can't explain it."

"I do as well."

I'm taken aback by his response, and an icy sensation trickles down my spine. "You do?" I hug Maddy tighter. "Do you think I should do what Arthur's asking me to do?"

"I think that's a decision only you can make."

Maddy begins to squirm in my arms, so I let him go. He pops up and scampers back to the discarded pillows and blankets.

"But regardless of your decision, we need to train," he says.

His tone makes me anxious all over again. I knot my fingers together. "I should train even if I don't help them take Area 19?"

Jonah scratches his chin. "President Camille has your ability, Hollis, and he wants you dead. Arthur wants you alive. I don't know what his plans for taking the Area 19 Testing Center look like, but whether those plans benefit you or not, honing your ability keeps *you* in charge. It makes you incredibly valuable, and as long as we are training, Mr. Evandrum will oblige you. We need to know what you can do. If you don't explore your ability, you're vulnerable on both accounts. In here and out there."

My words catch in my throat like shards of glass. "I don't want to do what Camille can do. He's a monster, and . . . I'm capable of it too. Ashton is proof. I almost killed him before the bombing. His ability doesn't even work anymore, and I have no idea why."

"I understand your hesitation, Hollis, but I don't think you have a choice." Jonah holds his cane like a lifeline. "I know your ability is vast and dangerous. Honestly, we haven't even scratched the surface of what you can do." He struggles with his words, his voice deepening. "But what if we need you? What if *our* people need you?"

My nose stings with the threat of tears, and I choke my way through the next sentence. "Jonah . . . I . . . what if, as we're exploring my ability . . . what if it consumes me? Camille said he couldn't let me live because I'd become like him. He told me it was inevitable." I shudder. "There can only be one puppet master. That's what he said. And Arthur didn't know Camille had my power until I told him. They all thought once they found me, I'd be able to march in and take Area 19 without resistance because no one could beat me. But Camille can. And I have no idea how I'm going to fight him—or if that's even possible."

Neither of us speak, and my breathing turns shallow. I bury my head in my hands, trying not to panic.

"I've lost myself before. When I hurt Ashton, I couldn't control it. I was so angry. I *wanted* to hurt him. That's why I gave up my ability in the first place. And in front of the Capitol building, I brought down a thousand men. I've never been so scared in my life because . . ." My throat closes, and my eyes burn with tears I can't hold back. "I thought I was going to lose you, Jonah."

"Hollis . . ."

"I told my friends that if the government killed you, then I'd never stop. And I'm scared that will come true. What if I become like him? What if I can't stop myself?"

Maddy, upon seeing me, runs over and hugs me again, bringing my attention to his innocent smile. "Don't be sad."

"Hi Maddy," I say, sniffling.

"Hi!" He smiles, brushing blond curls from his eyes.

"I'm not sad," I say.

"But you're crying." His little features crinkle with concern.

I wipe the tears away on my sleeve. "I'm okay, Maddy. I promise." I return his hug, giving him the biggest smile. "See?"

Jonah looks at me, the compassion I've come to know so well lighting his face. "Hollis, you are nothing like that man."

"How do you know?" I whisper.

"Because your heart is full of good." He leans forward in the chair, resting his arms on his knees. "Hollis, you have an incredible drive for truth and justice, and more importantly, you have a family here that cares about you. You've experienced friendship. Love. You know what it's like to *feel* now. The President doesn't have that, and that's what sets you apart from him. He can't feel the way you can. He doesn't know how."

Tap. Tap. Tap.

I jump, running a hand through my hair. "That must be Olivia."

Scooting Maddy off my lap, I hurry over to the large metal door and slide it open. Olivia Turrick stands in the hall, rocking up and down on her toes.

"Arthur said you wanted to talk to me?" She peers over my shoulder at Jonah and Maddy.

"Yes," I say. "Come in."

She walks into the training room, and her eyes trace over the disarray. Cushions, blankets, and pillows are scattered everywhere, and most of the chairs are overturned. Her posture stiffens.

"I'm just really messy," I say in a half-hearted attempt to explain the room's appearance.

"Oh."

I grimace. She definitely didn't buy that.

"Hi," Maddy chimes, waving at Olivia. "I like your blue light. I can make golden light!"

Olivia stoops down to his level, grinning. "Golden light? That's pretty cool."

"But the golden light isn't a circle like the blue light." He giggles and draws a circle in mid-air with his finger. "It's a wiggly line like this!" He traces a flowing pattern on the stone floor with his shoe.

"That's really special, Maddy." Olivia gives his tiny hand a squeeze. She looks up at me and rises from her crouched position. "What did you want to speak with me about?"

I catch Jonah's eye and decide to dive right in.

"First of all, I want to thank you for saving our lives. Without you, we would have been killed."

Olivia gives me a sad little smile, and my gut plummets. This girl's mannerisms remind me of the first time I met Tiffany after she teleported me to the underground compound.

"How did you rescue us from the platform? How did you find us?"

"The President was broadcasting the feed live worldwide. As

soon as we picked up the signal, I knew where to find you," Olivia explains. She shrugs. "I mean, it's the Capitol building, so . . ."

"Sorry, dumb question," I murmur.

"Then I transported myself to the platform and took everyone with me. Just in the nick of time too."

"Right." I clear my throat to gear myself up for the question I really want to ask. I bite my lower lip, contemplating how blunt I should be, but I choose to keep my voice level and controlled. "I want to know about that day in the forest. I saw your blue orb by the river."

Olivia's cheeks darken to a deep crimson, and she looks over her shoulder.

"Your people have been looking for me since I failed the Test, but you already found me. You knew where our camp was, and you didn't tell Arthur. Why?"

Olivia looks like she might make a break for the door. Her mouth parts, and her hands begin to shake.

"You were in the forest that day. I saw you. How did you find me?" I ask, taking a step toward her. "Why did you keep my location a secret?"

She backs away from me, shaking her head. Strained, she says, "I'm sorry. I have to go."

"Wait!" I advance on her.

"I have to go!" She exits and marches down the hall with a surprising burst of speed.

I run after her. "Olivia, wait!"

But with a flash of intense blue, she vanishes from the corridor. I stand alone, arms limp at my sides. Sweat creeps across my brow once more as a nasty wave of sickness overtakes me. If there's one thing I've learned since discovering the truth about society, it's that secrets do more harm than good. And it's clear that Olivia Turrick has a big one.

8

A MUSICAL VOICE HUMS THROUGH THE SPEAKERS OF THE mountain. "Mid-day Meal: 1145. Please make your way to Sector 12."

I grind my teeth together, grabbing a pillow and stuffing it against my ear. I'm lying on the largest couch in the training room, staring up at the vaulted ceiling. I've been trying to sleep, but the incessant instructions issuing over the speakers are driving me insane.

It's time for me to get up. Today is the first official meeting between our Council and their Board, and I'm not excited. Arthur Evandrum's curly handwriting stares up at me from the oak coffee table:

Miss Hollis Timewire,

I request the honor of your presence for lunch as we celebrate the union of our people. Kindly join the

Board in the dining hall at 1200 for refreshments and fellowship.

Sincerely,

Mr. Arthur Evandrum

I roll my eyes. For the last three days, Arthur's been away at the Area 7 Testing Center. Apparently, he left after showing Jonah and me the training room. And no matter how many times I've explained the situation to Beezee, Keith's detainment hasn't changed.

Her retort is seared into my brain: "Mr. Keaton's release is Arthur's decision, and Arthur's decision alone."

The speakers crackle, and my stomach clenches into a knot. I glance sideways at the itinerary Beezee provided me. It details the schedule of the automated voice. The text is an onslaught of one task after another, slotted out in military time.

```
0700: Rise

0715: Morning Meal

0800: Duty Assignment 1

1000: Duty Assignment 2

1145: Mid-day Meal

1230: Ability Training (16 years and older)

1230: Education Period (15 years and younger)

1800: Evening Meal

1845: Duty Assignment 3

2000: Duty Assignment 4

2130: Retire
```

Next to the itinerary, a map of the facility lies open, detailing the Sectors of the mountain. There are 27 total. I haven't made time to look through them all. I've only learned the bare minimum since everyone from the forest arrived.

Sector 12 is the dining hall. Sector 9 houses the East Rooms where my people are staying. Sector 2 is where they're holding Keith. Sector 7 is my training room. Sector 3 is the aircraft hangar. And Sector 15 is Arthur's office where Board meetings typically take place.

I groan, throwing the pillow onto the patterned rug below the couch. I make a mental note to ask Arthur to disconnect the speakers in this room. It's like an endless wall screen feed. I never used to mind these feeds back in society, but now that I've been disconnected from constant technology exposure for six months, it's irritating. Jonah and I don't need the distraction, especially considering what we're attempting to do.

I swing my legs to the floor and sit up. The soft fibers of the rug squish between my toes, soothing against my skin. I'm alone. Maddy is with Vianne, and Jonah is with Beezee getting another healing session. He's feeling better than before, but he still has a long way to go. I'm trying to avoid the negative thoughts that come when I dwell on Jonah's injuries, but it's proving impossible.

I better get going . . .

The maze of corridors stretches on and on. This mountain fortress is huge, and I scold myself as I weave through the endless halls. I should've studied the map of the Sectors. I'm on my guard here, and if Arthur thinks I'll ever relinquish that, then he's a fool. The problem is, Arthur Evandrum doesn't strike me as a fool.

I'm supposed to head straight to Sector 12. I've learned from Beezee that Arthur doesn't like to be kept waiting, but I want to check on my friends first. I'm worried about Candice. She hasn't been able to see Keith since arriving, and she's not doing well.

I hook a right past the next stone alcove, making a beeline for Sector 9. I walk through the double doors and stop at the third room in the hall. The door is slightly ajar. My fist hovers over the wood, but before I can knock, a soft voice floats from within.

"Ben, it isn't your fault," Candice says. "Camille was controlling you. You didn't stab Rosalie on purpose."

I freeze, wondering if I should leave or stay to listen.

"Ben, look at me. Please," she whimpers, breathing deep. "You can't blame yourself. Please . . . just look at me."

There's a moment of quiet, then a creak as someone shifts their weight.

"We're safe now."

I can tell Candice is trying her best to be comforting, but her tone breaks my heart, and Ben's silence is chilling. Flashes of the silver knife slice through my mind, and physical pain jumps down my spine. I couldn't stop Ben from plunging the blade deep into Rosalie's abdomen and tearing it out. Ben had always been such a goofball, but Camille broke him. I peek through the seam of the door. The ever-smiling boy is not smiling now . . .

I raise my fist and knock three times.

Candice startles then says, "Come in."

I push the door open and meet her gaze. Dark circles hang under her eyes, and her brown hair is unkempt. She's tucked under several blankets, sitting on a cot pushed against the back wall. Ben is sitting next to her. His lanky, boyish features are hollow. Empty. Like he doesn't have any strength at all. He gets up, and without looking at me, he lies down on a second cot and stares up at the ceiling with a blank look.

"Hi." I walk into the bedroom and sit on the foot of Candice's cot.

"Hi," she says.

"I came to check on you. How are you doing?"

Candice hugs her legs over the blanket and doesn't respond. She looks like she hasn't been able to sleep.

"Rosalie lost a lot of blood," she murmurs, pulling at her fingers. Her blue eyes space out, unblinking. "But Beezee said she'll be fine."

I place my hands on hers, and she stops fidgeting. "Candice, how are you?"

"Fine," she says. Her mouth trembles, and her teeth begin to chatter. "I'm still scared. But I keep thinking, 'It's done, and we're safe now,' so . . . I'll be okay."

I nod. "It's done, and we're safe now."

I don't know how true that is for me, but for everyone else, their fight is over. For the first time since the government's brutal attack, they don't have to worry about dying. No one is exposed to the elements, no one is going to get blown up, and no one is going to starve.

"Do you think they'll let my brother go?" Candice whispers.

Her eyes glitter with tears. Even exhausted and crying, Candice is pretty. Her hands shake in mine. "Do you think he could still be under the President's control?"

I give her a gentle squeeze. "He's not."

"They won't let me see him!" she says. "I've asked Beezee a hundred times, but she says he's dangerous. She keeps telling me I need to rest. But Hollis, I can't rest! I can't sleep! I'm scared for Keith. I need to see him. He's my brother!"

"He's okay. I've seen him."

"You've seen him?" she asks, her voice cracking. "Where is he?"

"He's in a holding cell in Sector 2."

"Why did they let *you* see him?" she demands, sitting straight up.

"I asked Arthur. He's taken a special interest in me and . . ." I pause, chewing on the inside of my lip. "We have an arrangement. I can ask for whatever I want, and he promised to give it to me."

Candice's tone rises in an alarming manner. "You went to see him and didn't even think to bring me along? I'm not the one who got stabbed, Hollis. I'm perfectly fine! I need to see my brother! Why didn't you—"

"OW!" I screech, pulling my hands away from hers as the heat of her ability scorches across my skin. "You burned me!"

Candice yelps, springing into an apology. "I'm sorry! I'm so sorry! I didn't mean to burn you!"

"It's okay," I say, wincing. "I'm alright."

"I'm just—I'm angry and scared. Who does this Arthur

person think he is? I can't even see my own brother?"

"You'll see Keith. I promise."

"Hollis, I don't like this." Her brow turns upward. "Aren't these people supposed to be on our side? I understand why they had to lock Keith up. He almost killed you, but I don't get why they're keeping him from us."

"They think Camille can still control him," I say. "But he can't. I used my power on Keith when I saw him. I couldn't do that when the President had him. And as soon as I see Arthur, I'm going to demand they release him. It'll be okay."

She runs a hand through her hair like she's trying not to burst into tears.

"Hey," I say, my tone soft. "Do you want to come to the dining room with me? It might be good to stretch your legs. Get your mind off things."

She shakes her head. "I don't have much of an appetite."

"Okay." I give her a smile. At this point, I'm definitely late to Arthur's lunch. "I should go. I have to . . . well, I'm expected to be . . ."

I stop speaking. I don't know how to say, "I'm expected to be at all of Arthur's Board meetings because I'm helping them take the Area 19 Testing Center." That's a conversation for another time. And I don't want to add to Candice's stress.

"I'm late," I say, moving to the door. "I'll speak to Arthur about Keith. You'll see your brother. I promise."

She nods, sniffling.

"Hey, Candice?"

"Yeah?"

"I'm glad everyone is okay."

"Me too."

I close the door and make my way to Sector 12 as fast as my legs will carry me. It takes another five minutes before I arrive. I peer through the small, rectangular windows installed into the metal. The room is a great stone hall with hundreds of long wooden tables that span the length. And it's packed.

I take a deep breath and nerves jut through me like skewers. I don't want to be here right now. I just want to sleep. But I don't have a choice. Gritting my teeth, I enter through the double doors, and chatter fills the stone to capacity. It brims over to the point of being uncomfortably loud.

Slinking down the left wall, I take care to stay out of people's way. As I continue, more and more eyes follow me. I've grown accustomed to this, but there are so many more people here. I'm nearly to the front of the room when my path is blocked by a gaggle of teens.

"You're Hollis Timewire, right?" A short, scrawny, black-haired boy chirps at me with gushing enthusiasm.

"Of course she's Hollis Timewire," a heavily freckled, plump girl snaps. Her tone is pompous. "Don't you watch the World News? Honestly."

"I watch the World News!" the boy retorts, hands on his hips.

The plump girl snickers. "Yeah, sure you do."

A third girl barges in, taking my hand. She shakes it vigorously. "You're really brave! It's so cool to meet you in real life!" She bounces up and down. "Is it true you broke into the Area 19 Testing Center?"

Overwhelmed by the attention, I retreat until my back is against the wall. I'm surrounded by a small crowd growing larger by the second, and I fight the urge to use my ability on them to get away. Voices call out on all sides.

"Did you really control all of those soldiers in front of the Capitol?"

"I heard you stole the secret weapon."

"Can you freeze me?"

"Yeah, show us your ability!"

"Do it!"

The chorus rises, and my power tingles in my chest, ready for my command. I swallow the knot growing in my throat as sweat collects on my forehead. "Excuse me, I need to—"

"Were you scared when the President was going to kill you?" the plump girl inquires.

The scrawny boy nods. "Yeah, did you fake that you couldn't use your ability on the platform?"

"Duh. She was faking. She's got a stupid powerful ability."

"Did you know you're the most wanted person in the world?" the boy adds.

"Show us your ability!" someone shouts.

"HEY!" a voice booms over the crowd. "ENOUGH!"

To my relief, Terrace DuPont is here, fighting his way through the throng and pushing people aside.

"MOVE!" he yells. "She isn't some spectacle to gawk at. She's a person, so everyone back off. Miss Timewire has somewhere to be." The teens appear stunned, so Terrace barks up again. "Well? Move!"

They scatter with disgruntled looks. Terrace offers his hand to me, and I take it. He leads me through the rest of the crowd, and we emerge past a sectioned-off portion of the dining hall. Velvet ropes are strung at intervals across a barrier of chairs that spans the width of the room. It seems Arthur's set up a V.I.P. area, and I'm glad to be out of the suffocating mob. Terrace drops my hand.

"Thanks for that," I mumble, feeling dazed.

He nods. "Anytime. I know you don't like meeting new people."

"It's fine," I say. "I don't mind."

"You're lying, but that's okay. It's good to be able to pretend you're fine. It's a useful skill."

I bite my lip, perturbed. I don't like that he's using his ability on me. It's invasive.

"Funny," Terrace continues, still marching to the front of the room. "So many people are annoyed when they first meet me. You'll get used to my ability soon, Miss Timewire."

I scoff. "I wouldn't count on that."

He eyes me over his shoulder. "You're late."

"I know."

"You stopped to visit your friends."

"Yes. *And?*" I can't hold back the edge in my voice.

"And you're late," he finishes.

Terrace steers me to a large round table set up at the end of the dining hall. Arthur Evandrum stands to his feet, motioning me to his right-hand side.

"Miss Timewire, welcome," he says.

I take my seat with flushed cheeks, wishing I were anywhere but here. Familiar, condemning faces meet mine. Eli Stone, our lead Council member, sits across the table, his cracked glasses askew over deep wrinkles. Libbie Lizette, the woman who built the forested compound with her ability, sits to his left, her mousy demeanor stern. And Caleb Stuart, the man who interrogated me during my trial, sits to his right. He strokes his wild gray mane, glaring at me. But his sour look is rivaled by Mr. Thomas's, the worst of my accusers. His bald head shines with sweat, and he clutches his mangled arm, staring me down.

With disgust in his voice, Mr. Thomas says, "This must be some kind of sick joke. What is *she* doing here?"

Arthur ignores him. "You're late, Miss Timewire."

"I apologize."

I keep my eyes down as Arthur turns back to his conversation with Eli Stone.

"Eli, I'd love to incorporate you and the rest of the Council onto the Board. Leading and protecting our people, especially in such a cancerous world, can be a precarious task. On behalf of everyone here"—he motions to the other Board members—"we welcome your input and leadership."

"Thank you, Mr. Evandrum," Eli Stone says. "We appreciate your kindness and hospitality." He glances at me for a fraction of a second, pushing his glasses up the bridge of his nose. "Considering recent events, you couldn't have shown up at a better time. We're truly grateful."

"Think nothing of it," Arthur replies. "We are overjoyed to have you here."

"Is no one going to say anything about this?" Mr. Thomas bursts out, gesticulating at me.

"Yes, Mr. Evandrum," Caleb Stuart says, sneering at me. "What is the girl doing here? Her presence is inapprop—"

"Miss Timewire is part of our Board," Arthur says, raising his posture.

Oh no . . .

The heat in my face intensifies, and I fold my sweaty hands together on my lap. This isn't going to end well.

"OUTRAGEOUS!" Mr. Thomas shouts, slamming his fist down.

Several Board members jump—me included—but Arthur appears unfazed. Mr. Thomas throws his good arm up in the air.

"She's a traitor on probation with us to prove her worth. A probation, mind you, that I never agreed with!" He looks around at the other Council members, a purple hue creeping across his cheeks. "You can't honestly expect us to allow this? She's dangerous. A criminal!"

Arthur presses his hands together. He speaks slowly, as if addressing someone stupid. "Miss Timewire is at my disposal. She's agreed to aid us in a very special task. She will sit in on Board meetings because I require her input."

"What special task?" Mr. Thomas growls. "What could you possibly gain from having her running about? I haven't changed my mind. I've said it once, and I'll say it again: She should be locked up!"

"Mr. Thomas," Libbie interjects, her thin hands clasped over her heart. "Perhaps you should—"

"I don't need *you* telling me what to do!" he roars. "This whole situation is absurd, and I will not stand for it!"

"Then, Mr. Thomas," Arthur says in an icy tone, "the Board no longer requires your services. You are dismissed. We have important business to discuss."

He gapes at Arthur like he's been slapped in the face. A hum of uncomfortable silence follows this, to which Mr. Thomas peers around, clearly expecting someone to come to his defense, but no one does.

"Now." Arthur flicks his hand up.

Terrace walks over to Mr. Thomas and raps on the back of his chair. "To another table, sir."

Mr. Thomas stands, shaking, his face livid. "Well, I never! You've not heard the last of this!"

He storms off, shoving Terrace aside and cursing at a group of boys blocking his path. He jostles chairs aside, knocking them over, and the commotion is so abrasive that the massive dining room quiets for a few seconds to see what all the fuss is about.

I turn away from Mr. Thomas's temper tantrum, my nerves shot.

"Please, eat," Arthur says, pointing to the platters of meat, fruit, and cheese as if nothing had happened. "Let's enjoy the afternoon and get to know each other."

My appetite is gone. I don't know whether to be happy or concerned, but one thing is perfectly clear: Arthur Evandrum has no reservations about getting rid of anyone who stands against me.

9

THE MEAL CARRIES ON WITH GUSTO AND FLOWERY language. I don't like all the pomp and circumstance, but I bear it with a fake smile and tight lips. I'm not one for politics—ironic, considering the position I'm in.

Arthur goes on and on between sips of red wine, and I patiently listen as he divulges a landslide of information upon my people. He boasts of his position as Chief Overseer, details the fully compromised state of Area 7, and shares that 83% of the world's Testing Centers have at least one undercover informant with an ability. Eli Stone is so enraptured by this that his mouth never closes for more than a few seconds at a time.

To my relief, Jonah joins the table fifteen minutes later. I'm so excited to see him that I grab a skewer of chicken and stuff it in my mouth. As soon as I do so, my appetite returns like a storm and my stomach growls.

"Ah, Jonah. I'm glad you could come," Arthur says. "Eat. We have plenty."

"Thank you."

"To our next order of business, Eli," Arthur continues. "Would any of your people be willing to join us at the Area 7 Testing Center?"

Eli Stone's eyes widen, and he almost spills his drink. "Mr. Evandrum, what exactly do you mean?"

"I would like to invite you to participate in what we've accomplished," he replies. "Over the past decade, we've secured the Area 7 Testing Center and infiltrated some of the highest government positions. We want you to join our team."

Eli Stone clears his throat, fiddling with his glasses. His wrinkles crease in worry. "Mr. Evandrum, you must excuse my hesitation, but I'm concerned about my people stepping foot in a Testing Center. I mean, just a few days ago, I thought we were the last group of people with powers on earth. This is all quite overwhelming."

"I understand, Eli," Arthur says. "Please, ask me anything you'd like."

"What is it that you do at the Area 7 Testing Center?" he probes, and my ears perk up.

"We stay up to date on society's scientific advancements, we use the Center's resources to find others with abilities, and we keep tabs on the President. We are also working on a series of projects—research, if you will. And thanks to Miss Timewire, we have furthered one *particular* project." Arthur turns to me with a haughty smile. "We've learned a great deal about our *beloved* President since you've arrived."

I nod, keeping my mouth shut.

"And young Maddy?" Arthur continues, musing. I clench my fork between white knuckles. "The secret weapon of a hundred years ago. Why, you've saved us quite a bit of work. We still have much to learn from Maddy, don't you think?"

I bite my lip, addressing the table stiffly. "Yes, sir."

"What's the research on?" Jonah asks.

Arthur leans back, wine in hand. "The Test."

"What about the Test?" I ask.

Arthur pauses, considering me, and his pale features ignite. "In due time, Miss Timewire," he says in a demeaning tone. He's speaking to me like I'm inept, and his mouth twists into a patronizing smile. "We're all on the same side here."

My ability surges through my chest and down my arm faster than I can catch it. I twitch my fingertips, Arthur's arm jerks, and red wine spills down the front of his crisp white suit. A few people gasp, and I stuff my hand below the table.

Jonah slides me a sideways glance, and I grimace. I shouldn't have done that, but it was involuntary. Arthur's snide response set me off.

Arthur sets his glass down and grabs a cloth napkin, dabbing the front of his jacket, but the red stain has already done its damage.

"I'm concerned," Eli Stone admits, trying to brush past the awkward moment. "My people's safety is my life's purpose. I'm sure you understand that . . . well, I have some reservations."

"Of course." Arthur places the cloth napkin on his lap and rests his elbows on the table.

"Is the Area 7 Testing Center safe?" Eli Stone asks. "If my

people volunteer to go there, will they be protected? Can you guarantee this? We would be out in society. People have died. Even now, those with abilities are being hunted across the globe."

Arthur's eyes light with sympathy, as if he bore the weight of the world. He reaches out and places a hand on the table in front of him, addressing Eli in a tender voice. "I promise you. Everyone will be safe. Area 7's security team is the best. They're people I've hand-picked—people I would trust with my life. And if we accomplish what we've set out to do with this research, no one with an ability will have to suffer and die at the hands of society *ever* again."

The table grows quiet. I'm even drawn into the certainty of Arthur's statement, and hope for a better world shines in my thoughts. But reality comes crashing down again with its iron fist. Arthur's statement seems too good to be true. What could they be doing at the Area 7 Testing Center that would ensure that no one with a power has to die ever again?

"I'll help," Libbie says. "If what you say is possible, then I want to help."

"Me too," Mr. Stuart chimes in. "If it's safe, then let's help."

Eli Stone's smile shines through his deep wrinkles. "We'll discuss the matter in private, if you don't mind, Mr. Evandrum. But it sounds incredible."

"Of course." Arthur is glowing from ear to ear. "Take as much time as you need. We can detail next steps when you're ready. But we should take today to celebrate!" He holds his wine glass high. "To partnership and the blessing of new friends."

"Here, here!" Libbie says, copying Arthur.

Glasses clink, and drinking ensues.

Arthur bows his head. "From the bottom of my heart, welcome. All of you."

"Thank you, Arthur," Libbie says. "You've been very gracious to us. We're so grateful you've allowed us to come here."

Arthur stands, walks around to Libbie, and grabs her hand. He plants a gentle kiss there, and says, "Not at all, Libbie. I was thrilled to learn there are more of us. It's heartening, especially in this dark time."

"It is."

I want to puke. Already, Arthur has everyone wrapped around his finger.

Batting away strands of blonde hair from my eyes, I ramp myself up for a grand exit. I don't want to be here anymore, but there's one thing I need before I go. I'm getting Keith out. Right now. He shouldn't be locked up, and with the meal drawing to a close, and Arthur slipping further under the influence by the minute, I have to make my request before anyone leaves. I need an audience for this.

"Mr. Evandrum," I say, speaking above the lingering conversation. I make sure I'm loud enough for all to hear. "I want you to release Keith."

His grin falters, but only for a moment before he chuckles. My hands burn with my ability, but I keep it at bay.

"Mr. Keaton is still an unknown danger, Miss Timewire."

"No, he's not."

Arthur cocks his head to the side. "Then please, enlighten me."

"Camille doesn't have control of him anymore," I say. "I used my ability on Keith when I visited him. He's safe. So let him out."

Arthur smiles at me. "No."

I spring to my feet, and it takes everything in me to keep my power contained.

"Why?"

"Say the President senses when the boy is around you and takes control of him again. You'd be beaten to death. I can't have that happen. We need you, Miss Timewire."

"That's not how my ability works," I say. "Camille only kept control of Keith because he grabbed him *before* Olivia teleported us. Once he relinquished control, that was it. We're too far away for him to grab Keith again."

"You can't know that."

"I can! *I'm* the puppet master here."

"Yes, you're the puppet master," Arthur drawls. "And yet, you weren't able to beat Camille at the Capitol. In fact, you've admitted to Jonah on several occasions that you recognize your inexperience, and that you and Jonah haven't even scratched the surface of your ability."

My blood turns to ice, and I glare at Terrace, seething venom. "*You* need to mind your own business and stay out of my private conversations!"

Arthur sighs. "Miss Timewire, the point is, we don't know. Perhaps Camille can't grab him again. But maybe he can. *You* don't know, and you're not strong enough to face Camille if he were to take control of Mr. Keaton. So, my answer is *no*."

I grit my teeth. "Keith is innocent, he's not dangerous, and he shouldn't be locked up. It's my fault he's in there, and that's not fair to him."

"Life's not fair," he says coldly.

My hands vibrate. Fine. He wants to play? Then let's play.

"You told me that you would give me anything I need for my training. *Anything* I need. I need Keith." I speak in a savage tone, my ability leading me. It rears up like a wild animal, purring in my chest. "Was that an empty promise to get me to cooperate? Were you lying? Because that tells me you're manipulative and not truly interested in helping me."

I've struck a chord. I can see it. Arthur's pale face turns flushed, and the vein in his neck thuds. He presses his hands together. "Why do you need Mr. Keaton to train? What does he have to do with anything?"

I glare at him. He's not going to steer the conversation his way. I won't let him. I don't need Keith to train, I just need him. He makes me feel safe and sane. Everything is alright when he's around, but Arthur doesn't get to know something that personal.

"You didn't answer my question. Were you lying to me?"

"Miss Timewire—"

"Mr. Evandrum." I speak boldly over him, unrelenting. "Do you shirk on your promises?" I give him a forced smile. "Of course, I don't *really* need your permission, do I? I could bring Keith out of that cell right now, and no one could stop me. You know it. I know it. Everyone here knows it."

I challenge his gaze, pulling my ability back to a low tingle to deliver the final blow.

"But as you said, we're all on the same side here, right?"

Silence stills the table, and I feel incredibly pleased with myself. The corner of Arthur's mouth twitches, but he squares his shoulders and passes off a collected posture.

"Very well, Miss Timewire. I'll release him. But he will be accompanied by an armed escort at all times."

"Fine," I say.

My power recedes from my hands. Keith doesn't need an armed escort, but that's a battle I'll win another day. I maintain a professional posture, not daring to let my excitement show. I'm ecstatic, especially for Candice. She needs this. I stuff my expression back, looking poised and pristine like a good little society member.

"Now, can you please sign whatever paper I need for his release?"

With a taut sneer, Arthur leans back, removes a pen and small notebook from his breast pocket, and begins to write. No one says a word as he scratches out a message. He signs his name in large, loopy letters, and hands me the paper.

I grab it with a smirk. "Thank you for the meal, Mr. Evandrum. This was lovely."

And with that, I march off past the velvet ropes.

IO

I SKIP DOWN THE STONE CORRIDOR ON MY WAY TO Sector 9, giddy with pride. I challenged Arthur Evandrum and won. The energy of victory surges through me as if my ability were celebrating too. Skidding down the remaining stretch of hall, I knock on Candice's door with several hard raps.

"Come in."

I tumble through the entrance, tripping over my feet. "Candice! Let's go get Keith. Arthur signed for his release." I hold the paper with his loopy signature high above my head.

She sits straight up, throwing the blankets off in a flurry. "Really?"

"Really."

Candice looks like she might cry for joy. She rushes forward and tackles me in a bear hug. I brace myself for the impact and stagger back, wincing as pain spikes in my ribs. But her reaction is worth it.

"Let's go get him," I say.

She disentangles herself from me. Skittering over to Ben, she dips her head down to tenderly kiss his forehead. "I'll be back," she whispers. "They're letting Keith out."

With a spring in her step, Candice exits the room, vibrating with excitement.

"Thank you, Hollis. I mean it. And sorry for getting upset earlier. I shouldn't have snapped at you about visiting him. He's . . . well, he's your boyfriend."

"Don't worry about it."

I mull over the word Candice just used with a smile. Boyfriend. Society doesn't use that word, but I like the way it sounds. The term gives me the most wonderful falling sensation, and my giddiness increases. Is Keith my boyfriend? We never really had a chance to talk things over in the forest, but when he saved me at the river, I knew he still cared.

As we make our way to Sector 2, I explain Arthur's stipulation regarding Keith's release, and Candice crinkles her nose.

"But that doesn't make any sense. Why does my brother need a guard if he's not under Camille's control anymore?"

I sigh. "My thoughts exactly."

We continue down the flight of dimly lit stone steps, emerging into the circular antechamber before the holding cells. Candice follows me to the middle door, but I stop her by holding my arm out.

"Let me handle the guard," I say. "Don't do anything until I've given him Arthur's note. Okay?"

She nods, clutching her hands together in front of her chest.

We enter the starkly lit holding facility, and I peer at the cells lining the back wall. Keith is sitting on the cot in 'B-9.'

The guard, clearly surprised by our visit, steps in front of me and Candice, blocking our path. He eyes us with disdain, clutching his machine gun as if ready to take lethal force.

"You again?" he says, disgruntled.

"Yes, me again," I say, equally as cold.

I shove Arthur's note in his face with a smug look. He grabs it from me, eyes raking over the handwriting like it might be a trick.

"Let Keith out. Arthur Evandrum's orders."

With a grumble, the guard lets us pass.

As we walk to Keith's cell, I notice another cell has an occupant. Pierce Bodegard leans against the glass of 'B-5' with his right hand balled into a fist. He stands broad-shouldered and stoic, but the look of hate he wears twists my stomach. His strong features only deepen my sense of unease. He was one of three people who attacked Jonah and me in the forest and tried to kill me by throwing me in the rapids. The Council arrested him for this. And unfortunately, they never discovered the identities of the other two boys.

I ignore him as I pass his cell. He scares me, and I'll never forgive him for messing with Maddy's head during the rescue mission. I have to remind myself that I'm safe now. He can't get out, and I have my power back. He's no match for my ability.

Candice and I run up to 'B-9' and bang on the glass.

Keith jumps, falling out of his cot and landing on the floor. He curses under his breath and then stands, clutching his chest.

"What the—Candice?"

"Keith!"

"What are you doing?" He beams at his sister. "Trying to scare me to death?"

She laughs. "I'm pretty sure that's what *you* were trying to do to *me*."

He shakes his head. "Funny."

"You're getting out!" She holds her hands up to the thick pane.

At this, Keith's face lights up. "You're getting me out of here?"

She nods. "Yup!"

Keith laughs and pushes himself off the glass. He sits down, immediately stands up, and then starts pacing back and forth, a goofy grin plastered on his handsome face. I haven't seen him this happy in a while.

The guard walks over, waving his hand at me. "Ma'am, you and your friend need to move back."

We oblige him, retreating from the cell door. The guard opens a panel next to the deadbolt and taps in a code. The door lights up then beeps. The guard places his hand against a scanner, and it flashes green.

With a hiss, Keith's cell door opens, and Candice pelts herself at her brother, launching into the most ferocious hug I've ever seen. Her voice grows thick with emotion as she embraces Keith.

"I thought we were going to die at the Capitol. And when you attacked Hollis, and they took you away . . . I'm so happy you're okay."

Keith hugs her tightly and rests his chin on the top of her head. His soothing words come out like a melody.

"I'm okay, little sis."

Candice pushes herself out of his arms then punches Keith on the shoulder.

"Ow! What was that for?"

"That was for scaring me, even though you couldn't help it." She squints at him, but then melts back into a smile. She turns to me with a wink. "He's all yours."

I roll my eyes, unable to help the grin that slides. I walk up to Keith, and he wraps his strong arms around me. I sink into his chest, and everything is right with the world again. With him, I'm safe.

"Hi," he breathes.

"Hi."

I drink him in. He smells of pine trees and earth, and his scent takes me back to the peace of the forest by the stream with the sun shining high. I tilt my head up, and his lips brush mine. We sink into the kiss like we've always done this. Electricity flies down to my toes, and the warmth of his skin pulls me in deeper. Home. If that were a feeling, it would be this. I'm home again.

"I missed you," I say.

"I missed you too."

He kisses my forehead and stares at me. This usually flusters me, but I feel something different this time. I don't know how to describe it, but my heart aches when I'm around him like I can't get enough. It's a type of affection I've never known. It's intense and overwhelming and effortless all at the same time. And the deeper I fall, the colder society becomes. I never would have had this depth of feeling if I were still there.

"I've got you," I say. "If the President takes control of you again, I've got you."

Keith gives me a gentle squeeze. "I know."

Camille's puppetry surges to the forefront of my attention. The way he stopped in front of Keith. His chilling words: "This one is a fighter. I can feel him. Strong-willed." He relished the fact that he could use someone who would fight him tooth and nail to never hurt me.

"I know how hard you fought him," I whisper, my eyes burning. "I tried to fight him too, I just couldn't . . ."

The shame of our near execution douses me. I let my friends down. Right before Olivia came, I gave up. I stopped fighting. I let my ability die in my fingertips because I couldn't beat Camille, but I should have fought until a bullet stopped me.

Keith tips my chin up with his hand. "Hollis, this wasn't your fault."

"I stopped fighting." Voicing it out loud causes my lungs to constrict. "Right at the end, right before they were going to shoot us . . . I stopped fighting. I shouldn't have done that. I should have died before giving up."

"It's okay."

His soft tone breaks my resolve, and I bury my head in his arms, battling with my tormented thoughts.

"No, it's not okay! I should have fought harder for you—for *everyone* in that room—but I didn't. He was too strong, and I gave up."

"Hollis, you fought," he says, stroking the top of my head. "You fought for us."

"But Camille was—"

"You fought for us," he says again.

I cling to him, taking in his embrace like a breath of fresh air.

"We're safe," he says. "It's over, and you won't have to face him again."

A spike of adrenaline fires through my blood. Keith doesn't know about Arthur Evandrum's agenda, and his innocent words spark a frightening thought. If I'm going to help these people, I'll have to face the President again.

Alvaro Camille won't give up society's crown jewel without a fight. And unfortunately for me, I *am* that fight.

———

II

———

I'M STANDING IN THE CENTER OF THE TRAINING MAT FACING Jonah as he leans on his cane. We're starting my training today, and the worst kind of nerves thunder through me. Maddy is with Vianne for the afternoon because Jonah thought it would be best to be alone. I agree. I don't want Maddy to see my power, especially since we're pioneering its limits.

This is my first training session since getting my ability back, and even though I'm anxious, familiarity follows me like a friend. I've done this before, and Jonah is with me.

"What should we do first?" I ask.

"Let's start with what we know," he says. "I'd like you to make me speak."

The revulsion I feel is so strong that I back away from him. I take several uneven breaths, upset with myself. Why am I acting like this? I know I have to train if I'm going to discover more about my power. I shouldn't be afraid.

"I'm sorry," I say, shaking my hands out and putting on a tough exterior. "Yeah, let's start there."

"Are you okay?"

"Yes. I just . . . I don't want to be like him."

"You're not like him, Hollis, but you *are* a puppet master. We need to work with what we saw Camille do. And once we've exhausted that, perhaps we'll discover something new to your ability—something Camille *can't* do."

I bite my lip, hating the position I'm in. "You really think so?"

"Yes. I do."

I pace the width of the mat for a few laps, brushing stray wisps of hair out of my face. "Why do you think we weren't able to control each other?"

Thinking back to when Camille slashed his palm over my chest gives me chills. His unsettling words snake through my mind: "I can't make you still. How interesting." On the one hand, it's comforting. That fact that Camille can't control me gives me leverage, but it's also scary. I have no power over him.

I scuff the sole of my boot against the mat. "How am I supposed to take Area 19 if I can't even touch Camille? Although . . . Arthur did say we would discuss what could be done about the President. Maybe he has an idea?"

"It's possible," Jonah concedes, scratching his dark stubble beard. "Hollis, do you remember the day I taught you about connection points?"

I nod, thinking back to the time I spent with Rosalie in the forest. Her ability allowed us to search my memories to find

Maddy, but there was a particular memory she couldn't stop. It was the moment Maddy appeared. She got stuck in a trance, pouring my memories into the forest, and I watched Tiffany get shot.

"You said that abilities can become connected," I recite. "The energy from one person can join with the energy of another. It's a link, or something like that."

"Precisely. A connection point is an interaction between biomarkers," Jonah explains. He shifts his weight over the cane. "My power's whole purpose is to connect to other powers and use them as if they were my own. Type twos can link to other people by nature of their ability, but that's not the same as a true connection point. It's deeper than that. With a connection point, the energy from each biomarker produces a unique effect that can only come from the combination. Like Rosalie being unable to pause the memory with Maddy. Until I witnessed it, I wasn't sure a connection point could happen with anyone else's power but mine. Do you remember what Rosalie said about Maddy after the memory?"

I hug myself and stare at the floor. "She said he was sad."

"Exactly. Rosalie's ability is about story. People's memories; their history. She sees the past, and with that comes an overwhelming amount of feeling. Maddy's emotions were strong enough to cause Rosalie to experience what he did. She felt what he was feeling, and it caused her to lose control over the memory. Maddy and Rosalie's connection point was tied to empathy."

"And your connection point?"

Jonah chuckles. "Curiosity, I suppose. My ability only works through connection points. Every time I use it, my biomarker forms a link with someone else's to produce the unique effect of me replicating their ability. Seeing Rosalie and Maddy's connection point made me realize something... There's no telling what kind of unique effect the combination of two biomarkers could produce. It depends on so many factors. The nature of the abilities themselves, being a type one versus being a type two, the way in which a person uses their ability, the depth of their understanding of said ability..."

I shake my head. "But I don't have a connection to Camille."

"And that's what got me thinking." He fidgets with his cane, tapping it on the mat. "This is just a theory. Most of what I study is theory, but what if the reason you and Camille can't control each other is because you carry the *same* biomarker? And by virtue of that, your abilities can never connect. I'm calling it an anti-connection point."

"An anti-connection point," I repeat, chewing on the phrase. It sounds compelling. I can see why Jonah loves to study abilities. They're so complex. I'm glad he has a grasp of this because it gives me hope that somehow, I'll stand a chance against Camille. "Well, I suppose we should begin..."

My words die in my throat. I sigh, rubbing my temples. Forcing my teacher to speak is the last thing I want to do, but I don't have a choice. Practice is the only way forward.

"Are you ready to try and make me speak?" he asks.

Rolling my shoulders out, I take a calming breath. "Yes."

Jonah gives me an encouraging smile, and this eases the knot of tension in my gut. "I'm with you every step of the way."

I stand across from Jonah, pressing my lips together in concentration. I need to clear my thoughts and focus. My hands vibrate, and I stand at the ready, but I don't proceed.

"I don't know where to start," I admit.

Jonah considers me for a moment. "Would you like me to try instead?"

"Are you well enough?" My eyes trace his deep bruising and land on his cane. His injuries still look severe.

"I'm well enough."

I shake my head. "No, it's okay. I'll do it."

"Alright. Whenever you're ready."

I hold my hands forward, and the buzzing electrifies me, pulling my mind into sharp focus. Jonah becomes still. Closing my eyes, I turn my thoughts back to the President's office where I was surrounded by my friends and forced to my knees. I can hear their voices, eerily joined together as one, jeering at me.

How did he do that? Did he force thoughts on them? My hands twitch, and the tingling in my fingertips strengthens. I impose all of my will over Jonah, pushing him to open his mouth, but nothing happens. He stays frozen in place, bound to my command.

I flick my wrist, releasing him. "I have no idea what I'm doing."

"Hollis, you don't have to figure this out by yourself. You're not alone this time. May I try?"

I drop my hands to my sides. "Okay."

Jonah discards his cane and holds his hands up. "Are you ready?"

"Yes."

His power stiffens my muscles instantly. I'm rooted in place, unable to move, and helplessness swallows me. It's horrible. I've only felt my own power one time before: the day I asked Jonah to use it on me so he could feel the beast.

Jonah's hands shudder, and the energy in me surges. It emanates from my gut and wells up through my throat. I feel like I'm going to vomit, but instead, a searing sensation rips through my esophagus as words are forced from me.

"My name is Hollis Timewire."

My ability is suffocating. I feel violated. It's as if a long rope that was coiled in my stomach has been violently pulled from my mouth. Then, the stillness in my body ceases, and I stumble forward, sinking to my knees. The dull ache in my ribs is back, and stars flicker around my vision.

I look up at Jonah. "You did that so quickly. How?"

"Say the words in your mind," he explains. "It's like a mantra. Repeat it over and over and force the words on me. Concentrate only on the phrase you want me to say until it happens."

"Force the words," I repeat.

"Use me as your mouthpiece."

I stare at him, brow furrowed. "You already knew what to do."

There can only be one explanation for this: Camille must have made Jonah speak during his brief time as a captive. And it wasn't to get information from him either. He wouldn't need to force his own words on Jonah to do that. Camille did it to torture him . . .

"He made you speak?" I ask, and my voice breaks.

Jonah's eyes sober. "He made me speak."

I hold a hand over my mouth, attempting to keep myself collected as my imagination runs wild. What other horrific ways did he torment Jonah?

"Did you fight him? Did you use your power?" I whisper. "Could you?"

"No."

His response cuts deep to my soul. The memory of Camille's puppets dragging Jonah, bound and gagged, into his office is scorched into my brain. Jonah was so badly beaten he couldn't have helped me even if he wanted to. Camille made sure Jonah couldn't fight, and something about this moment seals my determination. If I'm going to help change the world, then I have to be the best. I must be better than the President, which means I have several decades of practice to catch up on. I lock eyes with Jonah, and the ferocity of my ability pulses alive through my veins.

"Camille is going to regret not killing me," I say. "Because I'm going to beat him."

"Do it," Jonah says. "Make me speak."

I take control of him with a slash of my palm and channel the phrase, 'My name is Jonah Luxent,' through my mind over and over again, willing it onto him with all of my strength. Jonah gulps like he's choking, and I pour everything I have into the phrase until . . .

"My name is Jonah Luxent."

I gasp, releasing him, and he stumbles out of my grip. I'm

panting like I've run a mile. Sweat pours from my brow, and I wipe my nose with the flat of my hand.

"I did it," I say, electrified by the victory.

Something about having so much control makes me hungry for more. I don't want to stop. This power is better than the air I'm breathing.

Camille's words, though terrifying, are proving true: "Does it make you feel alive? Does it make you *hunger* for more?"

Yes. It does.

I've felt this hunger before. It's the part of my ability I fear the most because it makes me crave control. Power roars down my arms, and I drink it in. I'm going to get stronger, and Camille's going to pay.

"Let's go again," I say.

Jonah nods. "Whenever you're ready."

—

12

—

Sweat lingers in my nostrils, clammy against my skin. It trickles down my back with sticky tendrils. In the distance, dark clouds collect overhead, brewing over the Area 19 Testing Center.

Run.

My legs propel me down the sidewalk of the gray city block. One bound after another, like I have no say in the matter, just instinct.

Get home. Before they find you.

Advertisements flash from the street transit stops, bright to the point of hurting. Then, bold red text wraps itself around my arms, searing into my flesh with angry waves of pain.

I screech, trying to rub the words off of my skin.

Alert. Escaped convict. Extremely dangerous. If sighted, do not approach. Contact your local authority. Any information regarding the whereabouts of Hollis Timewire must be reported immediately.

My heart jackhammers through me as I pelt down the street. I can't be seen. They'll report me.

Charging forward, I sprint over the asphalt toward my housing unit. A few moments later, the cobblestone path leading up to the front door welcomes me, and with one last leap, I make it to the entrance, slamming my hand to the panel. It lights up, and the door admits me.

Gulping air, I shut myself in and sink to the floor.

"Hollis, is that you?"

"Mother."

She's standing in the entryway. Her flawless high cheekbones, thin nose, and silky blonde hair give me pause. It's like looking in a mirror. We're the same—delicate, like a flower. Placid hazel eyes meet my own, and for a spell-bound second, my lips part to say the words I know will rip her soul in two . . . .

I failed my Test. This is all a big misunderstanding. I'm not a Diseased One. I can't be.

"A Diseased One," I whisper in a trance.

"What was that, Hollis?" my mother asks in a soft voice.

I snap out of my hazed thoughts. I know the truth about the Test, and I have to tell her. My mother. My flesh and blood. I can't leave her here. We have to run. The military men are on their way with death at their heels.

"I'm a Diseased One."

I look at her and conviction chokes me. This is my chance, and I have to take it.

"Mother, come with me. This is all a lie! The Diseased Ones aren't murderers, the government is! Please, we don't have much time."

Her eyes flicker, emotion hidden beneath years of self-restraint. Her brow knits together almost imperceptibly. "Hollis, be reasonable. You need to go with them."

"No!" I run to her, grasping her hands and pulling her close. "Mother, listen to me. We have to go. Now! They're going to kill me, but you don't understand. The Test is a guise. The government lied about the Terror War. I have pow—"

Bang.

The foundations of the room shake with an ear-splitting crack, and the front door nearly comes off of its hinges.

"They are here to help you," my mother says with a tremor.

"Mother, please!" I drag her away from the front entrance. "We have to run!"

"They are here to help you," she repeats, this time slipping into a squeak.

"No, they're not!" I roar. "You have to come with me!"

Tears sting my eyes, and I keep a firm grasp on her hands, but the more I pull, the heavier she becomes. Then, my hands slip from hers. They're drenched in salty sweat that overwhelms my nose. The room turns from sour to rotten, and I gag, bile coming up my throat.

There's a burst of light that blinds me, and for a moment, I feel as though I'm being teleported, but when the light dies and my eyes readjust, the sight that greets me rips anguish from my throat. I scream.

"MOTHER!"

She's lying on the polished wood, covered in blood. It oozes around her mangled frame, her body spilling open like fruit that's been smashed against stone.

I sink to my knees, tearing out my hair and screaming so loud it scalds my vocal cords.

"NO! Stay with me! Please! Don't leave me. You can't leave me!"

I cling to her, cradling her in my arms. My heart slams inside of my chest with a rhythm of rage. They can't do this. They can't take her from me.

Bang.

The door splits off its hinges and smacks the ground, shattering the glass of the window adjacent to it. Wind tunnels through my dwelling, and men in beige military uniforms spill into the room, their machine guns pointed at my head.

With a roar, my hands extend from me, gripping them with an animalistic fury.

How dare they, the voice inside me growls. *How dare they kill her.*

My hands twitch and the group at my mercy writhes, their eyes bulging. Their faces flush purple with suffocation. I stand, my mother's lifeless body falling from my lap.

"YOU DID THIS!" I shriek, pulling them forward to kneel before me. My breath heaves, and my chest rises and falls in a symphony of agony. "MURDERERS!"

I own them. All of them. Every part—mine, to play with. To end. They will pay for their sins.

You know what you have to do, the darkness snarls. *Kill them.*

My hands tremble under the weight of my own power, and the military men are crushed, their skin sucked in toward their skulls. And like a switch, my ability floods them, and I scream as

I feel every cell in their bodies burst under the power of my fingertips . . .

. . .

I shriek awake, coming out of the nightmare with a curdling noise. For a moment, I can't see anything. All I can feel is a heavy object curling around my limbs, so I kick at it, desperate to be free.

The patterned quilt of my bedding tumbles to the floor, and I stare around at fresh white sheets. I'm in my bed in the training room, safe in the mountain, and small hands grab my own.

"Did you have a bad dream?"

A pair of big blue eyes looks up at me through a mess of blond curls.

"M-Maddy," I say, panting. "I—yes—I . . ." Adrenaline is still overdosing my senses, as if the threat of my dream were still present. "I'm . . . yes. A bad dream."

"It's okay," Maddy says, climbing up on the foot of the bed. He situates himself in my lap and snuggles up to my chest. "I get bad dreams too."

I take several soothing breaths, centering my thoughts on something real. My fingers curl around the fabric of Maddy's sweater, and I pull him in for a hug. He leans against my arm. Calmness descends upon me, and Maddy's little head tilts upward with a smile.

"Bad dreams are just dreams. And when you're awake, you don't have to be afraid anymore."

I return his smile, giving him a light squeeze. "Thanks, Maddy."

He squirms his way out of my lap, slipping off the bed and jumping up and down. "I'm hungry!"

"What time is it?" I look up at the clock on the wall, rubbing my eyes to clear the sleepy fog.

As if on cue, the musical voice sounds over the speakers of the mountain: "Mid-day Meal: 1145. Please make your way to Sector 12."

Maddy giggles, pointing up to the speaker. "Food time."

"Food time. Well then, let's go."

I extend a hand, and Maddy, vibrating with energy, takes it. I stand reluctantly, scooping the quilt off the floor and throwing it back on the bed. I'm not hungry in the slightest. That dream took everything in me and shattered it into a thousand pieces. It felt so real. My mother. Right there in front of me. Dead . . .

Maddy tugs me forward, dragging me to the door.

"I'm coming," I scold playfully.

I've started sleeping in the training room rather than the East Rooms. It's more secluded, and I like the privacy it provides. And here, I can keep Maddy as far away from Arthur Evandrum as possible. Maddy is my responsibility, and I've taken this to heart. I saved him from the government, and everything in me wants to save him from the darkness of this world because his innocence makes me believe good can still win.

"Will Vivi be there?" Maddy asks, skipping along. I follow him like a shadow and grab hold of the metal handle, sliding the door into the wall.

"We'll find her," I say. "Don't worry."

"Yay! Duck bill! Duck bill!"

The hand that isn't clamped over mine waves high in the air, and Maddy bounds faster, pulling me down the stone hallway.

I chuckle. "Hey, slow down!"

Vianne and I have taken turns watching Maddy, and ever since the forest, Maddy's been untamable in his affection for her. It's partly because of her impressions. Apparently, Vianne's duck impersonation is the best thing to ever happen to Maddy. I've only heard his joyous cackle once, but it was so spellbinding I couldn't help but laugh. It was the happiest sound in the world.

Five minutes later, Maddy and I reach the double doors leading to Sector 12. There are so many people packed into the dining room that the thought of going in makes me anxious, but Maddy yanks on my arm in his persistence, so I follow his lead.

As we enter, the throng pushes against us, and Maddy stumbles. I grasp his hand to keep him upright, and we enter the food line. It takes us nearly twenty minutes to get our bowls of porridge, and when we exit, Maddy jumps up on a chair, scouring for Vianne.

"Careful!" I chide. "Don't spill your porridge."

"I see Vivi!" He takes off, and I scurry after him, almost knocking over a mousy-looking boy in my pursuit.

"Sorry," I mumble. "Maddy, wait!"

Muttering "excuse me" under my breath way more than I need to, I maneuver through the crowd, barely able to keep up with Maddy. I spot Vianne a minute later. She's sitting with Ashton at a table hugging the far wall. They're huddled together, talking and laughing, and everything in me tells me to turn around and leave them alone. I don't want to talk to Ashton, but Maddy's already reached the table.

"Duck bill! Duck bill!" he cries, charging at Vianne.

She turns, a smile lighting up her porcelain features. Her hair changes from teal to shimmering lavender. "Hi Maddy!"

Maddy sets his bowl down in between Ashton and Vianne. "Hi Ash!"

"Hi Maddy," Ashton says, scooting over to accommodate him.

The moment I arrive, Ashton stiffens. He eyes me with a mixture of disdain and discomfort, and his whole demeanor shifts—like he's trying not to run away. Vianne must have told him I have my power back. Otherwise, why would he be acting so scared of me? Last he knew, I was powerless, and he had enough gall to destroy the wood stack I'd been working on and assault me, demanding to know what I'd done to his ability.

"I didn't mean to interrupt," I say awkwardly, taking the seat to Vianne's left. "Maddy just . . . ran ahead."

"That's okay," Vianne says.

She looks over to Ashton. He's gripping his spoon so tightly his knuckles are white. Abruptly, he stands, scooping up his half-eaten bowl.

"I'll see you later, Vi," he says.

"Okay." Her tone spells disappointment, but she doesn't push the issue.

Ashton stalks off, and we sit there in an uncomfortable silence. My eyes trace the thick gray boot covering Vianne's ankle, and sympathy pain creeps across my skin.

"Feeling any better?" I ask, trying to ease the tension.

Vianne nods. "Loads better. Beezee is amazing. The pain's more of a dull ache now."

"Good. I'm glad."

"Duck bill! Duck bill!" Maddy chimes, knocking over the crutches that lean against the edge of the table.

"Careful!" She shakes her head. "I swear, ever since I showed him that trick . . ."

Vianne faces Maddy, puckering her lips and furrowing her brow. Her face transforms, lengthening out from her nose into a flat bill of leathery yellow. She squawks, passing off a rather convincing duck noise, and Maddy bursts into a fit of laughter. His pitch carries above the noise of the dining room, and it fills me with warmth.

Vianne holds the form for a few seconds more, and then melts back into her flawless complexion. "I've gotten pretty good at 'duck bill' if I do say so myself."

I snicker. "You sure have." I stir the hot porridge with my spoon and take a bite. The warmth feels wonderful on the back of my throat. "I'm glad to see you're up and about, but I'm surprised you're not taking advantage of medical's room service."

"Can't stay in that sterile room," Vianne says, turning her nose upward. "Plus, it's only my ankle. I'm fine with the crutches. And Ashton's been helping me."

"Yeah, I've noticed. Are you two . . . a thing?"

Her pale face takes on a light pink hue. "Maybe?"

"I'm confused. He said all those terrible things to you. He forced you to show your scars." I swallow a knot as I recall Ashton verbally assaulting Vianne and savagely exposing her scars by suppressing her ability. He called her disgusting. He told her no one in the world would want her, and that was the moment I snapped. I lost control, and I attacked him. And somehow, in my rage, I did something to Ashton's power.

"I know," Vianne replies, looking sheepish. The pink tinge rises in her pale cheeks. "He talked to me about it. Back in the forest."

"What did he say?"

"He apologized."

"He apologized?" I gape at her, unsure of whether she's joking. "What did he say?"

Vianne's hair flickers to auburn, and she sobers. "A few hours after you left to rescue Jonah, it got dark. Maddy stayed with me in the alcove, like you asked. I was burning up, and I was in so much pain I couldn't think straight."

She pauses, tinkering with her spoon.

"The woman helping me left to go get some rags and water. She promised to come right back, but she didn't. And that's when I heard people crying. Everyone was crying, but I couldn't get up to see what was happening."

A shiver colder than ice slips down my spine. The broadcast. Camille's feed meant to reach every screen in the world. He wanted my people to see my execution. There's no doubt in my mind that Libbie's tablet picked up everything.

"And I didn't want Maddy to leave me, so I called out to see if anyone was around." Vianne's cheeks flush. "And Ashton showed up. He seemed . . . shell-shocked, and I knew . . . I just knew you were dead. That Jonah was dead."

"What did he say?" I ask, rapt into the story.

"He said the President had Jonah and everyone up on this

platform, and that they were going to shoot you all, and then the feed cut out."

"He didn't see the blue orb?"

She shakes her head, eyes glittering with sadness. "He didn't say anything about a blue orb. And then . . . I burst into tears. In front of Maddy and Ashton. And he . . . well, he didn't really know what to do. He just sat on the edge of the cot with me while I cried."

Something inside me breaks at the image of Ashton's kindness.

"I cried until I couldn't anymore, and then we sat in silence. Even Maddy went quiet." Vianne's enchanting voice is like a melody. She rubs the bridge of her nose with the back of her hand, sniffling. "And then he said, 'I'm sorry.' And those two words kind of . . . broke him, and after that he . . . he sort of . . . just said everything. He told me I didn't deserve to go through this, and what he did to me was cruel. He said he hates himself for it."

She takes a deep breath.

"And since that night, he's been nice to me. For those few days—the ones before we came here—he helped me. And Maddy too." She tilts her head, tightening her lips, like her next words will upset me. "Maddy's actually taken quite a liking to him."

At this, Maddy lights up. "Ash is funny."

I raise an eyebrow, looking down into his happy face. "He's funny, huh?"

"Yeah!"

I'm at a loss. Vianne's story doesn't make sense. So much has happened between me and Ashton. I don't know if I can put it in the past. I'd like to move on from what I did to him, but Ashton's sudden shift in behavior strikes me as odd.

"He's changed since he lost his ability," she adds, twirling a lock of her silky hair. It flickers to an off-white. "I mean . . . he used his ability to bully people, and now he can't do that anymore."

She lowers her voice, glancing around. "What happened? When you attacked him?"

I press my hands to my temples. "I have no idea. It's a blur. All I remember is feeling like I couldn't control what I was doing. I couldn't stop until Jonah used Ashton's power to suppress my ability. And then everything was over."

Vianne gives me a strange look. "Until Jonah what?"

"Until Jonah suppressed my ability," I repeat. "Then I stopped hurting Ashton."

Vianne's confusion grows, and she scratches her head.

I blink, mirroring her concern. "What is it?"

"You'll have to ask Candice to confirm," she begins, twisting the lock of hair tighter. "I mean, I was knocked out after you threw me into that table. But Jonah never suppressed your ability. Candice said he tried, but he couldn't. You stopped yourself."

My pulse picks up in an uneasy rhythm. "No, Jonah took on Ashton's ability and then suppressed mine. That's why I stopped."

Vianne shakes her head. "No, he didn't. Candice saw the whole thing. A lot of people did."

"I . . . No, that can't be right." Numbness spreads to the ends of my fingertips as my ability tingles beneath my skin. "I couldn't stop. I was trying to stop myself from hurting him, but the more I tried, the stronger my ability got."

The hair-raising voice reverberates in my head. *Kill him, Hollis. He deserves it.*

Vianne's pale cheeks drain of the color they'd gained before. "Hollis, you should probably talk to Jonah about the attack. I don't know what else to say other than you stopped yourself." She pauses for a moment then places a delicate hand on my shoulder, concern creasing her brow. "What did you do to him?"

"I don't know. This power . . . it's vicious."

"Hollis, you're shaking," she says. "Are you alright?"

"No. You weren't there. The President, he's like me. He's a puppet master."

Vianne nods, compassion written into her tone. "Candice told me everything. I can't imagine what you're feeling. I'm so sorry you had to go through that."

"He did terrible things," I say. "And I'm capable of that too."

She grabs my hand. "You'll figure this out, Hollis. I know it's scary, but Jonah will help you."

Her encouraging words settle some of my nerves. She's right. Jonah will help me. But I still feel alone. Arthur's grand plans for me are weighing heavier every day, and it's a burden I don't want to carry in silence. I scan around, making sure none of Arthur's guards are nearby.

Back in the forest, Vianne told me the story of how she got her scars. She told me about the dogs and how her parents died.

She was brave and decided to share the burden of her past with someone so she didn't have to bear it alone.

And now it's my turn. I don't have to bear this alone. I'm telling her everything Arthur told me. I need a friend I can talk to.

"We're not here by accident," I say. "These people have been looking for me. And they have big plans."

13

THE NEXT FEW DAYS PASS BY IN A BLUR. I'VE MASTERED forcing Jonah to speak, but the ease of learning this particular skill doesn't bring me any comfort. It's as if my brain has shut off, summoning focus only for what I need to get through the day. I'm still healing from my injuries in terms of stamina, and by evening, I'm completely exhausted.

Today, however, I'm not working on my ability. Arthur Evandrum has requested my presence at a Board meeting, and I'm dreading it. I stare at the note curled on the table next to my bed in the training room.

Miss Hollis Timewire,

Kindly join the Board in my office at 1400. I'd like to discuss what your role will be as we partner together to take the Area 19 Testing Center.

Sincerely,

Mr. Arthur Evandrum

I sigh, sweeping the paper off the table and crumpling it up. I sit at the end of my bed and count down the minutes until I have to go to Sector 15. I'd like to know how Arthur plans to use me to pull off his scheme—especially considering President Camille. The more I think about it, the crazier the idea becomes. It's festering in my subconscious like a cancer, and my dreams aren't helping.

Last night, I dreamt about her again. My mother's dead face turns vividly in my mind. I've missed my parents in the past for all the wrong reasons, but now that I'm on the right side of history, I miss them even more. It's strange and confusing, and all it's created in me is the desire to never sleep again, despite my fatigue. The nightmares I have . . . they're relentless and cruel. I can't catch a break, and it's eating me up inside.

"Hollis."

I jump, clutching Arthur's note to my chest with a squeak. Jonah, cane in hand, slips through the entrance of the training room and walks over to me, still harboring a limp.

"I didn't mean to startle you," he says. "Are you ready to go? The meeting starts in 15 minutes."

I eye the clock on the wall just below the speakers that house the musical voice. 1346. My stomach churns. "Yes, I'm ready."

I'm not, but what else am I supposed to say?

I stand, hugging myself. The only thing keeping me from ditching this meeting entirely is the fact that Jonah will be there, by my side and *on* my side. I don't have to do this alone.

I sigh. "Let's go."

The two of us leave the training room and walk in silence. I count the cracks in the flooring as we go, trying my best to keep it together. I'm drowning in the sea of a task much greater than I can handle. What if I can't help these people? What if I'm not powerful enough? What if there isn't a way to beat Camille?

"Something's bothering you." The statement rolls off of Jonah's tongue with a 'you-can't-hide-things-from-me' look.

He's right. I can't. I groan in frustration but resign myself to his soft gaze. I don't know how to talk about Camille and Arthur and the assignment I've been given, so I deflect. "I've been having nightmares."

"What about?"

"My mother."

"Your mother?"

"She keeps dying."

Jonah's taken aback by the blunt nature of my words. His face pales under the discolored bruising. "Are you alright? From your nightmares?"

"I don't know," I admit. "I haven't had time to process . . . the dreams. But bottling it up isn't going to help either."

Jonah's cane taps along the concrete. "I think that's wise."

"What if she isn't safe?"

The question slips from me so fast I don't have time to catch myself. I have no reason to think she isn't safe, but why is my subconscious dwelling on her? What's changed? Is it this place? Is it the task Arthur's thrust upon me? I don't know.

My teacher's response is chilling. "I think that if she were not safe, we would know," he says. "You're public enemy number one, Hollis. In all likelihood, your mother is deeply involved in the government's plan to kill you."

My heart sinks. He's probably right. She tried to turn me in after I failed the Test. She's a high-ranking lady, married to the head of the military elite. She may even have government escorts and armed protection in case I turn my "terrorist" activities toward her.

"I didn't think about that." Sadness claims me, but I push it away. Shifting my tone into a more playful, sarcastic one, I say, "But that's okay. I'll be traumatized on my own time. Right now, Arthur's requested my presence!"

I sweep my hand into a salute and give Jonah a grandiose bow.

He chuckles. "I see you haven't lost that fiery spirit."

"No, sir. I haven't."

A few minutes later, Jonah and I arrive at the double doors leading to Sector 15. The white hall beyond is unsettling, and I almost turn back. But I force one foot in front of the other, following Jonah until we make it to the door that guards the entrance to Arthur Evandrum's office.

Biting my lower lip, I place my hand on the panel, and it flashes to admit us.

"You're a Board member now," Arthur had said when he'd programmed my palm print into the bio scanner. "You'll need scanner access to come to meetings."

We enter, and the disturbing, society-like atmosphere twists my anxiety deeper. I gulp, swallowing spit against a dry throat.

Terrace sits at Arthur's left. And Hugo, Arthur's bodyguard, stands directly behind him.

Eli Stone, Caleb Stuart, and Libbie Lizette are present as well. They stop talking when I enter. Eli Stone gives me a curt nod, adjusting his cracked glasses. Caleb Stuart, however, strokes his thick mane of a beard with his nose in the air. He's not okay with me being here, but unlike Mr. Thomas, he's learned to hold his tongue.

"Miss Timewire," Arthur says, acknowledging my arrival.

"Mr. Evandrum."

He gestures to the black leather chair at his right-hand side. "Please take a seat. I'll be with you in a moment. We're just finishing up."

I slip into the chair, keeping my head down. Jonah sits next to me.

"Eli, I'm glad you've agreed to volunteer at the Area 7 Testing Center," Arthur says. "You'll be the perfect replacement as head of our search team. We're fortunate to have someone of your experience stepping into the role."

"I'm honored," Eli Stone says. "Finding people with abilities and offering them a safe haven has been my life's work."

"Replacement?" Jonah repeats, leaning forward. "I apologize for coming at the tail end of this, but could you clarify?"

Terrace clears his throat and answers in Arthur's stead. "The head of our search team had a nasty accident a month back and is . . . out of commission."

At this, my ears turn sharp. During the banquet, Arthur mentioned a series of projects happening at the Area 7 Testing

Center. Could that be what put one of their leaders out of commission?

"He's fine," Terrace adds, noting Jonah's unease. "But he's requested to be reassigned."

"Arthur, it's so kind of you to afford us with the resources of a fully functioning Testing Center," Libbie says, eyeing Evandrum with ravenous attention. She blushes. "My ability allows me to communicate with trees. I would *love* to join your ground team!"

Arthur turns to her with a charming smile. "How fascinating. That's something we could use. Consider it done, Libbie."

At this, Libbie nearly falls out of her seat. I crinkle my nose. Is she pining after Arthur Evandrum? I've never seen her like this before. I've only ever known her as stern and unyielding. Back in the forest, she was the one who suggested to the Council that I be executed for my crimes. Now she appears positively doe-eyed, like a schoolgirl who has a crush on someone who will never notice her.

"Speaking of fascinating abilities, Eli," Arthur says, folding his hands together. "The ability census? With a few hundred new additions to the family, I need to know who's here and what they can do—in particular, how many among you are type *twos*. You agree, yes?"

Eli Stone rubs the bridge of his nose and pushes his glasses up. "Yes, of course. Caleb and I will inform our people."

"Wonderful!" Arthur's voice rumbles over the table, and I jump. He hands Eli a folder. "Starting tomorrow, your people can make an appointment with Beezee-Day Jones, our head physician. Everyone will receive a health checkup and physical. And

Beezee's assistants will help catalog the abilities we've gained. Hugo will handle the scheduling." He motions to his bodyguard.

"And when will we be joining the Area 7 team?" Mr. Stuart asks.

"Jonah," Arthur says, disregarding Mr. Stuart as if he weren't present. "How many type two abilities do you have?"

Mr. Stuart, who's normally extremely aggressive, looks like he's going to burst. But he remains quiet—a stark difference from the man I knew in the forest who berated me during my trial and did his best to turn the Council against me during my probationary period.

"Six," Jonah replies. "Although . . . five, if you'd like me to be accurate."

Arthur's eyebrows knit together. "How do you mean?"

"Ashton Teel no longer has his ability."

At this, Arthur's whole demeanor changes, and his attention cleaves to Jonah as if they were the only two in the room. "The boy? Did young Maddy do this?"

I nearly blurt out Jonah's name to stop him from saying anything. I don't want Arthur to know what I did to Ashton. *I* don't even know what I did to him. It's going to provoke questions with no answers.

To my relief, all Jonah says is, "No."

"Speaking of young Maddy," Arthur continues, and the protective instinct I've been nurturing since Maddy's rescue roars to life in my chest. "Hollis, I'd like to ask you something."

He's using my first name . . .

What is he playing at? I'm trying to avoid his staring eyes, but they are glued to me, prying. I shift in my seat, perturbed.

"Okay, what is it?"

"What exactly can Maddy's ability do?"

"Why?" I ask flatly.

"He took away your power, correct?"

"Yes, and?"

"And then he gave it back, correct?"

My shoulders stiffen. "Yes. Why do you ask if you already know?"

"Is that all he can do?" Arthur poises a hand to his chin.

I open my mouth to spit out a retort I know I'll regret, but Jonah places his hand on mine under the table and answers for me.

"We don't know, Mr. Evandrum. But I trust you understand that this five-year-old boy is no longer an experiment. He's a child, and he's one of us."

Arthur purses his lips. "Of course." His fingertips tap the table, and an uncomfortable silence follows. After a moment, he sweeps the mess of folders into a neat stack and says, "Eli, Libbie, Caleb, thank you for meeting with me. I look forward to working with you, but for now, you are dismissed. I have matters to discuss with Miss Timewire. Hugo will show you out."

The stout, beady-eyed, bald man behind Arthur scuttles into action. He dips his head low, running his pointer finger and thumb over his burly mustache. He shuffles up behind Eli Stone and holds his arm out, gesturing to the Council members. "Right this way."

Chairs skid against the floor as the three of them get up from their seats. They exchange odd looks, and then, without conversation, they file out of the room.

Arthur fiddles with the stack of folders in front of him. He's staring at me to the point where I'm starting to feel uncomfortable.

"Miss Timewire, I asked you here today because I'd like to discuss the plan moving forward."

"Yes, let's."

"Upon your arrival, I showed you the extent of our reach. 83% of Testing Centers have undercover plants. It's been a long, tedious journey. But we're finally in a position to take over the government. *You* are the last piece."

"The last piece?" I repeat.

"You're the only person powerful enough to help us take Area 19. With its strong military presence, it would take too many resources—and lives—to secure it without you. You are the last piece to my puzzle. When this happens, all the Testing Centers must fall *together*," he says. "Including Area 19. A powerful strike across the globe. Only then can we gain the upper hand and turn the tables in our favor."

"And you're ready to do this?" I ask. My heartbeat picks up in my chest. "How? What's your plan?"

Arthur pushes the massive stack of files over to me. "Take a look."

I grab the top folder, flipping it open and scanning the contents. Bold text glares up at me along with a picture of a man. His brown skin complements his dark hair, and his body is toned with muscle.

Mateo Sebastian—Testing Center 89

Ability: Hardening.

Mateo can turn his skin into steel. When he does this, he is bulletproof, and his strength and stamina increase tenfold.

I grab the next folder. This time, there's a picture of a woman. She's scrawny and wears a sly smile.

Fiona Gafford—Testing Center 10

Ability: Sleep.

Fiona can cause sudden sleep to overtake an individual or a group of people. She can control the duration and intensity of the slumber.

I snatch open the next one.

Nicole Pak—Testing Center 142

Ability: Communication.

Nicole can manipulate the electromagnetic field with her mind and interact with or stop any electronic communication.

I move from folder to folder, scanning them quickly, and I'm overcome by the scope of this. There are so many powerful abilities—and so many type twos.

Frank Turner—Testing Center 47

Ability: Illusion.

Frank can create hypnotic visions that confuse the mind and transfix the body. He can control what someone sees by altering reality in their brain.

I grab one more. I haven't even made a dent in the monstrous stack...

Miles Maverick—Testing Center 113

Ability: Memory.

"Like I said, you're the last piece." Arthur adjusts the collar of his white shirt. "I have my people where they need to be, strategically placed with their abilities in mind. We're ready to take down the Testing Centers."

Jonah's wearing the same astonished look I am. He's still thumbing through folders.

"Some Testing Centers will require less force to take than others," he continues. "But Area 19 is by far the strongest. The Capitol City's Testing Center must fall with the others. It's the linchpin. That's why I need *you*."

He lingers on the last word with charm, and the hairs on the back of my neck stand on end. Even without his ability, he commands attention like no one else I've ever met.

"And how am I supposed to help you if Camille is there?" I ask.

So far, the only thing I've thought of is the only thing I'm not willing to do: use Maddy to take away the President's power. It's not removing Camille's power that bothers me, it's the risk of Maddy getting hurt. Maddy would have to physically touch the President to take his ability, and there's no way I'm letting Maddy anywhere near that man. How could we possibly restrain the President long enough for Maddy to use the golden light? As wonderfully simple of a solution as that would be, removing the President's power isn't feasible. He's too strong, and I'm not willing to fight Camille for control over Maddy. If he gained the upper hand, that would be disastrous.

I lean forward, keen to hear what Arthur has to say. He must have an idea. Judging from the folders, he's clearly been planning this uprising for a while.

"I've thought a great deal about what we've learned from you, Miss Timewire," Arthur begins. "It seems that my plan to collect you and have you take Area 19 isn't as cut and dry as I would've hoped. We've hit a little snag, wouldn't you agree?"

"Little?" I say. "Camille being a puppet master isn't little. We can't control each other. We're immune. Jonah thinks it's because we carry the same exact biomarker. I can't just barge through the doors of the Testing Center and take everyone under my power. Camille wouldn't let that happen. He's . . . unbeatable."

"Ah, so you've come to the same conclusion I have." Arthur claps his hands in a slow rhythm. "Bravo."

"Don't patronize me!" I retort. "I'm not a child. I fought him, and I lost. He's incredibly powerful. So, what do you propose we do? I'm on board with taking Area 19 if it means we'll finally be able to end the Test. But how?"

Arthur clears his throat and sits back in his chair, elevating his posture. His hands fold together in his lap. "Simple. When the time is right and you've trained your ability sufficiently, we assassinate the President."

"We *what*?"

"You disapprove? Then I assume you've figured out a way to defeat Alvaro Camille in your short time here?" He opens his hands like an invitation. "Please, do tell."

My ability hums in my chest. "I haven't. But we can't just storm in, take over, and kill the people who stand in our way."

"Why not?" Arthur's quick, dismissive tone rubs me the wrong way.

"What do you mean, 'why not?'"

"Shall I educate you on the goals of the current administration, Miss Timewire?" Arthur quips.

"Educate *me?*" Anger curls in my belly, and my hands begin to tingle. "Stop treating me like I don't know what's going on. I was raised in society!"

"Then you know just how far the government will go to rid the earth of us!" he snaps. "Area 19 *must* fall, or all of this is for nothing. Camille is unbeatable. You said so yourself. Taking the Testing Center can't happen unless he's out of the picture."

He leans forward aggressively, and even though he's not yelling, I shrink back.

"As promised, you may take all the time you need, and I will give you and Jonah anything you require to train. But once you're ready, Miss Timewire, there's only one way this ends. Camille's death will serve us all. Then, you take Area 19, and the others will take their respective Testing Centers. One deadly blow. All at once—all across the world. The end of the Test. And finally, after a hundred years of hiding, the end of the bloodshed of people with powers."

Quiet descends like a spell. I don't know what to say, and neither does Jonah. We're all staring at each other as the gravity of Arthur's plan sinks in. This all comes down to me. I must be strong enough to take on the military and anyone else who stands in my way. But killing Camille is the part I hadn't bargained for. It seems I can't beat him, but is ending his life the answer?

"My people have been ready for quite some time," Arthur says. "We're waiting on *you*. We take the government when you're ready to take Area 19."

Nerves settle in the pit of my stomach like a poison, and it makes me sick. I understand. Because of my ability, I'm in charge of taking down the strongest Testing Center. And when that falls, everything else will too—like dominoes. I'm the last piece in Arthur's plot.

14

THE NEXT MORNING, I MAKE MY WAY THROUGH THE PACKED dining room to join my friends. I'm exhausted because I couldn't sleep. I was tossing and turning all night thinking about Arthur's plan to assassinate Camille. I don't know why, but something about his proposal doesn't sit well with me. But I'm hoping spending time with my friends will be the distraction I need to get a clear head about the matter.

After a minute, I spot Rosalie's bright red locks. She's sitting next to Maddy, who's playing with the remnants of a breakfast roll. Across from them, Candice is leaning on a groggy-eyed Ben. She has her arms wrapped around his waist like she'll never let him go. To be honest, I'm shocked Candice got him out of bed. He's been so quiet since arriving at the mountain.

To my surprise, I also spot Olivia Turrick. She's perched next to Keith with a playful smirk. She waves at me, and I give her an awkward wave back. Ever since she ditched me outside of the training room, I thought she'd avoid me. It's clear she has no intention of telling me why she was in the forest that day. So why is she hanging out with my friends? Is she here to keep an eye on me as a favor to Arthur? I don't like this . . .

I jog the last stretch, arriving at the table and slipping into the seat next to Keith. I'm so happy to see him, but my happiness doesn't last long. A figure looms over us. There's a sour-looking guard in a beige uniform standing directly behind Keith. And he's hovering like a shadow.

My insides boil over when I notice the machine gun. If Keith tried to attack me—even though I know Camille doesn't have a hold of him—it wouldn't end well. The fact that Arthur's willing to take lethal force against Keith if necessary is not okay. I'm definitely going to talk to Arthur about this guard situation.

"Hi," I say, pulling Keith into a quick side hug.

The guard shifts his stance, as if ready to separate us, but he doesn't move any further.

"Hey," he says, hugging me back.

"Hollis!" Rosalie beams. "I'm out of the hospital!"

"I can see that." I return her smile and reach across the table to grab her hand. "I take it you're feeling better?"

"I am."

I chew on the inside of my cheek, unable to think of what to say next. I want to tell Rosalie and Ben that I'm sorry for what happened, and that I hate myself for not being able to stop Camille from forcing Ben to stab Rosalie, but this isn't the time or place. I want to speak with them privately—not in a crowded room, and certainly not in front of one of Arthur's guards.

"I'm so happy you're alright," I say.

"Olivia!" Candice pipes up, her face taking on a mischievous grin. She untangles herself from Ben. "What do you guys do for fun around here? No offense, but this place seems kind of . . . *regimented*." She slides a sideways glance at the guard lurking over her brother.

Olivia smiles, twirling a finger through a tight curl at the base of her neck. "No offense taken." She turns toward the guard, addressing him in a mocking tone. "It is kind of regimented, wouldn't you say, Erwin?"

Candice stifles a snort by trying to pass it off as a cough. The guard's mouth curls into an upside down 'U,' and he replies through stiff lips. "I suppose, ma'am."

"So formal, Erwin," Olivia chides. "Miss Turrick is fine, you know."

Candice buries her head in Ben's shoulder, and Rosalie gives her a swift kick from under the table.

She yelps. "Ouch!"

Keith turns to his guard with a smirk. "Erwin, eh? Well, I guess we're on a first name basis now. I'm happy to know a little more about you since you're stuck babysitting me."

Olivia taps her hands on the table in an odd tempo. She stares Erwin down—and while her demeanor turns more playful, Erwin's turns more sour. Is she egging him on? Without taking her eyes off him, she says, "Candice, instead of answering your question, how about I show you?"

"Olivia—" Erwin begins, but she cuts him off.

"It's Miss Turrick to you," she says curtly.

Candice looks between the two of them then flowers her hand open in excitement. A flame dances across her bare skin. "I would love that!"

Maddy claps upon seeing Candice's fire. "Orange light!"

"See, Erwin? She would *love* that," Olivia says.

Candice tugs at Ben's arm. "I am dying to have a little fun around here!"

Ben, who looks like he hasn't slept in days, lets air out between pursed lips, and Candice turns pink in the face. I can tell her comment was partially aimed at him. I don't think she meant to call him 'no fun,' but it came off that way.

Olivia's impish smile deepens. She stands, her tone spirited. "Come on, Erwin, let's show them Sector 1. It'll loosen you up. You're too serious."

"Yeah, come on, Erwin. Loosen up!" Keith echoes. "Hollis, want to go?"

My eyes dart between Erwin's grumpy countenance and Keith's smile. I don't know what Olivia's up to, but she's piqued my interest. "Absolutely. How about it, Maddy? Want to go on an adventure?"

"Yeah!"

"What's in Sector 1?" Rosalie asks, grabbing her finished plate and placing her used napkin and fork on it.

"Oh, you'll see."

"I like you," Candice announces. She stands up and punches Olivia in the shoulder. "I think we're going to be good friends."

"Careful with this one, Olivia," Keith adds, nudging his sister. "She bites."

"Shut up, Keith!" Candice snaps. She pulls Ben to his feet. "Let's go see what's in Sector 1. It'll be fun."

Ben remains silent. Shame festers in me as I recall the boisterous, overeager, card-trick-loving boy I met during the marble game—the very same boy I skipped rocks with by the river where he tackled Candice and tickled her until she begged for mercy. Now he looks empty. Like he's lost a piece of himself.

Candice whispers, "It'll be good for you." Then she lowers her voice to a volume quieter than I can catch.

"Let's drop off our plates first," Rosalie says.

Everyone follows her as she makes her way through the throngs of people crowding around the kitchen. I haven't eaten yet, but I don't want to miss out. My friends dump their cups, plates, and utensils into one of the large black bins that line the end of the buffet area. Then, we exit Sector 12.

"I don't like crowds," I whisper to Keith.

He grabs my hand and winks. "I know."

With Maddy on my left, Keith on my right, and the rest of the gang in tow, we follow Olivia through the maze of stone halls. We take one turn after another, until all the halls blend together, and my attention shifts out of focus.

Candice's energetic voice echoes off the stone as she tries to guess what could be so worthwhile in Sector 1.

"Do you have pool tables? We had pool tables back at our old compound. We had four of them. Do you know what a pool table is? I love playing pool!"

"Slow down, Candice," Rosalie says. "Don't forget to breathe."

"I don't know what a pool table is," Olivia says, "but I can guarantee you this will be better."

Candice nearly yanks Ben to the floor in her excitement. He stumbles, and she yelps. "Sorry, didn't mean to trip you!"

"That's okay," he says quietly. He puts his arm around her, pulling her into a hug that calms some of her bouncing energy. Her dark brown hair trails over her shoulder, and she wraps her arms around Ben's skinny chest.

"Just here," Olivia says, pointing to the double doors leading to Sector 1.

She barrels through them, and as I enter, I'm caught off guard by the shiny silver metal coating the walls, floor, and ceiling. It's like we've entered a hall made of mirrors. The bright, reflective surfaces cast doubles of each of us all over the place like a kaleidoscope. The other odd feature of this hall is the placement of the doors. They line the corridor, but only on the right, and each door has a rim of lights along the keypad—green or red.

"Woah!" Rosalie casts a nervous glance around. "What is this place?"

I keep a firm grip on Maddy's hand, making sure he's close to my leg. I glance down at him. His eyes are as big as saucers, and his little mouth hangs open in awe. The mirror effect in here is head-spinning.

Olivia stops at the first keypad with green lights. "This," she says, tapping in a six-digit code, "is the Holodeck."

Candice gasps. "No way!"

"You have Holo-tech?" Keith asks, just as impressed as his sister. "But this is military tech. How do you have this?"

I squeeze Keith's hand in excitement. "This mountain is an abandoned nuclear weapons lab. This *is* a military facility. I haven't used one of these since I was a kid!"

"You've used a Holodeck before?" Keith gapes at me. "When?"

"I experienced a Holodeck once when I was in primary school. It was amazing! My father's the head of the military elite, so growing up I got special privileges . . . except for the Test," I say with venom. "He sold me out quicker than Ben's super speed."

Keith gives me a sad smile. "I'm sorry he did that to you."

"Me too."

"Well then, what are we waiting for?" Candice bursts out.

Olivia pushes the door open. "Everyone in! Let's have some fun. And that includes you, Erwin."

Candice fights another bout of snickering as she leads Ben past Olivia. The guard utters a low growl, and this time, even I laugh. I agree with Candice, I like Olivia. She knows how to have fun. I'm not sure if I'll get answers about the forest anytime soon, but if I build some trust with her first, maybe I'll have a chance down the road.

Everyone files into the room, and it takes me a second to adjust to the brightness. We're standing in a perfect cube, about fifty feet in length, width, and height, and the entire space is nothing but light panels, all shining white. The illumination is almost uncomfortable.

The door clicks shut behind us, and a cheery musical voice echoes in the cube. "Welcome to pod 007. Please state your unique access code."

"5-6-6-1-0-1," Olivia says loud and clear.

"Welcome Olivia Turrick," the female voice chimes. "Would you like me to load simulation X?"

"No," she states. "Load Simulation Tutorial."

Lights along the floor spiral out in beats, a pattern of two short bursts repeating. "Loading Simulation Tutorial," the voice says.

Candice, who looks like she might die from the stimulus overload, whacks Ben on the arm, squealing in delight. Ben cracks the smallest hint of a smile.

Olivia looks at me, and then says, "Hollis, you'll know what to do, seeing as you're the veteran. Everyone else, go ahead and spread out, and follow Hilda's instructions."

"Hilda?" Rosalie inquires.

"Oh, that's the Sim voice," Olivia answers. "I call her Hilda."

Everyone spaces out, and I keep Maddy close to me. He's trembling, but with more excitement than Candice—if that were possible.

With a flash, the entire room changes, and all of us gasp as the brightly lit panels disappear. We're standing on a white sand beach at sunset. I glance around, drinking in the scene.

We're on the sand a few yards away from the ocean's edge. To our backs, the base of a dark rock cliff towers high, looming over the misty water. Rays of pink and orange burst across the horizon, and the ocean moves rhythmically, lapping up and down the seaside in even strokes—a symphony of saltwater. In the distance, columns of black rock jut up just offshore, peeking out of the fog that dances around the boundary of the simulation. Every so often, something gleams in my peripheral vision, like I can almost see the shimmer of the Holodeck's illusion.

A salty breeze tosses hair across my face, and as I brush the strands away, I smell the brine of the water and hear the screech of gulls bickering nearby.

I kneel to unlace my boots. "Maddy, take off your shoes!"

I remove my shoes with quick fingers and toss them behind me. My feet feel the smoothed granules of fine sand, and I close my eyes and raise my hands above my head, taking in the texture of the beach against my skin. The technology humanity's developed is incredible. It feels so real.

Maddy's shoes fly off, and then he copies me, holding his hands up against the breeze. His toes wiggle through the sand, and the rest of my friends follow suit.

Candice crouches, grabbing fistfuls of sand and letting it fall through her fingertips. "Keith, a real beach!" She squeals with delight. "Did you ever think you'd stand on a real beach?"

He laughs. "Well, it's a simulated beach."

She punches him in the chest.

He steps back, catching her hands. "Ow!"

"Why do you always have to ruin things? It's as real of a beach as we're ever going to get."

"Welcome to tutorial mode," Hilda says, her smooth voice carrying over the sound of the waves. "This is the Beach of Possibility. From here, you may select any number of locations, training simulations, and tactical gear. My program is designed to simulate real life. To start your tutorial, please pick up the nearest stone."

Hundreds of smooth turquoise pebbles appear, scattered along the sand. I reach for one, and as I grasp it, a shock of static zips across my palm.

"In the simulation, you may pick up anything projected," Hilda instructs, her soothing tone intertwining with the beats of the water washing up and down the shore. "My program produces a field of energy and light, creating boundaries that replicate physical objects."

At the water's edge, eight silver targets appear, one for each person present, and Candice squares her shoulders, a squint creeping across her brow. It's her 'game on' face.

"In the simulation, objects can interact with one another. Throw your stone at the target," Hilda instructs.

"Hey Candice!" I call out. With a heave, I chuck my stone, and it lands just off center, striking the surface of the silver with a thunk. "Beat that."

"Timewire, please," she scoffs.

She winds up her arm, taking a moment to aim. With a smack, the stone lands dead center, and she turns to me with a victorious grin.

"Nice shot!" Rosalie exclaims, throwing her own turquoise pebble. It falls short of the target, landing in the water beneath it. She scuffs the sand with her foot. "I've never had good aim."

"Neither has Ben," Candice snickers, nudging Ben in the ribs.

This comment seems to spark Ben's competitive nature because a smile hides in the corner of his mouth. "We'll see about that."

With a big wind up, Ben swings his arm forward, and his stone hurdles through the air, striking dead center with the loudest thunk yet.

He turns to Candice, this time, a real smile cropping up.

"You were saying?"

Candice was right. This is good for Ben. He's playing, and it's the first time I've seen him smile since the President's office.

"Okay, Maddy." I crouch next to him and point toward the waves. "See that target? Can you hit it?"

Maddy stoops down and selects the nearest turquoise stone. With a wild swing, he throws the rock forward, but it plows into the sand a few feet from us.

"Good try." I drop another stone into his hand. "This time, hold your arm up higher." I take his arm and lead him through the motion of throwing. "Like that. And give it some power."

Maddy takes another shot, and this time, his stone nicks the bottom of the target.

"I hit it!" he says, clapping his hands.

I beam at him. "Amazing job!"

"Hey Erwin." Olivia slides a cheeky grin at Keith's guard, who hasn't moved a muscle. "Why don't you give it a shot?"

But before he can make any kind of retort, Hilda's musical voice chimes up again. "Safety Protocol: enabled. This simulation is designed to ensure user safety. While the program creates real projections, these projections cannot cause harm. Any object, weapon, location, or person projected cannot hurt you. While the safety is enabled, the Holo-tech monitors all organic life forms and will stop any simulation that may cause injury or death."

A long oak table replaces the silver targets at the water's edge, and weapons of all shapes and sizes materialize across its surface. I swallow a knot as my eyes trace the array. Knives, broadswords, handguns, a bow with a sling of arrows, and an axe are laid out in a row.

Olivia steps up to the table, peering over her options. She selects a throwing knife then glances back at us. "Don't worry. Safety mode is protected with a password and retina scan. Only an admin can turn it off." She looks me dead in the eye, a smirk curling her mouth. "Hollis, may I?"

I know what's coming, and I want to say no, but I pass off a brave face and step up to the table. "Sure."

Olivia stands a few yards from me, and with a quick flick of her wrist, she throws the knife directly at my face. The blade flies, and my friends screech, but before it reaches me, it stops in mid-air and shatters into hundreds of glittering pixels. The pixels float there like an enchantment and then dissipate into nothing.

"See?" Olivia says. "Totally safe."

"Damn," I hear Candice mutter under her breath, clearly impressed by Olivia's aim.

Hilda's voice crackles to life once more. "To load a simulation, please refer to my library. I have hundreds of locations and combat exercises to choose from."

Against the sky, a screen appears. On it are three categories:

```
Category A: Location
Category B: Training Exercises
Category C: Level
```

"Hilda, what's category C?" I ask.

"Category C allows the user to set the difficulty of the combat my program creates. There are five settings: Beginner, Standard, Intermediate, Hard, and Expert."

"Most of us keep it on standard," Olivia says.

"Have you ever tried expert?" I ask.

"Once."

"And?"

She chuckles. "Even with the safety on, it was a little too intense for me. Plus, I come here to have fun, not fight."

"What are we waiting for?" Candice says, pulling Ben along behind her. She approaches Olivia. "Let's have some fun!"

"Alright, Miss Keaton." Olivia gestures to the skyline where Hilda's screen options burn bright. The rest of us gather around, gazing up at the menu. "Where would you like to go first?"

15

FOR THE FIRST TIME IN A LONG TIME, MY DREAMS ARE pleasant. They carry me through the night on the wings of one fantastical world after another. I slept in Candice's room after spending a good portion of the day in the Holodeck. It was nice to get away from the training room for a while. Olivia's invitation was just the thing I needed to get my mind off things.

But when I wake, it doesn't take long for worry to capture me again. I lie there in the quiet of the room and stare up at the ceiling. The Holodeck was wonderful, but it's not reality. Arthur's plan rushes through my mind, twisting my anxiety deeper: "When the time is right, and you've trained your ability sufficiently, we assassinate the President."

I turn over, trying to block him out, but this only sharpens his words.

"You are the last piece to my puzzle . . . We're waiting on *you*. We take the government when you're ready to take Area 19."

Why do I have such a problem with this? If Camille were out of the way, I wouldn't have to fight him, and I could take Area 19 without resistance. But it doesn't feel right. Something about my upbringing is holding me back. I was born and raised in society, not here, and even though I'm fully allegiant to my people, I know how society thinks. If people with powers are going to take over, shouldn't we do it with the utmost integrity? Shouldn't we show the world that we aren't monsters? That we don't kill?

I shove the thin blanket off of me and dress quietly so as not to wake my friends. I need to talk to Jonah. Maybe he'll know what to do, and maybe he'll be able to ease the conflicted feelings in my spirit.

After a brief trek through the mountain, I arrive at Jonah's room. I knock three times, and step back to wait. There's a scuffle and a groan, and then the door opens.

"Hollis?" Jonah's bleary-eyed face peeks out. "Is everything okay?"

"I don't know," I say. "Can I come in?"

"Of course." He opens the door further, and I slip past him, taking a seat in the chair next to his bed. I bury my head in my hands and take a few calming breaths.

Jonah walks back to the bed and sits on the edge. "What's wrong?"

"Jonah, what's the point of this?"

He gives me a strange look. "What do you mean?"

"Let's say Arthur's plan works. Let's say I take control of the Area 19 Testing Center, and the others take down their Testing

Centers. What's the point if everyone in the world still thinks that people with powers are evil?"

The tingling of my ability creeps up my arm, and I shiver.

"We just take over? Isn't that exactly what society thinks we tried to do a hundred years ago? The history of the Terror War runs deep. It led to the creation of the Testing Centers. Wouldn't we be feeding into the system we're trying to destroy?"

Jonah sighs and leans over, resting his elbows on his knees. "You've been placed in a particularly challenging position."

"I . . . yes, I have been."

"In many ways, what Mr. Evandrum's asked of you isn't fair." His brow furrows, and he scratches the stubble of his beard. "And you're right. I've been thinking the same thing. What these people propose to do is beyond anything I thought possible. To end the Test? To go back to society? It would be a victory for people with abilities, but the cost... I don't know if Mr. Evandrum's fully considered it."

At this, a huge weight lifts from me. The fact that Jonah's been thinking the same thing settles my nerves.

"Exactly," I add. "This isn't just about a building. It's bigger than that."

"Do you think taking the Area 19 Testing Center is a worthy cause?" Jonah asks.

His question surprises me, but I also don't have to think about my answer. "Yes, I do."

Jonah nods. "I do too."

"The Testing Centers were created to weed out people with the biomarker and kill them," I say. "That needs to stop. I just . . .

I can't help but feel torn about Arthur's plan to assassinate Camille. Am I crazy for wanting to keep him alive? He's evil, and he's had a hand in strengthening a system that's designed to kill us. I should be okay with his death, but I'm not. I just keep thinking... how are we supposed to go about changing the world when we're becoming what society fears the most by doing so?"

Jonah cracks the tiniest hint of a smile. It hides in the corner of his mouth and lingers there a moment.

"What?"

"You're a leader, Hollis."

"I'm a leader?"

"Yes."

I clasp my hands together in an effort to keep my voice steady. "I guess I didn't expect to be one."

"Good leaders never do."

His words give me courage, and right now, I could use all the courage I can get. I look at my teacher, and determination settles in me. Maybe there's a way for me to beat Camille. Maybe I can take the Area 19 Testing Center without bloodshed.

"I need to talk to Arthur," I say. "I need to tell him that I'm not okay with his plan. Will you come with me?"

"Absolutely."

Jonah grabs his cane and slips into shoes. Then, the two of us walk toward Sector 15. My mind is racing with every step. Arthur's not going to be happy with this. His entire operation hinges on my participation, but I'm not refusing to help them. I want to come up with an alternative that doesn't end in Camille's death—if that's even possible.

We arrive at the panel outside Arthur's office, and I look to Jonah for strength. He gives me a nod of encouragement.

"What if Arthur's not in there?" I ask. "It's still early."

"Then we'll come back."

"Right."

I take a deep breath and place my hand to the scanner. It flashes, and the door slides open. At the end of the oval table, Arthur sits hunched over folders. Terrace is with him, rifling through papers as well. They both look up.

"Miss Timewire. Mr. Luxent," Arthur says. "To what do I owe the pleasure?"

I step forward, adrenaline spiking through me. My hands begin to shake, so I stuff them behind my back.

"I need to talk to you," I say.

Arthur tilts his head, and his hands creep across the table, snatching up a ball-point pen. He scribbles out a note on a pad of paper. "What about?"

This is my moment. If I'm going to be a leader, then I need to lead.

"I'm not okay with assassinating the President."

Arthur continues to write, unfazed. "You don't have to be the one to kill him, Miss Timewire. You just need to take Area 19."

I swallow a lump, and my heart begins to race. "No, I mean . . . I'm not okay with anyone killing him."

At this, Arthur stops his work—and so does Terrace. They stare at me. Then Arthur's face turns from amused to cold.

"Excuse me?"

"I'm not okay with the assassination plan," I state.

"You're joking, right?" Arthur's tone verges on anger. He tosses the pen, and it skids a few feet down the table. "I asked you once. Let me ask you again. Do you know how to defeat Alvaro Camille?"

"No, I don't."

"Then how do you plan to help us take Area 19 from a fully realized puppet master?"

"I don't know."

The vein on Arthur's neck bulges, and his face flushes. "You don't know?" he repeats, his voice sinister. "Well, why don't you stroll up to the Capitol and ask *nicely*? You don't understand a thing, do you?"

My ability roars in my fingertips, and I have to hold myself back from grabbing him.

"No, *you* don't understand a thing!" I yell.

Terrace and Jonah flinch, but Arthur doesn't shrink away. He glares at me, his eyes boring into mine. He opens his mouth, but before he can say anything, I forge ahead.

"Society thinks we're mass murderers! They think the biomarker drove us crazy a hundred years ago and that we tried to take over by killing everyone. I used to think the Test was a *good* thing. That purifying the bloodline of humanity was *right*."

Sweat beads on my brow, and shame stirs in my belly.

"I believed the false history of the Terror War to the point of betraying the only people who ever cared about me!"

Power thunders through my arms, ready for my command, but I pull it back. I lower my voice to speak with a deliberate, slow cadence.

"What you have to understand, Mr. Evandrum, is that assassinating the President is *exactly* what society would expect us to do if we were going to take over. It will only reinforce the false narrative. If we kill him, people will see us as the monsters they've been taught to fear. But that isn't true. We're not murderers."

The vein on Arthur's neck ticks faster. "We aren't going to massacre millions of innocent people, Miss Timewire. Just *one*. And he's far from innocent."

"This has to be about more than a power grab. This has to be about changing people's minds. We have to do this the right way."

Arthur throws his head back and laughs—a deep, guttural, patronizing laugh that stirs my anger to new heights. "And what is the 'right way?'"

Silence extends between us. My tongue feels like sandpaper against the roof of my mouth, and although I can't see myself, I'm sure I've gone red in the face. I don't know how to answer him.

Arthur leans forward, sticking his pointer finger down on the table.

"Name *one* society member who will change their mind about us regardless of how we take over." His upper lip curls to expose his teeth. "You can't, can you? Because no one will believe us! All anyone understands is power—and *who* is in control."

I stand there, breathless. I wish Jonah would say something, but I'm not sure he knows how to answer Arthur's question any better than I do.

"How about I make you a deal?" Arthur asks.

The tingling beneath my fingertips heightens. "You like deals, don't you?"

"I do."

The air in the room is so thick it's suffocating, but I don't back down. "What deal?"

"If you can come up with a better idea, then I'll defer to you. But if you can't, then we'll take the Area 19 Testing Center my way—starting with killing Camille."

I open my mouth to retort, but nothing comes out. I don't know how to challenge him.

"When Miss Turrick brought you here, you agreed that changing the world is a worthy cause," Arthur adds. "But I'll ask once more. Miss Timewire, do you think changing the world is a worthy cause?"

My confidence plummets. "Yes."

He taps his fingers in a rhythm against the table's surface. "Shouldn't Camille be stopped at all costs? Shouldn't he be stopped from hurting anyone else? He's the figurehead of the institution we're trying to destroy. Shouldn't he pay for his sins?"

I'm fighting a wave of nausea that's clawing its way up my esophagus, and my mind feels like it's moving at a snail's pace. "He should, but not with his life. I still have so much to discover about my ability, and . . . and I'll train, I'll—"

"Then, Miss Timewire, I look forward to seeing what you come up with. The plan, as of now, rests on your shoulders, puppet master. We will reconvene to discuss this matter again in a month. You'll have discovered new and exciting portions of your ability by then, I'm sure. And you'll have regained your strength. Does that sound fair to you?"

"I . . . yes," I state. "That sounds fair to me."

"Excellent."

My head is swimming. I didn't expect him to make a deal with me. But one month? How am I supposed to figure out how to beat Camille in one month?

"Miss Timewire," Arthur says. "Should we find no alternative solution, we move forward with *my* idea. One way or another, what we've planned can't happen with Camille in the picture, I trust you know that. And our brighter future won't come without loss. It is the unfortunate nature of war."

"War?"

"Yes, war."

"I don't think killing is necessary to achieve what you want to do, Mr. Evandrum."

"Think what you will." Arthur's eyes narrow. "But you will soon learn that few things come without this kind of cost."

I stare him down, choosing my next words carefully. "And *you* will soon learn that I can be quite surprising."

"Then *surprise* me."

A chill crawls down my neck, but I keep my face determined, speaking with the boldness of my ability spurring me onward. "Don't worry, I will."

16

It's early morning and I lie awake in the training room. Jonah asked me to get a good night's rest in preparation for today's training, but my nightmares had other plans. And to make matters worse, I have to come up with a plan to stop Camille without taking his life.

That's something I have to start thinking about today, and even though I'm not working alone, coming up with an alternative to satisfy Arthur Evandrum is no small task. It feels impossible and completely unfair. I'm already trying to master an ability that feels beyond my control.

I lie awake with nervous jitters until I can't keep still any longer. Climbing out of bed, I begin to tidy up, mostly to give myself something to do. I don't clean for long before a tap comes from the other side of the metal.

I rush over to greet my teacher.

"Good morning."

"Good morning," Jonah says, limping through the door.

To my surprise, Vianne comes in behind him, leaning on her crutches.

Her hair flickers from creamy blonde to bright white. "Jonah asked me to help. I left Maddy with Ashton."

"Ashton?" I say.

"Ashton's good with him. I promise."

Even though this makes me uneasy, I trust Vianne's judgment. Ever since she told me he apologized to her for exposing her scars and calling her disgusting, it's changed my perception of him. Maybe losing his power is what he needed to turn into a decent person.

"Alright," I say. "I'll get Maddy when we're done."

Jonah walks over to the training mat. "Come on up, Hollis."

"What are we working on today?" I ask.

Vianne discards her crutches and hobbles over to the training mat, sitting at its center. I was under the impression we were going to brainstorm ideas to counter Arthur's proposal, but it seems Jonah has something else in mind.

I cross my arms. "We're not discussing Arthur's request, are we?"

"No," he says. "You're going to fight me for control over Vianne."

My stomach curls into a knot. "Why aren't we going to talk about Arthur's deal?"

"Do you have any ideas?"

"Well . . . no, not yet. But Jonah, we have a month. That's not much time."

He shifts his weight over his cane. "We had a month in the forest."

"Arthur's given you a month?" Vianne gapes at me, sweeping a hand through her silky hair. "To master your power? He can't be serious. I thought you told me Arthur was giving you all the time you need?"

I shake my head. "He's given me a month to figure out how to defeat Camille without assassinating him."

Vianne's hair turns bright red. "He's planning to assassinate the President?"

"Yes. And I don't want him to."

Jonah turns to Vianne with a sober look. "Vianne, I understand Hollis has chosen to share Arthur's plans with you, and I'm glad she's confided in a friend, but I think it's best if you don't discuss these matters with others."

"Yes, sir," she says. "I won't."

Jonah turns back to me. "Hollis, the reason we're not discussing Arthur's deal is because you need to get stronger—and fast." He taps his cane against the mat, moving closer to me. "Are you ready to work?"

"Yes. I'm ready."

I knot my fingers together, pulling at them one by one. Taking Area 19 the right way feels more important to me than honing my power, even though I know training my ability is critical. I feel a tension rising in me, pulling me in two different directions. What deserves more of my time—my power or coming up with the best possible plan to create a better world?

"Jonah, what if we can't come up with a plan in time?"

"Hollis, Arthur wants to assassinate Camille," Jonah says. "And you want to spare his life because of the political and social ramifications of an assassination. And while that is incredibly noble of you, you're not going to stand a chance if you can't control people like pawns the way Camille does."

My insides turn to ice. Jonah's right. My control compared to Camille's is childish—almost laughable. The President's words snake through my thoughts: "You have no understanding of the entity beneath your fingertips. You're an infant: juvenile in your control and rash in your emotions."

Jonah's brow furrows, and his voice runs as deep as his words. "I know you don't want to be like him, but you *must* learn to control your power like he does. You need to be able to take people from him. This has to be second nature. Like breathing."

"You think I can do that in a month?"

He smiles. "I've seen you do incredible things in a month."

I let air out between pursed lips, chewing on the inside of my cheek. "But that wasn't me. That was you and the rescue team. I didn't have my power. I didn't—"

"*You* are the reason Maddy is here," Jonah says, cutting me off. "You carried the vision of a brighter future for that boy, and his life has been spared because of your bravery. Your power doesn't define your purpose, Hollis. Your heart does. You did so much good without your ability, but now that you have it back, you have the chance to carry that vision even further."

Silence follows this, and heat prickles across my face. Does he really mean that?

"I admire what you said to Arthur: that this has to be about changing people's minds, and not another bloody grab for power," he says. "You grew up in society. You know what people think, and *how* they think. And if there's ever going to be real change, then you must step into the role Arthur's required of you. And I know it's not fair, but it's the reality of the situation."

I stand there with limp arms, struggling to get a grip on my quickening pulse. A wave of lightheadedness travels through me. If I'm going to do this, then I need to eat, sleep, and breathe being a puppet master.

Vianne gives me an encouraging nod. "I'm with you, Hollis. Okay? You can do this."

"Okay."

I appreciate Vianne's courage for volunteering. I'm glad Jonah's asked her instead of anyone else. She wasn't in the President's office, and that alone makes me feel better about forcing my will over her. She doesn't carry the trauma of what happened in that room.

My palms begin to sweat, and my fingertips fidget with one another. I knew this was coming, but I didn't think we'd tackle this part of my ability so soon. Given Arthur's accelerated timeline, I don't have a choice. I have to push myself if I'm going to get better.

I let my ability build in my chest until I can feel its buzz.

"Are you ready to fight?" Jonah asks.

"As ready as I'll ever be," I say.

Jonah continues in a serious tone. "I'm going to try something different today."

"What do you mean?"

"During this training session, I'm not your teacher and I'm not your friend. I'm Camille, and Vianne will stay under my power until you can take her from me."

My eyes trace his mending injuries. "Are you sure you're okay? I don't want to hurt you."

Jonah chuckles, squaring his shoulders and dropping the cane. "Don't worry about me. I've been taking on abilities longer than you've been alive."

I run my tongue along the inside of my teeth. "Right."

"I'm going to push you," he says.

"Okay."

"I'm not going easy on you."

"I don't want you to."

"I'm your enemy right now, in every sense of that word. Do you understand what I'm saying?"

My ability zips down my fingertips with a dash of adrenaline, and I breathe it in. "Yes, I understand."

"Hollis," Jonah says, and his gaze intensifies. "Don't hold back."

"I won't."

Jonah looks down at Vianne, who's still sitting in the center of the training mat. "Do you remember what we discussed?"

"Yes, sir."

"Very well then." Jonah's eyes turn sharp as he snaps his attention back to me. "Let's see who has more control, puppet master."

Jonah and I stare at each other, Vianne between us, and the air turns stale. Silence, so thick it hurts, creeps across the space. I hold my breath, waiting for the opportune moment to strike. Tingling fills me to capacity.

Jonah and I move simultaneously, grasping for control. But the instant I have her, the power is wrenched from my fingertips so violently that I'm thrown forward. Unable to catch myself, I land flat on my face, and my chin smacks the mat. Teeth dig into my tongue, and blood immediately pools into my mouth.

"ON YOUR FEET!" Jonah growls, his demeanor morphing into something I've never encountered from him. He flares his fingertips, moving in an eerie, energetic rhythm.

I spit blood onto the mat, wincing at the metallic taste. Power courses through my chest, and I leap to my feet, throwing my hands forward.

The effect is instantaneous. I feel a tug through my palms, and just as I'm about to gain the upper hand, the power is pulled from me again. Like the crack of a whip, I'm yanked down to the mat once more—this time to my knees.

"UP!" Jonah barks at me. "Is that the best you can do?"

Panting, I dig my hands into the mat and stand.

"What are you waiting for? An invitation?" he taunts. He starts to walk the outer rim of the mat, slow and calculated. "Take her back from me."

My ability sears under my skin, and for several seconds, Vianne is bound to both of our grips. I push further, forcing my power above Jonah's, but it's not enough. Jonah pushes back, stealing Vianne away, and a shock travels through my arms. I drop my hands, winded from the effort I've already expended. How is he this powerful at *my* ability?

"I thought you'd put up more of a fight." His tone dips into lazy, low notes. "I'm waiting for you to show me something."

My jaw stiffens, and my hands spiral forward, grabbing for control anew, but this time, I can't even feel Vianne. It's like she's shrouded in some kind of fog. I can see her sitting a few yards away, but I can't grasp her. Jonah's power is overwhelming, just like Camille's, and I'm beginning to lose control.

I tense, pulling everything I have into my fingertips, but as I cast my power toward Vianne, her neck tilts in a creepy, serpent-like motion, and words slither from her open mouth.

"You're not even trying!" she hisses, sitting statuesque. "I can feel you giving up."

Jonah's hands move in rapidly, forcing words from her.

"Weak," Vianne spits, her voice moving through cold inflections.

I fill my hands to the brim with power, straining to pull the reins of control from Jonah, and for a moment, I have her. My palms are on fire, and Vianne gasps, free from being Jonah's mouthpiece, but the victory is short-lived. The ferocity of Jonah's ability overtakes mine, and Vianne twists, facing me with wrath in her voice.

"Is that what happened with Rosalie and Ben?" She stares at me with unblinking eyes and her singsong grows more dangerous. "Did you give up when they needed you?"

My eyes blur with involuntary tears from the savagery of the power struggle, and I step back with shaking hands. My fault. Ben and Rosalie were mine to protect. I'm so overcome, I'm paralyzed. Jonah is forcing her to say this. Is that what he thinks of me?

"I didn't give up!" I cry. "I didn't!"

"LIAR!" she shrieks.

It's like I'm back in the President's office all over again, powerless and small. I twitch my hands, feebly attempting to pull Vianne under my ability, but I can't do it. I'm buffeted back by a power that feels a hundred times stronger than my own.

"Make your move," Jonah says. "Take her from me!"

"I'm trying!"

"You're not trying. She's still mine."

Sweat pours from my brow, and I ground my stance, sinking my heels into the mat. My arms shake with energy, and I latch onto Vianne, feeling her pulse thump alongside my heartbeat. Jonah and I are vying for her, but he still has the upper hand. Like a tug-of-war, I can't seem to dig deep enough to wrench them apart.

"You don't have it in you! Deep down, you've lost your fight!" he shouts.

Jonah's ability nearly pushes me away, but I maintain my hold, straining with everything I have to keep him at bay.

"Camille saw that in you," he sneers. "A little girl, scared and alone."

I stand my ground with streaming eyes, refusing to relinquish the small amount of control I've latched onto.

"Unable to save anyone!" Jonah spits, pulling me forward with a tug as we continue to struggle. "Unable to help your friends."

We shudder under the force of the deadlock. The energy between us is so intense that heat starts mixing with the tingling under my skin, and parts of my vision blur.

"Unable to do anything!" he roars. "Your power is nothing! Your fight is nothing! *You* are nothing!"

I snap.

Emotion, raw and pure, pours from my heart, and with every piece of strength I have left, my ability explodes. It shatters Jonah's grip on Vianne, and this time, he's thrown forward on the mat. He hits it with a slap, and I stand over him, breathless and triumphant, the tingling beast purring in my chest.

I won. Vianne is mine.

For several seconds, the room is quiet, except for the sound of panting. Vianne's porcelain features are flushed, and Jonah's bruised face is covered in sweat.

With a flick, I release Vianne from my ability. I'm shaking, my body feels numb, and a mesh of colored stars hangs in my peripheral vision.

"Right there," Jonah says, now speaking to me in the gentle voice I've come to know and love. "That's what you have."

Gingerly, he stands up, brushing himself off and gazing at me with kindness. His features have softened. The old Jonah is back.

"What do I have?"

"Your heart. That's what makes you two different. The President doesn't feel things like you do, and one day he'll pay the price for that. Your emotion is what feeds your *strength*. It drives you to excellence, and I am proud of you."

I mop my watering eyes with the back of my hand and sink down to the mat, exhausted. I suck in gulps of air.

"You did it, Hollis. You took the power from me."

"For a minute there, I didn't think I could do it."

"For a minute, neither did I." Jonah smiles. "But like you said to Mr. Evandrum, you can be quite surprising."

"Thank you for pushing me. I needed it."

"You're welcome." He turns to Vianne and says, "Are you okay to continue?"

"Yes," she replies. "I'm okay."

He nods. "We check in after every round. You let me know when you've had enough."

"Yes, sir."

"Hollis, stand up," he instructs.

I obey him, even though my legs are aching and my fingers feel numb. Jonah's hands rise in front of his chest, at the ready.

"You're tired, I can see that. But we're far from done. Camille didn't give you a break, so I won't either." Jonah's hands move. "Let's go again."

$$\text{17}$$

I'M WRAPPED IN A SOFT BLANKET, SITTING IN A PLUSH armchair in Sector 9, and Vianne sits across from me. She's tucked crisscrossed into her bed with Maddy fast asleep on her lap. His golden curls rest across his pink nose, and his little chest rises and falls in a peaceful rhythm. Tonight, I've opted to sleep in Vianne's room instead of the training room. It's late, I'm exhausted, and this morning's lesson shook me. I don't want to be alone.

I lean my head back, eyelids drooping. That training session was beyond draining. I have nothing left in me, and I just want to sleep.

Out of the corner of my eye, Vianne's hair changes from teal to purple. She bites her lip and stares at the floor, a furrowed expression coming over her.

"What's up?" I ask, keeping my voice low so I don't wake Maddy.

She looks up. "This morning was . . . intense."

"No kidding."

"I've never seen Jonah like that," she admits. "He was scary. And his ability is really powerful."

"Jonah's an excellent teacher," I say. "I needed him to push me like that. I'm glad he did."

She fiddles with a loose thread sticking out of her comforter, wrapping it around her pointer finger repeatedly. "I'm sorry you're having to train so hard. It must feel overwhelming."

"It is."

"Are you sure you want to do this?" Vianne asks. The thread coils around her finger tighter. "Arthur can't make you help him."

I let out a long breath, hugging the blanket. "I know."

"Then why are you choosing to? You don't owe these people anything."

"It's not that simple."

"Why not? We're safe here, Hollis. The President can't get to you or Maddy. You don't have to fight anymore. I know Arthur told you they're ready to take down the Testing Centers when you're ready to take Area 19, but that doesn't mean you have to do this. Changing the world isn't on you."

"It is though!" I say, frustrated. Maddy stirs but doesn't wake. I purse my lips, lowering my voice. "Somehow, by some random stroke of fate, I was born a puppet master. I have one of the most powerful abilities in existence, and I have a responsibility to do something good with it, especially because I exposed us. These people are ready to take back society, and whether I like it or not, I've been given the opportunity to help them do it. And you're right, I don't have to, but I *should*. I was born in society. I've lived out there *and* in here. I understand both worlds. Maybe everything that's happened to me has led me here on purpose."

Vianne leans forward, abandoning the thread. She speaks in a soft voice. "I just want you to know that you have a choice, Hollis. I don't want Arthur to bully you into doing something you don't want to do. That's all."

I sigh, fiddling with the hem of the blanket. "I know I have a choice. And I'm choosing to do this."

She gives me a sad smile. "Then I'll support you."

My eyes begin to water, and I bury my head in my hands. "I'm sorry I got so upset. I'm just . . . I'm exhausted."

"That's okay," she says. She peers down at Maddy and strokes the top of his head gently. "Is there anything else you want to get off your chest while we're at it?"

I smile, fighting off a dry laugh. But then, my face sobers as my attention falls on the little boy sleeping on Vianne's lap. My stomach twists as I recall Arthur's hungry and sinister demeanor upon meeting Maddy. And the questions he's asked me about him . . .

"Arthur wants to know more about Maddy, and I don't like it."

"But I thought you said he was a Chief Overseer? Wouldn't he already know everything about the 'secret weapon?'"

I shake my head. "Camille kept tight a rein on Maddy. Arthur's only been briefed on what he needs to know to operate Area 7. Other Testing Centers are required to transfer kids who fail to Area 19 because that's where Maddy was."

I run my fingers over the soft fibers of the blanket, deep in thought. Stealing Maddy dealt a blow to society. Citizens have no idea that they've placed their trust in an institution that doesn't have its secret weapon anymore. But Camille won't inform the masses that their insurance is gone. True, he made that broadcast luring me out of the forest to exchange Maddy for Jonah, but he never said what we took. If only society knew.

What would other Testing Centers do if they had someone test positive without being able to offload them to Area 19? Shoot them, most likely. But there are biomarkers that can potentially withstand a bullet, and others that can deal with the aftermath—like Jacob Ganiston, the ancient man I met at the old compound who could heal himself. He was murdered by the government and survived. Rosalie showed me his memories. I even asked him to tell me his story because he lived through the massacre . . .

"And that's not all," I say.

I think back to Arthur's steely, prideful gaze, sipping red wine over a white suit as he dismissed my question about their research at Area 7.

"These people are researching the Test. And by that, I can only assume they're looking into the biomarker—the one that makes us 'diseased.' That's one of their projects."

Vianne squints. "Strange."

I swallow a lump, gearing myself up to say something that frightens me more than Camille. "Arthur wants Maddy for something. I just know it."

Vianne's hair turns crimson, and her face flushes. "What do you mean?"

"Arthur has this weird obsession with abilities," I say. "He's been very accommodating to me, but it feels like I'm some kind of prize—like the only reason he cares is because of my power. He's been that way with Maddy too."

I clutch the folds of the blanket more fiercely. Fatigue is steadily making it harder to think.

"And he's not afraid to get rid of anyone who stands against me. I mean, when Mr. Thomas objected to my seat on the Board, Arthur threw him out. And Keith is still under armed guard for trying to kill me."

"Maybe that's a good thing?" Vianne offers, her tone kind. She shrugs. "I know it's scary, but Arthur seems like he's willing to protect you."

"But only because he wants me for my power." My throat closes, as I try to search for how to explain my unease. "It feels like I'm a pawn in a game I had no say in playing, which is another reason why I want to help these people take over. This has to be done right. The situation is so delicate. The politics, I don't..."

I scrunch my nose. Of all the career paths society could've offered me, being a politician was last on my list.

"Not one for politics, I take it?" Vianne asks, cracking a smile.

"Not at all."

"Well, I'm sure you're doing a fantastic job."

I chuckle. "If purposely spilling red wine on Arthur Evandrum's white suit constitutes 'doing a good job,' then I'm a natural."

Vianne gasps. "You didn't!"

I smirk. "I did."

A few moments of silence pass between us, and Vianne goes back to twisting the loose thread through her fingers. I watch her, falling into a tired haze as my eyelids grow heavier.

"I want to protect everyone . . ."

I let my head fall, and my eyes well with tears. I fight the sensation, breathing in through my nose and out through my mouth.

"I still feel like I have to atone for what I've done. If I hadn't betrayed everyone—if I had listened to Tiffany, then no one would have died. And then maybe . . . maybe we could've all just lived in peace."

Vianne shakes her head and says, "But then we would've never met Maddy. We wouldn't know about Camille or his power. We wouldn't be here. It's *good* here, Hollis. We have jobs, food, and shelter. There are so many new abilities to explore and people to get to know. This could be our home."

I smile at her, still working through the knots of guilt in my stomach. "Maybe you're right."

My body aches, and sleep is trying its best to claim me, but I have one more thing I want to share with her. I lean forward, resting my forearms on my knees.

"Olivia Turrick found me in the forest before we came here, but Arthur had to ask *me* where our camp was."

Vianne tilts her head in surprise. "Olivia found us?"

"Yes, and she won't talk to me. At least, she wouldn't the day I confronted her about it. I got the chance to spend time with her on the Holodeck, but … maybe if we both worked on befriending her? I need help. I have to know why she didn't tell Arthur our location in the forest to begin with."

"Doesn't Olivia work for Arthur?"

"She does."

Her brow furrows. "That's so strange."

"I know. What possible reason could she have for withholding that information from him? It doesn't make sense. What if Arthur doesn't have the best intentions for us?"

"I think your sense of caution is valid, but Hollis, Arthur's intentions can't be as horrible as you're imagining." Her hair flickers to a soothing off-white color. "These people took us in. They wouldn't have done that if they were planning on hurting us."

I click my tongue in frustration. "I suppose."

"And we're like them. We have abilities. We're all on the same side here."

A chill runs down my spine. Those are the exact words Arthur said to me. Maybe Vianne's right. Maybe I'm making a fuss over a good thing for nothing. Maybe I should count my blessings and be happy I'm helping people with powers crush our enemies and crush them swiftly. But my naïve trust of authority in the past and Arthur's rhetoric of war frighten me.

Am I ready for war? Am I ready to lead because I happen to be the girl whose power these people need? Is my distrust even warranted? Or I am afraid because I'm broken by what I've done and what's been done to me?

"I believe in you," Vianne says, giving me an encouraging nod. "Okay? You're not alone."

"Thanks."

Maddy's tiny chest continues to rise and fall. He looks so peaceful when he's asleep. It almost makes me believe we'll be okay.

"Vianne?"

"Yes?"

"Thanks for being a good friend."

She smiles. "Any time."

18

LIFE IN THE MOUNTAIN SLOWLY SETTLES INTO A NORMAL rhythm, and besides the occasional Board meeting, it feels like it did back at the old compound. It's strange to admit, but I've adjusted well, and Vianne's encouraging words have helped. She was right to confront me about my worries, and although I'll probably never get rid of the unease I feel around Arthur Evandrum, I've managed to find more peace since our conversation. This *does* seem like a good place, and for the time being, I don't have to worry about dying.

As I bustle through the crowded dining room, I spot my friends, and comfort warms my stomach. Candice is talking to Rosalie with animated and energetic gesticulations. Ben is slouched by her side, pale, but present. And Keith is sitting across from them, Erwin silently standing behind him with a gun slung over his shoulder.

I approach and nudge Keith's arm.

"Hollis!" He lights up with a boyish smile, pulling me into an embrace. I hug him back, and his warmth makes me wish I were eating with him alone. We've barely seen each other since his release, and I want to spend more time together.

I take the seat next to him, and lean close to whisper in his ear. "Maybe we could eat alone?"

He smiles, but before he can say anything else, Candice grumbles in irritation, "Damn needle! My arm still hurts."

She rubs the flat of her arm opposite her elbow where a small flesh-colored bandage sits pressed against her skin.

"Your arm?" I say.

"That stupid physical we have to do. I don't know why they had to draw my blood. I'm perfectly healthy. I did enjoy showing off my power though," she adds with a smirk. "I think Beezee was impressed by my fire. Have you done yours yet?"

At this, I remember Arthur's request for an ability census to take stock of all the newcomers—as well as a general health checkup.

"No, I haven't," I say. I hate needles. I hate blood. I don't want to get pricked.

"You haven't signed up yet?" Candice asks, perplexed. "That bald mustache all but forced me to." She knots her arms across her chest, squinting and passing air between tight lips.

Rosalie chuckles. "Bald mustache?"

"Well, I don't know his name!" She throws a hand into the air.

"It's Hugo," I say, grinning. "But I like 'bald mustache' better."

"Me too," Rosalie snickers.

I give her a warm smile. "Rosalie, you look amazing, by the way."

She beams. "Thanks! I feel amazing. Clean bill of health. I just finished my last healing session with Beezee yesterday, I don't feel nauseous anymore when I walk, and I got my physical done early. They have *plenty* of my blood. You know, with the knife wound and all." Her voice plays into light, comical notes, and Candice laughs.

Ben drops his spoon on the floor then swears under his breath, ducking below the rim of the table to retrieve it. Rosalie and Candice exchange quick glances. When Ben resurfaces, Rosalie back-peddles, guilt written into her countenance.

"Sorry, Ben. I didn't mean to say it like that. It's not funny, I know." Her freckled face takes on a pink hue. "I'm okay, I prom—"

"It's fine," he replies, but his rough tone says otherwise.

"Ben." Rosalie's eyes begin to sparkle. "You know I don't blame you, right? You had no control over what you did. It's not your fault I got stabbed."

"Even so. I'm the one who stabbed you."

"But you're not to blame. Camille is. And I'm not mad at you, I'm just happy we're both alive."

He nods and gives her the faintest smile, forcing it through his tired eyes. "I know."

Candice pats Ben's shoulder, leaning on him and taking his hand. Keith puts his hand on top of theirs, and Rosalie and I follow suit. For a moment, the five of us sit, holding hands at the center of the table. All of us were in the President's office that night, and all of us were part of his game. We nearly died, but we didn't, and as we sit together, hand in hand, a strange peace fills my heart.

"It's done," I say. "We're safe now."

"We're safe," Candice says, giving Ben a soft kiss on the cheek.

After a minute of no conversation, our hands fall apart, and I nudge Keith's foot with the toe of my boot, hoping he'll take the hint to dismiss us from the group. Thankfully, he does.

"Hey, I think Hollis and I are going to eat a few tables over," he says.

Candice's eyebrows jump up and down quicker than Ben's wit. "Aww, lover boy's going on a lunch date!"

My face burns hot, and Rosalie giggles. Even Ben cracks a smile.

"Shut up, Candice!" Keith hisses.

"Make me." She waggles her finger.

I pull on Keith's arm, dragging him away, and Erwin follows us with a scowl, readjusting the machine gun on his shoulder.

"I'd like to apologize for my sister," Keith says.

"It's fine."

He points to a vacant table six spaces down. "Let's take that one."

I maneuver my way around the packed tables and sit down at the one Keith indicated, rolling my eyes at Erwin's sour attitude. The fact that Keith *still* needs a guard when it's perfectly clear that he's not a danger to anyone irks me. The next time I see Arthur, I'm putting an end to this.

I stare at Erwin as he takes his position immediately behind

Keith. "Do you mind? Can't you give us some space?"

"No, ma'am. Mr. Evandrum's orders are to—"

"I know what his orders are!" I snap. With a sigh, I lean back against the chair and listen to the voices of the crowded dining room rise in a chorus of vibrant chatter.

"How are you?" Keith asks. He hesitates before saying, "You know, since I nearly beat you to death?"

"I'm doing better. My jaw doesn't hurt much anymore. And my ribs are as good as new."

I reach for his hand, and a ball of emotions wells up in my stomach. I want to tell him everything I told Vianne. I want to share my worries and fears about this place, but I can't do that in front of Erwin. I must wait until we're alone. Truly alone.

Instead, I turn my nerves into another conversation I've been meaning to have with him. Earlier, Candice used the word "boyfriend," and I'm scared of it in a good way. I never had a romantic relationship in society. And if I were still living there, I'd have been assigned a husband. I didn't entertain romantic thoughts as a child; I was raised to bury them. And while I've broken free from many of society's toxic ideologies, I'm still new to the freedoms I'm enjoying.

"I have a question." I let go of him and stuff my hands into my lap to stop them from shaking.

"What's up?" he asks.

"Do you remember the marble game?" I ask.

"Yeah, that was the day I met you."

A flutter settles in my stomach. "Why did you ask me to play?"

He gives me a curious smile. "I thought you'd like it."

I laugh. "No, I mean, why *me*? I was the creepy new girl with the dangerous power."

"Creepy?" Keith raises an eyebrow, teasing. "I wouldn't say you were creepy, more like 'spine-chilling.'"

"Hey!" I kick him lightly under the table, noting that Candice has heavily influenced my behavior. "Watch yourself!"

Keith's joke gives me all sorts of twisty, warm feelings, and I grin.

He leans forward. "I invited you to play because you looked like you could use a friend. Plus, I thought, 'if this girl can take on an entire group of Testing Center employees and escape her Test, she must be pretty badass.'"

My face flushes, and heat prickles across my skin.

"Turns out, I was right." He winks at me. "You're definitely a badass."

I grin. I didn't feel like that back then, but I can also recognize how powerful I was—even at that point. I controlled an entire room of people intent on killing me because of adrenaline and sheer dumb luck.

I bite my lower lip. "When did you start liking me?"

Nervousness skitters through me. Why do I feel so awkward? It's just Keith. I've known him for over seven months now.

Keith tussles a hand through his dark hair, and without missing a beat, says, "The day you did the magic trick with Ben."

Ben's unexpected kiss comes screaming to the front of my mind, and I want to melt into the floor. That card trick ended with Ben Bryson kissing me full on the mouth in front of the entire dining room.

"Ben's card trick? Are you serious?"

Keith shrugs. "You seemed so open to trying new things in a world that was so different from the one you grew up in. And I found that attractive." He shifts in his seat, straightening his shoulders. "You didn't seem to care about people's perception of you. You were bold, and I thought, 'I want to get to know this girl better.'"

I smile. "No one else turned your eye?"

"Not really," Keith says. "The girls I grew up with felt more like family. It was a pretty small world down there." He looks around, chuckling. "I guess it's a much larger world now that we're up here."

I nod, scouring the massive room. "Yeah, up here you could pick anyone you want."

Keith smiles. "I already have."

The warm, happy feelings sharpen like a crescendo of instruments playing together in harmony, and I avert my eyes from his brilliant blue ones. "You want *me*? Even though I got people killed because I betrayed everyone?"

It kills me to ask him this after such a sweet sentiment, but I need to know how he really feels. He doesn't owe me his affection.

Keith's brow turns upward with sadness. "I'm not going to lie and say my feelings for you weren't challenged by what happened."

He stops talking for a few seconds like he's wrestling with how honest he wants to be.

"Please don't hold back to spare my feelings. You can tell me the truth," I say. "I'd prefer it, actually."

He smiles, but it's not the same as his joking smile from

earlier. "After the bombing, I had to think about what I wanted. I realized I didn't know you as well as I thought I did. I was angry and grieving the loss of so many people I'd known and cared for my whole life . . . You did a horrible thing, Hollis, but I stand by what I said to you at the river when those thugs tried to kill you. I don't think you deserve to die. You did an amazing thing by saving Maddy. You grew into what our people stand for—hope for those who are outcasts in this world simply because of their blood."

He pauses, taking a deep breath.

"I'm proud to have been part of that rescue mission. I felt like my parents were with me that day, watching over me."

When Keith flew me up to the ceiling at the old compound, he shared about his parents dying on a mission to search for more people with powers. He told me he was proud to be their son, and I can only imagine how eager he must have been to participate in rescuing Maddy from the government.

"Sounds stupid, I know," he breathes. "Thinking like that. I know my parents are gone."

"It's not stupid at all," I say. "It sounds beautiful. And I bet they *were* with you that day. I mean, without you, we'd have been stuck on the roof of the Testing Center with no way of escape. We'd have been shot."

"I suppose I *did* save the day," he says with a teasing inflection.

"You suppose?" My tone falls into light playfulness again. "You were amazing."

Silence ensues, and I chew on my lower lip, wondering whether I should break it or wait for him to continue. I speak up again, my stomach fluttering with anticipation.

"Thank you for being honest with me," I say. "I know I hurt you, and I'm deeply sorry. I understand that doesn't change anything. For what it's worth, I want you to know I'm with you, and I want to fight for people with powers like your parents did. I hope that one day I can live up to the responsibility I've been given as a puppet master. And I hope you can forgive me for what I've done." I speak quickly, tripping over my words to get everything out. "And I understand if you don't want to be with me. If you don't want to be my . . . boyfriend."

I look down, my heartbeat thundering. What if he says he doesn't want this after all? What if, by my invitation, he decides he'd rather break it off. I'd have to live with it. I'd have to understand, because how could I not? I hold my breath, hoping that I haven't just ruined one of the best things life's thrown my way.

"Hollis?" Keith's soft voice carries my eyes back to his.

"Yes?"

"Will you be my girlfriend?"

I break the tension in my chest with a joyful laugh, relieved by his words. "Yes, I'd like that very much."

Keith offers his hand to me, and I take it, feeling so happy I could shout.

"Careful," Keith says, nodding back to Erwin with a smirk. "He's allergic to happiness."

Erwin's scowl deepens, and I snicker. "So . . . we're okay?"

"We're okay."

Boom.

A thunderous crash makes everyone in the dining area jump, and I almost topple out of my seat. Heart ramming itself into my ribs, I launch to my feet. "What the—"

Bang.

The noise echoes from the other end of the room, and shouting cuts clear across the space. People are beginning to stand on tables and chairs, keen to get a look at what's happening.

"What the hell are you doing?" a familiar voice yells, strangled. "Let me go!"

"Get off!" a second voice shouts.

"Stop it! Stop it!" a girl screeches.

I leap on top of my chair, straining to see over the crowd. Dozens of other people join me, and within seconds, the entire dining room falls to a hush as the shrieks grow louder.

"Get off of him!" another girl squeals.

"LET ME GO!"

"HELP!"

Several men in black attire are wrestling with two boys and two girls, pulling them up from their seats. They are all screaming at each other, and as I crane my neck above the horde of people to see, I make out one of their faces amidst the scuffle.

My mouth drops open. "Is that . . . Ashton?"

Without a second thought, I sprint across the dining room, pushing my way through the throngs of onlookers to get closer to the commotion. Keith follows close behind.

Thud.

"GET OFF—"

"LET THEM GO!"

The cries sound over the uncomfortable murmuring of the room, and my adrenaline piques. Out of the corner of my eye, I see that Rosalie's followed me as well. She's sprinting so fast she nearly runs into me. Narrowly missing one another, we both cover the remaining distance between us and the men in black.

I arrive just in time to see Vianne attempting to pull a man off of Ashton. Her crutches are on the floor and she's hopping on one foot. To her left, Maddy is cowering in his seat, his little hands pressed over his mouth. And Audrey is fighting with another guard, trying to pry him off of Darren. He shoves Audrey backward and she crashes to the floor, unable to catch herself on her only leg.

Both Ashton and Darren are grappling with the men, but the struggle doesn't last long. The guards gain the upper hand, and within moments, the boys' wrists are cuffed behind their backs—with two men holding Ashton and two men holding Darren.

At this, Darren uses his ability, and his wrists pass right through the cuffs like mist. For a second, I'm unable to think clearly. I'd forgotten that Darren's ability lets him pass through solid matter. I've only seen it twice before—when I first met him during the marble game, and then again over a game of Cutthroat.

"He's a phaser!" the guard on Darren's right yells.

Darren tries to run, but Taser prongs fly through the air, burying themselves deep in his shoulder. He slumps to the floor, convulsing, and Audrey and Vianne scream.

"STOP!" I cry.

My fingertips are electric, and in an instant, the four guards, as well as Ashton and Darren, are under my ability—and their mouths are clamped shut. The people who can see the spectacle gasp at the use of my power, and a significant portion of them back away from me, creating a large ring. They've never seen my ability in real life, even though they all know what I can do. Everyone stares at me. Some with shock, others with trepidation. But I ignore them.

I march up to the man who tased Darren and bring him to his knees, control washing over me so powerfully I take a deep breath to soothe the intense tingling.

"What is going on here?" I demand, my fingertips ablaze.

I flourish my hand to open the man's mouth.

Eyes bulging, he stammers, "Orders f-from Mr. Evandrum, Miss!"

"What orders?" I spit, forcing his face upward with a flick of my pointer finger.

"We were told to take Mr. Ashton Teel and Mr. Darren Mitchell into custody."

"For what reason?" I ask, my voice running dangerously close to a growl.

"Because they tried to k-kill you," he squeaks, strangled under the ferocity of my hold over him. A vein on his temple begins to swell.

I stare at him a moment, mouth askew. "What are you talking about?"

"In the forest, they were the ones that tried to kill you," he says, gasping for air. "That's what I was told, Miss! We are to bring them into custody because they tried to kill you."

The forest. The boys who attacked me. The river. I gape at him for several seconds before coming to my senses. "How do you know about that?"

"I don't know, Miss! I'm just following orders!" he says, lips turning blue. He sputters, unable to move a muscle.

"Hollis, you're hurting him!" Keith shouts, pulling my shoulder. "He can't breathe!"

I relax my hand, and the man inhales deeply, able to breathe freely now, but he's still bound to my control.

I glance between Ashton and Darren before addressing the man on his knees. I speak to him spitefully, channeling my ability into the command. "Don't hurt them, and don't use that Taser again."

I flick my hand, releasing the four men. They stumble forward to their hands and knees but recover quickly. Ashton, now free from my power, begins his struggle anew. But Darren lies curled on the floor in a stupor. The two men who grabbed him earlier pick him up and restrain him. And this time, he doesn't fight back.

"Hollis!" Vianne whimpers, looking between me and Ashton. "What's going on?"

"I don't know."

Audrey, who's still sitting on the floor, eyes me with contempt, but doesn't say anything. She looks to Vianne instead. "Darren tried to kill Hollis? What are they talking about?" she demands.

Vianne locks eyes with Audrey. She's shaking, so Keith answers in her place. "Audrey, back in the forest, there were three people that attacked Jonah and Hollis, and they tried to kill

Hollis by throwing her into the rapids. Pierce was one of her assailants, but we never figured out who the other two were."

I walk up to Vianne, stooping to pick up her crutches. I hand them back to her and say, "I'll sort this out. Okay?"

"Okay," she says, looking like she might cry. Her hair changes from brown to platinum blonde with hints of silver.

I move to Audrey next, offering her my hand. She hesitates, but takes it, and I help her stand. "I'm sure this is just a misunderstanding."

I turn back to the man in charge, glaring at him. "Well? Let's sort this out. If Arthur gave the order, then let's bring this to him."

He addresses me hesitantly. "We're to place Mr. Teel and Mr. Mitchell in block—"

"I don't care what your orders are!" I snap. My power tingles, ready for my command. "We're sorting this out right now. So please, lead the way." I gesture across the room then turn to Rosalie. "Rosalie, come with me. I need your ability."

"Absolutely." She rolls the sleeves of her sweater up, and her bright red hair dances around her shoulders.

I lower my voice, glancing between Ashton and Darren. "Do you think it's true? Do you think they helped Pierce?"

"There's only one way to find out, right?"

"Right." I look to the man in charge, arms crossed. "Well? Let's go."

He falters, clearly afraid of me. He takes a step back and straightens his shoulders. "Miss, Arthur's in a meeting. Our orders are to take them down to cell—"

"Well, I'm giving you *new* orders," I say. "You've arrested two of my friends, and we are going to sort this out. Now, I can *make* you walk up there, or you can use your own two feet. Which will it be?"

The guards share apprehensive looks, but after brief reluctance, they nod.

"Good," I say.

I approach Keith, who's eyeing Ashton like he's ready to throw a punch. I step between them, grabbing his hand and pulling him away. "Can you stay with Maddy? Please?"

Maddy's still shaking in his seat. Keith's brow furrows like he's going to protest and say he needs to come with me, but he doesn't. "Yeah, I'll stay with Maddy."

"Thank you," I say, leaning up on my toes and giving him a quick kiss on the cheek.

Keith walks over to Maddy and crouches next to him, speaking in low, soothing notes.

An uncomfortable ten minutes of travel later, our odd group arrives at the door of Arthur's office in Sector 15. I don't even knock. I just place my hand to the panel, it flashes, and the door opens. Rosalie and I enter, and the four guards detaining Ashton and Darren file in right behind us. The room quiets at the sudden interruption.

Arthur swivels in his black leather chair to face me, agitated.

"Miss Timewire," he says. "What an unpleasant surprise. What is all of . . . *this*?"

His dismissive manner boils my blood, and I have to fight with my power to keep it contained. I take a deep, calming breath. "That's what I'd like to know. You gave orders to have Ashton and Darren arrested?"

"Yes, I did," he says, as if he were bored. "They, like Mr. Pierce Bodegard, were at the river that night and made an attempt on your life. And while Mr. Bodegard is now under our custody, Mr. Teel and Mr. Mitchell are not."

"How do you know about the river?" I ask, but I already know the answer, and my stomach flips in irritation. "Terrace?"

Arthur smiles, folding his hands together. "Mr. DuPont has an incredibly *useful* ability, don't you think?"

I scoff. I hate the fact that Terrace's ability is so invasive, but it *is* useful. Still, he knows too much. "Do you mind if I check before you detain them?"

Arthur sits straight up, suddenly interested. "What do you mean?"

"Rosalie?" I point to Ashton.

Ashton, hands cuffed behind him, begins to struggle again, fighting the men's grip on him, but they hold him firmly in place.

"Come on, Simmons!" he yelps. "It's me. You know me! I'm an ass, but I'd never kill anyone."

Rosalie stares into his face, flowering her hand open with a sad look. "I hope you're right."

Dark mist pours into the large stone room, and the Board members gasp, leaping up from their seats as Ashton's memories seep into the middle of the oval table. Arthur stands, gaping at the foggy substance. Within seconds, the forest materializes in the midst of the room, and with it, three shrouded figures erupt from her fingertips. It's Pierce, Darren, and Ashton, all crouched behind a clump of thick bushes just beyond the clearing where I cut wood. Then, Jonah and I appear. We are walking away from the pile of stumps.

The memory sharpens on Pierce as he twitches his hand toward me.

"Jonah, I still have the axe. Hold on. Let me run and put it back," my translucent counterpart says.

"Alright," he replies. "I'll wait here."

I stare at the memory, my heartbeat thudding through my chest and into my ears. Ashton, Pierce, and Darren move quickly, pulling masks over their faces. Ashton stoops low, grabbing a snapped-off branch and holding it like a bat. In a flash, he swings it through the air, hitting Jonah in the back of the head. The crack of his skull against the weapon makes me want to scream. Jonah crumples to the ground, and Ashton tosses the branch into the thick of the trees.

"Okay, let's go," Pierce murmurs.

"No mistakes," Darren whispers. "This has to be perfect."

Ashton nods. "That bitch dies tonight."

"Jonah?" I hear myself calling out.

"Shh!" Ashton hisses. "Let's go around." He motions the other two forward, and the memory zooms in on me.

"Jonah?" my silvery figure calls out again.

The fog of the memory streams off of Arthur's oval table, and the temperature of the room drops.

"That's enough," I say to Rosalie, placing a hand on her shoulder. "I don't want to watch this."

At my request, Rosalie pulls the memory back into her palms and stares at me, her face littered with fresh tears. I'm physically shaking—like my chest is going to explode. It takes everything in me not to walk up to Ashton and punch him in the face. The truth is, I understand why he did what he did. I took away his home, and somehow, his ability. He lost everything because of me. But the anger I feel toward him is making it hard to keep calm.

Rosalie approaches Ashton, her lower lip trembling. "I hoped you were telling the truth."

Ashton's mouth thins out, and his shoulders stiffen. He doesn't say a word to her. Instead, he turns away, finally sinking into the guards' grip and ceasing his escape attempts. Arthur's bored look from earlier is replaced with an impressed one as he stares at Rosalie like he's never seen anything like her.

"It's Miss Simmons, is it?" he asks, giving her a small bow.

She tucks a strand of hair behind her ear. "Yes, sir."

"What an *unusual* ability. Quite remarkable. I could find a useful place for you here, my dear."

I step in front of Rosalie before she can reply to Arthur, eyeing the boys. Darren is still in a daze from the Taser, but Ashton is seething.

"You were right," I say. "They tried to kill me."

"Indeed," Arthur replies, pressing his hands together fingertip to fingertip. "I'm detaining them for your protection, Miss Timewire."

I walk up to Ashton, bringing myself a few inches from his silently resigned face. His jaw is set. I peer at him, resentment curling in my heart for how he assaulted Jonah and tried to throw me into the rapids, but something else stirs there too. I almost feel . . . sorry for him.

I take a deep breath and speak with all the sincerity I can

muster. "I never meant to hurt you, Ashton. I hope you know that. And . . . I apologize for everything I've done to you. I know what I did was wrong, and I'm sorry for hurting you. I hope you can forgive me one day."

Ashton's eyes widen, and his lips part, like he's going to say something. The moment stretches on between us, and we hold each other's gaze, but then he closes his mouth and looks away.

"Remove these boys from my office," Arthur instructs.

"Right away, sir."

There's an awkward scuffling as the men escort Ashton and Darren from the room, and Rosalie and I are left standing with everyone staring at us.

I give Arthur a stiff nod. "Sorry for the interruption. We'll show ourselves out."

We turn to leave, but Arthur's voice stops me.

"My first priority is keeping you safe, Miss Timewire," he says. "They tried to kill you. You understand, don't you?"

I pause by the door. "I understand."

"You're valuable to us. We need you."

"I know."

Rosalie gives me a sideways glance. Hooking her arm in my own, I steer us out of the room and into the hall, exiting Arthur's office. Rosalie waits until we're a fair distance from the room before speaking.

"I don't believe it," she breathes.

My mind is buzzing. Ashton and Darren? Ashton makes sense, but I never thought Darren hated me enough to try to kill me. Is it because of Tiffany's death? Is it because of Audrey's amputated leg? I never spent any time with Darren and Audrey after the bombing, but I always got the feeling that he liked her, and when she got hurt . . .

"That's crazy," Rosalie says, mopping her eyes. "I can't believe Ashton would do that."

"Yeah," I say, slightly numb.

"And Darren too." Her throat constricts. "He's my friend."

"I know."

I continue to walk with her, our arms looped together, my brain shuffling through a myriad of chaotic thoughts. Arthur's proved it once again—he's willing to remove anyone who stands against me.

19

Cold fog trickles across cracked pavement, and dark clouds gather above a silent city. I'm alone, my feet scraping against the sidewalk as I hurry home.

Mother will be expecting me.

I gather my school-issued blazer tight about me, shivering in the frigid breeze. A storm is coming. Around the corner of the block, a group of black vans screech, and I wait until they pass before crossing the road. The street transit stop glows bright in the falling light of dusk, and gaudy advertisements flicker in rapid succession.

If I'm not home soon, mother will worry.

I tuck a strand of loose blonde hair behind my ear and forge ahead. The end of the block is close, so I pick up the pace to a light jog, my heart rate thrumming in even beats. But when I turn the corner of the street, the Area 19 Testing looms into view, towering above me.

What? Why am I here?

Crack.

Thunder and lightning explode directly over my head, and I scream, shielding my face from the brilliant strike of electricity. Its energy is so great that the air itself buzzes. Then, rain soaks the earth and seeps through my clothing, drenching me.

This is not where I need to be. Mother wants me home.

I turn my back to the Testing Center, and a scream that pierces the very depths of my soul laces my veins with adrenaline.

"HOLLIS!"

I spin around, searching for the woman who just cried my name, but no one is there.

The voice shrieks again.

"HOLLIS!"

The hairs on the back of my neck stand on end, and my eyes rake over the city block, scanning for the source of the guttural cry.

Panic spurs me into a sprint. I don't know why or how, but instinct is drawing me to the daunting, glittering building ahead. Society's symbol for purity and worth. The Testing Center is where I must go.

I sprint over the soaked pavement as another crack of thunder splits the sky open with the force of a bomb. I'm thrown to my hands and knees. Aching pain travels up my legs, but I push past it. Sucking in rattling breaths, I launch forward anew, until I'm standing on the marble steps of the monument.

"HOLLIS!" the woman shrieks.

And this time, my heart stops. I know that voice . . .

"Mother?"

"HOLLIS, HELP ME!"

"MOTHER!" I shriek, peering up the panels of reflective glass. They're littered with rain. My eyes climb higher until they land on the slender figure of a woman drenched to the bone. Her hair is plastered against her clammy skin, and she's standing on the bitter edge of the roof, weeping and hugging herself.

Fear jumps down my throat with its suffocating hands, and I fight to scream. But it's like my voice is slugging through a bog. I'm suffocated, clawing out each word.

"Mother—get away—from—the edge—you'll—fall!"

Her frightened gaze meets mine, and she nods, taking a step away from the sheer drop.

"I'm coming mother!" I call up to her. "I'm coming!"

I spin on my heels, but my path is blocked by three military men. They're on me like ants to rotting food, and ice stabs through my veins. Their rough hands grab me, dragging me down the slippery steps of the Testing Center and out to the street.

"NO!" I scream, fighting them. "Let me go!"

My hands flail, and my fingertips sear with tingling, but no ability comes. My control is gone. And the men grow in number, multiplying and filling the street to the brim.

Dozens of them.

Hundreds of them.

Thousands . . .

"HOLLIS!"

The men drag me to the center of the street, where a huge

metal throne sits as high as the nearest housing unit—the same throne from the Test. They force me, kicking and screaming, into it and fasten cuffs to my wrists and ankles. Then, a gun is trained on my head, and my body goes numb.

Boom.

The next crack of thunder is so loud that my chest rattles. Blinding light strikes the steps of the Testing Center, fracturing them down the center so that the very earth beneath us quivers. Chunks of marble fly in every direction, and as the dark spots in my vision fade, the black, unfeeling eyes of Alvaro Camille stare through me, his face inches from my own.

I writhe in my restraints, hands floundering for control of an ability I don't have. I'm powerless, and Camille's wicked smile scorches my flesh.

"HOLLIS, HELP ME!" my mother screeches. I can't get to her, and I can't free myself.

Camille brandishes a silver knife, sliding the tip of it against my neck.

"Foolish of you to come here, Hollis," he sneers, pulling the knife away. "Now we can finish what we started."

I struggle, desperately fighting to free my arms and legs, but I'm bound to the throne, unable to escape.

Camille draws his arm back, and before I can even gasp, he plunges the knife into my abdomen. The pain is unlike anything I've ever felt—sharp, hot, puncturing torture that rips through my flesh like tissue paper.

Every nerve in my body is on fire in agony.

My vision blurs, my skin blisters, and my heart thuds in an

ever-increasing rhythm like it's going to rupture. With a dark cackle, Camille steps back from me, and lightning cracks again over the street, striking the metal throne and splitting my bones.

.   .   .

I scream awake with a voice that shreds my throat like shrapnel. A pair of strong hands shake me, and I wrestle them, caught in the limbo between sleep and consciousness.

"Hollis! Hollis, it's me!"

I grasp the wrists of the man standing over me, grappling to free myself before realizing it's Jonah who's grabbing me.

"Jonah!" I gulp, ceasing my efforts to fight him off. His cane is on the floor, and the armchair he was sitting in is knocked askew.

I sit up, panting with sweat clinging to my clothing and hairline. As I survey my surroundings, my panic diminishes. I'm in the training room, it's late in the evening, and I must have dozed off after finishing another grueling session.

Jonah kneels by the bed, staring at me. "Hollis, you're white as a sheet. What did you dream about?"

I swallow, the back of my throat dry. I struggle to speak through my heaving breaths. "My mother—the President—I . . . I died. He stabbed me." My eyes water, and a burning sensation follows. "I couldn't escape. I didn't have my power. I tried to save her, but they tied me to the metal throne. They—"

Jonah's hands steady my shoulders, and I bow my head over my lap. I feel like I'm going to be sick.

"Hollis, are you having these dreams every night?" he asks.

"Well, not every night . . ."

We lock eyes, and I take a few moments to calm myself down from the vividness of the nightmare.

Jonah's brow creases in concern. "You've mentioned these dreams before. They seem to be getting worse. For a second there, I couldn't wake you. Are you okay?"

I shake my head, tucking myself into a ball as Jonah releases my shoulders. I choke back a whimper. "No, I'm not okay."

Stress is working its way into my every moment, suffocating any peace I might feel here in the mountain. The dreams about my mother, the enormous responsibilities I've been given, and the leadership role I've taken are almost too much. I'm adamant about taking the Area 19 Testing Center in the *right* way. Society can't view us as the monsters history says we are, but I haven't come up with anything. And as I've internalized the idea of changing society's mind about people with powers, it makes me think of my mother.

What about her? She's family. I have no idea what she thinks of me, but maybe I can talk to her. Maybe I can change her mind about me. Maybe she'd come back with me. I have to start somewhere, and she seems like the perfect place. I can't get her off my mind. She's in my sleep—some nights more potently than others, but she's always there.

"Jonah," I say, my voice cracking. "I want to go see my mother."

I brace myself for his protest. I've been thinking about voicing this to him for the past few days, I just haven't had the courage. I don't want him to shoot the idea down, but considering the insanity of it, I wouldn't be surprised if he did.

I'd be leaving the protection of the mountain and stepping back into society.

Jonah's brow furrows. He sits on the floor by the side of my bed, considering me, and a minute goes by before he speaks.

"Explain."

Relief washes over me. I'm grateful he didn't immediately tell me how dangerous this would be. "Do you remember when Arthur challenged me to name one society member that would change their mind about us?"

He breathes out between tightened lips. "Yes, I remember."

"Maybe my mother could be the one," I say. "Maybe I could make her see that we're good? That people with powers aren't a threat, and that I'm not a terrorist? We're just trying to live peaceful lives. The government has been lying to her."

Jonah gives me a melancholy smile, resting his hand on his cane. "Tiffany thought the same thing about you."

At this, my heart aches, and guilt consumes me. "I know."

"Do you think seeing your mother will change her mind?"

I'm fighting the urge to cry. Changing her mind about people with powers isn't the only reason I want to see her. These nightmares are scaring me. What if Camille's done something to her? I can't shake the feeling that something's terribly wrong.

"Jonah, I think my mother is in danger," I say. "I know you said that she is probably involved in the government's plan to kill me, but what if she's not? What if she's not safe? Why am I having these dreams about her?"

I sweep the tears beading in my eyes away with the tips of my fingers, but I can't stop them from coming.

"She's my family," I continue earnestly. "And if people with powers are going to take over, then I want her to know we're not evil. We're not here to repeat history, we're here to change it. And I stand by what I said before—this has to be about changing minds and hearts, not about grabbing power. Maybe I can start with her. And then I can show Arthur that it *does* matter how we do this."

Jonah folds his hands together, still sitting on the floor. "If you were to go to her, would you ask her to come back with you?"

"Yes," I say without missing a beat. "Of course."

"Would you force her to come?"

I chew on the tip of my finger, thinking of Tiffany and how she forced me to hide with them underground. I know now that it was the best choice—the *only* choice—and if Tiffany hadn't teleported me out of my home when she did, I'd be dead. But my mother doesn't have the biomarker.

"No, I wouldn't force her to come with me."

"Have you thought about how you could achieve a visit like this? The whole of society saw you vanish during the public broadcast of your execution. You're the most wanted person in the world."

I cling to the folds of the quilt, frustrated. "Are you saying I shouldn't do this?"

"Hollis, you're incredibly powerful, but you're not invincible. You can't go traipsing into the city without a plan. I'm sure Camille's put extra precautions in place since your last visit. He's intent on killing you."

"I know."

"And I'm sure Arthur wouldn't like the idea of you leaving the mountain," he adds. "You're not a prisoner here, but I bet if you asked, he'd say no."

My stomach squirms. Arthur definitely wouldn't approve of this, but he doesn't have to know. This is my business. Besides, he's the one who mockingly suggested that not one person from society would be on our side regardless of how we took over. Maybe I can prove him wrong.

"I'm not planning to ask his permission," I say with an aggravated edge. "He doesn't own me."

"You're right. He doesn't." Jonah grips his cane and stands up, walking back to the armchair and readjusting it. He takes a seat and shakes his head. "I don't like the idea of you leaving the mountain, Hollis."

I pick at my cuticles. I've been mulling over bits and pieces, imagining what it would be like to step into my home again and see my mother. To talk to her face to face. The thought of it thrills me, but I haven't labored on the details of accomplishing a visit.

"I was thinking of asking Olivia to take me there, but if she tells Arthur that I'm planning to leave the mountain . . ."

"That could be challenging," Jonah concedes. "Olivia is your only way in and out. And she works for Arthur. Do you trust her?"

"I don't know."

Jonah sighs. "What about a disguise?"

"I suppose having one would be smart," I say.

"Any thoughts?"

I give Jonah a humored look. "Do you have any ideas? You're the one who's good at planning things."

"On the contrary, young lady, *you're* the one with the good ideas." He smiles. "I'm simply here to guide them."

I chuckle. "Well, Vianne gave me a pretty good disguise when we rescued Maddy, but I'm not sure if she'd want to go back to the city with me."

Jonah leans back in his chair, resting both his hands on top of the cane. "I think you're right."

"I won't know until I ask her," I say, speaking quickly. "If Vianne disguises me and Olivia teleports me directly to my housing unit, then I could slip in and out undetected. And I could control anyone I perceive to be a threat. The three of us could make this operation clean, quick, and manageable. I just need to make sure Arthur doesn't know about it."

Jonah closes his eyes, rubbing his forehead. He looks like he's trying his best to not condemn my plan. "Can I ask you something, Hollis?"

"Of course."

"If you go to her, are you willing to accept that your mother may try and turn you in all over again?"

My heart drops. I hadn't thought about that, and the idea dampens the hope I felt moments ago. All I can think to say is, "Maybe she won't."

"Perhaps, but I think it's important you plan this venture without any expectations," he says. "It took months and a bombing to change your mind about the government. Your mother likely won't change hers with one conversation."

The word 'bombing' crushes my spirit, and my stomach churns.

"And another thing to consider," Jonah continues. "Unfortunately, Arthur *and* Camille will likely find out about this one way or another."

I sit straight up, dread zipping down to my toes. "Why? What makes you think I can't pull this off without them knowing?"

He taps his foot against the floor. "Putting aside Olivia's hopeful discretion and your stealth throughout this visit, if your mother doesn't come back with you, she'll likely report sighting you. Camille will know you were in the city. Arthur will too. Are you willing to take the *high* chance that this will become public? That Camille will likely twist this visit with your mother for political gain in the eyes of society? You come from a prestigious family, Hollis. Your father is the head of the military elite, his wife is a high-ranking society member, and his daughter became the 'leader of the second Terror War,' or so Camille has dubbed you. This won't come without consequences."

Fear seizes me. I can only imagine what warped news reports could release worldwide about my terrorist activities as a result of this decision. Would I do more damage seeing my mother than good? Maybe she wouldn't tell the government about my visit, but that's a big maybe.

"Do you think it's worth it?" I ask, my lower lip trembling.

"I think only you can answer that, Hollis," Jonah says. "But I will say that even if your mother reports you, you may plant a seed in her heart. An idea can be as powerful as an ability."

Wadding the quilt up, I toss it to the foot of the bed and sit crisscrossed, staring down at the floor. "Do you think this is selfish of me? Going to see my mother with all the negative publicity I've already given us?"

Jonah laughs grimly. "I think the government will continue to use fear and manipulation of the masses regardless of your actions, Hollis. Camille's already done so, and he will continue."

I fiddle with a thread sticking out of the long sleeve of my shirt, pondering this. Camille will continue to use me as a scapegoat, no doubt, but it won't deter me from doing the best I can to be the change I want to see in the world.

"You're right," I say. "But I don't care. I want to go see her. Maybe this visit *will* plant a seed, and maybe that's all I can hope for. I have to try."

Jonah smiles, spinning his cane under his palm. "You know what?"

"What?"

"You've come a long way since I met you," he says. "You're growing up."

Warmth spreads into my heart, and I smile back. "You said to me once that no one would expect anything from a sixteen-year-old girl. I don't think Arthur knows what he's signed up for, because I'm going to initiate change *my* way—and if he doesn't like it, tough. He's not a puppet master."

Jonah chuckles, shaking his head. "He's certainly not."

I fold my arms across my chest, resigning myself to the task at hand. "Now all I have to do is convince Olivia Turrick to take me to the city."

"Hollis?"

"Yes?"

"I think it's best you don't share your plans with anyone other than Olivia and Vianne."

"Yes, sir. I'll keep this to myself."

"Then you have your work cut out for you, young lady." He clears his throat. "I'd say get some rest, but I think that's in poor taste."

I scrunch my nose, stifling a laugh. "I agree."

20

"THERE WE GO, SWEETHEART," BEEZEE SAYS, CAREFULLY positioning a needle and vial to extract a sample of blood from Maddy's arm. Her long black braid is weaved into a tight bun, her scrubs pressed flat against her tall thin frame.

Maddy and I are in the medical ward in Sector 10 for his physical. I sit on the examination table with him, my arm around his shoulder. Beezee's speed and precision are impeccable, and after ten seconds, the small vial is filled with dark red liquid. She pops another vial onto the needle's funneled end, collecting a second sample. Then a third and a fourth.

"All done," Beezee chimes, unsticking Maddy and setting the vials into a test tube holder on her rolling cart. "Well done, Maddy."

Maddy squirms, holding out his arm. "It hurts."

"I know," Beezee says in a honeyed tone. She puts a cotton ball over the prick mark opposite Maddy's elbow. Unwrapping a bandage, she presses it flat against his skin. "Good as new."

"Good job, Maddy," I say.

"Why did you need to poke me?" Maddy asks, looking up at Beezee.

"I'm here to make sure you're a strong, healthy, growing boy." She smiles down at him. "And your blood can tell me a lot about you."

"Do you know about the golden light?" Maddy asks, perking up.

"I sure do." Beezee tosses the bandage scraps into the waste bin in the corner.

"About that," I say, speaking quickly. "I know Arthur's requested everyone demonstrate their ability to you, but in Maddy's case, I'd like you to take my account of it instead. No need for any accidents to happen."

She bows her head. "Of course."

"Thank you." I sigh in relief, grateful I don't have to fight Beezee over this.

Beezee pats Maddy on the knee. "I hear you have quite a special ability. Is that true?"

He claps his hands together. "The golden light!"

"Yes." She hands him a piece of red candy and a cup of juice. "Drink up, and then you can eat the treat. You've earned it for being so brave today."

Maddy takes the candy and fiddles with the bright plastic wrapping, giggling with delight.

"Maddy, drink the juice first," I encourage him. "Or you won't feel good."

Maddy uses both hands to handle the large plastic cup, and then sips it, slurping some of the juice. It dribbles down his chin. "That's cold!"

Beezee grabs a clipboard with a stack of papers and begins to fill out Maddy's profile. "How old is he?"

"Five," I say. "Well . . . a hundred and five if you want to be accurate."

Maddy, after wrestling open the wrapping, pops the candy from the plastic and begins to suck on it.

"And can you please describe the nature of his ability?" she continues.

"He can take a person's power away by sucking it into his hands," I say. "He took my power away not too long ago. But he can also give it back. He's definitely a type two, and his ability physically manifests as golden light that spirals out of his palms. For now, that's the extent of what we know. But since he's so young, he may have more parts of his ability that will come out with time."

Beezee scratches down my notes, glancing over the form and rifling through to a different page. "Any history of illness?"

"Not that I know of." I rub Maddy's back in gentle circles.

Beezee's pen flies across the clipboard. "From what you've observed, do you have any concerns about his health?"

I shake my head but add, "He's been cryogenically frozen for most of his life. I'm not sure if there are any long-term side effects associated with that?"

Beezee clicks her tongue. "When cryostasis was invented in 2381, there were a myriad of issues—botched coma inductions, blood clots, paralysis, seizures, strokes, heart failure . . . the list goes on. But we've improved the technology by leaps and bounds since then. A lot can happen in a few hundred years. Two hundred and sixty-six to be exact!" She pauses, hands on her hips. "As far as I'm aware, there's not been any significant side effects documented from Cryo sleep in well over a hundred years. Although . . . I've not read a case study of anyone who's been in Cryo for as long as Maddy. But you shouldn't worry. The technology is very safe."

"That's good that Cryo is safe," I mumble.

It's been almost eight months since I failed my Test—five months at the old compound, one month in the forest, and almost two months here in the mountain. The year is still 2647, but I feel like I've lived several lifetimes through all this mess. Maddy, however, has lived through so much more . . .

"His blood sample should tell me plenty," Beezee says, waving her hand. "I wouldn't worry about it, and I'll let you know if something concerning comes up in his bloodwork."

"Thank you."

"Now, let's see here," Beezee says, flipping to the last page of the clipboard. "His blood pressure looks good, heart rate is normal, his lungs sound great, and his overall physical appearance doesn't raise any concerns." She sets the clipboard on the rolling table with the test tubes of Maddy's blood. "I think he's good to go."

"I appreciate it, Beezee."

I hop off the table and pull Maddy down with me. He wobbles, clinging to my arm. "I'm a little dizzy."

"I took your blood, sweetheart," Beezee explains. "You'll feel dizzy for a little bit, but you'll be fine soon."

"Drink the rest of your juice," I say, gently prodding him. He listens and downs the last few sips. "Good job, Maddy."

Maddy and I make our way to the door, but Beezee stops me. "Hollis?"

I turn back toward her. "Yes?"

"You need to do your physical soon. I'm just about done with everyone else. I expect to see you here when you can find a moment. I know you're busy training, and Arthur's got you going to all his Board meetings—*that man*—but you're not exempt. I need a blood sample from you."

I grimace. "Yes, ma'am. I'll find the time."

"Good, now run along."

I turn to leave when a thought occurs to me. I linger in the doorway, still holding Maddy's hand. Clearing my throat, I try to keep my tone even and relaxed. "Beezee, what do you use the blood for? I thought about being a medic when I was younger. I'm just curious what a blood workup entails?"

Beezee sighs, folding up the crinkled paper Maddy sat on. She tosses it into the waste bin, rips a new sheet from the roll, then lays it across the examination table. "You have an interest in medicine?"

"Yes," I lie, and my heartbeat picks up.

"Well, without getting too long-winded, we get a count of your red and white blood cells and measure your hemoglobin levels. We screen for things like anemia, a blood infection, or cancer. We do a metabolic panel and a lipid panel. But part of what we do—and I'd say the most important part—is categorize and analyze the biomarker that gives people their *specific* ability. It's quite fascinating."

I bite my lip to keep my devouring interest at bay. I don't want to sound too eager. "And is that . . . one of the projects you do at the Area 7 Testing Center?"

Beezee gives me a sideways glance. "In a manner of speaking."

"Could you elaborate?" I ask hopefully.

Beezee ducks below the cart and pulls out her large medical bag, rummaging through it. "I'm sorry, child. But some of what I do is . . . well, for lack of a better word, *classified*. But I'm sure Arthur would talk to you about it if you asked him."

I stifle a scoff. "Right, of course."

My stomach sinks. I was hoping to get more information out of her, but for now, I got another piece of the puzzle. Whatever this project is, it definitely involves blood, and what unsettles me most is that all of my people have just offered it up willingly.

"Thank you," I say, "And do you know where Olivia might be this morning?"

"That girl is like the wind," Beezee says, shaking her head. "I couldn't tell you. Although your best bet would be the Holodeck."

"Got it. Thank you."

I dip out of Beezee's examination room. Picking up Maddy, I hoist him onto my hip and speed through the sterile corridors, keen to get back to the part of the mountain that doesn't smell like chemicals.

"See Maddy? That wasn't so bad, was it?"

Maddy tucks his head on my shoulder. "But my arm hurts."

"I know."

"Where are we going?"

"We're going to find Olivia. Do you remember the blue orb that took you here?"

Maddy nods. "I like the blue light."

We continue down the maze of corridors, and now that we're a good distance from Sector 10, I set Maddy down and hold his hand as we walk.

Just then, the musical voice of the mountain chimes. "0800: Duty Assignment 1, please make your way to the appropriate Sector."

"Um," I murmur, coming to a fork in the hallway. "The Holodeck is to the left. At least I think it is . . ."

I silently scold myself for not having the layout of the mountain down by this point, but it's so much bigger than the old compound. Since Jonah's talk, I've been mulling over how to approach Olivia about helping me see my mother, and I've settled on an idea that I hope will work.

After another five minutes, Maddy and I arrive at the Holodeck in Sector 1. The kaleidoscope of mirror-paneled walls greets us like a dazzling light display, and I shield my eyes from the brightness.

Maddy scrunches his nose, pointing up at the walls. "All the lights!"

I laugh. "You sure do like lights."

As I scan the hall, there's only one door that's red. The rest are green and unoccupied. We walk over to the red-lit door, and I knock five times. I step back to wait, hoping I haven't just interrupted a stranger's Holo program.

A minute passes by, so I raise my hand to knock again, but just as I move to do so, the door slides open, and Olivia pops her head out.

"Oh, Hollis."

She checks the hall beyond, faltering when she sees we're alone. Her dark skin glistens with sweat, and she wipes her forehead with the back of her hand.

"Hi," I say. "Sorry to interrupt. Can I talk to you for a minute?"

She hesitates, looking back over her shoulder. "Um . . ."

"Please?" I add, noting her uneasy stance. She probably thinks I'm going to ask her about the forest again, and the vivid image of her darting away from me and disappearing in a flash of blue arises.

She steps out of the Holodeck, shuts the door behind her, and says, "Sure."

"Thank you."

Olivia kneels with a smile. "Hi Maddy. How are you?"

"Hi!" He waves at her. "I got stuck with a needle, so I got a piece of candy."

"Did you now?" Olivia stands, hands on hips, eyeing me warily. "What's up, Timewire?"

I glance down the hall to ensure we're alone. "Before I ask you . . . what I'm about to ask you," I say, and my heart begins to race. "I want you to know that even though I have no idea why you didn't tell Arthur where to find my people, you must have had a good reason. And even though I don't know that reason . . . I trust you, and I trust your judgment. If you're not comfortable sharing that with me, or you *can't* share it . . ." I pause, gearing myself up for the statement I know will drive my curiosity insane. "I accept that."

Olivia's offensive stance relaxes as if a heavy weight had just been lifted from her.

"I don't know you, but you saved my life," I continue. "You rescued me from Camille, and for that, I'm incredibly grateful. Regardless of how you found our camp in the forest, I believe you had, and *still* have, my best interest at heart. So, I can live with not knowing, if that's what's best."

She squares her shoulders, checking the hall as I had just done. Her dark brown eyes meet my hazel ones.

"Thank you for trusting me," she whispers.

Her response only confirms my suspicions. I believe she's trying to keep something from Arthur, and because of Terrace's ability to learn things about a person just by being around them, she's chosen not to share something important with me. My ability is stronger than hers, and Terrace's ability to learn is directly connected to the extent of someone's power. Arthur's words slink through my mind: "The more powerful someone's ability, the more he can learn. Like your favorite hobby, for example. Or perhaps, your favorite color. Or other *deeper* things."

Olivia rubs her palms together. "What did you want to ask me?"

"Given your discretion before, I was hoping you could keep something else from Arthur?"

At this, her interest piques. Without hesitation, she grabs my wrist and says, "Not here. In the Holodeck."

I obey, and Maddy and I follow her back through the door and into the room of flashing lights. It's uncomfortably bright in here, and Maddy squints, clinging to my leg as the room shuts.

"Welcome to pod 009. Please state your unique access code," Hilda's automated voice states.

"5-6-6-1-0-1," Olivia says.

"Welcome, Olivia Turrick," Hilda chimes. "Would you like me to load simulation X?"

"Hilda, activate Privacy Mode."

The room flashes bright orange then dims to a reasonable level. "Privacy mode enabled."

"Hilda, furnish the room."

Two couches, a dining room table with chairs, a coffee table, and a rug appear in the midst of the room. Light blue throw pillows and a matching blanket pop against the gray upholstery.

"Hilda, create building blocks," Olivia adds.

Brightly colored blocks of blue, red, and yellow materialize in the center of the rug, and Maddy's face lights up. He lets go of my leg and runs over to the blocks, sitting down on the carpet. He starts sorting them into groups, babbling to himself.

Olivia motions me over to the couch, and we both sit. She stares at me with a look so intense I'm momentarily speechless.

"I'm good at keeping secrets," she says.

"Good. That's what I need."

Olivia's enthusiasm to help me hide something from Arthur puts me on edge. I didn't think she would assist me so willingly. If anything, her attitude makes me more wary of Arthur. Why would one of his most trusted employees be so eager to do something behind his back? But I can't ask her that.

I take a deep breath. "I need you to teleport me to the city a few blocks outside of the Area 19 Testing Center. I want to see my mother. And I'm almost certain Arthur wouldn't be happy about me leaving the mountain, considering that my safety is his top priority."

Olivia sits straight up, a grin playing on her lips. "You're damn right he wouldn't be happy."

My stomach churns. "I can't get there on my own. I need you."

"Looks like you need a *chaperone*," she says. "I'm in."

"Why? Why are you willing to help me?"

She shifts on the couch. "That's *my* business. For now."

"Fair enough." Everything in me wants to question her further, but I hold back. "I didn't think you'd be this cooperative."

"Like you said, you don't know me."

I give a dry laugh. "I definitely don't."

"You want to see your mom? I'm pretty sure she wouldn't want to associate herself with the 'leader of the second Terror War,' but I'm interested. Why go see her?"

I hesitate, uncertain of how honest I should be with her. She's surprised me so far, but part of me knows the only way I can enact the type of change I want is to be honest. "Arthur wants to take over the Area 19 Testing Center and stop the Test worldwide."

"Yes, I'm aware."

"And while I'm more than on board with this, Arthur plans to assassinate the President."

"He *what*?" she hisses, her voice razor sharp.

"So, he doesn't tell you everything," I note.

She scoffs. "I'm more of an ability to him. And a convenient one at that."

I knot my hands together, adjusting my position on the couch. "I couldn't have said it better myself. I want to go see her because I refuse to be a part of more violence. Killing the President isn't the answer. It can't be. I want to change society's mind about us, and an assassination isn't going to do that. But maybe I can start small. Maybe I can start with my mother. That's why I need to go see her, to talk to her, to . . ."

I trail off, emotion growing thick in my throat.

"To try and make a meaningful difference?" Olivia offers.

"Yes."

Olivia tucks herself up on the couch, facing me with the same intense look. "We have a lot in common, Timewire."

"We do?"

Out of the corner of my eye, Maddy's hard at work, building a tower with the colored blocks. He carefully selects the blocks in a pattern, creating a pillar of yellow, then blue, then red.

"What's your plan?" she asks.

I recount the conversation Jonah and I had the previous day, and she listens carefully, nodding occasionally, but never interrupting. And when I finish, she leans back with a quizzical look, hand to her chin.

"We have to go to the city on a day where Arthur isn't in the mountain," she says. "Because if he went looking for you, for any reason, and you weren't here . . ."

I brush a hand through my hair. "That wouldn't be good.

How can we get him to leave the mountain?"

"Well, Timewire, it seems your clandestine request came at *just* the right time," she says with a sinister smile.

My pulse accelerates. "What do you mean?"

"In a week, Arthur has his Quarter Review. He travels to the Area 7 Testing Center for the day, and all departments give him their progress reports. That's when we'll go."

The tension in my body increases tenfold, and my shoulders ache. I roll them out, trying to loosen my stiff muscles. I didn't expect to see my mother so soon. What if I can't think of what to say to her? What if she doesn't want to come back with me? What if she reports me?

"That soon?" My voice comes out feebly.

"Arthur leaves the mountain all the time," Olivia says. "But he comes and goes as he pleases—he's a Chief Overseer. I can't guarantee a day where he'll be gone other than once every three months. He never misses the Quarter Review. If we want to do this, it has to be then."

I grip the edge of one of the throw pillows. I can't wait another three months for this opportunity if Arthur's only given me one month to come up with a plan to take Area 19 without assassinating the President. And at this point, I have even less time than that. This may be my only opportunity to talk to my mother before Arthur makes his move.

"Okay," I say. "Let's do it."

Olivia's mischievous grin deepens. "Excellent."

"Don't tell anyone," I say, tension settling in the pit of my abdomen.

She stifles a laugh. "This isn't my first illicit away mission.

Don't worry, Timewire. Your secret's safe with me. And, just a tip," she adds in a serious tone. "Don't look Terrace in the eye. It helps him."

So, I'm right. At least partially. Olivia isn't telling me something because of Terrace's ability. And direct eye contact helps him discover more about a person. Good to know.

Crash.

All of Maddy's blocks tumble to the ground, and he looks around at the mess, mouth half open. His big blue eyes well with tears. "My tower!" he cries, sitting down amidst the wreckage with a frown.

I jump up from the couch and kneel by his side. "How did it fall?"

"I couldn't reach," he says, weepy-eyed. "It was too tall."

"Do you want to build a new one with me?"

His smile snaps back in a flash, and I barely have time to brace myself before he tackles me with a hug.

"Woah!" I grunt. We tumble to the floor.

"Can we build a tower as big as you?" Then, he points to the ceiling of the Holodeck. "As big as the lights?"

I laugh, lifting him off of me. "Maybe not as big as the lights, but we can try."

He claps, jumping up and down. "Yay! Yay! Yay!"

Olivia hops up from the couch, crouching next to Maddy. "Look at all this. Can I help build the tower too?"

Maddy nods, scampering about to retrieve the blocks that skidded from the rest of the pile. "You have to change color every time," he says, grabbing a yellow block. "Yellow is first." He places it directly on the carpet. "Then blue." He stacks the next one. "And red." He finishes the first pattern and stares at me expectantly.

"Yellow. Blue. Red." I stack the next three. "Like that?"

Maddy giggles. "And we have to build it as high as the lights!"

"As high as the lights?" Olivia cranes her neck, looking up at the ceiling. "Hilda, add more blocks."

The room flashes, and a couple dozen additional blocks appear in the midst of the carpet. Maddy immediately starts sorting them into piles based on their color, bustling about like this is the most important task in the world.

I mouth a "thank you" to her.

"It looks like you've done this before, Maddy," Olivia says.

He nods, his arms so full of blocks I can barely see his face behind them. "Sissy liked to build towers."

Olivia sits crisscrossed on the carpet, helping Maddy unload the blocks into their appropriate piles. "Who's Sissy?"

"My sister," Maddy says, and his little face falls, brow turning upward. "I called her Sissy."

The video of Maddy's twin sister's murder claws its way through my thoughts. A man who could spew silver from his hands broke into Maddy's room to destroy the government's secret weapon. Little did he know that the weapon was a pair of twins: a boy with the ability to take someone's power and a girl with the ability to find people with power. He killed the little girl, but he was shot before he could kill Maddy. It was one of the reasons I fell for the lie and betrayed my people. Back then, I was so convinced of the biomarker's supposed "brain mutation" that I was willing to give my power away for a chance to go back to society.

"Sometimes . . . I miss her," Maddy whispers. The corners of his mouth dip downward, like he's trying to hold himself together. "I'm . . . sad."

At the word "sad," Maddy drops the blocks and holds his hands up to his face. My heart breaks. From all I've observed from this sweet boy, I know that he values happiness and light over everything else. The words he spoke to me by the river the day he gave me back my power are forever in my heart and soul: "Don't be sad."

"Maddy, come here." I speak softly, trying to keep my own tangle of sadness at bay. I open my arms to him, and he walks over. Scooping him into a hug, I prompt him to sit on my lap. "It's okay to be sad sometimes."

"I don't like sadness," he sniffles. "It's cold. But the golden light makes me feel warm. Sissy made me feel warm."

I choke on the ball of emotion welling up in my throat. "I know. Sadness *is* cold, and my power is warm. I've felt that too."

"How do you stop feeling sad?" Maddy asks, looking up at me as I cradle him.

"I remember that I have people like you in my life." I smile, tightening my hold around him. "Then I don't feel so sad anymore."

"Like Vivi and Ash?" he asks.

"Yeah. Like Vivi and Ash." I look up at Olivia. "And new friends that come in unexpected ways. Like when we came here."

Maddy rubs his nose with the flat of his hand. "New friends?"

"Yes," I say. "There are a lot of wonderful people here with special powers just like Sissy. We all have our own unique type of light. Many aren't gold like yours, Maddy, but the light is still there in all of us. Remember that."

He smiles. "I'll remember."

I lock eyes with Olivia, and something seals between us. This odd, covert friendship is not what I anticipated, but with her as an ally, this mountain doesn't seem so scary. A confidence I can't explain emerges in me. In one week, I'm going to see my mother again for the first time since Tiffany teleported me from my home.

$$\underline{\qquad}$$

21

$$\underline{\qquad}$$

ROUGH HANDS SHAKE ME AWAKE, AND I JOLT, COMING out of a deep sleep, disoriented. Olivia is standing over me. She pries me up from the warmth and comfort of the mattress with clammy hands.

"Hollis!" she hisses. "Arthur needs you in his office. Now."

I wipe my eyes, looking up at the clock on the wall through a thick blur of sleep. 0417. It's the middle of the night. I turn to Olivia, perplexed. Her face is perspiring, and her dark complexion is ashen. A wad of tight curls is pressed flat against her head like she's been yanked out of bed too.

"What is it?" I ask, tripping over my feet in the semi-darkness as she pulls me along. Nasty thoughts assault me, seizing me with icy fingers. If Arthur wants to see me in the middle of the night after a secret conversation with Olivia about going to see my mother, then . . .

"Does Arthur know about what we talked about?" I whisper.

"No idea." She takes me by the wrist forcefully. "If you don't want to be blind, close your eyes."

"Wha—"

Before I can finish, the brilliant blue orb of her ability engulfs us, and I shut my eyes tight. The icy sensation is awful—and almost more than I can bear—but it's over in seconds, and when I open my eyes, we're standing in front of Arthur's office. The panel on the door blinks, ready to accept my palm.

"Just keep your head," Olivia murmurs with a tight jaw. "And don't say anything stupid." She holds her hand up to the scanner. The door flashes then folds into the wall. The large oval table greets me, but this time there isn't a crowd. Only three people are seated at the far end: Arthur Evandrum, Terrace DuPont, and Hugo.

"Thank you, Miss Turrick, for your promptness," Arthur says, swiveling in his black leather chair. He presses his hands together.

Olivia pushes me forward. "Of course, sir." She slips from the room, vanishing like a wisp of smoke and leaving me alone with the three men.

Arthur's white mane is slicked back with gel, but instead of his normal suit and tie, he wears black cotton pajamas. "Miss Timewire, come sit."

His voice is more gruff than usual.

The panic I felt upon waking a mere minute ago sharpens, but I can't let it show. Taking a deep breath, I stride over to Arthur, glaring at him. "You didn't have to kidnap me from my bed, you know."

Arthur scoffs. "This was hardly a kidnapping."

"What do you want?" I fold my arms across my chest, putting up a brave façade.

"We have a problem."

Ice fills my veins, and my heart sinks. He *knows*. Somehow, he knows about my plan to go see my mother. That's the only thing I can think of. And my hazy, sleep-deprived brain can't come up with another explanation on the fly.

"What's the problem?" I ask, trying to keep my furiously beating heart at bay.

He gestures to his right with a curt nod. "Have a seat."

I hesitate but decide to listen, sinking into a leather chair and gripping the armrests with white knuckles.

Arthur stands, tapping on one of the wall screens behind him. It flickers through several menus before opening to a video feed of the vast Presidential suite where my friends and I nearly lost our lives. President Camille sits at his desk, hands folded, his dark eyes directed straight at the camera.

"We received this nineteen minutes ago," Arthur says, turning to me. "It's for you."

All thoughts of Arthur discovering my plan dissolve, and anxiety fires through my chest, stealing my breath away. I stare at the screen as the feed begins to play.

The President clears his throat, his countenance as somber as society allows. "Citizens of the World, I come to you with grave news. Tonight, a terrorist attack devastated the Area 34 Testing Center. At 1:14 am, an explosion leveled half the building, killing a hundred and seventeen workers and injuring twenty-three more. First responders are at the scene, helping the trapped and wounded as I broadcast this."

My stomach drops, and adrenaline pulses with my frantic heartbeat. I grip the armrests tighter, holding my breath.

Next to Camille, a second feed plays on the screen, showing an aerial view of the burning wreckage of Area 34. Smoke, concrete, and bent metal twist together as a chopper cam zooms in, framing the obliterated Testing Center ruins. Camille pauses, stiffening his stance.

"Citizens, this is the work of the terrorist leader Hollis Time-wire and her accomplices."

My ability roars in my palms and I stand, propelled by the animalistic fervor. I stare at the screen.

"You must be prepared for what is coming," Camille breathes, his chest rising and falling in an eerie rhythm. "Every man, woman, and child must be on their guard. The Diseased Ones are on the rise, and they've struck at the heart of our Society once more. It is my sincere belief that these creatures plan to eradicate the very institution that keeps us safe: the Testing Center."

What? How could he know our plan before we've even started it? My mouth tastes like ash. The feed of the blazing, fiery wreckage continues from a new angle. A second chopper is covering the devastating blaze as tiny fire engines pour water onto the inferno.

"The second Terror War is as real as the first," Camille says, directing his growing aggression toward the camera lens. "A hundred years ago, society failed to eliminate these *cockroaches*, and now we are paying the price."

Camille straightens his tie and places his spindly hands down on the desk like two spiders.

"Tonight, I will be more transparent with you than *any* leader before me. And I do this for your safety, so that you will be informed of the nature of this threat. The Diseased Ones are not diseased in the way you *think*."

"What is he doing?" I gape at the feed as tingling thunders through my limbs.

"They have evolved *differently* than us," Camille continues. "It is not just a brain mutation. It is deeper than that. The biomarker that beats in their blood creates fire from their hands, ice in their veins, and sulfur from their mouths. They are creatures with the unnatural ability to steal away your minds, hearts, and thoughts. They have *power* that you know *nothing* of—power that, for a century, the Testing Centers of this world have strived to eliminate. We are fighting against animals that outmatch us in every conceivable way. This is not a simple matter of bad blood. The Diseased Ones have supernatural powers that infest the very chemicals of their minds. They cannot be reasoned with, they cannot be tamed, and they cannot change. It is *their* destruction or *ours*, and they've proven it once again. The Testing Center that burns tonight is their doing. War is here."

Camille's hands creep back toward the edge of the table, but his black eyes never waver from the camera, like they can see me, like they know me.

"Effective immediately, the military divisions of each Area will deploy to your dwellings. We will patrol the streets of our cities, the homes of our people, and the crevices of this world to find where these beasts are hiding." The black of his pupils enlarge. "I will leave no stone unturned in my search for Hollis Timewire. She is the head I will crush under society's foot. And once she is dead, I will not cease until our world is rid of the Diseased Ones for good."

The destruction of the sweltering Testing Center rages behind Camille's wicked words, and the gravity of the moment descends on me like an avalanche.

"Do not be deceived," the President says. "Our very existence is at stake. So, I charge you, Citizens of the World, to report *anything* you see—any hint of a suspicion. I have reason to believe they are among us now, in disguise, biding their time, waiting to strike—just as they did tonight. To burn us. To *kill* us all."

The camera angle zooms in on Camille's face, and the footage of the scorching Testing Center cuts out.

"And now, as this emergency broadcast sweeps every channel of every screen in the world, I know you're listening, Hollis." He smiles, portraying an emotion he shouldn't in front of the world. "Come out to play, cockroach. I will take great pleasure in crushing you."

The camera cuts to black, and I stand in a silence that sucks all the strength from my body.

Arthur swivels back toward me, his lips pursed. "Like I said, we have a problem."

My skin crawls at the President's last word. *Cockroach.* I'm so numb I can't think. Camille just bombed a Testing Center full of workers, blamed it on *me*, told the world we have supernatural abilities that can't be reasoned with, and declared a worldwide manhunt. In one act, he's instilled more fear into millions. My knees buckle, and I sink into the nearest seat, looking weakly up at Arthur.

My first thought about Camille's manhunt involves the mountain.

"Do you think he'll look here?" I ask, heart racing. "Is this place safe? Beezee said the mountain had so much radiation at one point that it's a no-fly zone, but—"

Arthur cuts across me. "What's your plan?"

"My plan?" I repeat, rubbing sleep from my vision. "What do you—"

"Yes, your plan. The President's stunt tonight accelerates our timeline." Arthur drums his fingers on the oval table. "Last Board meeting, I gave you and Jonah a month to come up with a way of taking the Area 19 Testing Center *without* killing Camille. What have you discussed?"

I fumble, and the alarm in my voice increases. "That was barely two weeks ago! We haven't come up with anything yet."

"What have you been doing?" Arthur demands.

"Using the Holodeck," Terrace says, staring at me deadpan. "Twice now."

Anger curls in my belly, and Olivia's warning comes to mine. Don't look him in the eye. But I can't help it. I twitch my hand directly at Terrace's heart, staring at him fiercely. For a brief moment, I grab him with my power and growl, "Stop using your ability on me!"

Terrace tenses, overcome by the force. At this, Hugo lunges, arms outstretched like he wants to strangle me. I raise my free hand toward his face and grab him too. He halts, mid-step, suspended with his limbs at awkward angles. They are both *mine*, and control washes over me, building in my chest. It's like breathing fresh air, and the monster purrs, spurring me on.

"Now, let's everyone relax," Arthur says, holding his hands up.

"Relax?" My muscles tense. "The President just bombed the Area 34 Testing Center and blamed it on *my* terrorist activities!"

"Release them," Arthur instructs.

I glare at him but back off, and the tingling in my palms vanishes. Terrace gulps, adjusting the collar of his bed shirt and breaking eye contact with me. Hugo, at Arthur's steely gaze, begrudgingly steps away and resumes his position near the wall screens.

Arthur leans back in his chair. "So, you don't have a plan?"

"I've been training, like you've asked me to. I don't have a plan yet. But Jonah and I will—"

"Then consider *mine*. You saw the destruction. The President deserves to die for what he's done. And killing Camille takes care of your puppet master problem. When we kill the President and take the Testing Cen—"

"NO!" I shout, interrupting him. "You really think society will go quietly into the arms of their worst enemy when we take over? Camille is breeding fear and hate. He's breeding people who will fight back against us. We won't stand a chance at making a better world if we kill him. We need to take over with him *alive* because then we can show everyone that we aren't monsters. This can't be a bloody power struggle and—"

"This already *is* a bloody power struggle, Miss Timewire," Arthur shoots back, his eyes narrowing. "People *have* died! People will continue to die! Is that what you want?"

"No. Of course not."

"Then what is your alternative? Camille wants you dead and blew up a Testing Center to lure you out of hiding. This doesn't look good for us."

I shoot him a dark look. "Really? I hadn't noticed."

Arthur's upper lip curls in displeasure. "Sarcasm doesn't become you."

"I don't care." Power tingles in my fingertips, but I pull it back. "I'm not agreeing to an assassination. I'm not ready to face Camille yet, but I will be. I *will* come up with a plan."

"Give me an alternative," Arthur says, pushing the issue further. "What could you possibly come up with? You can't beat him, Miss Timewire. You're immune to each other. You can't control him, and he can't control you. What on earth makes you think you can keep this man from his own bloody end? He can't be President in the world we hope to make."

"Then why don't you kill him already?" I shout, standing up so quickly my chair skids back a foot. Anger seethes in me, boiling over. I don't normally raise my voice to authority figures, but Arthur's an exception. "Why do you need me at all? Kill Camille and take your Testing Center!"

Arthur shrinks back in his seat at my ferocity but collects himself swiftly, placing a hand to his forehead. He mutters in a quiet voice. "I need you."

"And why is that again?"

He looks me up and down, sucking in a loud breath. "We can't take the Area 19 Testing Center without your power. There are too many military men and not enough abilities to stop them. It would be a massacre. You *must* help us. You are the only way we can do this without anyone with powers dying. And you're the only one who can help us maintain order after it's done."

"So, you *do* care," I say. "And here I thought you were just a blood-thirsty leader hungry for power that isn't yours."

Arthur rockets up from his seat, and I flinch.

"I am nothing of the sort!" he hisses, eyes bulging. The vein on Arthur's neck turns purple, and an intense moment of silence follows. We stare at each other, both leaning over the table.

I slide back into my seat, looking him full in the face with a ferocious and eerie calm. I know I still have all the power.

"Let me make one thing very clear. I don't have to help you do anything. I'm choosing to help you. *Choosing* to, and I need more time. You're a Chief Overseer, an esteemed member of society. Tell me, in your expert opinion, how likely is it that Camille will destroy another Testing Center in his attempts to lure me out?"

Arthur's brow furrows, and his upper lip bends, exposing his teeth. He speaks like he's reluctant to answer my question. "In my expert opinion, it is a possibility. However, this seems like a PR stunt to instill more fear into the masses and drag your name through the mud—and it's given him an excuse to impose extra patrols, invade people's homes, and heighten security worldwide. It would be . . . foolish of the President to continue to damage the institution he's looking to uphold."

"So, in your expert opinion, we have time?"

"Not much," he murmurs. "Leader of the second Terror War."

"Don't call me that!" I spit.

Arthur's knuckles turn white, and he bows his head ever so slightly. "My apologies."

"Save your apologies! I don't want them. What I want is for you to understand that killing Camille will drag *our* name through the mud," I say, matching Arthur's inflections perfectly. "And it would be foolish to continue to damage the institution *you're* looking to uphold."

The intensity of my conviction fuels me, and I stand there, panting and shaking.

"If I were still a society member, and I saw the Diseased Ones kill my beloved President in a power grab that ended in the total takeover of the Capitol City's Testing Center, I'd never yield. I'd believe the false history of the Terror War even more—I'd probably join the military to fight!"

My chest heaves, but I push the point further.

"That was me—a drone in a world of no emotion with a dark and frightening history. The path to a perfect society is perfect obedience. I would obey!"

"You don't need to recite that garbage to me, Miss Time—"

"Citizens are already brainwashed!" I point to the wall screen. "And that burning Testing Center is driving the lie further and branding the false narrative deeper in the minds of those who don't know how to think for themselves. No. There will be no more blood on my hands."

I forge ahead, brazen.

"Now that Camille's done this, I believe it's more important than ever to keep him *alive* when we take power. It's important that people see us for who we really are. That we're not a people of death and destruction, that we *never* were. Our actions matter."

Arthur, Terrace, and Hugo exchange quick glances, like they're communicating something to which I'm not privy.

"*My* actions matter," I say. "I've learned that the hard way, and a lot of innocent people have died because of it. But I've changed. I'm not going to be anyone's puppet."

"Curious choice of words," Arthur muses.

If I could shoot daggers with my eyes, I would. I shove the leather chair out of my way. It skids across the floor with a hair-raising screech, and I place both hands flat on the oval table. "I'm going back to bed."

I turn away from them and march straight for the sliding door.

"Miss Timewire?" Arthur says, stopping me just shy of the exit.

I spin around. "What?"

"Use your time wisely. Camille isn't a patient man. And neither am I."

Scoffing, I trudge off without answering him. I wish I could slam the door in his face. Instead, I storm down the hall. When I'm far enough away, I stop, lean against the cold stone, and slide down to a crouched position. Hugging my knees, I take huge gulps of air. My heart thuds violently, and stars twinkle around the edge of my vision.

I thought I had more time. When I came here, I thought

things would be different—that I'd feel safe from the government. But now they're breathing down my neck. Camille wants me dead, but I never imagined he'd initiate a terrorist attack and blame it on me to draw me out. Am I crazy for wanting to spare his life? Is it foolish to think there's a way to take over without killing him?

Bile rises up my esophagus. Innocent people died tonight, and part of me feels guilty for not wanting to charge into the fray to stop Camille from hurting anyone ever again. But I'm not ready. I'm not strong enough. Jonah and I have worked on forcing people to speak and battling for control over *one* person. I'm nowhere near where I should be.

Part of me is ashamed I haven't progressed further. Every time I talk with Arthur, the pressure builds, crushing me from every direction. I need to excel at my power because so much depends on it. The people I love must stay safe. I made the decision to push for a peaceful resolution, but is that even possible? The leadership thrust upon me because of my power is almost too much.

I want to be a kid again, to fall deep in love and experience the sweet passions of a vibrant life—to live in peace with no worries and enjoy my youth. I want to be happy. In a way, I envy Candice and Ben's relationship—their freedom to be with each other, to spend time with each other. I don't know if Keith and I can have that when I'm plagued with the task of a war I never wanted. It's ironic that the daughter of the head of the military elite who wanted nothing to do with that career is now leading the charge.

And mother . . .

I shiver, clutching the fabric of my pants tight, still crouched in a fetal position on the floor. With the increased security of the city, is seeing her worth the risk? I know deep in my soul I wouldn't feel right abandoning her, but is she too brainwashed for my visit to matter?

Even as I ask the question, determination kindles a fire in me. Camille can't keep me from her or from fighting for the world I want.

I bow my head, resting it on my knees, and the frantic pitter-patter of my heartbeat slows. I sit there for several minutes, taking long, soothing breaths and tracing the cracks scattered across the hall with my eyes. I begin to count.

Three. Four. Five.

I furrow my brow, staring at the stone floor in a haze.

Six. Seven. Eight.

There are times I still wish I didn't have this power, even though I'm grateful for it. I know I'm meant to be this way. Maddy has taught me that. But my power is a tool to Arthur. A means to an end.

Nine. Ten. Eleven.

If only Camille wasn't a puppet master. If only there were a way to beat an unbeatable power.

Twelve. Thirteen. Fourteen.

Too bad there isn't anyone with a power stronger than mine . . .

I sit bolt upright, wide-eyed. "A power stronger than mine!" I say aloud, breathing heavy again.

I scramble to my feet, electrified. How did I not think of this before? Jonah. I need to see Jonah right now.

With a burst of speed, I sprint through the double doors leading out of Sector 15. After racing through the maze of endless halls, I arrive at his room. And even though it's the middle of the night, I knock on the door without ceasing as loudly as my knuckles will allow. A scrape, a tumble, and a muffled groan comes from within.

A second later, a groggy-eyed Jonah appears in the doorway, his bed shirt crinkled and his hair askew. Upon seeing me, urgency overtakes his sleepiness.

"Hollis, what's wrong?"

"I have a plan."

Jonah rubs his eyes. "A plan?"

"I know how to beat Camille."

Jonah's lethargic haze evaporates, and his shoulders straighten. "What? How?" He peers down the empty hall then pulls me forward. "In here."

I scurry into his room, and Jonah shuts the door behind us. He flips on the bright fluorescent lighting and pulls a chair over, sitting down.

"I can't believe I didn't think of this sooner!" I say, pacing back and forth.

"Think of what?"

"Ashton Teel! He's the only person who can beat me."

Jonah tilts his head, and I can tell from the growing excitement on his face that he understands where I'm going with this.

"When Ashton had his power, he could stop me," I say. "He could suppress my ability! I'm a puppet master. I'm nearly invincible. But not to him." I bite my lip, hating myself for what I'm about to say next. "Him . . . and Maddy. I thought about using Maddy's power before, but I couldn't think of a way to incapacitate the President long enough for Maddy to use the golden light. But if Ashton suppresses Camille's ability, and we drug him so that he's unconscious . . ."

"We could take Camille's power away," Jonah whispers.

The deafening quiet that follows this statement attacks my ears.

"Yes. I just need to figure out what I did to Ashton's power and reverse it."

This could work. With Ashton's help, we could keep Camille alive. We could show society we aren't evil and put the President on trial for his crimes. And everyone in the world could watch.

"No more bloodshed," Jonah says.

"No more innocent deaths," I add. "And with Camille out the way, I can take the military easily, and we can end this on *our* terms. Peacefully."

Jonah takes a few steps back, hand to his forehead, looking at me in disbelief. I clench my sweaty hands into fists, relishing in the beauty of this plan. If this works, we can make a better world. There's only one thing standing in our way, and my stomach twists as I remember the demonic voice of my ability and Ashton Teel's curdling screams.

What the hell did I do to his power? And how can I get it back?

22

"JONAH, WE HAVE TO GO SEE ARTHUR."

"Right now?" He looks up at the clock on the wall. "It's the middle of the night, Hollis."

"That didn't stop him from snatching me out of bed," I mutter.

"What?" he says, alarmed.

"Olivia woke me up," I add, noting Jonah's unease.

I spend the next few minutes catching him up on the President's broadcast. As I speak, Jonah's face turns paler with each word. "Camille bombed the Area 34 Testing Center?"

"Yes," I say. "And he blamed it on me. He wants to lure me out."

"Then you shouldn't go see your mother."

My heart plummets, and despair clouds the elation I felt about my plan to defeat the President. "But Jonah—"

"Hollis, if Camille is increasing security in the city, it's not a good idea. I was hesitant before, and I heard you out because I know you're powerful, but—"

"Jonah, I have to!" I cry, pleading with him. My eyes well with tears, and all thoughts of talking with Arthur vanish. I approach him and grab his hands, speaking with earnest. "I have this horrible feeling. Like she's not safe. These dreams that I've been having . . . they're not normal. Something isn't right. I just know it. I have to see her! Please don't forbid me to go. Please! I can't disobey you. I couldn't do that. Please, Jonah!"

Jonah's taken aback by this. He stares at me, his brow knitting together. After a few seconds, he says in a gentle voice, "Hollis, sit down a moment."

I drop into the seat next to his bed and wipe the tears from my face. I can't believe I'm crying like this. I feel embarrassed. Tonight's been so overwhelming.

Jonah kneels in front of the chair, peering up at me. "Talk to me. What's going on?"

I bow my head, emotion strangling me. Tears fall fresh, and one slips down my cheek and into my mouth. "I respect you too much to not listen to you. If you told me not to go to the city, I would obey you. Because . . . you're my family, and I love you. So, please don't forbid me to go to her. I *have* to see her."

I look at him, afraid to say anything more. For all the things this wonderful man has done for me, for all the moments he's mentored and stood up for me, for everything he's given me, I could never defy him. My own father wasn't as present or caring as him. There was always important military business to attend to—and I was second to that. But Jonah? He's been more of a father than my own flesh and blood.

Jonah sits on the floor, frail and tired, but his face is full of compassion. He told me once that his ability doesn't just allow him to take on other abilities. It also allows him to feel other people's emotions. And in this moment, I know he understands me.

"I love you too, Hollis," he says. "I can see how much this visit means to you. I won't forbid you to go to her."

I let out a whimper and hide my face in my hands until I've mopped up my tears. Sniffling, I sit up, taking a few deep breaths. "I don't care that Camille's heightened security in the city. I can pull this off. I've talked with Olivia, and we have a plan. I won't get caught, and even if someone sees me, my power is strong enough to keep me safe. You have to trust me."

"I do trust you, but with the added security measures, I think it's best that Olivia doesn't transport you into the city."

"But Jonah, don't you think walking through the city to get to my home would be more dangerous? Even if Vianne disguises me?"

Jonah scratches his beard, still sitting on the floor. "I have a better idea. What if Olivia transports your mother to you?"

I shake my head. "I said I wouldn't force her to come here."

"That's not what I meant. What if you talk to your mother outside the city? Then you could avoid the extra security Camille's put in place altogether." He studies me. "Is there a place like that?"

The best childhood memory I have with my mother comes to mind. The little pond on the outskirts of Area 19.

"Yes! Do you remember the story I told you about skipping rocks with my mother when I was younger? She took me to a pond. It's only a few miles from my house. Jonah, that's perfect!"

He smiles, eyes drooping with fatigue. He shifts his weight to stand, and I reach out to help him up. He sits on the edge of the bed with a sigh.

"Sorry I woke you," I say. "But do you think you're okay to stay awake? We need to talk to Arthur. I have to tell him my plan for Camille, and I want to see Ashton."

Jonah looks up at the clock again. It reads 0458. Forty-one minutes since Olivia yanked me out of bed. He tilts his head. "I'm guessing you don't want to go back to sleep?"

"Not in the slightest. I can't. Not after what Camille just did."

The burning wreckage of the Area 34 Testing Center claws its way through my brain. It's all I can see. And now that I've come up with a way to stop Camille without killing him, I have to let Arthur know. Maybe then I'll get some space to work on my ability in peace instead of constantly being hounded for answers about a plan I never thought I'd have to come up with.

"I need your help, Jonah. Something tells me Arthur won't be happy about me wanting to see Ashton."

Jonah stands, grabbing a soft gray robe hanging from the corner of his bed. He pulls it on and fastens the belt around his waist. He grabs his cane then says, "after you," motioning to the door.

I walk up to him and give him the biggest hug. Through anything, even with no sleep, I know I can always count on Jonah. "Thank you," I whisper.

Jonah returns the hug, wrapping his arms around me. "You're welcome. Now let's go tell Arthur what we've discovered." He releases me, and I scamper to the door, pulling it open with a fresh spring in my step.

We move quickly back to Arthur's office, taking the hairpin turns of the mountain at a breakneck speed. Olivia really does have a convenient ability. It would be nice to teleport anywhere in an instant.

Ten minutes later, we come to the double doors of Sector 15, and I slam them open, ready to breathe fire at Arthur Evandrum. I walk up to the sliding door of his office, Jonah in tow, and place my hand to the scanner. It flashes and admits us.

To my relief, Arthur, Terrace, and Hugo are still present, all huddled over some folders at the far end of the oval table.

"Miss Timewire. Mr. Luxent," Arthur huffs. He looks up and closes the top folder, quickly tucking it under his arm. "To what do I owe the pleasure of this visit?"

I march up to him. "I have a plan."

Arthur perks up, but his dismissive mannerisms linger. He adjusts the collar of his bed shirt. "Well, that was quick. Look at what can happen when you put your mind to it."

"Just listen!" I snap.

He folds his hands together. "Please, enlighten us. What have you come up with, puppet master?"

Terrace and Hugo look to one another, then Terrace fixes his gaze on me. Our eyes connect briefly, and adrenaline shoots down into my stomach. Don't look at him. I break eye contact, keeping my attention solely on Arthur.

"Ashton Teel, the boy who tried to kill me back in the forest," I begin. "His ability is to suppress other people's abilities. And when I first met him, he was the only person who could control me because he could temporarily take away my power."

I grip the back of the nearest chair, bracing against it for support.

"Here's my plan," I say. "Olivia teleports me and Ashton to the President. Ashton suppresses his power. We drug him and bring him back to the mountain. Then, Maddy takes away his ability. I will help you take the Area 19 Testing Center and the Capitol, and I will also help you maintain control as our people step into power. We keep Camille alive and broadcast to the world that we're not the creatures they've been taught to fear— that we only want to end the bloodshed of people with powers and tell everyone the truth about the Terror War. We let citizens know that we will strive to create a new world where we can all coexist *peacefully*. Camille will be tried by our people and pay for his crimes in prison. And we will broadcast his trial to the world so they can witness that we are a people of our word. No more bloodshed. No more Testing Centers. No more Test. Just peace—where people with and without powers can finally be together and move past this horrible stain of history."

I square my shoulders, feeling incredibly pleased with myself. And although I can't see him, I feel Jonah's presence right behind me, encouraging me. Arthur taps his pointer finger on the table.

"You forgot to mention one little snag, Miss Timewire," he says. "Ashton Teel doesn't have his ability anymore, does he?"

I hold the chair tighter. "I'm aware."

"Then your plan doesn't work." Arthur cocks his head to the side, studying me. "Why is that? Something *you* did?"

Jonah steps forward now, addressing Arthur in a respectful, yet firm tone. "Yes. Back at our compound, Hollis and Ashton were involved in an incident that led to Ashton's power disappearing. We aren't sure what Hollis did, but we will find out. And once we do, hopefully, we can reverse it."

Arthur's curious look deepens, and he opens his mouth, but Jonah cuts in before he can say anything.

"We require access to Ashton for training. I know he's detained—and for good reason—but I request that you release him. Only for training sessions of course."

I'm relieved Jonah asked Arthur about Ashton's release instead of me. He likes telling me no, even though he promised to give me anything I need to train. But unlike Keith, I truly need Ashton to work on my ability. The fate of the world depends on it. And if he denies this request, I'll march down there and free Ashton myself.

Arthur doesn't acknowledge Jonah. His attention is all on me. "I wonder as to the nature of this 'incident' Mr. Luxent speaks of. What did you do that made Mr. Teel so keen on killing you? I believe, if I recall correctly, he said 'that bitch dies tonight.' He's not safe."

My power tingles at my fingertips. "When Ashton tried to kill me, I didn't have my ability. I was powerless against him. That's not the case now. He can't hurt me."

"Ah, but you want it to be the case again?" Arthur asks.

"What are you talking about?"

"You somehow figure out how to give him back his power. Then he can suppress your ability. He may attack you again. You wouldn't be safe."

"Then have Ashton escorted by armed guards," I say, heat rising in my face. I take a step toward Arthur. "You had no problem sticking an armed guard on my boyfriend like he's some kind of animal! Did you hear a word I just said? We can do this without killing Camille. I need time with Ashton to figure out what my power did to his."

"Fine. He may train with you with an armed guard present. But Terrace will accompany you," Arthur says.

"No. Absolutely not. Terrace isn't welcome."

Arthur leans back in his seat, disdain in his tone. "My terms or this doesn't happen."

"I don't need your permission!" I growl. I push the chair out of my way, stepping even closer to him. "You keep going back on your promise. I need Ashton to train."

Terrace holds his hand up, and I halt. My eyes trace his ginger hair, but I avoid full eye contact. "I may be able to help," he says. "You don't know what you did to Ashton's power? Just by being around him, I may be able to glean helpful information. It could lead you to discover what you've done."

Jonah and I exchange glances, then Jonah says, "Very well. Mr. DuPont, you may observe. But I am in charge of what we do and don't do with Mr. Teel. Is that clear?"

Terrace nods, and my heart plummets. I don't want Terrace there. I don't want him anywhere near me. He'll report everything we do directly to Arthur. And on top of that, what if he discovers my plan to go see my mother?

"Jonah, I'd prefer privacy," I say.

"I understand, Hollis, but given that we don't know what you've done, I think Mr. DuPont's ability will be of use to us."

I sigh, resigning myself to this fate. I'll do my best to not look him in the eye and pray he'll remain ignorant. If he's busy using his ability on Ashton, maybe he won't use it on me.

"Terrace, let's go," I say, turning away from him.

"Now?"

"Yes. Now."

I hook Jonah's arm and pull him out of Arthur's office quickly. I whisper to him, "Don't look Terrace in the eye, and don't let him near me."

Seconds later, the scuff of chair against stone issues from the room we've just left as Terrace scrambles up. He joins us in the hall. Jonah steps in between us to provide a buffer as we continue down the white corridor.

"Well, well," Terrace muses. I can practically feel his eyes boring into me. "You've come up with quite the plan, haven't you? If I'm being honest, I didn't think you had it in you. But you've held your own against Evandrum. Consider me impressed."

I don't respond. Instead, I keep my gaze forward and continue walking toward Sector 2 where the holding cells are.

"I like you, Hollis," Terrace says, his tone slippery. "You've got a fighting spirit. You don't give up easily, do you?"

My muscles stiffen as if I were under my own power. Even with Jonah walking in between us, Terrace feels much too close. I swallow a lump that's formed in the back of my throat, fighting the urge to turn my head toward him.

"Curious," Terrace continues, still intently staring at me. And even though I'm not looking at him, I can feel fragments of information leaving me without my consent. "This mysterious incident. You attacked Ashton because he was harassing someone. It was ... vicious. Hmm ... let's see. Vianne Evolet? Mr. Teel and Miss Evolet have certainly gotten cozy since arriving at the mountain. Does she like him?"

My hand twitches, but Jonah grabs my wrist, shaking his head.

"Mr. DuPont, let's cut the small talk," he says. "You're accompanying us because you've offered the services of your ability, not the pleasure of your conversation."

Out of my peripheral vision, I see Terrace turn his attention toward Jonah, and the knotted feeling in my stomach ceases. "Of course. I'm here to help."

"Good," Jonah says, leaning heavily on his cane with each step.

Terrace's icy voice slithers into my ear. "Anything for Miss Hollis Timewire."

23

SECTOR 2'S GLOOMY, CAVE-LIKE ENTRANCE LOOMS OVER us. It's hard to see in such dim lighting, but Terrace moves ahead, jogging to the middle of the three doors. He pulls it open and ushers Jonah and me through.

The rapid change from near darkness to excruciating brightness is unpleasant. Blinking to clear my strained vision, I scan over the holding cells. Pierce, Darren, and Ashton are being held here now. The same snide guard eyes me with disdain, but I ignore him.

"Sir," the guard says, saluting Terrace. "What's the reason for the visit?"

"Release from Cell D-3," he says. "And I'll need an armed guard escort."

"Right away, sir," the man replies, readjusting the gun in his hands.

Jonah and I follow Terrace and the guard as they approach

the row of cells marked 'D.' I spot Ashton sitting on a cot with his legs tucked up and his head resting back against the wall. He looks up at our approach. The moment he spots me, he jumps, backing away from the door of his cell.

"What is this?" He glances between Jonah and Terrace.

"Face the back and put your hands on the wall above your head," the guard instructs in a gruff tone.

"Jonah, what's going on?" Ashton demands.

"Ashton, obey the guard. I'll explain. I promise."

Ashton's contemptuous look deepens, but he listens, turning slowly and placing his hands against the back wall. The guard taps on the panel next to the deadbolt, entering a code. Then, he places his hand against the panel, and it turns green.

The glass door slides sideways, and the guard enters. He cuffs Ashton's hands behind his back and grabs him by the upper arm, escorting him over to us.

"Thank you," Terrace says. "Please accompany us to Sector 7."

"Of course, sir," the guard replies, pushing Ashton roughly ahead of him. "Walk."

"Jonah, what the hell?" Ashton says, wide-eyed. The corner of his mouth twitches, and perspiration forms on his brow.

"Ashton, it's alright," Jonah says. He approaches the guard and speaks in a forceful manner. "Don't push him."

The guard glares at Jonah but says nothing. He turns away, stiff-shouldered, keeping his weapon at the ready.

Terrace rubs his hands together with an off-putting grin. "Ready, Miss Timewire?"

I give him a curt nod, feeling like I might be sick. "Yes. I'm ready."

"This will be fun," Terrace muses in a near singsong. "Let's go."

The five of us make our way back through the dark cave entrance. We walk in silence, taking the halls of the mountain at an uncomfortably fast pace. I'm anxious, and sweat creeps down my back. Whatever I did to Ashton, that evil voice was involved. Since getting my power back, I've only heard it once more—at the steps of the Capitol when I brought the military men to their knees. It felt like a guide, spurring me toward Jonah. But with Ashton, it felt like a monster ready to kill its prey. I don't know much about this part of my ability. Camille asked me if my power speaks to me yet. It has, but only in extreme circumstances.

A shiver zips across my skin. I'm going to have to get it to speak again. Somehow, that's part of this puzzle. I can feel it.

Tingling prickles my fingertips as we continue our trek to the training room. I stare at the back of Ashton's head, hating myself for what I did to him. His blood-soaked face, trembling hands, and screeches of "demon" haunt me.

"Right this way, Mr. Teel," Terrace says, directing him to the entrance of the training room.

My chest constricts, and lights dance around the edges of my vision as we enter the massive room. The guard pulls Ashton up to the training mat, and Jonah and I follow.

"Please uncuff him," Jonah says.

The guard scowls but obeys, unfastening the cuffs and standing behind Ashton, practically breathing down his neck.

"Stand by the door," I instruct the guard, waving him away from us. "This is unnecessary. I'm fine."

The guard doesn't move. He doesn't even register what I've said. Instead, he glowers, keeping close to Ashton. I turn to Terrace, raising an eyebrow and throwing my hand up.

Terrace says to the guard, "You may stand by the door."

"Yes, sir," he says, obeying him without hesitation.

Ashton eyes me apprehensively, rubbing his wrists. "Is someone going to tell me what the hell is going on? Why have you dragged me here in the middle of the night?"

"Ashton," Jonah says, approaching him calmly. "We brought you here to figure out what happened when Hollis attacked you."

Ashton's eyes widen, and he takes a step back.

"I need to ask you a few questions," Jonah continues. "Can you tell me what happened?"

"Why?" Ashton glares at Jonah. "What's this really about?"

Jonah and I exchange quick glances, and I take a tentative step toward Ashton. He shrinks back as if I were brandishing a sword at him.

"You stay away from me!" he hisses.

"I want to restore your power," I say.

Ashton's brow turns upward, and some of the panic in his face diminishes. He looks me up and down like he's trying to decide if I'm telling the truth. His watery gray eyes finally fix themselves on my hazel ones, and his upper lip curls. "You want to give me back my power? Is that even possible?"

"I don't know," I admit. "But I'm certainly going to try."

"Ashton, I need you to tell me what happened that day," Jonah says. "The smallest detail could help us figure this out."

Ashton falters, considering us. "She . . ." He pauses, shaking his head and backing away from me. His hands tremble, and his dirty blond hair sticks to his forehead.

"Take your time," Jonah says. "Don't look at her. Look at me."

He focuses his gaze on Jonah. "She grabbed me with her ability and . . ." He stops to collect himself, physically shivering. "She held me there. I . . . I felt like I was burning. Like I was on fire."

I draw in a sharp breath, holding my hand over my mouth. I can almost hear the memory of him screaming.

"And I felt like she was . . ." Ashton struggles with his words, eyes darting to me then back to Jonah. "This is going to sound crazy, but I'm not crazy. I swear!"

"I don't think you're crazy, Ashton," Jonah says softly.

He grits his teeth and shudders. "It was like my ability was pulled inside out."

"Inside out?" I repeat.

Ashton ignores me. His attention is still locked onto Jonah. "She took my power, and I felt this tug inside of me. My skin started to crawl, and I could feel my power changing, turning inside out—like when someone takes off a glove, and then . . . I couldn't feel it anymore. It was gone. No tingling in my fingertips. No power in my chest. Nothing. It was gone. And then she stopped."

His words spark something in me. Vianne said something similar when we were discussing the attack over lunch.

"Jonah!" I exclaim, knotting my hands together. "Vianne told me that you tried to stop me from hurting Ashton with your ability, but you couldn't. I thought you used Ashton's ability to suppress mine, but she said I stopped myself."

"You did," Jonah says. "I couldn't stop you. When I got to you, Ashton's ability wouldn't come to me. I felt nothing."

"Then how is Ashton alive?" My voice is faint. I shift my weight from foot to foot. I'm trying not to pace because I don't want to spook Ashton. He already looks like he's ready to make a run for it.

"What are you talking about, Timewire?" he growls. He exposes his teeth and squares his shoulders, like he's ready to fight me, but his shaky demeanor tells me he's far from attempting anything.

"My power has a voice," I explain. "And it told me to kill you." Ashton's clammy face pales, and I look to Jonah, perturbed. "If you didn't stop me, how is Ashton still here?"

Jonah furrows his brow, hand to his chin. "I don't know."

"Am I . . . like Maddy, somehow?" I ask. "Is his power completely gone?"

Jonah scratches his beard, deep in thought. "Ashton, may I try something?"

Ashton nods and Jonah walks over to him, placing his palm on Ashton's chest and closing his eyes. He remains still for a minute before removing his hand and shaking his head. "I can't feel anything."

"May I try?" Terrace offers, flourishing a hand in front of his chest.

"By all means," Jonah replies, stepping out of the way.

Terrace approaches Ashton, creeping up to him and getting far too close for comfort. His eyes bore into him, and Ashton fidgets. He looks away from Terrace, but the moment he does, Terrace grabs his chin and forces his face back toward him.

"Look at me," he commands.

The room is dead silent. Nobody breathes. Nobody moves.

"I can sense it." Terrace nods slowly. "His ability is still there."

Terrace releases Ashton's face, and Ashton pushes him away. He balls his hands up, trying to put on a brave façade, but whatever Terrace just did shook him. He looks like he's going to vomit.

"If his ability is still there, why can't Ashton or Jonah use it?" I ask.

"That's the question we need to answer," Jonah says. "Hollis, I'd like to ask what happened from your perspective now."

Ashton scoffs, kicking the mat. "She attacked me! That's what happened from her perspective."

"I know that!" I retort, heated.

Jonah holds his hand up to stop Ashton from saying anything else. "Hollis, *why* did you attack Ashton?"

I shake my head, thinking back. "He was taunting Vianne. Teasing her about liking Ben and then ..." I close my eyes, visualizing the scene. Ashton advances on Vianne in my mind's eye. His hands cut through the air, and scars blossom across her face and neck. "He forced her to show her scars by suppressing her ability. He called her disgusting."

Ashton's eyes begin to water, and he rubs his nose with the

flat of his palm. I can see his look of shame. I know he hates himself for what he did. Vianne told me so.

"I snapped. I was angry. I'd never felt anything like it before. Then my ability took over, and I couldn't stop myself."

"You were angry?" Jonah repeats.

"I was so angry," I say, nodding. "It's like something in me couldn't let go of him until it was done."

Jonah tilts his head. "Until what was done?"

"I don't know. It was almost like . . . like I was just watching it happen. I wanted to stop. I could see what I was doing to him. I could see the blood. I had so much control, but I couldn't do anything about it. My power poured itself out until it was empty, and then my hands stopped buzzing. That's why I thought you suppressed my ability using Ashton's power," I finish.

Jonah glances between me and Ashton then starts pacing back and forth, his cane tapping on the training mat. The noise echoes off the high stone walls. "Terrace, you can feel Ashton's ability?"

"Yes. But it's not quite . . . the same."

"What's that supposed to mean?" Ashton sneers.

"It means that you don't feel the same to me as any other person in this mountain," Terrace answers, running a hand through his ginger hair. "I can feel abilities and secrets. The longer I'm around someone, the more I learn. But you . . . you feel different. And not like the powerless of society. I can tell when someone doesn't have an ability."

Jonah stops pacing. "Hollis, what was different about this encounter with Ashton? You've used your ability plenty of times before, but why did you hear the voice when you attacked him?"

I stand there, searching myself. What was different about this? I've felt angry before. I was angry when the government was going to execute Jonah. I was angry when Ben stabbed Rosalie and I was at the mercy of the President. I was angry when I finally discovered the truth about history.

"I wanted justice?"

I shake my head. That can't be it. I've wanted justice many times before. And I've used my ability with justice in mind.

But something dawns on me. Every time I've used my ability, I've controlled it, but there have been three instances where *it* controlled *me*. The first was the morning of my Test. Instinct took over, and the demon voice guided me out. The second was my encounter with Ashton. It told me to hurt him. And the third was at the steps of the Capitol when Jonah's life was at stake. In each case, I yielded fully to the power in my palms. I was simply a witness—present, but completely overcome. My ability was in charge.

I raise a hand to my forehead, staring at Jonah with wide eyes.

"It controlled me," I whisper.

The room falls silent. I stand there, arms limp. My ability buzzes, alive beneath my fingertips, like the demon within is confirming what I've just spoken aloud. My plan to defeat the President depends on Ashton getting his power back, and now that I know there's a power still in him, I'm going to find it. I grasp the folds of my sweater to dry my clammy hands and look up at Ashton.

"I know how we figure this out. I have to let my ability control me again."

$$\overline{}$$

24

$$\overline{}$$

I SIT ALONE IN THE FAR CORNER OF THE DINING ROOM, mulling over the training session I had with Ashton. My stomach growls, and I ladle another spoonful of hot vegetable stew over my tongue, savoring the salty flavor. The warmth soothes my nerves. Dinner is, in my opinion, the best meal of the day because I get to wind down afterward instead of going to a training session or a Board meeting.

I didn't end up trying anything on Ashton because I don't know how to trigger the voice of my ability to speak to me. Just thinking about it makes me uneasy, but I'm certain it's the way forward. The best thing for me to do is explore this part of my power on my own because I'd hate to do something else horrible to an already traumatized teenager. I can't make things worse for Ashton. I don't want to hurt him. I want to help him. I need his ability, but beyond that, I need his help. Jonah and I didn't tell him the real reason behind the training session. We only told him that we wanted to restore his power.

Was that the right call? Not being totally honest with him? What if I figure out how to reverse what I've done only to have him refuse to help me kidnap Camille?

I sip another spoonful of stew.

I should go down to the holding cells and talk to him. I don't know how I'm going to get him to trust me, but maybe if I'm truthful about my intentions, it will make a difference.

My eyes glaze over as I stare out across the crowded dining area. For the most part, people leave me alone when I'm by myself at the periphery of the room. But many still ogle at me—something I don't think will ever change.

"Damn!"

There's a clatter of metal utensils and a storm of swearing. The man at the next table over ducks to retrieve his fallen spoon.

"You're so clumsy," the woman sitting across from him says, laughing and dipping her head low as she bats her heavily lidded eyes.

"Shut up, Lanie," the man says grumpily, although his smile says he's not mad. "I'm exhausted."

"Well, good thing the Ability Festival is coming up," a second woman chimes in. She's a lot taller than the first woman and towers over the table. "Only a few weeks now!"

I perk up. Ability Festival? What's that? I take another spoonful of soup, looking down at the gray speckled pattern of the tabletop but keeping my ears sharp.

"About time too," the man mutters, stretching his arms over his head and leaning back in his seat. "I'm overworked."

"Me too, George. Me too," Lanie says. She leans over the

table and strokes George's arm. Then, she turns to the taller woman and speaks in a commercial announcer voice. "What about you, Claire? You need a break? Feeling overworked and underappreciated?"

She says this like she's quoting someone.

"Lanie!" Claire scolds, drawing herself up even taller. Her long neck cranes over them. "It's not a break. It's a time to honor and celebrate people with powers—to celebrate our culture. To preserve our history! Because God knows the government isn't going to do it. It's important work."

Lanie and George snicker, and Lanie rolls her eyes. "This isn't my first Ability Festival, honestly Claire. I know what it's about. You sound so stuffy."

George leans over like he's going to whisper in Lanie's ear but speaks much too loudly for the gesture. "It's because Claire might get a seat on the Board. She's got to act all proper now. You know? She's got to act like she actually gives a damn about procedure and rules."

Claire sticks her nose up and retorts in an aggressive manner. "I *do* give a damn about procedure and rules. That's not a bad thing!"

Lanie holds her hands up like she's surrendering. "Just jokes, Claire. We're having *fun*. You should try it sometime." She turns to George, nudging him on the shoulder and scooting closer to him. "Are you going to ask me to dance this year?"

George eyes her with a frown. "You know I don't dance. I'm here for the booze." He glances at Claire. "And the *break*."

Lanie sighs, putting on a fake pout and batting her eyes at

him once more. "Oh, come on. Just one dance? It won't kill you. I promise."

"The booze? Really George?" Claire says, folding her arms across her chest. "What a lovely sentiment."

George shakes his head and addresses Claire in an apathetic tone. "Look, I'm all for recounting the true heritage of our people and dispelling the 'Diseased Ones' nonsense for the little ones—powers are to be celebrated, blah blah blah—but I'm in it for the alcohol."

"One dance?" Lanie pesters. "Just one."

"Lanie, I'd rather act in one of those God-awful plays," he says.

Lanie looks affronted. "You're a terrible person, you know that?"

George shrugs. "It's true. I don't know why you put up with me."

"They are re-enactments, not plays! And they are not God-awful!" Claire huffs.

"Right," George says. "Of course they aren't. They are tributes to our forefathers." He says this with a dramatic flick of his wrist. "And they're for the children."

Claire frowns at him, baring her teeth like she might breathe fire. "They *are* tributes to our forefathers. You shouldn't be so disrespectful."

George chuckles. "Would you relax? You take everything a little too seriously."

A hand furiously waves in front of my face, snapping me out of my eavesdropping so abruptly that I nearly knock my bowl of stew over. It's Olivia Turrick, and she looks like she's seen a ghost.

"Come here!" she hisses, grabbing me by the wrist and pulling me up from the table.

I trip over the chair. "What is it?"

Without a word, she marches us toward the exit of the dining room, never relinquishing her firm grip on me. I follow her in haste, a thousand things flying through my mind—all of them horrible.

We exit the double doors of Sector 12. The second we're out, she lets go of me, looks around to make sure no one is near us, and says in a hushed voice, "Arthur is leaving tomorrow for the Quarter Review. He moved it up because of the bombing at the Area 34 Testing Center. We leave for Area 19 the moment Arthur's out of this mountain."

My blood runs colder than ice, and my hands begin to shake. "Tomorrow? What? That's—that's so soon. I . . . I'm not ready."

"We go to your mom tomorrow or we don't go at all. I told you I can't guarantee a time when Arthur is gone other than the Quarter Review. This is our only chance." Her brown eyes glisten against her dark skin. She puts her hands on her hips. "Well, are we doing this or not?"

I bite my lower lip, interlocking my fingertips and placing them on my forehead. I'm going through with this. The Area 34 bombing didn't change my mind, and Camille's threat of increased security worldwide doesn't scare me. I haven't talked with Vianne yet, but considering Jonah's idea of meeting with my mother outside of the city, I don't need a disguise. Vianne doesn't have to be involved. It's safer for her to stay in the mountain. And if anything were to happen to me, at least Maddy would have someone.

I blow air out between pursed lips, locking eyes with Olivia. "Yes, we're doing this."

She grabs my hand and pulls me further away from the double doors of Sector 12. "You have a plan?"

"Yes."

I glance over my shoulder to ensure we're alone, and then I recount what Jonah and I discussed about the pond just outside of Area 19.

"Are you okay with that?" I ask. "You'd teleport the two of us to the pond first then teleport directly into my home and bring my mother to me. Jonah thinks it's best I don't enter the city at all."

Olivia rubs the back of her neck. "Jonah's wise. And yes, I'm okay with that."

"You've got guts," I say, brushing a loose strand from my face.

"So do you. You know you're like . . . the most wanted person ever, right?"

I give her a dry laugh. "Don't remind me."

Olivia scuffs the sole of her shoe against the stone floor of the hall. "And, just so you're prepared, if Arthur finds out you left the mountain, there will be hell to pay—for both of us."

"Good thing he's not going to find out."

A group of four kids accompanied by three adults appear at the end of the hall, making their way toward the double doors of Sector 12 for mealtime. Their chatter sets my teeth on edge, and Olivia and I slink back against the wall, falling silent as they pass.

Once they're through to the dining area, Olivia locks eyes with me again.

"I'll hang around Arthur's office, and when he's gone, I'll come get you." She gives the hall one last sweeping look. "Get ready to go. It could be as early as the middle of the night."

"Great, looks like this might be the second night in a row of you yanking me out of bed," I say sarcastically.

A grin plays on Olivia's lips. "Yeah, sorry about that."

"That's okay. You're not the one who bombed a Testing Center."

"Good point." Olivia steps away from me a few paces. "Hey, Hollis?"

"Yes?"

"I hope this meeting with your mom goes well. See you soon." She gives me a sad little smile, once again reminding me so much of Tiffany it hurts. "Also, close your eyes if you don't want to be blind."

With a pop, the blue orb expands into the hall, and I shut my eyes tight. But even with that, the flash of blue bleeds through my eyelids. Olivia's left me in a heart-pounding silence.

This is it. In only a few hours, I'm going to see my mother.

25

I LIE AWAKE IN THE TRAINING ROOM, STARING UP AT THE ceiling in the near darkness. Maddy is with Vianne. I made sure to check in with them after dinner. I also told Jonah what Olivia told me. I didn't want to go to my mother without him knowing.

Before going to bed, I packed a small bag with the bare minimum—a tiny amount of food and meager medical supplies. Just in case. Now, I wait.

The clock on the far wall reads 0437. I've been lying here far longer than it takes to fall asleep, but I don't know if sleep is possible. My nerves are shot, and my anxiety is holding steady at close to fight-or-flight. What am I going to say to her? How can I explain that everything she's ever known is a lie? How will she respond? In a perfect world, she'd believe me. She'd come back with me. She'd leave society and join us. But this is far from what will likely happen.

I hope she doesn't scream for help. I don't want to use my

ability on her, but I will if I have to. Even though I won't force her to come back with me, I will force her to keep quiet if needed. By doing this, I'm risking Olivia's life as well as my own, and I'll do anything necessary to keep the two of us safe.

My eyelids droop, so I close them, but no matter how hard I try, rest evades me. Agitated thoughts circle over and over in my brain as I drift through one scenario after another. And my stomach is tense beyond comfort.

Readjusting myself under the covers, I check the clock again. 0449. Time is dragging at a snail's pace, and the longer I lie here, the worse I feel.

Tap. Tap. Tap.

I sit bolt upright, throwing the covers off of me. Hastily, I shove my feet into my burgundy-laced boots, grab my bag, and jog to the door. It slides open, and Olivia stands there, dressed in dark colors and combat boots.

"Arthur's just left," she whispers.

My heart leaps into my throat.

"Are you ready?"

I nod, feeling weak in the knees. My ability tingles down my fingertips. The control pulsing through my body is calming, and I take several deep breaths, allowing my power to wash over me in waves.

Olivia checks the hall then steps into the training room, closing the door behind her.

"Alright, Timewire. Let's do this," she says, hooking my arm with an iron grip. "And if you don't want to be blind—"

"Close your eyes," we finish together.

The blue orb expands like a rattling creature, engulfing us in brilliant light. First, warmth covers my skin, then coldness rips through it, jerking us forward with a snap. Darkness surrounds us, then striking brightness, and with a thud, my feet find purchase on damp earth.

The chilly air of early morning mixes with the scent of stagnant water. I steady myself on Olivia's arm, taking in our surroundings. It's not quite sunrise, but the first hints of light play across a horizon overcast with clouds. We're standing at the edge of a pond, and in the distance, the towering gray walls of Area 19 jut up from the ground like sentinels.

Reeds brush my shins in the soft breeze, and clumps of dried bushes hug the periphery of the body of water.

"It's so much smaller than I remember it," I breathe.

Olivia pulls me over to the nearest bush, tugging me down to a crouch. "Stay hidden until I'm back."

She relinquishes her grip, and before I can say another word, the blue orb swallows her, and I'm left alone at the edge of the silent pond.

The scent of earth and decay trickles up from the soggy ground, and I scoot back toward a patch of dry dirt, keeping low. Sitting down to ease the strain on my muscles, I tuck myself into a ball and take soothing breaths. If I don't breathe, I'll pass out from apprehension. If everything goes to plan, Olivia shouldn't be gone long.

My eyes scan over the tiny pond, which is more of a large half-dried-up puddle with rotting twigs and oblong stones protruding from the surface of the water. It's not like it was when my mother skipped rocks with me. It's dead now.

Water striders glide over the still surface, making tiny ripples in the muck. I count them, watching them dance in zig zags.

"I just . . . need . . . to breathe . . ." I whisper.

A light gust of wind picks up the loose strands of my messy bun. I wrap my arms around myself, pulling my jacket in tight. It's still early enough for the cold to be unforgiving. Gray clouds hang ominously above the city. It feels like it did the day we rescued Maddy.

A spark of light appears at the edge of the pond, and I jump to my feet, heart pounding into my ears. The blue orb is here, growing larger until it touches the water. After a moment, it bursts to reveal Olivia and my mother. Olivia slinks back from her quickly.

Seeing my mother steals all the breath from my lungs. She's more gaunt and skinny than I remember. Her blonde hair is unkempt, and her normally porcelain skin is wrinkled. Dark bags hang under hazel sunken eyes. She's like a ghost, standing there in a white silk nightgown.

She raises a bony hand to her chest, clutching the collar of the gown. Her lower lip trembles, like she's doing her best to contain the emotion she's not supposed to show.

"Hollis?" she breathes.

"Mother." The word catches in my throat, thick and heavy.

She peers at me like she's unable to believe I'm here. "Is that really you?"

My eyes begin to water, and my heart fills with overwhelming affection for her. She's here. Right in front of me. A few feet away. With all my soul, I want to run to her, but as I take a step forward, she yelps and her whole body spasms.

I stop and hold my hands up. "I'm not going to hurt you. I promise."

"Are you . . . real?" she asks with a whimper.

"Yes, I'm real."

I want to fall into her arms. Everything in me wants to embrace her, but I can't scare her. I need to be strong. I don't know what's happened in the past eight months, but judging from her appearance, nothing good.

Speaking in the calmest tone I can, I say, "I just want to talk. Is that okay?"

Her eyes rake over me. "They questioned me about you. They—" She gulps, and her voice shakes, each word laden. "I said, 'I don't know.' I said, 'she's never exhibited any . . . signs.'" Her body jerks like she's been shocked by a cattle prod. "They asked me where you went. I said, 'I don't know.'"

A pit forms in my stomach, and it makes me ill. She's a shell of the woman I knew before. What has the government done to her? "Mother, did they hurt you? Are you safe?"

"I . . . I didn't raise you to be . . . a monster," she murmurs.

She's white as a sheet, shivering in the cold of rising morning. I cautiously take another step toward her.

"No, mother, you didn't. You raised me to be good. And I am. The Diseased Ones—we aren't like what you've been told. We don't have bad blood, and we don't have an incurable disease. We have powers. *Good* powers. We can do incredible things. But the people in charge of society want people to fear us. The government's lied to you."

Her sunken eyes sparkle like she's on the brink of bursting into tears, but she draws herself up, puffing out her thin chest. "No. N-no."

A tear falls down my cheek, landing in the dirt below my feet, and anger burns in my belly for what society's taken from me—for what it's done to her. And with all my heart, I loathe Camille for it. He may have everyone else fooled, but I'm going to expose him to my mother. He's convinced the world that the Diseased Ones are the problem, even though he's a Diseased One himself. She deserves to know the truth.

"Mother, the President is like me," I say. "He has a power. He's a Diseased One. And he says we're evil, but we're not. He's a liar, and he's using his power to keep everyone living in fear."

My mother's face pales, and she places a thin hand over her mouth. Her eyes grow so wide that fear slinks through me, and adrenaline ticks with my rapidly increasing pulse. She's not saying anything. Why isn't she saying anything?

"Did you hear what I said? Camille is a Diseased One."

Still, she remains silent, but something rouses behind her eyes. She's trying her best to remain emotionless. I can see it. But what I just told her changed her whole body language. Something is not okay—and now, she's looking at me like she's never seen me before.

I speak up again, attempting to keep my voice steady.

"When I failed my Test, I was so scared. I thought, 'there's no way I'm like them. They're monsters. Murderers.' I even tried to come back to you when they took me. You saw the girl who took me. You saw her power."

My mother speaks barely above a whisper. "You vanished. Right in front of me."

"Yes, I did. That was the girl's ability. She rescued me because the government would have killed me."

"You were with *them*."

"Yes."

She's shivering so violently I want to reach out and hug her, but I don't move. "They've brainwashed you."

"No, mother. They helped me see the truth. The biomarker doesn't make us go crazy. It gives us special abilities, and the people who run the world are threatened by that. They wanted to put a stop to something they didn't understand and couldn't control. But we're just people!"

"You bombed a Testing Center. You started a war."

She says this like she's reciting it.

"No, I didn't. Camille did. Mother, he's a Diseased One! He's blaming me so that everyone thinks we're monsters." I keep my tone steady, even though I want to cry. I can't frighten her. "I didn't start this war. The government did."

"No." She shakes her head, and her teeth begin to chatter in the frigid breeze. "You're lying."

"I've never lied to you."

I'm fighting with the emotion that's building in my chest. I want so badly for her to believe me. Wind whips my mother's hair across her face, but she doesn't swipe it away. She's quivering— and staring at me with empty eyes.

I move carefully, drawing closer to her frail frame. "Can I show you? Can I show you my power?"

She hesitates, trembling like she wants to run, but she can't take her eyes off of me. Sweat coats her pallid forehead, clinging to her hairline. Then, something in her shifts, and like a burst dam, she lets out a guttural cry with a sound that rips my heart open.

"You had to be perfect!" she cries, clutching her gown with bony hands. "No mistakes. My little girl, the *only* thing I had to show for myself. You were *everything* I had to offer society. And you did all I raised you to do. It was perfect. No one knew . . . No one!"

My eyes brim over with angry tears. Her words are strange. I don't understand them, but I quell my anger because it's not for her. It's for Camille. It's for the woman who placed the tracker on Tiffany. It's for the people who used Maddy. It's for everyone who's hurt people with powers.

"What do you mean no one knew?" I ask.

Her eyes crease with anguish. I've never seen her show emotion like this. She's always been perfect—pristine beyond explanation. Her mouth shudders, but she doesn't speak.

"Mother, what do you mean?"

"It c-can't be . . ." she stammers.

"What can't be?" I say, feeling more confused by the moment.

She stifles a moan, shaking her head like I'm not understanding her. Then, she covers her face as if to rein herself back in from the emotional outburst.

I can't let her suppress this. Whatever's happening, maybe this is the way to reach her. I take the chance, crossing the remaining distance between us and grabbing her fragile hands with tenderness.

She gasps the moment we touch.

"Don't push this down, mother. *Feel* this!" I beg. "Feel what you're feeling. I don't know what's going on, but I know you've had to be so strong, never letting your guard down. Never expressing a thing because of father's position in the military. The wife of the highest-ranking military official in the Capitol City itself." I take a breath, and my lungs burn as the wind tosses between us. "Growing up, I watched you. You were graceful and proud. You were everything I aspired to be. The very jewel of perfection—*my* mother."

"You h-had to be perfect," she says, barely above a whisper. She's paralyzed within my grasp, still fighting to kill the emotion she's unleashed.

I squeeze her hands gently. "Don't push this down. *Feel* this. I know your whole life changed because I was the first one in twelve years to fail the Test. And I can't imagine what you've been through since."

"I told myself I would n-never . . ." she says, crying.

I pull her hands to my chest, right over my heart. And even though I don't know what she's talking about, I want her to know that feeling what she's feeling is okay. She shouldn't have to suppress it any longer.

I brush the strands of hair away from her face. "Mother, it's okay. No one is here to stop you. No one is watching you. It's okay to feel this. *That's* what the Diseased Ones showed me. That life can be beautiful and hard—all at the same time. That it's messy and wonderful. And sometimes, there isn't a perfect way."

I'm battling the constriction in my throat. My whole life, I've addressed her so formally. Mother. She's more than that. I want to use the word Olivia uses. It's warmer and full of the deepest kind of love.

"Mom," I whisper. I smile through my tears, hopeful. "Change is coming. Soon. And then you'll see. We aren't the monsters you've been taught to fear."

Her bony hands grip mine tighter, and her trained face trembles, but her eyes . . . I can see it. Something deeper is about to come alive in her. Her malnourished face is inches away from mine.

"Before my Test, I would've said I admired you. But there's something more I need to say. And I had to learn this feeling the hard way." I choke on my words, and my wrists turn numb. "I *love* you, mom. And I know you're scared. I don't know what you've been through or what they've done to you, but you don't have to pretend to be okay right now. Please . . . *talk* to me."

She collapses forward, leaning on me with a sob. I embrace her, shielding her from the wind that's picked up to an uncomfortable level. With all my self-restraint, I hold back from breaking down too. My lips vibrate from the cold as dark clouds gather in the bleak break of dawn.

"Hollis, you're not safe here," she says. It's like she's come out of a haze. As if, for the first time in her life, she's finally lucid. "He's going to kill you."

Again, her words seem so strange. I know I'm not safe here,

and she knows it too, so why would she say that? I hold her tight as we tremble together in the cold.

"Hollis, I'm sorry." Her hushed, yet vividly clear voice sends a shudder down to my toes, causing the hairs on the back of my neck to stand on end. "I was a coward. The morning of your Test, I thought they finally discovered the truth about you."

I loosen the embrace and hold her at an arm's distance so I can get a better look at her. She's so pale she looks like a corpse.

"What do you mean?" I ask. "Are you talking about the Test?"

She shakes her head slowly, eyes brimming with tears. She speaks in a frenzied tone. "I thought they were finally coming for me. That somehow, they had figured it out. But once I realized you'd failed, that you were a Diseased One . . ." She lets out a moan, panting like a wounded animal. "I knew I was safe—that still, after all these years, no one found out. And in that moment, I realized I had to let you go if I wanted to live. I knew they would kill you for being a Diseased One, but I told you they were there to help you. And I hate myself for it!"

I hold her firmly within my grasp. "That no one found out *what*?"

"You're not s-safe here, Hollis," she says again, wide-eyed.

"I know I'm not safe!" I say, raising my voice. "Mom, what are you talking about?"

She trembles, eyes wild, and something in her breaks. Words tumble from her in a torrent. "I tried to get pregnant—for so many years. I tried. Your father and I tried. I had to bear children. I *had* to! It was my civic duty. But no matter how many times we tried, I couldn't . . . we couldn't . . . and everywhere I looked, the other first ladies of society were bearing children. I . . . I couldn't be the only one who didn't!"

My lips part, and my heart pounds all the way up through my head.

"He always had his eye on me. At all the high society parties, he always took notice of me. A glance. Over and over again. Just a glance, but with so much behind it . . ."

Adrenaline floods my system.

"I devised a plan. One evening, at a dinner party at the Capitol, where all of the highest-ranking members of society were present, I made my move. I had to bear children." She fights with herself, openly weeping. She looks me in the face. "And it worked. I got pregnant with you. And your father . . . he never knew. He thought you were his—all these years."

My vision tunnels, and my face begins to tingle.

"You looked so much like me. It was perfect," she says, stroking my head. "No one knew. Not a soul. Not even *him*."

I grip her like a lifeline as my voice shakes beyond my control. "Wh-who?"

Her eyes glisten. "President Camille."

All of the blood drains from my face, my sight blurs, and tingling overtakes my entire body. Power roars in my chest, very much alive. Everything comes screaming at me all at once, and clarity hits me with the force of a storm. The reason I have the biomarker, the reason I'm a puppet master—I'm the daughter of the President.

And my mother, who could never breathe a word of her

treachery, had to stand and watch as her only daughter was ripped away from her for failing the Test. She didn't know Camille had the blood biomarker. How could she? My mother did what she had to do to give society what was expected of her—an heir. And for all these years, she kept the secret, because if it got out, she would have been put to death.

I'm crying, sucking in mouthfuls of air and holding my mother by the shoulders, unable to believe what she's just said. Camille is the reason I'm a puppet master.

"He doesn't know," she says, her voice catching in her throat. "Camille doesn't know."

I'm numb within her arms.

"I'm sorry, Hollis!" she cries. "I'm so sorry."

Crack.

Lightning strikes over the city, and rain drizzles from the brewing clouds above. The water feels like icy needles pattering against my skin.

"Come back with me!" I implore her, trying to overcome the shock reverberating through every part of my body. The rain comes down heavier, and I pull her close. "I can protect you. You don't have to be in society anymore."

She shakes her head. "No. I can't."

"Yes, you can!"

Her voice runs through wild inflections. "I thought that if I was perfect, then everything would make sense one day. I've always obeyed. Always. I... I don't know what to believe anymore."

"That's okay," I say. "I was there too. I didn't know what the truth was either. But I didn't have to find out alone. Please, mom, let me help you. Let me show you."

She whispers the next words so softly I can barely hear her. "I'm afraid."

"You don't have to be afraid. Come back with me."

We stand inches apart in the downpour, looking into each other's eyes. I can see so much of myself in her. We're so alike—every feature a near perfect copy. It's like looking into a mirror.

"No," she whispers.

"Mom . . . please." I break down in a sob. "Please!"

She peers at me, and for the first time in her life, smiles. A look so warm and tender—graceful beyond her years. Her tears mix with the rain, and her thin lips part. She pulls me into an embrace, gripping me so tight it hurts. Her lips brush my ear.

"No."

She releases me then steps back, her nightgown as soaked as the earth beneath her feet. She tilts her head, looking me over with years of pain in her eyes.

"I love you, Hollis."

Then, her face dampens to a deadpan, her eyes glaze over, and she turns back toward the walls of Area 19, walking feebly toward the towering city.

"Mom!" I call after her, strangled. "Come back!"

She grows smaller, the sheets of rain blurring her figure. I strain my eyes, holding a hand up to shield myself from the rain. My chest feels like it's going to explode.

"MOM!" The wail that escapes my lips scares me. My ability tingles to my fingertips, and I fall to my knees in the mud, holding my head in my hands and screaming. "COME BACK!"

Hands grab me. It's Olivia. She kneels in front of me, soaked to the bone and wearing a shell-shocked expression. "Hollis, we have to go."

She tries to pull me up, but I fight her.

"MOM!"

"We have to go!" she says, hauling me to my feet forcefully. "I'm sorry, Hollis."

Before I can scream again, the orb expands, rattling and electric. It swallows the two of us, and in a flash of blue, we're thrown forward. The icy sensation sears my skin, and seconds later, my feet slam into the concrete of the training room. We're back in the mountain, and Olivia grips me in a fierce embrace, cradling my head as I weep into her chest.

26

I SIT ON THE RUG IN THE TRAINING ROOM, LEANING BACK against the couch with my knees up to my chest. My face is buzzing, and my body is stiff. So much adrenaline is pumping through my blood I feel faint. And everything is numb.

Olivia made me drink a glass of cold water and sit down. Then, she told me she'd be right back. I don't know how long I've been sitting on the floor. It seems like an hour, but it's probably only been a few minutes.

My ability itches beneath my fingertips, crawling down my arms in an eerie, pulsing rhythm. Power expands in my chest as I breathe. In and out. So much power. If I move, it might explode, so I sit perfectly still, processing the information I've just learned.

I'm the daughter of the President. A second puppet master. I can't believe it's true, but the more it sinks in, the more it makes sense. It's a cruel joke—the worst kind of waking nightmare. How could a duplicate puppet master exist if it's such a rare and overpowered ability? Blood. That's how. I'm his secret progeny, and that's why we can't use our abilities on each other.

There's a scuffle in the hall just beyond the closed door, and I look up. The voices are so loud I can clearly hear them.

"You're not coming in with us!" Olivia shouts.

"Mr. Evandrum's orders! I must accompany Mr. Keaton anywhere he—" a gruff voice begins.

"I'll deal with Arthur *and* the consequences!"

The door opens, and Keith and Jonah file into the room. Jonah grabs Keith's arm and pulls him away from Erwin. Erwin tries to enter, but Olivia pushes him back against the wall with so much ferocity that he gasps. Her forearm braces against his upper chest, her face inches from his.

"Get out of here!" she snarls. "Or I swear on my ability, I'll teleport you out of this mountain and strand you somewhere until we're done."

Erwin gulps, breathing heavy, pinned against the wall. "You'll pay for this insubordination," he says. "Arthur *will* hear about this."

"I don't care!" she snaps. "If you don't walk away in five seconds—"

"I'm going," Erwin mutters, pushing Olivia off him and glaring daggers at her. He straightens his guard uniform then stalks off, his nose in the air.

Olivia slips into the room, closes the door, then points Jonah and Keith to me. They both run, crossing the space between us in seconds. Keith crouches in front of me, his brow creased together in concern. Jonah follows suit, discarding his cane and sitting on the rug.

"I didn't know what to do," Olivia says, placing a hand to her forehead. "I thought of you two first. I . . ."

"Hollis, what happened?" Keith asks, clearly confused—and rightly so. I never told him about the plan to see my mother. "Are you hurt?"

My shaky breaths come out uneven and labored. I must be white as a sheet because Keith reaches over to the side table next to the couch and grabs the glass of water. He hands it to me, and I take it, downing it quickly. My mouth still feels drier than sand.

"Hollis, what is it?" Jonah asks. He's looking at me like he did the day I told him the government was coming to bomb us. "Is everyone in the mountain safe?"

I nod slowly, trembling. Keith grabs my hands, and the warmth of his skin pulls my attention away from my hammering heartbeat. The tingling in my fingertips subsides, and I look into his brilliant blue eyes.

Whimpering, I lean forward, and he wraps his arms around me. I sit in his embrace, trying to bring myself to say it. But the words won't come. They refuse to leave my mouth, strangling me instead. It's a brutal poison to choke on.

Jonah and Keith look at each other. Then, Jonah looks up at Olivia, who's perched on the armchair wearing the same shell-shocked expression I am. "You went to the city with her. What happened?"

"What do you mean you went to the city? To Area 19? Hollis, you went back to the city?" Keith asks, rapid-fire.

Olivia shakes her head. "I'm sorry, Jonah . . . this is Hollis's story to tell."

Keith loosens his tender hold around me, moving a strand of hair from my cheek. Worry lines his face like words inked onto the page of a book.

I have to say it. I have to tell them.

Taking a deep breath, I look Jonah in the eye and say, with trembling lips, "There's a reason I'm a puppet master. I didn't get the biomarker by chance."

Jonah pales, and his mouth parts, a gut-wrenching understanding lighting his tired face. He knows, but I still have to say it out loud.

"I'm the daughter of the President," I whisper, shuddering. "I'm his blood, and he doesn't know."

The silence that follows hurts my eardrums. It's so quiet I want to scream, but I sit, leaning against Keith's chest, with nothing left in me. I went to see my mother to convince her that people with powers aren't evil, but I never imagined this.

After a few minutes, I find my courage and my voice. I tell Jonah and Keith everything my mother told me. Tears stream down my face as I recount the tale. I'm glad Olivia brought Keith. I haven't been able to tell him anything for fear of Arthur finding out something through Erwin. Now I can include Keith in this mess, and it gives me a great amount of relief.

I talk until my voice turns hoarse, sharing everything with Keith. I move from the encounter with my mother to Arthur's plan for Camille. Then, I share my plan for Camille. The words run from my tongue like a river until I have nothing left to say. I even tell Keith about Terrace's ability and the overbearing pressure it's put on me.

After I finish, I fall limp against Keith. Sharing this with him makes me feel like a boulder's worth of weight has fallen from my shoulders.

He holds me tight, his voice gentle and soothing. "Oh, Hollis, I had no idea. I'm so sorry you've been put in this position."

I close my eyes, feeling the rise and fall of his chest. He always makes me feel safe. He's been there for me time and time again. When he flew me down from the rooftop of the Testing Center when we rescued Maddy, when he stopped the three boys from throwing me into the rapids, when he spoke out against Mr. Stuart's accusations the night Jonah and I were attacked, when he punched Pierce in the face upon finding out that he was one of my attackers . . . Keith is steadfast, and my feelings for him have only grown. I'm safe.

"I'm sorry I didn't tell you about Arthur's plan before," I say, choked up. "When you told me I wouldn't have to face Camille again, that it was over . . . I wanted to say something, but there was so much going on. Arthur placed one of his guards with you, and I couldn't—"

Keith shakes his head. "You don't have to apologize, Hollis. You did the right thing. It sounds like this Terrace person's a real piece of work."

"He is," Olivia says.

Keith looks up at her. "Thank you for getting rid of Erwin. I can't stand him."

"My pleasure," she says, looking over her shoulder. "He's an ass. It felt good to get in his face."

"Hollis?" Jonah's soft voice brings my attention back to him. "Do you think your mother will report seeing you?"

I shake my head, still leaning against Keith as we sit on the rug. "No, I don't think she will." My eyes well with fresh tears, and a lump thickens in my esophagus. "It felt like she was going to come back with me. For a moment, she was *so* present, but then she just . . . slipped away."

My mother's eyes glazing over with societal composure will haunt me for the rest of my life. She came so close—close enough to tell me she didn't know what she believed anymore.

"I hope she doesn't," Jonah says. He rubs his forehead. "If she does, Camille might try something else to lure you out. Hollis, you need to take time alone with yourself and your power. You need to figure out what happened with Ashton. Quickly. And we need to practice fighting for control over a large group of people. If you want to spare Camille's life, you have to figure this out. I wish I could help you, but I can't hear the voice. Only you can."

Jonah's grave tone sends jitters through me.

"You think tapping into that voice is the answer, right?" Jonah asks.

I swallow, feeling unsettled. "I do."

"Then do what you must to hear it again. And know that I'm with you every step of the way."

My heartbeat picks up, pattering uncomfortably. Jonah's right. I need to figure this out. I hope against hope that mother will remain silent, but I can't know for sure. The clock on taking Area 19 the right way feels like it's ticking down to zero, and the worst part about it is I don't know when time will run out.

27

Over the next few days, the mountain comes to life with the hustle and bustle of preparation. When I ask Olivia what's going on, she tells me about the Ability Festival, and I'm reminded of the conversation I overheard in the dining room. The event is fast approaching, and people scurry about, all smiles, as they come together to transform the stiff concrete halls of the compound into a festive and cheerful sight. It's odd to witness everyone's excitement when celebrating is the last thing on my mind.

Discovering Camille is my father has made me physically ill. I can't sleep and I don't want to eat. Jonah's had to encourage me to get something into my stomach, but all I've managed to do is swallow a few spoonfuls of soup and take a bite of some bread.

I'm the daughter of the President. What a cruel twist of fate. The man who has driven so much fear and hate into the hearts of citizens is the reason for my existence. I'm crushed. And what

I thought was a random anomaly of biology was a deliberate choice—I have the biomarker because Camille does. I'm a puppet master because my mother slept with him to conceive. In so many ways, I was never meant to be, but I'm here, fighting this fight because Camille has forced me to. I'm the face society's been brainwashed to hate, and I'm angry. He named me the leader of the second Terror War, and now I'm striving to end this so everyone can see him for what he truly is: a tyrant. Sparing Camille's life, in my opinion, is even more critical to the takeover than it was before. People with powers have to be above reproach. I have to be above reproach because I'm the leader both sides are scrutinizing. Whatever happens, the blame falls on me—Camille's made sure of that. But I won't let him win.

■　■　■

After returning to the mountain, I took a day to sit alone with myself and my power. I followed Jonah's advice, but I couldn't hear the voice. I tried letting my power fill me to capacity and holding it there as long as I could. I tried commanding it to speak. I even tried to meditate—something Keith suggested. Nothing happened. But I'm not giving up. It will come. It has to.

Arthur has not returned from the Quarter Review yet, and I'm incredibly grateful. I don't know how long he'll be gone, but it's a pleasant break from the hounding pressure. I don't need him to remind me that everything hinges on getting Ashton's ability to work again.

I haven't talked with Ashton about the plan. If I go to him without an ounce of an idea of how to fix his power, then what's the point? I'm waiting for the right time, and I'll know it when it comes.

For now, rather than focusing on what I can't control, I'm focusing on what I can. Today, Jonah and I are working on fighting over a large group of people. At the very least, I need to be prepared to take people away from Camille long enough for Ashton to suppress his ability.

The packed dining room is clearing out from the midday meal, and Jonah and I follow closely behind Terrace, who weaves his way through the crowd. Terrace moves quickly, hopping up on one of the round tables. He clicks a small bead on the collar of his suit, and his voice issues over the speakers of the Sector.

"Attention all, if you would like to volunteer for a training exercise, please stay seated at your table once you've cleared your meal. Miss Hollis Timewire requires people to practice her ability."

All over the room, eyes find me, and my face turns hot as Terrace continues to speak.

"This is optional, but if you choose to stay, you will be at Miss Timewire's disposal for the remainder of the next hour. And you will experience her ability. All non-volunteers must exit Sector 12 in the next five minutes. Thank you."

He clicks his collar again, steps down from the table, and nods to me, swiping his ginger hair from his eyes.

"Hard to have private lessons when you require so many *puppets*."

He savors the last word like a fine wine. He's not wrong, but I dislike that he felt the need to say that to me.

He stalks off, and I turn to Jonah, shaking my hands out like I've dunked them underwater. My skin is clammy, and my tongue is dry, but power buzzes in my chest, ready and waiting.

I examine the room as people file out, but a significant portion of them have stayed—at least three hundred. Maybe more. It's a larger group than I anticipated. A fair amount of them probably volunteered out of curiosity.

"Jonah, do you think you can control this many people to fight it out with me?" I ask, thinking back to how it felt to bring the military to their knees at the steps of the Capitol. I used all of myself in that moment, and I heard the voice.

Jonah leans his cane against the nearest chair and scans over the volunteers. "I'm not sure. I knew at some point your ability would surpass what I'm capable of, but I didn't think it would happen so soon. I'll do my best to help." He raises an eyebrow. "Do you have any suggestions?"

I stifle a dry laugh. "You're asking me for tips?"

"You're not just a student anymore, Hollis. I'm learning from you as well. You're the puppet master, whereas *I* am a far less useful copy."

I blow out air between tight lips, collecting my thoughts. When we fought over Vianne, Jonah didn't have to focus on the number of individuals. His attention was locked on to her, and her alone. He's also never controlled a large group before, so battling it out over one puppet was easy for him. Taking a group is far more demanding. It requires treating the group like a unit and pouring out every ounce of available power.

"Take as many people as you can and only focus on that.

They are not individuals; they are a collective. One cohesive unit," I instruct. "And don't think about keeping them from me. I'll worry about that. Just give everything you have until you can't handle it anymore. Like, when you feel it in your chest—let that fill you until it feels like you could burst. Then let it all go, out from your hands and into them."

Jonah nods, squaring his shoulders and positioning his hands toward the volunteers. He takes a deep breath and closes his eyes. After a minute, he extends his hands in a flash, and a portion of them gasp, frozen under his control. Per usual, a few people curse out loud, more out of surprise than anything else.

"Good, now hold it," I say to him. I stand on the nearest chair so that everyone can see me and speak loudly over the room. "Anyone who isn't frozen, please stand by the wall."

Of the roughly three hundred people, a large number of them get up from their seats and walk to the edges of the room. I count the remaining volunteers. Forty-four people are under Jonah's control. I sigh. It's not as big of a group as I would've liked, but it will have to do. Jonah won't be able to take any more.

I jump down from the chair and breathe in power until my fingertips vibrate.

"Ready?" I ask.

Jonah nods.

My hands cut through the air, and for about ten seconds, Jonah struggles to keep everyone under his control. But this time, it's much easier to steal them. With a swift flick of the wrist, I tug them under my control, causing Jonah to stumble.

A moment later, however, I feel the pull through my

fingertips as Jonah steals them back. We fight, pushing and pulling in a rhythm until we're both sweating. Every time I feel his power, I push myself harder. When I was at Camille's mercy, he took my friends away with such ease it was like I didn't have an ability at all. I can't let that happen again. I must be stronger.

I close my eyes, reaching back to the desperation I felt battling the President. Camille's words come to me: "We are different from the others, Hollis. Our ability isn't as simple as the biomarker, but I think you already knew that. Does it speak to you yet? Have you tasted its power? Tell me, Hollis, are you afraid of it? Or does it make you thirst for greatness?"

We are different from the others . . .

There's no doubt in my mind that Camille meant the voice. As far as I know, no one else with an ability has it. He and I have a monster only we can hear, one that gives us incredible power. But how does he tap into it? Does the voice come to him on its own? Or can he summon it? How does it help him maintain the kind of ferocious control that can't be broken?

When I faced him, I felt suffocated under his power. I was unable to take anyone away from him—even to the point of not being able to feel them at all. It's like the people in the room weren't present to me.

If I can tap into the voice the way Camille does, maybe I'll stand a chance. I only need to control the people around him long enough for Ashton to suppress his power. That means I need to be able to beat Camille for a few minutes at most.

I have no idea what to do or where to begin, but the voice is the key. I need to hear it again. And the only conclusion I've come to so far is that I've heard the voice in moments where I've given in. *It* controlled *me*.

So that's what I must offer. Myself.

Help me, I think, hoping that this will do something.

My hands shake, buffeted by the power. I push Jonah away, straining against him, but he still has a firm grip over the group of forty-four volunteers. Perspiration collects against my hairline as I fight, and the tingling of my power grows.

Help me, I think again, pleading with it.

I grapple with the wildness building in my chest, pushing myself harder. I have to find it. It's the monster I need to win, the beast I must learn from. And this time, I'm not afraid. I don't have that luxury. Closing my eyes, I breathe power in like the forest air—crisp and poignant. It rattles through me, overpowering to the point of uncomfortable, but I relish it.

I'm ready. Help me. Teach me.

A deep growl rumbles in my head, so present it feels like a dark presence is lurking directly behind me. The hairs on the back of my neck stand on end, and fear jumps down my throat. I freeze in place, unable to fight the physiological response—the involuntary biological urge to self-preserve. To run. To hide. To get away from this place.

It's here. Right behind me. More present than it's ever been. And everything in me turns to ice that slithers through my veins, closes around my neck, and steals all the breath from my lungs.

Hollis, it snarls in my ear.

I begin to shake. With trembling lips, I whisper, "Teach me."

It growls so deep my chest hurts. Right behind me. It's right behind me. I want to turn around and look, but I dare not. I don't want it to leave, so I embrace the chilling sensation and let it fill me, even though my heart is thundering into my ears.

You do not think big enough, it whispers. Its presence grows stronger, more tangible. My ability snarls, but only to me. What I'm hearing is not something Jonah can. *You do not understand.*

My voice shakes. "What don't I understand?"

You do not have control, it hisses.

Everything in me is screaming at me to turn around. To look at it. But I don't move. I stand facing the puppets, the darkness inches from me. "What does that mean?"

Let go.

My hands tremble, still caught in a deadlock with Jonah. I'm fighting with all my strength, but I still can't steal them away from him.

"Let go of what?" I ask, teeth gritted.

The creature's deep hiss curls my insides. *You are doing this alone when you do not have to.*

"Show me," I say, feet slipping on the concrete from the strain of holding onto the group of volunteers.

Let go. The words creep over my shoulder like an anthem. *Let go.*

I'm sweating through my shirt, the fabric clinging to my underarms. A tense knot is rising in the pit of my abdomen, and as I struggle to keep everyone under my grasp, I can't shake the nauseating feeling of failure. I'm going to lose. I can barely hold on.

"Fine," I breathe. "Take it. Take control."

I yield, letting go of the group of forty-four, and immediately, the tension in my abdomen releases. Then, with explosive power, my ability streams down my arms like a viper striking its prey and sinking its teeth in deep.

With a snap, the volunteers fall under my control, and Jonah staggers forward, now powerless. He swipes his hands, trying to take them back, but I don't budge. They are mine. I can feel them, the scent of their skin, every breath they take, every beat of their heart. I can see them, down to the hairs on their head, down to the very molecules of their anatomy. I can hear the pulses of blood rushing through their veins ... Everything becomes razor sharp.

The creature rattles right behind me, so close it's nearly tangible.

Do you understand?

I'm glued to the puppets dangling from the end of my fingertips, focused in a way I've never experienced. It's incredible. I feel like I could run miles on end and never grow weary. This creature is a part of me—the perfect symbiote. One that will not relinquish its prey for anything or anyone. And with it, I cannot lose.

We are control, it growls, its voice reverberating through my head.

"We are control," I repeat.

My eyes dart from one person to the next rapid-fire, and yet, it feels as though I'm able to linger on each to such a degree that I've memorized them. Their faces. Their forms. Their energy. If they are strong or weak. If they have any fight in them.

I finally understand. *We* are the puppet master. *We* are control. It's not surface level anymore. The connection I feel to the people under my ability is intimate—as personal as a lion sinking its teeth into a gazelle. The power I have. The undefeatable, vicious, absolute control. It's the most invigorating feeling in the world.

My attention snaps to Jonah, and I tilt my head, studying him. He's struggling against the hold I have in vain. He can never break this. The mere attempt is absurd.

Jonah drops his hands, turning to me. "I can't even feel them. How are you doing that?"

"I just gave in," I whisper, staring at Jonah with an eerie calm. Every feature of Jonah's face turns sharp—every pore in his skin, the way he blinks, the sweat clinging to his brow, his dark brown eyes and stubble beard. The way his face catches the light. "I get what Camille was saying. That we're different."

"Do you hear the voice?" Jonah asks, hoarse.

"Yes." My head tilts the other direction. I'm so intent on him that I can smell the faint hint of coffee on his breath, and I can hear his heartbeat.

The already perturbed expression on Jonah's face deepens. He takes a step toward me, holding his hands up like he's trying to calm a beast ready to charge him.

Power ripples under my skin, and I drink it in, the creature growing even stronger. I could do anything. Anything at all.

My ability's deep snarl vibrates my chest. *More. Take more.*

I face the room, eyes darting to all of the people standing against the walls. My hands fly, fingertips splayed through the air.

All three hundred of them are under my power—so effortlessly. Mine. And it's here, right behind me, like a deadly shadow feeding the drive for absolute control.

"Hollis . . ."

My eyes lock onto Jonah once more, and I stare at him, unblinking. He's free of my control, still holding his hands in front of his chest with his palms open. He moves closer, taking cautious steps.

I could control him too. If I wanted . . .

"Let them go," he says calmly. With a steady hand, Jonah reaches out and places it on my shoulder.

The moment we touch, I gasp, and my power extinguishes. All around the room, people stagger—some dropping to their knees, others coughing and sputtering. Angry and scared voices bristle around the dining room.

A man a few yards away from me sputters, blue in the face. "What—the hell—was that?" I look at him, unsettled. He sucks air in, clutching his chest. "I couldn't—breathe!"

Adrenaline pumps through my blood like fire.

"I'm out of here!" The man turns away, stumbling toward the door. At this, most of the room hurries to join him, scattering to collect their things. They file out in earnest, pushing each other to get through the double doors of the Sector.

I stare at the receding crowd, panting.

"Hollis?" Jonah has a firm grip on my shoulders now. He looks me straight in the eyes. "Is it still here?"

I shake my head. "No, it's gone."

Sweat drenches Jonah's brow, shiny in the bright fluorescents. "Your eyes . . ." he whispers.

"My eyes?" I repeat. "Jonah, what?"

"They were completely black."

A shiver prickles across my skin. Camille's eyes did the same thing right before he started the broadcast to publicly execute me. At the time, I didn't recognize what was happening, but now I understand. It was his ability enhancing his senses, heightening everything about his unbreakable control. It was feeding him strength and stamina, and I, a mere mouse in my ability, never stood a chance.

The statues I saw at the Capitol: a bear, a lion, a wolf, a crocodile, a viper. This power is like those creatures: an apex predator. And now I see this power as he does. It's so much more than myself. It's my complement, my companion, my means for absolute control.

"Jonah, I'm okay," I say, grabbing his hands gently. He's looking at me the way he did when I hurt Ashton—shock lingering beneath feigned calm. "I think I figured it out, and that means I'm one step closer to undoing what I did to Ashton."

"Hollis, what happened to you?"

I pause, mouth askew. I don't know how to describe what I saw and felt with the voice. All I know is that I understand what it can do.

"I . . . I need time to think," I say. "I'm sorry, Jonah. I can't explain it right now, but I promise you, I've got this. I won't hurt anyone."

Jonah picks up his cane, fiddling with the top of it. "I'm glad you were able to hear that voice, but when you're ready, you need to tell me what happened."

I nod. "I will."

"Why don't you join your friends in the aircraft hangar?" he suggests. "Beezee told me they're helping decorate for the Ability Festival. Just . . . take some time to get your mind off things and rest. Please. You need it."

I don't want to decorate. I've just unlocked a part of my ability I never thought I could, and with the pressure building on me from all sides, helping set up for the Ability Festival seems out of place, but I respond by saying, "Good idea."

I turn away from him and walk toward the double doors of the Sector, deep in thought. I've figured out a piece I hadn't before. This isn't just a biomarker, it's a creature willing to give me the control I crave.

I understand. *We* are control.

28

I WALK DOWN THE LONG HALLS OF THE MOUNTAIN IN A trance. I did it. I got my ability to speak to me, and the power it gave me is sweeter than honey. Now that I've heard the voice, I want to learn more. I've never seen so clearly. What a rush. It was like every sense in me heightened a thousand-fold. The way they felt under my fingertips, the way they appeared so sharply in focus, how I could hear the imperfections of their breath, feel the rhythm of their heartbeats, smell the scent of their skin . . .

My footsteps tap unevenly against the concrete as I head toward the aircraft hangar. Even though I'd rather be doing anything else, Jonah's right. I need to get my mind off things, and decorating seems like the perfect distraction. The weight of discovering the President's identity and the exhilaration of unlocking a new part of my power are sending my thoughts into a tailspin. It seems odd, even absurd, that these people are gearing up for a celebration when I've been gearing up for a war.

But maybe decorating is the few hours of simple bliss I need. I haven't been able to spend much time with my friends since the Holodeck, and I know it will be good for me.

Jogging down the last stretch of concrete before the entrance to Sector 3, I push open the double doors and slip through. The room is bustling with activity. Boxes of decorations, ladders, and people are scattered everywhere. I scan over the scene quickly and spot my friends over by the far wall. Muttering "excuse me" to the group of men blocking my path, I make my way over to them with a spring in my step.

"Would you hand me that string of beads, Candice?" Rosalie asks, her vibrant red hair done up in a messy bun. She's standing on a ladder that's tilted against the wall, and Keith is holding it steady at the base. Erwin is at his side, scowling.

"Sure thing," Candice says.

She weaves around Ben, who's sitting on the floor digging through a large box. Bouncing up on her tippy toes, she hands the beads to Rosalie, smirking at Keith with a mischievous grin. "You know, you could fly up there and do this for us. Just saying."

I run up to Candice, tackling her from behind with a hug. "Yeah, because I'm *sure* Erwin would be *so* cool with Keith flying up there."

She yelps, clutching her chest. "Hollis!"

Ben and Keith chuckle, but Erwin shoots me a dark look. The last time I saw him, Olivia pinned him against the wall and threatened to teleport him out of the mountain if he didn't leave Keith alone with me—something Arthur's bound to hear about soon. I ignore Erwin and address my friends. "I'm here to help decorate."

"Perfect!" Rosalie chimes. "I'm glad you're taking a break from training."

"Yeah," I say, smiling weakly.

"You need to branch out and have some fun," she says, stringing the first section of yellow beads around a hook on the wall.

"True," Candice adds. "You're always so serious."

"I am not always serious!" I retort, putting my hands on my hips. "And I know how to have fun."

"Sure you do," Rosalie says. She gives me a sarcastic wink.

Candice snickers, tossing her dark brown hair over her shoulder. She pops a flame onto her pointer finger, and it dances around before she blows it out.

"Move over then," I say to Rosalie, half amused, half exasperated. "Let me string the beads."

Rosalie descends the ladder and gestures me forward. "All yours."

As I climb up, Keith's hand brushes mine. His bright blue eyes twinkle, and he smiles. "Are you doing alright?"

He's asking me about Camille. Only he, Olivia, and Jonah know about what I found out from my mother, and for now, I'm keeping it that way.

I lower my voice so the others don't hear me. "I'm as good as I can be."

I reach the top of the ladder and continue to string the yellow beads over the hooks.

"Look at all of this stuff!" Ben exclaims, still rifling through the largest box. He surfaces, clutching a one-foot-tall wooden figurine of a woman holding her hands in front of her stomach, palms facing upward. She's wearing a golden robe and closing her eyes. "They've got some strange decorations. I wonder where this one will go?"

Candice walks over to him and plucks the figurine out of his hands. She turns it over, examining the woman's face. "She looks creepy."

Ben snatches her back. "Hey! I was looking at that." He sets the wooden woman on the floor, gazing at her with a scrunched up nose. "Yeah, she does look creepy."

"Where should we put her?" Candice asks, snickering.

Ben shrugs. "Don't know."

Rosalie scoops the figurine up and dumps it back into the box. "How about in there?"

"I'm excited for this Festival. It's such a good idea, celebrating our abilities! I can't believe we never came up with an event like this back at the old compound," Candice says. She squats behind Ben and wraps her arms around his shoulders. "I hear there's an ability show-off, kind of like a talent show. And there's a dance! You're going to ask me to dance, right?"

Ben grins back at her as he extends a lanky arm behind him, tussling Candice's hair. "I don't know. Maybe."

"Maybe?" Candice repeats, indignant. "You better ask me to dance, or I'll hunt you down."

"You couldn't catch me. I'm too speedy."

"Ben Bryson, you better ask me to dance!"

Keith leans out from under the ladder, chuckling. "Ben, you're treading dangerous waters, my friend. It doesn't matter how fast you can run, my little sister *will* find you."

"Damn right." Candice jumps up from her crouched position and folds her arms across her chest. She slides a sideways glance at Keith. "Are you going to ask Hollis to dance?"

Keith looks up at me with a boyish grin. "Of course."

My cheeks flush, and a wonderful feeling flutters through my stomach. I continue stringing the beads. "I don't know how to dance."

"Don't worry. I'll teach you."

Candice aggressively attacks the nearest box, pulling it open with so much force that part of the flap tears. She mutters under her breath, "At least my brother knows how to be a gentleman."

"Hey, Candy?" Ben says, walking over to her.

"Yeah?"

"Would you like to dance with me during the Festival?"

She glares at him then softens her fiery gaze, melting into happiness all over again. "Yes, I would."

Ben pulls Candice into a backward hug and begins to rock back and forth. "Can't wait."

"I'm out of hooks," I say. The remaining string of beads trails down the ladder, only half done up.

Ben disentangles himself from Candice. "Hollis, let me up there. I'll put in more hooks." Ben ushers me down from the ladder, and we switch places. He climbs to the top, looks around, then sighs. "Candice, can you hand me the roll of adhesive?"

She grabs the roll, runs over to the ladder, and holds it up to him. "Here you go."

I glance at the box of decorations immediately to my left, and something catches my eye. Shuffling through the chaos, I pull out a large puke-colored bow. I gawk at it for a moment. It's old and horrible with a sticky residue lining its rim and hair jutting out of the frills. I wrinkle my nose, holding it up to Rosalie. "What the heck is this thing?"

Ben flashes an overtly obnoxious smile at the two of us and tilts his head to the side. "It's a bow."

"I know it's a bow!" I shoot back at him.

"Here," Rosalie says. She snatches the oversized bow from me, walks up to the ladder, and sticks it to Ben's ankle. "Now it's Ben's bow."

"Hey! Get that nasty thing off of me!" he yelps, twisting to reach for the ugly thing. He flails and loses his footing on the top rung of the ladder. Ben slips, and Keith dives into action, leaping up from the ground and flying to catch Ben before he hits the concrete.

The three of us girls gasp as Keith lands safely back on the ground, Ben awkwardly sandwiched in his arms. Rosalie, hand over her mouth, bursts into an apology, while Candice, seeing that Ben is uninjured, bursts into laughter.

Candice crouches on the floor, holding her stomach in mirth with tears streaming down her face. Ben untangles himself from Keith and throws the bow back into the box. "That thing is gross." He shakes himself, as if the bow were still clinging to him. He turns to Keith. "Also, thanks for that."

"No problem," he says, eyeing his sister, who's still curled over in laughter. "Hey, don't laugh too hard. Ben almost got hurt."

She gets up from the floor and walks over to Ben, wrapping her arms around his middle. "I'm sorry. I can't help it."

Ben hugs her back. "It's okay. It was kind of funny."

She grins, wagging her finger at Keith. "Always there to save the day, huh?"

Keith grins. "You know it."

"Oh shoot!" Rosalie smacks her forehead and looks over the mess of boxes. "I was supposed to get this string of lights from the hall. Beezee said the middle section of the wall needs lights."

"I can grab it," I offer. "Besides, I need to log more hours of 'fun,' right Rosalie?"

She scowls at me. "Ha. Ha. It's just down the hall." She shoos me with her hands.

"Alright, I'm going." Then, in a sarcastic tone, I add, "You can always count on me—Miss Fun!"

I duck as the puke-colored bow flies through the air, narrowly missing me. I skip through the crowded aircraft hangar, calling back to her. "Not quick enough, Simmons!"

After a minute, I enter the hall and scan over dozens of boxes. The labels are faded and hard to make out, but I find the right one. Scooping it into my arms, I lean it on my hip and turn to head back into the hangar, but a strange sight stops me. Lights are hanging themselves a few yards away as a man stands there, twirling his hands over his head. His fingertips dance in a beautiful rhythm, and I'm momentarily transfixed.

I move closer, setting the box down by my feet. I know this man. "You're George, right?"

He turns around, and the lights stop hanging themselves.

"I overheard you talking to your friends about the Ability Festival," I say quickly, noting the look of concern that crosses his features. I have no doubt in my mind he knows my name, but for me to know his name . . .

"Sorry, I didn't mean to interrupt," I say sheepishly.

"Hollis Timewire," he says, nodding to me. "Pleasure to meet you."

"I have a friend with your ability." I point to the lights. They remind me of the floating marbles. Audrey made them fly through the air with her telekinesis the day I met her.

"I'll have to meet your friend," he says. He goes back to work, his fingertips flying through the air. "It's great to have your people here. How are you adjusting?"

"Well," I say. "Thank you."

"That's good to hear. It's been a wonderful relief to have the extra help."

"Oh, it's no trouble. Decorating for the Festival has been fun."

"Well, that too," George says, chuckling. The lights hook themselves one by one, glittering down the hall. "But I was referring to the Area 7 Testing Center. It's been a load off to have more people added to our staff so that our research teams can focus."

"Oh. Right, of course."

I bite my lower lip, scuffing the sole of my boot against the concrete. Maybe I can get George to talk about what they're doing at Area 7. From my brief conversation with Beezee during Maddy's blood draw, I know these people are working on the biomarker in our blood. And from what I've gathered from George's conversation with Lanie and Claire, he likes to take breaks and wants to drink booze. He also sounded like an ass, which means he probably has an ego I can stroke.

"So, you work at the Area 7 Testing Center?" I ask.

"Sure do. I'm a scientist."

"That sounds fancy." I layer adulation into my tone. I've never flattered someone before, but I'm determined to get some information out of him. "You must be very smart. I didn't do well in school. All that math, I just couldn't wrap my head around it." That's a lie. I held high marks in every subject, especially science. "What do you do as a scientist?"

George smirks, adjusting his shoulders and standing a little taller. "I'm the brains behind the operation. Sure, there are plenty of smart people on my team, but I'm the one doing the real work."

"Really?"

"Yes, ma'am. My job is demanding. And it requires a steady hand and a sharp eye."

I giggle, adding just the right amount of daring to my words. "A steady hand? That sounds dangerous."

"Pouring chemicals is delicate work." His hands flourish, and the last of the lights hang themselves. "One slip up and the whole batch is ruined."

Batches of what? It sounds like they're working on a serum of some sort, but I can't be sure.

"You're a chemist?" I ask.

"Indeed I am."

"That sounds even fancier than being a scientist." I twist a lock of my hair, taking care to keep the charm in my voice. "Have you ever ruined a batch before?"

George's smugness deepens, and he brushes off the front of his shirt. "Never. That's why Arthur chose me to head up the team. My work is excellent."

"I take it these batches are going well?" I give a bashful smile, lowering my eyes and scratching the top of my head. "I'm sorry, I don't know how to speak science."

George chuckles then shakes his head. "I can't say too much, little lady. It's top secret right now. Although . . . Everyone will know about it soon. Personally, I don't see why it has to be so secretive."

I give him a mysterious look, raising an eyebrow. "Sounds enticing."

"It is."

"That must be why you're the brains," I add, hoping this will get him to say more. "I'm sure not everyone can understand it like you do."

He puffs out his chest, jabbing a thumb against his heart. "It is *my* formula after all."

At this, his face pales. He clears his throat and checks the watch on his wrist. He mumbles something I can't catch then says, "It was nice to meet you, Hollis, but I really should be going."

I smile innocently even though my insides are jumping with victory. "It was nice to meet you too. I guess I'll see you around."

He storms off, muttering under his breath.

A formula? It has to be for some kind of serum. What could they be working on that requires such delicate precision? The pieces I've gathered are making me feel more and more uneasy.

What is Arthur cooking up in the lab at Area 7?

I sigh, grabbing the box of lights at my feet. As much as I'd like to investigate further, figuring out what's going on at the Area 7 Testing Center will have to wait. I have more pressing matters to concern myself with. Once the Ability Festival is over, I'm going to use the voice to figure out what I did to Ashton, then Camille will be out of the picture. Area 19 must remain my focus, because one way or another, these people are going to take over society, and I must be there to make sure it happens the right way.

29

THE NEXT WEEK PASSES WITH CHAOTIC ENTHUSIASM IN preparation for the Ability Festival. It's all anyone can talk about, and as the excitement grows, my stress diminishes. Arthur still hasn't returned to the mountain, I've been able to take a break from training, and nothing horrific has happened in society—which means my mother didn't report me. But more importantly, it means she's safe. If Camille found out I visited the city, there'd be a news broadcast, and her loyalty to the government would be called into question.

To my relief, I've also stopped having nightmares about her. I'm heartbroken she didn't come back with me, but I'm still hopeful. She's questioning her beliefs, and that's something I never thought would happen. Maybe I can visit her again once we've taken charge, and this thought gives me courage.

I'm also feeling rejuvenated by my friends. It's been nice to hang out with them and feel like a normal teenager. To forget, even for a few days, that this entire operation hinges on me is a wonderful feeling.

With the Festival days away, the mountain is unrecognizable. Lights hang above our heads in every room, dazzling the eye and charming the spirit, and most of the harsh fluorescents are off, shrouding the mountain in a soft glow.

The dining room is now a banquet hall. Individual tables have been pushed together to create long lines that fill the length of the room, and red velvet tablecloths drape over every available surface. In addition, wall screens hang around the perimeter of the space, displaying digital fireplaces. It's a truly cozy and festive atmosphere.

But the most astonishing transformation is the aircraft hangar. It's fully furnished for the opening ceremony with nearly a thousand golden fold out chairs set in sections. There's lights and beads and bows and satin drapes everywhere. It's breathtaking.

"Where are we going?"

Maddy's excited voice floats down the softly lit hall. I grip his hand, walking at a quick pace toward Sector 13. I've not been to this part of the mountain before, but I'm meeting Vianne there. It's the storage Sector, and according to the map Beezee gave me, it houses boxes of extra clothing, books, furniture, and other miscellaneous items.

"We are going to see Vivi," I say. "She said she has a surprise for me."

What surprise? I couldn't guess.

"Vivi!" Maddy chimes with a huge smile. He pulls me forward, and I jog a few steps to keep from tripping.

"You like hanging out with her, huh?"

He giggles, nodding vigorously. "Duck bill! Duck bill!"

I laugh. "That's quite a trick Vivi does, isn't it?"

Clutching the map in my free hand, I hold it out in front of me, looking over the labels for Sector 13. I'm supposed to go to the fifth storage unit on the left, and after another minute of marching, we find it. I pull open the door, and Maddy darts in, finding Vianne within seconds and pelting her with a hug.

"Woah!" Vianne says, patting Maddy on the top of the head. "Hi, Maddy."

"Vivi!" Maddy sings.

As I enter the classroom-like space, I'm met with colorful chaos. Dresses hang on rolling racks in every direction, several full-length mirrors lean against the far wall, and boxes sit in a large pile to the right of the door. Shredded cardboard and plastic bags litter the floor as well.

"Hollis! You made it."

Vianne is stunning. She's wearing a golden silk gown that falls in elegant tapered layers down to her ankles. It shimmers, flowing around her delicate frame as she moves. And the U-shaped neckline of the dress is dotted with small white rhinestones.

I glance around the cluttered room with a curious smile. "Alright, I'm stumped. What's the surprise?"

"We are getting you *dressed*!" she exclaims. Her hair flickers from dirty blonde to brilliant white.

I look over myself. "Funny, I thought I was already wearing clothing."

"No, no!" Vianne chirps. "I mean dressed *up*!"

"Dressed up?" I eye her hesitantly.

She gives me an exasperated look and disentangles herself from Maddy. She pulls me further into the room. "You have to dress up for the opening ceremony. And for the dance! The Festival is a formal event."

"What? No!" I say, shaking my head.

Heat crops up in my face. I've never worn a dress before, but I don't want to tell her that. Only high society women are allowed to wear dresses. Children are to wear their school uniforms and state-issued attire. I always wanted my mother to help me pick out my first dress when I came of age, but that part of my life has passed. And it hurts that I can't have that moment with her.

I stumble over my words. "In society I . . . I've always been told what to wear. I don't—"

"Good, then I'll tell you what to wear," Vianne says, grinning. "Since you've had loads of practice."

"But—"

"No buts!" Vianne drags me over to one of the rolling racks. "Beezee told me we can wear anything that fits. Rosalie and Candice got their dresses yesterday."

I purse my lips.

Vianne folds her arms across her chest. "Come on! Everyone in the mountain is dressing up for this. You can't be the *only* one who doesn't wear something nice for the opening ceremony. As if you need another reason for people to stare at you."

"Hey! Low blow."

"What? It's true. Plus, you have a date. I'd give anything to have a date, but Ashton's not—" Her enthusiasm falls, but the moment is short-lived. She plasters on a smile. "Keith is going to be dressed up, so you have to dress up too. Now come on, I'll help you find something to wear."

I sigh, resigning myself to her request. "Fine."

"Yay!" she squeals, clapping her hands together.

This causes Maddy to giggle, and he copies her, clapping his hands as loudly as he can. He totters over to us, rubbing his nose with the flat of his hand. "Can I dress up too?"

"Of course you can." I kneel down and give him a big hug. I point to one of the boxes by the door. "Why don't you explore what's in there for me, okay?"

"Okay!"

With a determined look, Maddy scampers over to the box and pulls it open.

"Let's see what we have here," Vianne says, rifling through the dresses on the nearest rolling rack.

I watch her, completely beside myself. At home, I wore one of two things: My casual clothing, which consisted of a gray sweater and shirt with a set of solid-colored slacks, or my school uniform—a navy blue skirt with leggings, a button up maroon blouse, and a navy blue blazer. Dressing up is only for high-ranking society members, and only for important political events. Doing so otherwise is considered vain. Inappropriate. But I have to remind myself that I'm not a part of society anymore. I'm a part of this new and beautiful culture, and even though I'm nervous, I should embrace it.

Vianne gasps so loudly I jump.

"What?" I say.

She turns toward me slowly, holding her hand to her mouth.

"Hollis, this is perfect for you."

She pulls a thin, floor-length, dark teal dress from the rack. A sash is sewn around the waistband, and several layers of polyester frame a slit that extends from the bottom of the dress to knee height. Long silk sleeves end in cuffs that button around the wrists, and the neckline hangs low in an elegant 'V.' The dress cascades to the floor, flowing from the hanger.

"Well?" Vianne squeaks, holding it out. "Try it on!"

I take the dress from her, staring at it, and the soft fabric slips through my fingertips.

"What are you waiting for? Go change behind those racks." She points to the corner of the room.

I slip away in between the racks of clothing. I lay the dress over a stray box and unzip my jacket, pulling it off inside out. I take a deep breath, removing the rest of my clothing and stepping into the dress. After zipping up the back, I walk over to where Vianne is eagerly waiting.

When I step out from behind the racks, she squeals. She grabs my hand and pulls me up the mirror leaning against the wall. I blink, looking at myself. I don't recognize the girl staring back. My eyes trace the fit of the dress, trailing up my hips and lingering over my neckline. Loose strands tickle my forehead, and I tilt my head, taking in the feel of the silk against my skin. My leg slides from the slit, and the dress flows like an enchantment at my touch.

I feel . . . pretty.

"Hollis, it's *gorgeous*!" Vianne breathes, mouth open in awe.

I turn to the side, taking in the dress from a different angle. It's like it was made for me. Just for me. A ball of emotion wells up in me as I think of my mother, and my eyes begin to water. I look just like her . . .

Vianne moves closer to me. "Hollis, what's wrong?"

I smile, letting the emotion rush through me. "It's perfect. Thank you."

She nudges me. "Wait until Keith sees you in this."

I blush, running my fingertips across the delicate skirt. Butterflies zip through my stomach. "Yeah?"

"Girl, yes!" she says.

A quiet thunk issues from behind us. I turn over my shoulder to see Maddy wearing a bright blue feather scarf and a large orange hat. He's sitting inside a box and giggling. With a flick, he tips the brim of the hat up and peers at us.

Vianne laughs. "Looking good, Maddy."

I walk over to him. "I love the scarf."

"It's soft!" He strokes it against his face.

"Okay, mister," I say in playful seriousness, squinting down at him. "I'm going to have to try that feather scarf on."

His blond curls toss around his forehead. "Try this one!" He procures a second scarf from the box, waving it above his head. I snatch it up, swinging the bright green feathers around my neck and posing.

"What do you think?" I ask Maddy.

He claps his tiny hands. "Feathers!"

For the remainder of the afternoon, I spend time with

Vianne and Maddy, playing pretend. From one fanciful, clashing outfit to another, Maddy's abounding joy lifts my heart. He's so full of happiness that I forget about all of my troubles, and before we know it, the automated voice crackles over the speakers of the mountain.

"Evening Meal: 1800. Please make your way to Sector 12."

Vianne looks up at the speaker in the corner. "I guess we lost track of time. We better clean up and get going."

After a few minutes of hustling, the box of miscellaneous clothing is packed and in order. Vianne and I change out of our dresses, and Maddy discards his feather scarf. With my dress in hand, I walk into the hall with Maddy, and Vianne follows close behind.

I touch her shoulder. "Hey, would you mind if I talked with Maddy alone for a moment? We'll catch up to you."

Vianne tips her head to the side, and her hair changes to a deep auburn. "Sure." She stoops down to Maddy's level and morphs her face into the duck bill. "I'll see you in a minute, little one."

"Duck bill!" Maddy cries with delight.

Vianne stands up then makes her way down the hall, vanishing as it turns toward the end of the Sector.

I sigh, taking Maddy's hand in my own. I sit down on the cold stone, folding my legs up crisscrossed. "Maddy, can you sit down a moment? I have to ask you something."

Maddy peers at me with big blue eyes and sits down in front of me. He grabs hold of his feet and rocks himself back and forth.

"Maddy, do you know who President Camille is?"

He nods slowly. "He is the one in charge."

"Yes, he is." I collect myself, taking in a deep breath. "Camille has an ability. He is like us."

Maddy's eyes sparkle. "Does he have the golden light?"

I shake my head. "No, his power is like my power." My hands turn clammy and my pulse quickens. "Do you remember when you used the golden light on me? The day you met me?"

Maddy nods again. "You looked sad."

"Yes." My throat closes as awful memories from that day attack me, but I push past it. I have to do this. I have to ask him. He shouldn't be part of this mess—this war. But there's no alternative if Camille is to remain alive. "Maddy, I need you to use the golden light on President Camille. Are you able to do that?"

He stares at me, crinkling his eyebrows. "You want me to use the golden light?"

"Yes."

My hands begin to shake, and I place them on my knees. I hate that I'm having this conversation with this sweet boy. It's not fair to him. He shouldn't be in the middle of this anymore. He's only a child.

Maddy blinks, gazing at me with a peculiar calm. "Why do you want me to use the golden light?"

A shiver runs through me. The way Maddy's looking at me . . . it's like he's older. My breath is coming out shaky. I don't know how to do this. How do I tell a child that I need him to help me so Arthur doesn't kill Camille? How could I possibly begin to explain the ramifications of what this means for the world? I can't.

"Camille has hurt a lot of people," I whisper. "And the only way to stop him is to take his power. I'm so sorry I have to ask you this, Maddy, but are you willing to use the golden light?"

"Did he hurt you?" His question pierces me like a dagger.

"Yes, he did."

Maddy's orb eyes lock on to me, and he stands up, placing his tiny hands on either side of my face. I exhale sharply at his touch. He stares at me with a look I've never seen from him, intent and purposeful.

"I will use the golden light," he whispers.

My heart twists in two different directions, and I choke back a whimper. The fact that he's willing to do this breaks me. I want to protect him at all costs, but this is something I can't do without him. And even though I hate the fact that Maddy will be close enough to touch that vile, soulless man, Camille will be unconscious from the drugs when we kidnap him. He won't be able to hurt Maddy.

"Thank you, Maddy."

I grip him in a hug, and as he wraps his arms around my neck, it rekindles the fight in me. I will not fail him.

———
30
———

THE MORNING OF THE ABILITY FESTIVAL ARRIVES WITH anticipation, and I spend it getting ready with my friends. Candice looks stunning in her flaming red and orange dress, perfectly suited to her ability. Rosalie wears a cream-colored, floral-patterned gown with puffy sleeves. Vianne is adorned in the golden dress she wore before. And all of them lose their minds over my dress, an odd form of attention that makes me feel special, unlike the rest of people's gawking.

Candice insists on putting a light face of makeup on me, and once she finishes, she drags me in front of the mirror propped against the side table of her room, gushing over how her brother is "just going to perish" over how gorgeous I look.

As we continue to prep ourselves—a task I never imagined could take hours on end—excited jitters build up in my stomach until I've lost the appetite I'm supposed to have for the evening banquet.

A sharp rap on the door brings us out of our fawning, and Rosalie bounds over to open it, her beautiful red curls tossing around her shoulders.

"Who's there?" Vianne asks as she applies lipstick.

"It's Olivia," Rosalie says.

She's not dressed up like the rest of us. Instead, she wears dark clothing and combat boots. She leans against the door frame, looking directly at me.

"Arthur's back. He wants to see you."

Olivia's quiet tone sends frisson down my arms. I move to her side as quickly as my feet will carry me, and all of the happiness I felt moments ago vanishes. I look back at my friends who appear bewildered. "I'll meet you guys for the opening ceremony."

With that, I step into the hall, following Olivia as she walks away from the door. We trudge several yards until we're next to the double doors leading out of the Sector.

"What does Arthur want?" I ask.

My thoughts fire in rapid succession. I haven't seen Arthur since the Area 34 bombing. I've seen my mother since then too. Does he know I left the mountain? Does he want a progress update on my training? On Ashton? Why does he need to see me now, mere hours before the Ability Festival is set to begin?

"I—" she falters, and then goes silent.

It's only now that I notice her eyes. They're puffy, like she's been crying, and anxiety clenches my stomach. Did she say something to Arthur about my mother? I grab her by the shoulder and turn her to face me.

"What's wrong?" I ask.

"Nothing," she says, stiffened. "I'm fine."

"You don't look fine."

She exhales sharply through gritted teeth. "It's nothing."

She moves to push open the doors, but I block her path.

"Hey, haven't I earned *any* trust? I haven't said a word to you about the forest. Not a word. Like I promised. Even though it's eating me up inside. And I took a risk by coming to you about seeing my mother. You could have reported me to Arthur, but you didn't. You helped me. Why? What's wrong? Because it's not 'nothing.'"

Olivia grabs my upper arm and swings me around with such force I gasp. She pushes me against the wall, eyes watering, then looks up at the double doors of the Sector, where a tiny camera presides.

"Close your eyes," she growls.

Without another word, the blue orb engulfs us. Cold attacks me and light blinds me, and after a horrible moment of feeling like my lungs are about to pop, my feet slam into earthy ground. Wind tosses my hair, water rushes in the distance, and the scent of pine lingers in the air. We're in the forest by the river, standing on the muddy bank where Maddy gave me back my power.

Olivia releases my arm, glaring at me. "You want to know why I was in the forest that day?"

I step back, fighting the panicked tingling that's reared up in my fingertips. I nearly freeze her in place for fear she might attack me, but I hold my power at bay.

"Because I wanted to leave!" she shouts. "I wanted to get away from Arthur!"

My heartbeat pounds into my ears, and adrenaline ticks through my veins. "Get away?"

"I'm just an ability to him," she says. "I'm not a person. I'm at his beck and call because of my power—constantly! I don't have freedom. And I don't have the liberty to tell him no. I owe him *everything*!"

Her chest heaves with the ferocity of a cornered animal, and her hands ball into fists.

"So, when he asked me to find you, I did. But instead of bringing you back to him, I wanted to join you. You and your people. Because living out in the elements seemed like a better deal than living one more day under Arthur's thumb!"

She takes a step toward me, and out of instinct, I retreat.

"There you were, living happily with a whole other group of people with powers, and I knew if I brought you back, Arthur would use you like he's using me."

She brushes her bleary eyes with the back of her hand.

"I was lying to him," she continues. "Saying I hadn't tracked you down yet, even though I found you immediately after your compound was bombed. And I fought with myself to leave the mountain—to leave and never come back. And I almost did. But when you and your friends got captured by Camille, Arthur saw the broadcast. He knew where you were, and he sent me. I *had* to save you and bring you to him. I didn't have a choice!"

Silence extends between us, and the late afternoon sun beats down with merciless heat. Birds are chirping in the distance, adding to the melody of the water as it tosses itself over submerged rocks.

"How did you find me after the bombing?" I ask, locking eyes with her.

"Arthur doesn't know everything about my power. No one does."

"Olivia." I say her name with a spark of aggression. "How did you find me?"

She's panting like she's just finished a sprint. Wiping away a loose strand from her face, she tilts her head, studying me. She puts her hands on her hips. "I can teleport to a person just by thinking of them. I don't have to know where they are—or anything about them. I can just go. And it's been hell hiding it from that sneak, Terrace. I'm good at it now, but I can't hide everything from him."

I approach her cautiously, closing the gap between us. "Why do you owe Arthur everything?"

Angry tears spring to her eyes, and she steps back, her brow creasing upward. She looks like she's going to scream, but her words come out strangled. "The Area 7 Testing Center is still a Testing Center. You know that, right? Arthur still tests people and runs it as he should in society's eyes—even though it's fully staffed with people that have powers."

My stomach drops like I've missed a step, and perspiration collects on my brow. Olivia continues, resentment seething from her. And what she says next nearly stops my heart . . .

"I owe him everything because three years ago I failed the Test."

My mouth drops, and the tingling of my ability returns so forcefully it's hard to breathe. Power rumbles in my chest, and stars waltz around my vision. Olivia Turrick failed the Test? She was born in society like me? I gape at her, unable to believe it.

"And instead of the worldwide news broadcast you got when you failed, Arthur took me in. Faked my death. I went in for my Test, and I never came out. Brain aneurysm—that's what they told my family. They said it was a freak accident."

Tears stream down her face freely now, and she doesn't wipe them away.

"If I had tested at *any* other Testing Center, I'd *really* be dead. And that kid who failed almost thirteen years ago wouldn't be the latest news. You'd have heard of me instead—another Diseased One the government eliminated to keep the world safe! But society never knew about me. No one does. *That's* why I owe Arthur everything."

My pulse pounds into my ears, and as I stand facing this broken young woman, my heart aches. I don't have words. Three years ago, Olivia Turrick was a citizen of the world. She believed what I believed. If anyone understands the identity crisis and ingrained lies I've had to overcome, it's her.

My feet move, and before I know it, I throw my arms around Olivia and hug her as tight as I can. She fights my grip, but I don't relinquish. I grip her fiercely with unrelenting compassion, and after a moment, she sinks into me, hugging me back. We stand there on the bank of the river, holding each other.

After a minute, I release her. Tears blur my eyes, and I choke back a sob. "You're from society?"

Olivia twists her foot into the dirt. "Yeah. And I managed to keep it together. Damn, Hollis. What were you thinking? Going back to Area 19 like they were going to welcome you with open arms."

"I wasn't thinking," I say, sniffling.

Olivia looks out over the river. "We need to go. Arthur's expecting you."

My stomach knots, and my palms turn clammy. "Why were you crying? You still haven't answered."

Olivia's eyes darken. "Arthur knows I kicked Erwin out when I brought Keith to you. He wants to know what happened. And I won't . . . I won't tell him." She marches up to me, fierceness in her demeanor. "Don't look at Terrace. Don't! And don't say anything stupid. Okay? I . . . I trust you. We have to go."

She grabs my upper arm, and the blue orb expands around us with a brilliant burst. In seconds, I'm standing in front of the door to Arthur's office, and Olivia puts her hand to the scanner. It flashes and admits us.

Olivia pushes me forward, and I step into the stone room.

"Thank you, Miss Turrick," Arthur says. "That will be all."

"You're welcome." She ducks out of the room and vanishes down the hall.

"Miss Timewire, you look stunning." His eyes trace my dark teal dress, and heat rises in my face. I don't like the way he's looking at me. "Please, sit."

Out of my peripheral vision, I can see Terrace staring at me, but I don't look at him. I keep my eyes glued to Arthur's.

"What do you want?" I ask, disregarding his request to sit. I keep my demeanor respectful, even though I'm itching to snap at him. "My friends are waiting for me."

"How's your training? Have you discovered anything in my absence?"

Arthur leans back in his seat. His beady stare makes me want to look away, but I don't.

"It's going well. Jonah and I made good progress while you were away. I'm close to discovering what I've done to Ashton."

This is not, strictly speaking, a lie. I'm closer, but I still have no idea how to give him his power back. I run my tongue along my teeth, blowing air out slowly.

"That's good to hear." Arthur tilts his head. "Terrace told me something interesting."

I have to fight myself to keep my gaze off of Terrace. "Did he?"

"Miss Turrick brought Keith to you in my absence *without* his guard."

My hands shake so I stuff them behind my back. My heartbeat thuds louder. "Yes, she did."

He raises an eyebrow. "What was that about?"

"With all due respect, Mr. Evandrum," I say, and the polite words taste like poison, "that's none of your business."

"None of my business?" he repeats.

"Yes. None of your business. Don't you trust me?" I add the last sentence hoping it will appeal to Arthur's better senses—if he has any.

He grits his teeth, and the vein on his neck ticks. "Of course."

Nothing could be less believable. I bite the inside of my cheek to stop myself from saying something nasty.

"Good." I fold my arms across my chest, an idea sparking.

"Then release Keith from his guard. He's not a danger. That's been proven ten times over. And I'd like to enjoy the Festival with him *alone*, if that's alright with you. I've earned a break. Don't you think? We all have."

Everything in Arthur's face says he doesn't want to grant this request, and he stays silent for nearly a minute. I almost speak up again, but then he says, "Very well, Miss Timewire. Enjoy your time."

He pulls a paper toward him, scribbles a note in large loopy letters, then signs it. He stands, walks over to me, and holds it out.

"Give this to Erwin."

I take it, reading it over.

Mr. Keith Keaton is free to go. You are no longer required to guard him. Thank you for your services.

Mr. Arthur Evandrum

I look up at him, bewildered, but I decide against questioning this. I give Arthur a curt nod. "Thank you. Am I free to go?"

"Yes, you're free to go." Arthur holds my gaze with unsettling intensity. "Have a good evening with Mr. Keaton."

I fold the note, clutching it tight, and exit Arthur's office as quickly as my legs will carry me. I march through the pure double doors and head toward the aircraft hangar where the opening ceremony will take place. My mind is buzzing. What just happened back there? Arthur didn't push me. He didn't pry. And he released Keith without a fight. I shake my head. I don't have the emotional energy to ponder it. Keith is free, the Ability Festival is about to begin, and I'm going to have a night of fun for a change. The secrets I've learned and the questions I have can wait one more day. Tonight, I'm not a leader, I'm just a kid.

31

UPON ENTERING THE AIRCRAFT HANGAR, I WADE THROUGH the crowds of beautifully dressed partygoers and make my way over to Erwin. I shove Arthur's note in his face. "Read it."

He snatches it from me, readjusting his gun and frowning. His eyes scan the paper, landing on Arthur's curly signature. He crumples the paper in his fist and mutters something I can't catch, but it doesn't matter. Keith is finally free.

I give him a patronizing smile and wave him away. "Bye."

Erwin glances at Keith then gives him a stiff nod. "Mr. Keaton, you're free to go. Arthur signed for your release."

He stalks off, nose in the air, his gun slung over his arm with the barrel pointed toward the floor.

"Good riddance," I huff.

Keith, who's dressed in a gray suit and white shirt, tussles dark brown strands from his face. His smile makes my stomach flutter, and my heart skips with happiness. His bright blue eyes trace the dress I'm wearing, and his mouth parts.

He steps closer to me. "Hollis, you look . . . wow . . . you look beautiful."

Heat creeps over me like the tide coming in, but I'm hopeful the soft glow of the lights that hang above us helps hide what I'm sure is a fiery blush. The nervous jitters are wonderful.

"Thanks," I breathe. "You look beautiful too."

Keith laughs, brushing off his suit. "I believe the word you're looking for is handsome?"

"You look handsome," I say, grinning, and the desire to kiss him burns strong. I miss him. It's silly. He's standing right in front of me, and I miss him.

I look over my shoulder, making sure Erwin is out of sight instead of lurking. To my relief, I don't see him. There's only the growing throng of excited, dressed-to-impress partygoers, and for the first time since arriving in the mountain, even though we're in the middle of a crowd, I'm finally alone with Keith.

My abdomen squirms with the kind of happiness I've only ever felt with him. "I've been waiting."

"Waiting? For what?"

I throw my arms around him and kiss him full on the mouth. He catches me, sinking into the embrace, his soft lips moving tenderly against mine. Like a shock wave, my ability tingles through me, and I'm filled to the brim with joy. After several seconds of his wonderful warmth, we break apart, and he gives me that boyish smile that makes me all fluttery inside.

He pulls me closer. "Well, that was unexpected."

"You're free!" I squeal, rocking up and down on my toes. "Finally!"

"I'm surprised Arthur agreed to it."

"I don't know why he did, and to be honest, right now, I don't care." I wrap my arms around Keith's middle, and he hugs me. We rock back and forth a few times. "I'm just happy I can spend tonight with you without that hovering, grumpy shadow of a man."

"Me too. Want to find our seats? I think I saw everyone come in a minute ago."

"I'd love to."

We make our way through the sections of chairs, moving to the back of the hangar, where we spot Candice, Ben, Rosalie, Vianne, and Maddy, who are all seated and chattering away.

"Keith!" Candice's excited cry rises above the babble. She jumps up from her chair and her red dress whips around her waist. "You're here without Erwin? Thank goodness. About time."

"Hey little sis, you look nice."

Keith and I shimmy into the aisle of fold out chairs, taking our seats at the tail end of the row. Candice grins, her eyebrows wiggling up and down. She grabs Ben and points toward her brother. "Ben, look who's wearing a collared shirt. An honest miracle. I swear."

"Ah, yes!" Ben chimes, following Candice's playful manner. "Your brother's looking fine."

"Yeah, he normally dresses like a slob." She snickers at the jab.

Keith leans back in his seat with a charming smile, and without missing a beat, says, "Hey Candice, when I said you looked nice, what I meant to say was that dress makes you look like a girl. And it's quite a pleasant change."

Candice's mouth drops open, and Rosalie and Vianne giggle, but Ben lets out the biggest guffaw of all, which was the wrong choice because Candice whacks him over the head.

"Ow!" Ben holds his hands up, shielding himself from his girlfriend's energetic fury. "Why do I always get clobbered?"

Keith raises an eyebrow. "Nature of dating my sister. Sorry, friend. You signed up for it."

"You take that back, Keith Keaton!" Candice says, squinting at him fiercely.

"You want me to take back saying you look like a girl?" Keith muses, hand to his chin. "You sure about that?"

Candice's face turns as red as her dress, and Ben leans in, giving her a quick kiss on the cheek. "You look amazing, Candy."

Her stern face hardens, and she huffs at her brother, exasperated. "Keith!"

Keith holds his hands up. "Okay! Okay. You look good, sis. Ben's a very lucky guy."

She folds her arms across her chest, melting back into a smile. "Damn right he is."

"Hey, I think they're starting," Rosalie says, pointing up front.

She's sitting next to Maddy, whose big orb eyes get even bigger as the lights all around the room dim. The stage at the front grows bright, and a hush falls over the crowd. I crane my neck to get a good look, but I don't have to strain for long. A large wall screen mounted high above the hangar flickers on, displaying a view of the stage.

Arthur Evandrum, dressed in a shining white suit, walks on,

and everyone cheers. The clapping is so thunderous it's almost uncomfortable. The live feed zooms in on the podium where he places a sheet of paper. He clicks the collar of his suit, and his voice sounds over the space.

"Ladies and gentlemen of the mountain, welcome to the thirty-sixth annual Ability Festival."

Once again, everyone cheers—this time even louder than before. And I join in, raising my voice to holler with the group.

After a minute, Arthur raises his hand, and the room quiets. "It is my pleasure to officiate the opening ceremony. But first, I want to welcome the newest addition to our family. I am speaking, of course, of the people from the forest. It is an honor that you are joining us tonight. I am humbled by your bravery and courage in the face of adversity. We hope you will find this celebration to be a refreshing time to pay tribute to the powers that make you who you are. We face a frightening world beyond the safety of these walls, but you are part of this fight, and we thank you for the trust you've placed in us."

His hands slide up the podium, resting on the top.

"This night is a celebration of our journey from the brink of extinction to the brim of success. But most importantly, it is a celebration of our abilities, because they make us unique—not diseased, as the World Order would have us think. Our powers are what help us create a culture of beauty and astounding tenacity. Every power is precious—every drop of blood that courses through our veins is a gift. And one day soon, thanks to the heroism of many in this room, including Miss Hollis Timewire, we will share this wonder with the world so that they may know: we are not to be feared but *revered*."

Arthur stands proud, bolstered by the audience. I shrink back into my seat, a twisty sensation tying my stomach into a knot. Again, I'm thrown into the spotlight—not the literal one, but by mentioning my name, Arthur may as well have invited me to stand on stage. And that's a lofty sentiment. Revered? I don't think society will revere us any time soon.

The applause dies down. Then, Arthur sobers, speaking in a reserved manner.

"We have come a long way since the massacre, and out of honor for the brave souls that perished along the way, I ask that we start the evening with a moment of silence."

The room grows still, the silence heavy. It presses in on everyone with bitterness. I've never truly pondered the death toll of people with powers. A hundred years ago, so many died, and now that I know the truth, it breaks my heart in a way it couldn't have before I took the Test.

I grip Keith's hand. He gives me a gentle squeeze, and then the moment of silence ends.

"Thank you." Arthur bows his head, hand over his heart. "As is tradition, please stand for the ability pledge."

The creak of over a thousand chairs sounds in a chorus as everyone rises. My friends and I follow suit, looking around, lost on what we're supposed to do. Words appear on the wall screen behind Arthur's head, and voices soar together as one, reciting it:

```
My life I give to my people. With my power, I
fight for justice as our forefathers did before
us. With my mind, I seek ways to better my
ability. With my heart, I pledge allegiance to
the cause of creating equality for all with the
```

biomarker. And with my feet, may our march toward a better world always continue.

I don't say the words. They seem innocent, but something about everyone saying this in unison leaves a sour taste in my mouth.

"Please be seated," Arthur says.

The creak of chairs trickles across the room again as everyone sits, and the wall screen shines above like a beacon. Then, a video begins to play.

A woman, dressed in a silver pantsuit, sits in a large plush chair with a bookshelf behind her. She looks like a society member, but her eyes are kind, and her demeanor is welcoming instead of stiff. She wears rectangular glasses, and her brunette hair flows delicately down to her shoulders.

"We can't forget what happened to us," she says, her words silky. "We can't deny it. As we learn from antiquity, that's the first step in erasing history. If we ever forget the massacre, it may happen again. And it is for this reason we must preserve the stories of our ancestors—the people who had to fight to survive."

Her fingers fold together, resting gently on her lap.

"If you've been fortunate enough to be raised in our hidden world of powers, shielded from the Test, hidden from society, and well cared for by our leaders, then it is your duty to remember. For every person with powers to come, you must *remember* so the bloody stain of history remains in the past."

The woman's voice is enchanting—even melodious—like a spell, and as she speaks, the room grows so silent that no one dares to breathe. I listen to her recount the events of the massacre, and it's like Jacob Ganiston is speaking. I've been transported back to the night that ancient man told me his story. His friends and family were taken by the government, drugged, and murdered by the thousands—and he survived because his ability was to heal himself. Rosalie showed me Jacob Ganiston's memories when Tiffany rescued me from the government, and I didn't believe it. But with all my heart, I do now, and shame fills me as the video continues to play.

Wise, captivating, grief-stricken words flow like a river from her lips. It's hopeful and troubling and awe-inspiring all at the same time.

"And even though recounting this tale weighs heavy on our hearts," the woman says, bowing her head low, "we must continue this practice. Thank you for your listening ears, your willing hearts, and your courageous minds. May this year's Ability Festival lift your spirits and ignite your powers to new heights. Enjoy your time as we celebrate our unique and beloved way of life."

The lights in the room come up, and Arthur strides back to the podium, adjusting his tie. He stands there without saying a word, gazing over everyone with a fierce countenance. He holds his hands in front of his stomach, palms facing upward, and closes his eyes. Everyone in the room copies him, holding their hands to match his and closing their eyes as well. This continues for an uncomfortable amount of time, and Keith and I exchange weirded out looks. Stillness captures the room. It stretches on and on, holding us captive, and then it ends, and everyone opens their eyes.

Arthur clears his throat, and his voice booms over the room, causing me to jump. "Have a lovely evening. Let the festivities begin!"

The crowd springs to their feet, chatter explodes around the hangar, and my friends and I exchange a round of confused looks.

Ben fiddles with the cuffs on his suit jacket. "Well, that was . . . interesting."

"That was weird," Candice adds. She pops a flame onto her pointer finger then blows it out. "But never mind that! Let's go to one of the ability workshops!"

She pulls Ben to his feet. Rosalie and Vianne stand as well, Maddy alongside them.

"Workshops?" Rosalie says.

"Talent show? Workshops?" Candice waves a hand over her head as she exits the row. "I don't remember what they call it. I just want to go so I can show off."

Ben laughs. "That's my girl."

"And you're helping me show off," she says, grinning from ear to ear.

Ben slides her a sideways smile. "I'm helping? This is news to me."

Candice cups her hands around her mouth and leans over to whisper in Ben's ear. His face grows more mischievous by the second. Candice pulls back then gives him a quick peck on the cheek.

"Onward!"

She thrusts her fist into the air and pulls Ben after her.

Maddy, carried up in all the excitement of Candice's energetic disposition, grabs Vianne and Rosalie's hands and clambers forward.

I turn to Keith and shrug. "I guess we're going to a talent show."

My dress dances around my ankles, soft against my skin, and the nervous butterflies I felt earlier intensify. I have no idea what to expect, but I'm excited.

Keith shakes his head. "I'm not sure what my sister said to Ben, but this ought to be good."

We funnel in behind the masses exiting the hangar, and after a good trek through the softly lit halls, our group finds its way to Sector 17—yet another part of the mountain I'm unfamiliar with. As we enter the black-box, theater-like room, the lights that twinkle above us sparkle like a limitless diamond sky. It's so vivid that it looks like we're outside.

Maddy stares up, enraptured. So does everyone else filing into the enchanted space. Standing round tables draped in black cloth are set up in intervals throughout the room, and wire strings of lights are balled up into fishbowls at the center of each table, adding to the soft glow ambiance. And at the front, there's a raised silver platform.

A girl in a stunning earth-green gown steps onto the platform, sweeping her thick raven hair behind her shoulder. She surveys the room, dark brown eyes darting over the growing number of faces. Her rosy porcelain complexion lights up as she calls out in a lofty voice, "Alright, guys. You know what this is about. Let's go. Someone get up here."

Candice bounces up, unable to contain herself, but Ben catches her around the waist and holds her back. "Not first!" he hisses. "Candice, we're not going first!"

She knots her arms together. "Since when do you have stage fright? Mister magic card tricks. You love attention."

"Not first!" he says again. "See? Look. Someone is already up there."

"Chicken," she mutters, looking defeated.

A tall, odd-looking man with a crooked smile steps into view, hauling a large bag over his shoulder. A murmur bristles through the room, like everyone already knows what he's going to do. But those of us who are new stand, eyes glued to the platform, waiting with bated breath. The man crouches then pulls out twelve red balls, ten foam disks, six bowling pins, five knives, and two plastic hoops.

"I wonder what he's going to do with those," Vianne whispers to Maddy, hoisting him up on her hip so he can see.

I hook my arm around Keith's, craning for a better look. For a second, the man stands in silence. Then, with a loud pop, there are six of him, and he's juggling all of the objects he removed from the bag. There's so much to look at so fast that my brain spins. Two of his duplicates are on their hands, balancing the disks on their feet. One duplicate does back handsprings around the platform with the two hoops circling around an arm and a leg. And the other three toss the red balls and knives and pins between themselves in a captivating triangular pattern.

Cheering ensues, and Maddy claps, giddy.

"Wow, impressive," Ben murmurs, hand to his chin, studying the man. "I wonder if I could move fast enough to juggle all of that by myself."

I feel a light tap on my shoulder, and I turn around. It's the girl in the earth-green gown.

She sticks out her hand. "Siena Rose."

I take it, and we shake. "Hollis Timewire."

"I know."

My face flushes. Of course she knows who I am. "Right."

Siena's hooded dark eyes glint. "I suppose we won't be seeing your ability tonight? Or am I mistaken? I mean, you put on quite a show the other day in the dining hall. Three hundred people. But you've done more than that. A lot more."

My stomach flips. From the way she's speaking to me, I assume she must have been a volunteer for the training session where I heard the voice again.

"Yes, I've controlled more," I say.

"I volunteered out of morbid curiosity," she says. "Although, I didn't think I'd stop breathing."

I grimace. "Sorry about that."

She pulls a lock of raven hair through her fingertips, eyes hovering on mine. "All's fair, I guess. I stayed for the session."

"So, Siena . . . what's your ability?" Keith asks, clearly sensing my discomfort.

Siena turns to him, a sly grin curling the corners of her thin mouth. She pulls a small satin handbag from a hook on her dress and procures a tortilla chip. She holds it delicately between her fingertips then turns from Keith to me, grabbing my hand and placing the chip on the flat of my palm.

"Eat it," she says.

I shake my head. "Excuse me?"

Her hooded eyes grow more impish. "Look, I know you low-key suffocated me the other day, but I'm not going to poison you. Eat it."

Siena tilts her head, her raven hair tumbling to the side. She's staring at me intently, so I place the tortilla chip between my lips, pushing it onto my tongue awkwardly. I chew it up and wrinkle my nose at the texture.

"It's stale," I say.

I stand there, waiting for something to happen, and with a rush, an overpowering and tangible sadness seizes my chest. I gasp as the sadness sinks to my gut, and tears fill my eyes.

"Hollis, are you okay?" Keith asks, speaking quickly.

I take a gulping breath, staring at Siena. She raises her hand, snaps her fingers, and the feeling vanishes as quickly as it had come.

"What was that?" I ask, wiping the brimming tears from my eyelids.

"I'm a mood eater," she says, matter of fact. "I impart emotion on food. Whatever emotion I want. It's thrilling and kind of boring all at the same time."

"You impart emotion on food?" I repeat.

Siena points up to the platform. "Your friends are up."

I look over to see Ben and Candice flexing and stretching. Ben rolls his shoulders out, and Candice pulls her brown hair into a disheveled bun.

Ben shouts over the crowd in his best announcer voice, reminding me of the time he performed the card trick at the old compound. "Ladies and gentlemen, get ready for a spectacular show of flashy proportions!"

Candice flings her dress about her, and the way the skirt moves makes it seem like she's already on fire. Her hands flower open and flames spurt upward in an arc. At her cue, Ben runs around her with his super speed, and her fire grows, lengthening into a column that towers upward, lighting up the entire room. Then, Ben switches his running route, zipping around Candice in an oval, expanding the distance between himself and her fire. The flames grow even larger, flickering in proportion with the growing wind created from Ben's speed.

Everyone oohs and aahs as they finish. The flames die, Ben halts—fully visible again instead of a blur—and the two of them take a bow.

Keith slow claps, clearly amused. "Those crazy kids."

I giggle. "We're kids too, you know."

He pulls me closer. "Yeah, I guess we are." His hand brushes my waist, and the butterflies flutter through me once more.

As Candice and Ben exit the stage, a boy who looks to be a few years older than me jumps on stage, dusting his fingers through his spiky jet-black hair.

A girl from the front calls up to him. "Let's go, Yang!"

"Hey, Yang, do Evandrum!" another girl sings.

"No, do DuPont," the first girl says, snickering.

I watch Yang, unsure of what the girls mean. His hands obsessively brush through his hair as if he's looking in a mirror, and he grins down at the audience. Clearing his throat, he puffs out his chest, speaking with loud, clear diction, and the hairs on the back on my neck prickle.

In the carbon-copy tone of Arthur Evandrum, Yang asks, "Is everyone having fun tonight?"

The crowd cheers, and the two girls in front chortle, hands over their mouths.

"Well, that won't do," Yang continues in a sarcastic tone, now posturing himself like Arthur. He wags his finger. "We can't have fun. None of that. Back to work!"

Laughter echoes around the room. Yang struts across the platform, pulling his shoulders back until he's standing absurdly straight. He holds a hand to his chest.

"Newbies, it is an honor you're joining us. We hope you find this place to be a strict and dull home."

"Now DuPont!" the girl in front shouts, cackling.

"Careful now," he says, holding his finger up to his lips, his voice now identical to Terrace DuPont's. "Don't let anything slip or I'll tattle." Yang's bold, unashamed swagger drips from his tongue—a perfect twin of Terrace's voice. His ability is uncanny. "For I'm the biggest tattle there is!"

Keith whispers to me under his breath, "Looks like you're not the only one who doesn't like DuPont."

I grin, feeling a little too pleased with this boy's spectacle. "Apparently so."

"Now Beezee!" the girl cries, doubled over in mirth.

"Come get your checkups, child," Yang says, his voice changed to match Beezee-Day Jones. He swaggers around, sweeping an imaginary braid from his shoulder. "Don't forget to give your annual blood donation. You know how important that is, child. Give us your blood."

The mirth from the audience at the mockery continues, and Yang switches to voices I've never heard before, each as unique as the next. He flies through impression after impression until a woman shoos him off the platform with a stern look that could kill. She curses him out with words so quick I can only catch the phrases "damn mimic" and "so disrespectful."

"I'm starving." Candice sweeps her red dress to the side, bending down to scratch her ankle. She steadies herself by holding onto Ben's arm.

"Already?" Vianne sets Maddy down from her hip, and her hair turns to a pleasant shade of light pink.

Maddy jumps up and down. "Me too! I'm hungry."

"Well, Maddy, I've heard the banquet hall is open all evening!" Rosalie exclaims. She crouches to Maddy's level, her cream-colored, floral-patterned gown bunching up around her. "Want to head over there?"

"Yes!" he squeals.

"I could use some food too," Keith adds. He nudges me. "Shall we go?"

"Sure."

After another trek through the glowing halls, our group arrives at the lavish banquet hall. The tables, adorned with red velvet cloth, are stuffed to capacity with the most extravagant platters of food I've ever seen: cured meats and cheeses, colorful fruits and berries, candied nuts and raw vegetables, cakes and sweets—all laid out in decorative patterns. And the largest of the platters hold garlic roast chicken, glazed ham, and baked potatoes. The smell of the feast is mouth-watering.

Ben's eyes are as wide as saucers, and he pelts off toward the nearest table, leaving Candice behind. She hollers after him and runs in his wake, but she's unable to keep up with his super speed.

Vianne whispers behind me so that only I can hear. "Rosalie and I have Maddy. Go enjoy your time with Keith."

She scoops Maddy into her arms, and she and Rosalie take off down the line of long tables until they vanish into the masses of partygoers.

Keith and I find a more secluded spot near the end of one of the banquet tables. He pulls a chair out for me, and I sit, eyeing the beautiful bounty. It looks incredible, and I grab a plate, piling on a bit of everything. The food is melt-in-your-mouth, straight-out-of-a-dream delicious, and the fact that I'm sharing this evening with the person I most wanted to share it with makes everything all the more wonderful. We spend the next hour talking and eating until we're so full it hurts, but I don't regret any of it.

"That was amazing," Keith says. He leans back in his seat, hand over his stomach.

"I don't think I could take another bite!"

Keith's brilliant blue eyes glow in the soft lighting, and I catch myself staring at him. A warm, wonderful feeling fills me, and I take a deep breath, drinking in the bliss. This night is exactly what I needed.

"You look gorgeous," Keith says. He extends his hand to me, the biggest smile brightening his face. "Would you like to dance?"

I look around, nerves hitting me. "Here?"

Keith laughs and shakes his head. "Sector 17 has a ballroom next to the black-box theater."

"Oh." My stomach flutters like I missed a step. I don't know why I'm so nervous. It's just Keith, and even though I have no idea how to dance, I know it will be wonderful with him. My face flushes, and I lean into the feeling, embracing the unknown. "I would love to dance with you. But I can't promise I won't step on your feet."

He winks. "I'll take my chances."

I take Keith's outstretched hand, and he pulls me to my feet. The enchanting atmosphere of the mountain makes this feel like a dream. We hurry through the halls, heading back to Sector 17, and all the while, I'm trying to remember how to breathe.

Entering the ballroom steals away what little breath I have left. It's like the black-box theater—sparkling with tiny lights that litter the ceiling, creating the illusion of standing under a moon-less, starry night. Wall screens add to the ambiance, displaying swirling colors that float around the room, jumping from screen to screen. And the most beautiful music swells around us. The space is packed to the brim with partygoers who dance across the dark wood floor in sweeping formations. I can't help but stare at them.

"Woah," I whisper.

Without a word, Keith leads me through the crowd to the center of the dance floor. His right hand holds my left up while his other one finds my waist. I rest my free hand on his chest, and he pulls me close so that our faces are an inch apart. We begin to sway to the growing music, and as he leads, I find myself following with ease, as if I've known how to dance all along.

We stare at each other as the spell-binding melody continues. Keith pushes gently on my lower back, turning me under his arm. His hand catches mine, and now I'm dancing with my back to his chest, arms crossed over each other.

I close my eyes, feeling the sway of his body against mine, and the music rises, moving from one beautiful verse to the next. Keith spins me again, turning me to face him and pulling me in tight.

"Hold onto me," he breathes, and I follow his lead.

He wraps his arms around my waist, and I hook mine around his neck. Slowly, Keith and I rise together, our feet leaving the dance floor. He flies us up among the glittering lights, high above the ballroom, and as we turn round and round, our foreheads touch.

Keith's breath is warm against my face, and my ability tingles down to my toes. His strong hands steady me, and his lips brush mine. I sink into the kiss and warmth travels through every limb, filling me with the most powerful sense of belonging. I never want this moment to end.

We spin, lowering to the floor, locked in the embrace, and my feet land softly. My breath is heavy with desire, and after we break apart, I stare at him with a new longing. This kind of touch is bringing forward feelings I didn't know I could have. Everything about this is perfect.

"That was like magic," I murmur.

Keith smiles, swaying me back and forth. This feeling—this night—it's everything I didn't know I needed. I want to kiss him again. And as we continue to sway, I rest my head on his chest, breathing in the comforting scent of pine trees and earth. Somehow, he still smells like the forest . . .

Pop.

A loud sound shatters over the ballroom, the music stops, and all of the lights extinguish, casting everyone into darkness. People around us scream, and I clutch Keith, the blackness so deep I can't see anything at all. My heart jumps into my throat with a spike of adrenaline.

"What's happening?"

Then, crackling comes from the speakers, and all of the wall screens turn back on. There, on the displays mounted around the room, a live feed of the steps of the Area 19 Testing Center cuts through the darkness. And as the camera angle pans up to the roof, my heart drops and my body goes numb. I'm staring into the reality of my nightmares . . .

My mother is standing on the bitter edge of the roof, tears streaking her gaunt face. She's emaciated—her arms rigid at her sides, and her mouth pressed shut. To either side of her, dozens of people stand stiff, all the same—statuesque frames and mouths closed, bound under the only ability that could produce a look like theirs.

The camera zooms in, and shrieks like smashing glass come from the audio as one by one, starting at the end of the line, people step off the ledge of the Testing Center, falling to the steps below. Thud after thud sounds as bodies tumble down to the steps, breaking against the white marble.

It's as if it happens in slow motion. I look into my mother's terrified face, which is blotched red and smeared with tears. She's so clear—as if I could reach through the screen and touch her . . .

Then, she takes a step into nothingness, falling down the towering heights of the Testing Center and smacking the steps with a bone-shattering crack.

The scream that tears my throat burns worse than fire. My knees give way, and my heartbeat hammers into my face. Keith sinks to the floor with me, cradling me in his arms as we both stare up at the bloody carnage. More of the line tumbles to the marble—bones splintering and flesh squelching.

The screen glitches, and a new feed begins to play. It's President Alvaro Camille, and he's beside himself with grief, fully portraying it on live television. His normally kempt white suit is disheveled, and his dark hair is askew. He looks at the camera, clenching and unclenching his fists.

"Citizens, we have seen this girl's monstrous power before." His voice is laden with emotion. "Hollis Timewire is now murdering us out in the open. Her ability allows her to control every muscle in someone's body. We saw it the day she came to announce the initiation of the second Terror War. We saw it at the steps of the Capitol when she brought a thousand of my men to their knees in an attempt on my life. And now again, at the very Testing Center where she failed the Test."

Camille's chest heaves, and his voice turns to pleading.

"Take me instead. Spare these innocent lives. Please end the killings! Take me in exchange for these citizens. I'm at the Area 19 Testing Center. End this now. Please! Don't take any more lives. If you have an ounce of humanity left, Hollis Timewire, you will come out and face me."

He buries his head in his hands, lingering there. Then, he looks up at the camera slowly, and his stare pierces my spirit. For the smallest fraction of a second, the monster of his ability peeks through, the black in his eyes grabbing hold of my throat.

The feed cuts out, and the entire mountain is cast into darkness. Then, the harsh fluorescents return, razor sharp, and I sit limp in Keith's arms, stunned, the image of my mother's body falling from the immense heights of the Testing Center permanently scorched into my soul.

32

"I HAVE T-TO GO," I STAMMER, CLAWING AT KEITH'S forearms. My feet slip against the dance floor as I try to stand, but Keith grabs my upper arm.

"Hollis, no! You can't go. Camille will kill you."

I fight his strong grip. "I have to go," I say again, heartbeat pounding in my ears. "He just killed my mother. He's . . . he's going to keep killing people."

I push him away, everything in my body numb with anguish. That emergency broadcast cut across every screen in the world. He wanted to make sure I was watching. I'm gulping the air, trying my best not to sob, but I can't stop the cascade of tears that fall from my cheeks onto my dress. I attempt to stand again, but Keith isn't letting me.

"Hollis, no!" he repeats, holding me back.

My hand launches forward with the ferocity of a viper striking, and I grab Keith with my ability, forcing him away from me. He skids a few feet and gasps as if I'd struck him across the face.

"Keith, you can't save me from this!" I shout. The room's already palpable silence grows deeper. "No one can."

My chest heaves, and another bout of tears brims over, blurring my vision. I wipe them away, rage building in my gut. He killed her. Camille killed her. I stumble forward, and everyone in the ballroom backs away. I'm met with looks of pity—even fear. The anger in me is boiling over, and my ability vibrates through my limbs, alive with wrath. I want to kill him.

The cozy days in the mountain have come to an end, and the part of me that craved the small sense of normalcy I felt here is gone. I look back at Keith, grief closing my throat. The wonderful boy who would do anything to protect me can't rescue me now . . .

With trembling lips, I say, "Don't follow me."

I march out of the ballroom. My hands flood with tingling, and the fury in me sharpens. He killed my mother. She's dead.

Just beyond the doors, I stop walking. I'm so overcome by my ability that all I can see is stars. My vision tunnels, and as I reach out to steady myself on the cold stone, the reality of the situation crashes over me. Camille set this up to win. I must go to him. If he kills me, then he's a hero in the eyes of the world, but if I kill him, he's a martyr—and the lie sinks its teeth deeper into the neck of society.

I want to scream, to tear out my hair and burn the Testing Center to the ground with him in it. But I can't. I will not let him do this to me. He doesn't get to change the future I want to create. He is going to pay for what he's done to society's face, and I will make the world see him in all of his ugliness. Rage cuts deep to my bones. Even though I want to rip his heart from his chest, I must keep him alive. Society has to know the truth about him—and about me.

I charge down the hallway. Everyone I pass shrinks away, like I'm the monster Camille says I am, but I leave their staring eyes and gaping mouths in my wake. They can't help me. There's only one person in this mountain who can.

Sweat clings to my hairline as I run down the steps of Sector 2. The ominous, cave-like entrance is just ahead, and I barge straight through the middle door, adrenaline thudding with my pulse.

The guard on duty startles, holding his gun up and aiming it at my chest. "Stay right there! What are you—"

I grab him with my ability, speaking in a growl that compels his obedience. "Out of my way!"

The man's body seizes under my command, and he sputters. I flick my wrist, and his gun clatters to the floor. Then, I release him, and he falls to his hands and knees, gasping.

I stand over him with wrath in my veins. "Move. To cell D-3. Now."

He clambers up, scarcely able to move his legs fast enough, and we sprint straight to cell block D. Ashton Teel springs to his feet, alarmed at the sight of me.

"What are you doing?" he demands.

I channel my power into the man under my will. "Open his door."

With a jerk, he types in a code on the panel and places his palm to the scanner. It lights up, and the glass door slides open.

"Get out!" I order the guard. Tingling enters my chest, and I have to take a deep breath so I don't hurt him. He stumbles toward the exit, eyes bulging, helpless to do anything but obey me. The door clangs shut behind him, and I turn toward Ashton.

"Timewire, what the hell?" he says, his voice shaking. He's pressed against the wall of the cell like an animal caught in a trap.

"Ashton, I need your help," I say, my voice thick with emotion. Another wave of grief threatens to spill over, but I shove the feeling down. "President Camille is using his ability to . . ." I swallow painfully. "He's using his ability to throw people off of the Testing Center, and he's not going to stop unless I go to him."

Ashton's face shifts from frightened to something I can't name. It's different from curious. His shoulders, a moment ago tensed, now begin to relax, and he leans his head to the side, examining me.

"And how is that my problem?"

I have to stop myself from grabbing him with the ever-growing fury of my power. I flex my hands, taking control of my breath.

"I need your ability," I say. "I can give it back to you."

He doesn't speak. Instead, he stares me down, his face unreadable.

"A puppet master is nearly invulnerable," I continue. "But not to you. You're the only person who can help me. If you suppress his power, we can drug him. Then Olivia can bring him back to the mountain, and Maddy can take away his ability. It's the only way to do this without killing him."

A peculiar smile curls his lips. "You want *me* to help you kidnap the President?"

"Ashton, I need you." My voice trembles. "Please."

He pauses, his back still pressed against the glass, but he doesn't appear scared of me anymore. He slides a hand through his dirty blond hair, and his words slink from him, cold and unyielding. "All the power in the world, Timewire, and you still can't stop Camille?"

"No, I can't."

His tone simpers, and he speaks slowly. "After everything that's happened? You can't be serious. I tried to kill you, and you're coming to me for help? You must be desperate."

"I can't do this without you."

Ashton shakes his head, exhaling sharply. He pushes himself off the glass and takes a step toward me, his watery gray eyes unwavering. "You can give me my power back?"

"I . . . yes, I can."

He strides all the way up to me, his face towering over mine, but I don't shrink away. "I want my freedom, Timewire. It's because of *you* I'm in this hellhole."

"Done," I say.

He sneers. "You don't run this place. Evandrum does."

"Evandrum gives me what I want."

"Well, aren't you special." Ashton crosses his arms, his lips pressed into a smirk. "If I help you, you can guarantee my release?"

"Yes."

His eyes narrow. "Why should I risk my life for *you*? Give me a reason."

I gaze at him, struck again with remorse for what I've done to him, to his home, and to his power. "I can't take back what I've done, Ashton. And I regret it every day, but if I don't stop Camille . . . if I don't keep him *alive*, then we won't have a better world to go back to. I don't expect you to be my friend or to even care what happens to me, but I do expect you to care about people with powers—about the life *all* of us could have if I stop him. These people are taking over society one way or another, and I've just run out of time to stop Camille's assassination. Evandrum won't wait any longer. And if he kills Camille, I don't think the world will ever understand the truth about us. Please, Ashton. I need your power to end this peacefully. It's the only way we come out of this as the good guys."

We gaze at each other, suspended in uncertainty. He doesn't have a reason to do anything for me, and I'm not sure my appeal will change his mind. The silence between us stretches on, and I can't get a read on him. He's hiding his thoughts as well as a society member, but when I open my mouth to speak again, he beats me to it.

"Okay, Timewire, give me my power back."

The knot of tension in my chest releases, and power overwhelms my palms.

"I can't promise this won't hurt," I say.

I hold my hands over Ashton's heart and will the voice into existence. The presence arrives stronger than before, darkness hovering mere inches from me, and it snarls with pleasure, filling me to capacity with its strength.

I can hear Ashton's rapidly increasing heartbeat. I can smell the salted sweat on his brow. I can see every pore of his face, zoomed in and crystal clear. Every sense in me heightens a hundred-fold, and the predator of my power whispers in my ear.

Hollis.

"I need to give Ashton his power back," I say. "Teach me."

He is a threat to us.

"No, he's not."

He can beat us.

"Teach me." My arms shake with the severity of the power stockpiling in my body.

He is too powerful for us.

"Then why didn't I kill him before?" I demand. "Why is he still alive? What did I do? You said, 'kill.' Teach me!"

The voice snarls, as if reluctant to listen, but in my mind, a memory comes to me as clear as if I'd gone back in time:

"Well, the biomarker is just a result of gene expression," I hear myself say. *"I learned about it in biology class."*

"Gene expression?"

Tiffany's friendly voice stuns me. It's so real and so present that I can't believe she's not standing in front of me, alive once more.

The memory of me continues to speak, *"It's like a light switch. Some genes in our body only turn on at certain times. That's why the government tests people at sixteen. It's when the gene that produces the biomarker turns on. I guess it's when someone's biologically mature enough."*

The memory ends in a flash, and I gasp like I've been thrown into an icy river. I'm back in Sector 2, standing in front of

Ashton, pouring my power into his chest.

The creature of my ability growls, *do you understand?*

"The biomarker is a switch," I murmur, mouth parted. "And I turned it off."

Yes.

It makes sense now. The voice of my ability didn't want to kill Ashton, it just wanted to kill his ability. When I attacked him, I controlled him to the point of turning off his power. The predator within perceived him as a threat because he could beat me. He was stronger, and at my most primal, I couldn't have that.

I know what I have to do . . .

Inhaling deeply, I dig my heels in and pour out my power with intention. Ashton's face contorts, but he doesn't cry out, and as my ability intensifies, my hands turn from hot to scalding. I shake under the force. My heightened senses hone in on his blood—to his cells. The very feel of him under my fingertips is nothing but pain, but I'll bear it all to give him back his power. He said he felt like he was on fire when I attacked him, and that's exactly what the sensation is—fire, pure anguish. I scream. Everything in my body feels like a thousand daggers stabbing me over and over again, but I don't stop. It's not done. My ability is telling me to wait—just a few more moments.

I hold on, my entire body quaking uncontrollably. And the longer it lasts, the worse the agony gets, until I'm sure I'm going to die from the pain. At last, my hands stop tingling, my arms go limp, and the power surging through me dies. I stumble back from Ashton, and blood drips from my nose. I wipe it away with the back of my hand.

"Did it work?" I ask, panting.

Ashton flexes his hand, inspecting it. "Let's find out."

He advances on me, and I stumble back until I'm pressed against the thick glass of the cell. My hand springs forward in defense, filled again with tingling, but then my power is snuffed out, suppressed under Ashton's newly returned ability. He pins me against the wall by my throat, towering over me, his haughty face an inch from mine. And with his free hand, he strokes the side of my face.

I'm barely able to breathe.

"Are you afraid?" he hisses, his breath stale in my nostrils.

I stare up at him defiantly. "There are far worse things to be afraid of."

A taunting smile curls his lips, and he scoffs. "You're something else, aren't you?"

"Apparently so."

The moment between us lingers, and I'm not sure what to do, but then Ashton backs off. He swipes his hand, and my power returns to me. Silence falls between us.

"Why did you give me my power back knowing full well I could have just killed you?" Ashton asks.

"Well, I figured . . . I almost killed you. You almost killed me. We're even, right?"

He shakes his head, amused. "Damn, Timewire. You've got some guts."

"I know."

With Ashton on my side, this night might actually go to plan. All I need is to find Olivia and get the sedative from

Arthur. I don't know how long I have before Camille starts throwing more people from the Testing Center—all I know is I have to hurry.

I jog toward the door, ushering Ashton to follow, and wrath settles in my fingertips. "Let's go see Evandrum. We're out of time."

———

33

———

ASHTON AND I ARRIVE AT ARTHUR'S OFFICE MINUTES LATER, out of breath from the run through the labyrinth of the mountain. I slam my hand against the panel, and the door opens. Crossing the threshold feels like a death sentence; the eyes of nearly a dozen familiar faces greet me, unnervingly quiet.

Eli Stone, the lead Council member of our old community, sits stunned in a black leather chair with Libbie Lizette and Mr. Stuart on either side of him. They're attending to him as if he'd just fainted. Terrace DuPont and Hugo stand stiff behind a shell-shocked Arthur Evandrum. And Olivia Turrick and Beezee-Day Jones lean against the wall, clutching each other for support. All of them wear grave looks, but the face that breaks my heart and makes me want to stay is my teacher's. Jonah's brown eyes brim with tears, and I run to him.

"Jonah!"

He wraps his arms around me, and I sink into him.

"I have to go," I say, strangled.

"I know." Jonah's deep voice is thick with sadness. He squeezes me tighter, and as my head rests against his chest, I push back a sob. I don't want to go, but Camille's not given me a choice. I wipe my eyes, and he gently releases me.

Arthur's face is as pale as his hair, and he's trembling. He grips the collar of his white suit jacket like a lifeline.

"I did it, Mr. Evandrum," I say. "I gave Ashton back his power. And we're going to the Testing Center. I'm going to stop Camille."

Arthur's lips part, and he rises from his seat slowly. "You did it?"

"Yes. Ashton can suppress the President's ability. We can do this without killing him."

His shocked eyes soften, and something passes between us. He's looking at me like I'm finally a leader. Then, he speaks in the most respectful tone I've heard. "I must admit . . . I didn't think you could do it. But I was wrong. Please forgive me."

I exhale sharply. I never pegged Arthur as a man who would ask for forgiveness. He always seemed too proud. We stare at each other for several seconds, and I give him a curt nod. He bows his head to acknowledge me. And in this moment, we finally feel like equals.

"Do you have the sedative?" I ask.

He turns to Beezee. "Beezee-Day, please get a syringe of sedative for Miss Timewire. Quickly."

Beezee clasps her jittering fingers together. "Olivia, dear. Let's go."

Without hesitation, the blue orb envelopes the two of them, and with a blinding flash, they vanish.

Jonah's worn face searches mine. He looks beside himself with anxiety. He leans over his cane then sinks into the nearest chair. "Hollis, be careful."

"I will."

"Don't hesitate. You have to strike first. Do you understand? You're strong, and Ashton's power is to your advantage, but Camille's still a dangerous man—even with a suppressed ability."

"I understand." I grab his hand, trying my best to comfort him. "This will be over soon. You'll see. It's going to be okay."

I'm not sure I believe my words, but it's all I can offer him.

"Hollis?" Jonah's voice is weak.

"Yes?"

He does his best to smile. "You can beat him. I know you can."

Arthur fiddles with his sleeve, perspiring. "Miss Timewire, are you sure you're ready to do this? Because if you go to Camille, this happens tonight. You understand, yes? My people are prepared. All the Testing Centers must fall *together*. We can't give society time to regroup."

My heart rate spikes. "I understand."

Arthur looks at me like he's seen a ghost. "After all these years, it's time. We take society back tonight."

My ability hums in my chest. "Yes, we do."

Arthur leans over the table. "Miss Timewire?" He pauses, and the severity of his tone deepens. "You can do this."

His words stun me. For the first time since arriving at the

mountain, I feel like Arthur Evandrum is on my side. I gather myself, speaking quickly.

"Once we've drugged him, Olivia will bring Camille to the mountain. And I'll stay at the Testing Center to keep it secure." I turn to Jonah. "Tell Maddy it's time. Okay? I've talked with him about the golden light. He knows what he's supposed to do."

Jonah nods grimly. "Okay."

The blue orb expands from nothingness, pulsing as it grows, and I shield my eyes. Olivia and Beezee have returned with the syringe, and my ability rumbles in my palms, ready for the fight. Olivia, sedative in hand, walks over to me and Ashton.

"Are you ready?"

"Yes." I look to Ashton. "Are you?"

Ashton peers over the room of grave faces then back to me, his jaw set. "Let's go get the bastard."

"Hollis, how are we doing this?" Olivia asks. "Where do you want me to teleport us?"

My ability fills me to capacity, and my hands pulse at my sides. Arthur's looking at me with eerie calm. Something behind his eyes is unsettling, and it reminds me of the Chief Overseer of Area 19. She was the woman I betrayed everyone to prior to the bombing. Even with Arthur's sudden show of support, I don't want to be around him, and I don't want to talk in front of him.

I lean into Olivia and whisper so that only she can hear me. "Take us to the pond."

Arthur's steely gaze hardens, but he remains silent.

"Jonah," I say, and everything in me fights back a sob. My brow creases upward. "I'm going to beat him."

Olivia, Ashton, and I grab hands, and with one last glance at Jonah's face, I close my eyes, and the orb sweeps us away. Seconds later, my feet slam into hard dirt, and I rapidly take stock of my surroundings. The musty scent of stagnant water wafts through the evening air. The dried up bushes that line the pond are barely visible in the dark, and the three of us huddle together, our breath coming out in puffs in the crisp breeze.

"Here's the plan," I say. "Olivia, you teleport me to Camille—just outside of whatever room he's in. Then, I'll go to him. I need him to see me. *Only* me. Give me *one* minute. I'll be okay. He can't use his ability on me. Then, teleport Ashton and yourself into the room. Ashton, you suppress his power, and Olivia, you stab him with the syringe. We need the element of surprise to pull this off. I don't want him grabbing either of you with his ability."

Olivia's brow glistens with sweat. "Okay."

Ashton nods. "Let's do this."

I take a deep breath, and a spasm of fear settles in my gut, making me weak in the knees. Gritting my teeth, I pull power into my hands. I have to be ready to freeze anyone in that room. The three of us exchange determined glances, one last look of shared camaraderie before the quest—my enemy and the girl who also failed the Test, all together in this fight.

"I'm ready," I say.

Olivia's ability encircles us, and in a burst of blue, we leave the deserted pond behind. Seconds later, I'm standing alone in a sterile white hallway in front of an ornately decorated golden door. It's the same door I entered in search of the Chief Overseer when I betrayed my friends nearly nine months ago.

The Area 19 Testing Center. Somehow, everything always leads back to this place . . .

I inspect the frame. The side panel's been damaged, and the door hangs slightly ajar. With my power surging in my palms, I push the door open to reveal the blinding white room. President Camille sits alone at the grand arching desk, and when he sees me, his mouth splits into an evil smile.

"Welcome back, daughter," he says, standing at my presence. "I knew you'd come."

My hands sear with the ability I can't use, and my anger builds to new heights. "You killed her."

"I did." There's no remorse in his tone—only depravity. "Did you really think she'd come back with you?"

His words are a slap in the face. He knew I went to see my mother? Did she report me? Did he find out some other way? I want to scream, but I bite my tongue. Any second now, Olivia and Ashton will appear. I just need to keep him talking.

"Did you know?" I ask. "Back at the Capitol? Did you know?"

Camille sneers, the black in his eyes growing. "That you were my daughter?" His head tilts to an unnatural angle. "No, I didn't. Clever woman, your mother. But not clever enough."

Any moment . . .

I'm strangled by the emotion I'm holding back. "You're not going to win." My hands ball into fists as I say the words I said to my mother the last time I ever saw her. "Change is coming."

Flash.

Olivia and Ashton appear out of thin air directly behind

Camille. Ashton's hands are outstretched, and his power pours into the President to snuff out his ability. Olivia launches herself at him, the syringe coming down toward the flesh between Camille's neck and shoulder. But Camille catches Olivia's wrist, holding the syringe at bay, and she shrieks as he lifts her into the air, dangling her an inch off the ground. His free hand points toward Ashton, and Ashton begins to shake uncontrollably, but he doesn't freeze. He's still free from the President's control.

"Oh my!" Camille taunts, as Olivia struggles in his iron grip. "And who are you, young man? You have quite a powerful ability."

"Hollis, I can't hold this for much longer!" Ashton cries. "He's fighting me!"

Then, several things happen at once: I spring into action, trying to cross the distance between myself and Camille, Olivia claws at the President's arm, and a gunshot shatters my eardrums.

The silver weapon smokes, clutched in Camille's dominant hand, and Ashton collapses to the floor, gasping for air. Blood soaks through his shirt just below his ribcage, pooling around him at an alarming rate.

"ASHTON!" I screech.

"That's better," Camille says. He releases Olivia and slashes his hand over her heart.

"NO!"

With both hands, I grab for Olivia, and the two of us fall into a deadlock, battling it out for control of her. I will the creature inside me to come alive, and it obeys, curling behind me to give me strength. Camille's hold over Olivia shrinks, but I can't shake him.

"You're stronger!" he snarls, licking his lips. "You understand, don't you?" The whites of his eyes completely disappear, and the guttural growl that issues from him sends a shiver down to my bones. "But you can't beat me, daughter. My voice is greater than yours!"

His monster pushes back against mine, and Camille hurls his palms toward the wall, carrying Olivia in his wake. With a crack, her head smacks against the wood, and she falls limp next to Ashton. A gash pours blood down the side of her face, and the syringe skids several feet across the white tile.

"OLIVIA!"

Camille flexes his hand, staring at me with merciless glee, and then he points the gun at Olivia's head, knowing full well I'm too far away to stop him.

With a cry, I do the only thing that could save them. I direct both of my palms toward Olivia's crumpled form, and with all of my strength and all of my will, I command her to teleport herself and Ashton to Beezee. Olivia told me once she could go to any person just by thinking of them. So the only name I repeat over and over again in my mind is Beezee-Day Jones.

The orb comes to life, drawing electric breath and expanding around them. It swallows them whole, and as they disappear, Camille unloads the magazine into the residue of blue that lingers on the floor.

But it's too late. They're gone.

"NO!"

Camille's enraged scream shatters the air in the room, and he looks up at me, feral. He slams his hand over a button on the curved white desk. Screeching as strong as an earthquake shakes the foundations of the room, and I stumble, trying to keep my footing. Thud after thud echoes from all around us, metal scraping against metal.

"Do you hear that, daughter?" Camille says, unhinged, the monster within growling deep. "That's the sound of our latest security upgrade: 12-inch thick, military grade, steel doors. The Testing Center is impermeable."

He rolls his sleeves up, baring his teeth. "You're not going anywhere, and this time, no one is coming to save you."

My eyes grow wide.

"Run, run, little mouse," Camille says, sweeping the tail of his suit jacket behind him. "Let's see how your power compares to the great Puppet Master."

―――

34

―――

The syringe of sedative lies a foot from me, and I lunge, scooping it up with tremoring hands. Camille's soulless black eyes dart to the needle, and I stumble backward, turning away from him to run through the golden door.

Panic blinds me as I sprint down the white hall. My heart is pounding so hard I'm starting to see stars. Camille was ready for me, and now I'm alone, trapped in the Testing Center, my only hope clutched between sweaty fingers. How am I supposed to get close enough to inject him?

I make it past two sections of laboratories, taking a left then a right. But when I round the next corner, I skid to a halt. A hundred feet away, a dozen people stand silent, staring with unblinking, sunken eyes, their heads bowed so that their chins almost touch their chests. Then, in unison, they creep toward me, keeping their gaze trained ahead.

Grounding myself, I pull tingling into my hands, and the

creature rattles—a guiding force. I throw my hands forward, but nothing happens. The unit of zombie-like employees continues, slowly inching closer and closer.

I channel the tingling anew, pouring it from my fingertips with all my might, but still, nothing changes. Cold sweat trickles down my back. What is going on? Why can't I feel them?

With a crack of static, the speakers of the Testing Center come to life, and I jump as Camille's voice sounds directly over my head.

"How do you suppose this ends?" His maddened words echo off the tile. "What has that fool, Jonah, taught you?"

I spin around, but Camille is nowhere in sight. The horde crawls closer, now fifty feet away, and I try again, willing the voice awake. The darkness hovers right behind me. *Pay attention,* it sneers.

Camille's high, clear voice cuts through the starkly silent halls. "Why don't you save yourself the trouble, daughter? I can make your death quick. Why draw this out?"

I retreat as the dozen puppets advance. Splotches of black and blue streak across my vision. Why can't I freeze them? In a frenzy, I slam open doors left and right, frantically looking for the stairs. I find them four doors down and pelt into the concrete spiral.

With burning lungs and strained muscles, I descend the steps. *Bang.* The door splits open, and the group under Camille's power follows me, now picking up their pace.

"Help me!" I cry, desperate for my ability's lead.

It growls. *Do you not see?*

"See what?"

The speakers assault my eardrums. "I took my time with your mother, you know. She suffered greatly. She was a traitor, after all."

His words are like a blow to the chest, striking deep. But I don't have time to dwell on the horrible things he must have done to her. The slithering unit of the President's minions charges down the steps, gaining ground, and I scream. Leaping down the last flight, I burst into the lobby, my dress catching on the door hinge. I yank it free, and it tears.

"She said she'd do anything if I spared you," Camille jeers. "So I told her, in great detail, *exactly* how I was going to kill you."

My heart drops into my stomach, and fear grabs me by the throat. There, in the middle of the lobby, sits the metal throne—the same one they strapped me to when I failed the Test, the same one from my nightmares. It towers high, set upon a pedestal of black stone with cuffs sprung open on either armrest.

I spin around as a hand grabs my shoulder. The puppets are upon me, and I splay my hands, power searing my fingertips, but they're impervious to my attempts for control.

The nearest man arrests my arms, and I kick out, flailing my limbs. The two of us tumble to the floor. His grip loosens just enough for me to get free, and I scramble to my feet, sprinting away from him toward the glittering doors. I gape up at the thick steel just beyond the glass, towering high like a sentinel of death. Camille wasn't lying. This time, I'm not going anywhere.

The speakers crackle again. "Did Jonah teach you I don't play fair? Your time is almost up, little mouse."

The horde closes in, and I shriek, this time a dozen hands restraining me. I'm lifted from my feet, and even though I writhe, I'm no match for them. They move as one, dragging me to the metal throne, and nothing I do has any effect on them at all. Power runs through me as deep as my blood, but it builds in vain. What has Camille done to make them invulnerable to me?

"Help me!" I screech again, pleading with the voice.

Look at them, it commands. *Do you not see?*

I search the faces crowded around me, still struggling to free myself as they pull me closer to the throne. Their gaunt, unfeeling eyes are glued to mine, and their mouths sag open, but I don't know what I'm supposed to see.

Can you smell them? The voice builds in my head, growling louder. *Can you hear them?*

The group pushes me into the chair, and my back slams against cold metal. I'm fighting them with everything I have, still clutching the syringe, but I can't get free. Cuffs clamp over my wrists and ankles, and someone snatches the needle away. Then, one of the puppets shoves a wad of cloth between my teeth and ties a length of cord around my mouth, gagging me. Now that I'm restrained, the puppets retreat, standing to either side of the throne.

From the end of the lobby, Camille appears, a wicked look engraved in his hungry features. He procures a silver dagger from his suit jacket, and as he approaches, I thrash, hyperventilating through the gag. I'm so overcome by the tingling in my body I can scarcely stand the sensation.

I'm going to die . . .

The President steps onto the black stone pedestal. He brings the tip of the blade to my cheek, pressing it just hard enough to break skin. Blood beads down the side of my face, and pain slices through me like fire.

"I'm disappointed in you," he says. "Even with the voice, you're still weak."

Hollis, my ability whispers, *what have I taught you? Look at them.*

And even though I don't want to, I take my eyes off of Camille and place them back on the people standing around us. And this time, I see it—a shimmer, so quick I think I've imagined it—and something clicks in my brain. The creature has given me one thing I never had before: razor-sharp senses as powerful as an apex predator. And the people gathered here have no scent, no heartbeat, no blood, no breath . . .

I understand.

They're not real. None of this is real. The people who chased me are projections of light and energy, mere Holo-tech, and that's why I can't freeze them—why my power can't even feel them. The only real person in this lobby is Camille.

Find the flesh and blood controlling these projections, my power hisses.

The President's lips curl in pleasure, and the knife digs deeper. "I've waited for this. You're going to die like your bitch mother, and I'm going to savor the light leaving your eyes."

Gritting my teeth against the acrid fabric in my mouth, I direct power from my chest into my palms.

Flick.

The pent up energy within me explodes, and the monster sharpens my senses until I can feel every breathing, flesh-and-blood person in the Testing Center. There are twenty-three people left in this place. And even though I can't see them, I can sense them. I've never grabbed anyone who wasn't right in front of me, but instinct and the creature work together as one, and I take them under my control.

Mine.

Their heartbeats, their muscles, their very blood—all of it belongs to me. With authority, I compel them to end the simulation and delete the Holo-file, knowing beyond a shadow of a doubt that they have no choice but to obey the puppet master who commands them.

There's a glitch and a flash. Then, the metal throne, the black stone pedestal, and the dozen puppets vanish with a pop. Camille and I crash to the floor, falling several feet from the spot where the light and energy projections held us, and my body smacks against the marble.

Pain spasms everywhere.

Free from the restraints, I pull the gag down, gasping for air. Camille's face changes from stunned to enraged as he realizes what I've done.

I dive for the syringe, and he dives as well. But I'm closer, and my fingers close around the vial. I bring my arm down, aiming the sharp tip at his neck, but he knocks it aside with a mighty blow that nearly shatters the bones in my wrist.

I screech, tumbling backward but still managing to cling to the sedative. Camille rises from the floor, wearing a feral look.

The black in his eyes expands, but it doesn't stop there. Every muscle in his body swells until the sharp rip of fabric leaves the white suit jacket in tatters on the marble. His teeth elongate, his fingernails grow, and his stature heightens to monstrous proportions. He's still a man, but the creature inside has manifested itself physically onto his body.

The statue I saw at the Capitol of the conglomeration of the five creatures on the body of a man comes screaming back to my mind. The blend of a bear, a lion, a wolf, a crocodile, and a viper—he looks like that. And the howl of rage that issues from the depths of his soul turns my skin to ice.

"I WILL RIP THE FLESH FROM YOUR BONES!"

His hands tear the control of the Testing Center away from me, and my power quivers under the force. It feels like my palms have been branded with a hot iron.

Run, Hollis. Run.

I obey the voice, crossing the expanse of lobby before making it to the second stairwell that hugs the side of the building. My lungs feel like they're about to burst, but I don't stop. I take the steps three at a time, rocketing up several floors before grabbing the handle of a door that leads to level five.

Camille's deranged words rumble through the stairwell, echoing around the spiral. "You can run, daughter, but you can't hide! I will *find* you."

Stars hang across my vision, sweat soaks my dress, and blood drips from the knife wound on my face. And still, I clutch the small vial—my only hope of beating him. Camille's brutish transformation is seared into my brain: savage teeth, sharp claws, and bestial strength—of all the things I imagined his power could do, it was never that. How am I going to get close enough?

My body shakes. I don't know how much more strain I can take. My bones ache from tumbling from the metal throne to the marble, and my wrist stings from Camille's sharp blow, but I press forward because I have no choice.

Just ahead, the hall dead ends, and in a panic, I pull open a door to my right, plunging into the small, brightly lit room. The door clicks shut behind me. An examination table sits in the center of the space, covered in sterile paper, and a cabinet rests against the far wall. I back into the corner, holding the needle up like a knife and fighting to calm my racing breath.

The silence is suffocating.

Seconds turn into a minute, and a minute turns into two. Then, out of the quiet, just beyond the closed door, a snarl creeps through the seam of the frame, guttural and thirsty for my blood. And the doorknob turns.

35

THERE'S A HAIR-RAISING CREAK AS THE DOOR SLIDES OPEN to reveal the beast. My fight-or-flight response pushes the adrenaline in my body over the edge. I'm shaking so violently I can barely keep a hold of the vial, and my knuckles turn white, gripping my only defense. I'm dead if I lose this syringe.

Camille fills the entire entryway, towering above me, his breath heavy. He licks his lips, and his slimy tongue runs over canines an inch long. My heartbeat tunnels into my ears. The only thing between us is the examination table . . .

Camille leaps with bared claws at my exposed neck, and his brutish body slams into the table, knocking it over. I dive to my right just in time.

The table skids, crashing into the cabinet, and glass shatters over our heads. Taking my chance, I try to stab again, but he's too quick. His claws slash through my dress. They catch on my calf muscle, and I scream in agony. Skewering pain wracks my leg, thundering up to my hip, and blood seeps from the gash, soaking the teal fabric.

I have to get out of this room. I need to find people I can control. Without my ability, he's too strong.

Jumping to my feet, though every muscle in me protests, I lunge through the door. The slash on my calf pulses white hot, and my vision blurs, but I keep moving. I race down the hall, leaving spatters of blood in my wake.

"Where are you going, little mouse?" The President rockets into the hall on all fours, hunched over with a hungry gleam in his eye. He dips his head down and licks the dribble of my blood off the tile. Prickling with pleasure, he growls low, "You taste *so* sweet."

Find them. Control them. The voice of my ability is back, guiding my hands. *They are your shield.*

I'm filled with tingling, and I follow the creature's lead, reaching to find the twenty-three people I felt before. My fingertips vibrate. Camille still has everyone under his command, but he's distracted with me. His control is fractured. I can feel it. And my ability extends with invisible tendrils, snaking through the halls of the Testing Center.

Eight people are on level six—the floor directly above us.

Hurry, the voice says.

Goosebumps sting my skin, and my pulse thuds louder. He's right behind me. He's going to catch me. I hurdle toward the stairs as the President gains ground. Everything in me wants to look back, but I don't.

Ten feet. Five feet. Two feet . . .

His snarling brushes the hairs on the back of my neck, and I crash into the door, throwing my body against it to narrowly escape Camille's claws. He skids on the tile and overshoots the opening, which gives me the fraction-of-a-second head start I need to charge up the stairs.

My footsteps jar off the walls, echoing around the spiral. Just a few more moments and I'll have a chance.

"You're a slippery one, aren't you?" Camille's unhinged words follow me. "I'm going to tear you apart, and I'll *relish* showing the world your mangled flesh—the leader of the second Terror War, defeated at last. And society will know how *great* their leader truly is!"

I exit the stairwell onto the white tile. Here, the floor plan is open, and three glass-walled laboratories space evenly across the level. Eight people stand ahead—three in the first room, four in the second, and one in the last.

With a cry, I throw my hand forward, pulling the vibrations from my chest into my fingertips, and I take them away from Camille. The darkness rattles behind me, growling in victory.

The eight puppets lurch under my command, and I direct them out of the laboratories. They encircle me, and I hold my arms at the ready, the syringe still clasped in my dominant hand. Camille stalks through the door, emerging with fangs exposed. His look of rage pierces me, but this time, the panic I felt in the lobby isn't present. The darkness of my ability prowls by my side like a guardian—my mentor, my teacher. And now that I have puppets, I'm every bit as dangerous as the President.

Camille stops in his tracks, raising himself up from all fours to stand like a man again.

I call to him in a loud voice. "Do you remember what you said to me at the Capitol?" Blood still seeps from the wound on my leg, but the creature within dampens it. I'm so full of power I'm hungry. Nothing else matters but the beast standing a dozen yards away.

Camille sneers, running his tongue along yellowed teeth, and a cold smile splits his mouth. "I said a lot of things at the Capitol, daughter."

"Then let me remind you." I tilt my head and stare him down with a cold smile of my own. "There can only be *one* puppet master."

He throws his head back with a wild yowl of laughter. "And you think it's going to be you? You're *weak*. Even now, I sense the fear in you."

"Your trick didn't work," I say defiantly. I breathe in power like fresh air, and the puppets around me shudder. "I beat your Holo-simulation. And now I'm going to beat you. I'm not the timid girl I was before. I understand the beast, just like you said I would."

Camille screams, and his fingertips fly. I feel a tug through my palms. He's trying to take the puppets back from me, but with every fiber of my being I cling to them—the salted sweat of their skin, their terrified eyes, their fluttering heartbeats. Down to their bones, I own them, and the dark voice coils around me, strengthening my resolve.

I push back, the vibrations so strong they hurt. And his attempt to steal them away from me fails.

"They're *mine*," I snarl.

The President hisses, and for the first time, his face flickers with uncertainty. His hands twitch, but nothing happens.

"Your eyes are black, little mouse," he taunts.

"Then you should be *very* afraid." The eight people move in unison, bound under the precision of my control. "Restrain him!"

They charge forward, crossing the space between us in seconds, and he thrashes at them. His hands grasp for control, but this time, I'm stronger. And even though he claws at them, drawing blood as they close in, the puppets grab him and hold him down. He writhes, biting and kicking, but he can't escape.

I rush forward, raising the needle high over my head and aiming for his chest. But with a mighty crash, a huge blur of a figure collides into me. I smack the tile floor so hard my lungs spasm. For a moment, I'm stunned, lying there unable to draw breath.

The puppets under my power falter, and Camille takes the opportunity to wrench himself free. His hands move, slashing the air like a blade, and I'm surrounded—not by my own group of puppets, but by a different set. I stare up in horror at fifteen new faces. Camille just called the remaining people in the Testing Center to his aide . . .

"Bring her to me," he commands, a demented grin twisting his face.

The mob closes in, and hands grab every inch of me. They drag me to my feet, yanking my arms behind my back. Fingers twist through my hair, nails dig into my flesh, and bodies press around me. It's suffocating. The horde moves as one to close the distance between us. Then, the puppets pull my head back, exposing my neck to Camille's razor claws.

You still have eight, my power whispers. *Fight.*

With all I have left, I channel tingling into the people still under my control, ordering them to my side. They barrel past Camille and into the mob, pushing back. There are so many people around me I fear I'm going to be crushed to death. Fists and limbs and faces are everywhere, and I'm caught in the middle, the smallest in stature of the bunch.

My puppets wrestle with the President's puppets, and amidst the chaos, though my people are outnumbered two to one, I'm able to twist myself free. I stumble away, retreating as quickly as my legs will carry me. I'm sweating and bleeding. Every muscle in me throbs. But I keep going—all the way to the end of the level. There are no stairs here, only two large windows. The three glass laboratories now shield me from Camille, creating a see-through barrier.

He tears at his own hair, shrieking so loud it shakes the air in the room. Veins, thick as small snakes, pop from his neck, and all around his black eyes, tiny red blood vessels burst. With a powerful tug, I'm thrown to my knees as he pulls every puppet away, stealing them for himself. All twenty-three people—bound under a new master. And I'm left with nothing.

"I must admit," he says with a heaving chest, "I've misjudged you. I thought killing you would be easy. I thought I'd even have time to play with my food!" He snaps his fingers, and the puppets enter the first of the laboratories. They pull open cabinets and upend drawers, shattering glass and overturning lab equipment until the work room is trashed. After this, they exit and fan out, forming a line that sweeps from wall to wall.

I reach for them anew, vying for control, but Camille's latch is too deep. I can't get a foothold. I cling to the syringe, trying my best not to collapse. Hues of purple and red hover just along the lines of my peripheral vision. Stars mesh together with the blinding lights. And the pain in my leg sharpens once more, throbbing with each hammer of my heart. I'm going to pass out . . .

"What are you going to do now, daughter?"

He leers, relishing in the power he holds. His claws dance through the air, and the people bound under him move together. Scalpels and scissors and needles and knives glint in the harsh fluorescents, clutched between stiffened hands.

"You're out of puppets and out of time." He flicks his wrist. "Kill her!"

36

I've never considered how I would die. Ever since the Test, death has been stalking me like a shadow, but I keep getting away. The creature of my ability guided me out of the Testing Center when I failed. *You know what to do, so do it*, it said. And Tiffany rescued me from my home—she even took a bullet for me. Keith saved me from the three boys at the river, his sweet words forever impressed upon my memory: "You don't deserve to die, Hollis. I don't care what people say. You don't." And when all hope was lost, and I couldn't fight anymore, Olivia teleported me away from the Capitol—away from Camille—and her charmed phrase, "of course there are more of us," broke my understanding of the world wide open.

I've been spared over and over again. Maybe there's no reason or rhyme to it. Maybe it's luck or fate or whatever they call it these days. Or maybe I'm the person in the story people die for even though I haven't earned it. Whatever it is, I'm here again, staring death in the face like an old friend. He's come to call, and this time, there's no one to shield me.

I raise my hand feebly toward the horde of puppets, taking what power I have left into my fingertips. The array of sharp weapons is seconds away from tearing me to pieces. This is it. I don't know if I can take them back . . .

The voice rumbles stronger than an earthquake in my head. *NO. WE SURVIVE.*

The darkness detaches itself from my back and slithers around to look me full in the face. Red eyes burn like hot coals. Its black snake-like body hovers a foot away, coiling and uncoiling in mid-air. I gape at the creature, heart rattling in my chest. What am I seeing? Am I going mad?

It bows its head low to acknowledge me, and without words, it tells me that I'm the only soul in the room who can see it. The mist of its ethereal body shifts in and out of focus. Then, the creature shatters into a thousand peppery flakes with a screech.

Time stands still . . .

A snow globe of black swirls in the air. It's like magic—peaceful and impossible and frightening all at once. And as I reach out to touch it, I'm thrown out of the present and into fragments of memory that appear as a kaleidoscope of color.

I'm standing in the middle of the training room back in the mountain, and Jonah is with me. "You're not like him, Hollis, but you are a puppet master. We need to work with what we saw Camille do. And once we've exhausted that, perhaps we'll discover something new to your ability—something Camille can't do."

"*You really think so?*" I ask.

"*Yes. I do.*"

Flash.

Crying bitter tears, I sit with Jonah in his room. He's kneeling in front of me with a gentle, fatherly look.

"*Talk to me. What's going on?*"

"*I respect you too much to not listen to you. And if you told me not to go to the city, I would obey you. Because . . . you're my family, and I love you. So, please don't forbid me to go to her. I have to see her.*"

He looks up at me with a worn face. "*I love you too, Hollis. I can see how much this visit means to you. I won't forbid you to go to her.*"

Flash.

Wind whips around me at the dried up pond. My mother and I embrace, holding each other tight. I don't want to let go. She's weeping openly, and her lips brush my ear.

"*I love you, Hollis.*"

Flash.

"*What do I have?*" I ask, facing my teacher.

Jonah's staring at me, and his response strengthens my resolve. "*Your heart. That's what makes you two different. The President doesn't feel things like you do, and one day he'll pay the price for that. Your emotion is what feeds your strength. It drives you to excellence, and I am proud of you.*"

Flash.

"What if I become like him? What if I can't stop myself?" My eyes blur with tears.

"Hollis, you are nothing like that man."

"How do you know?"

"Because your heart is full of good. Hollis, you have an incredible drive for truth and justice, and more importantly, you have a family here that cares about you. You've experienced friendship. Love. You know what it's like to feel now. The President doesn't have that, and that's what sets you apart from him. He can't feel the way you can. He doesn't know how."

Flash.

I'm sitting with Maddy and Olivia on the floor of the Holodeck, and the blocks lay strewn across the rug. I cradle Maddy in my arms.

"How do you stop feeling sad?" he asks.

"I remember that I have people like you in my life. Then I don't feel so sad anymore." Olivia and I lock eyes, and I smile. *"And new friends that come in unexpected ways. Like when we came here."*

Maddy peers up at me. *"New friends?"*

"Yes. There are a lot of wonderful people here with special powers just like Sissy. We all have our own unique type of light. Many aren't gold like yours, Maddy, but the light is still there in all of us. Remember that."

"I'll remember."

The memories come faster now, blending together into a symphony.

My friends and I sit, holding hands at the center of a table in the dining hall as we share an unspoken moment of camaraderie.

We nearly died in the President's office at the Capitol, but we didn't, and peace fills me knowing that we made it out alive . . .

Keith and I are dancing in the ballroom, flying high above the others, locked in that wonderful kiss. We spiral together to the enchanting music. His lips are sweeter than anything I've tasted. Home. He's home . . .

Olivia and I hug each other fiercely on the muddy bank of the river. She's from society too. For everything we've been through, for every lie society has told us, for all that we've lost. We're here. We fought. We survived . . .

Maddy's melodious words drift through the air. Over and over again he says, *"Don't be sad."*

Then, Vianne's voice blends with his. *"I believe in you. Okay? You're not alone."*

And now I'm standing at the steps of the Capitol with a sea of military men before me. I will not let Camille kill Jonah. I will not let him take Jonah away from me. I cry out into the torrent as my hands grasp control over every person before me. No one is going to die today . . .

The kaleidoscope of memories stops, and I'm pulled back to the present, where the peppery mist once more lingers in the air. It's perfectly still. The mist coalesces, forming the snake-like creature. It gazes at me with red eyes and coils in a looped pattern.

Do you understand?

Tears brim, spilling down my cheeks. "Yes."

Then draw your strength from them, it says. *We survive.*

The creature bows low, paying respect to its master. With a screech, it dives, rushing back into me, and a surge of energy fuels my hands. Tingling consumes every cell in my body.

Then, time resumes . . .

Camille's puppets swing their weapons at my head. My hands explode toward them, and in my heart, I think of Jonah and Keith and Maddy and all of the people who love me for who I am, despite everything.

I wrench all twenty-three of them away from the President. They freeze, inches from me, suspended in a run. Control washes over me, and the creature roars in victory, relishing in the triumph.

I flick my wrist.

They drop their weapons.

Metal clashes against tile.

Camille's look of astonishment seals my certainty. They are *mine*. I raise my hand, pushing power into the people under my will. They turn to face him, and I open their mouths, forcing them to speak as one. Their voices sound together in an eerie chorus—my mouthpiece.

"Your reign of terror is over, Camille. You're done hurting people, and you're done blaming everything on me. You're going to pay for your crimes, and the world will finally see you for what you are: a dictator and a coward."

Taking a deep breath, I command them forward. "Hold him down!"

Camille shrieks, trying to tear them away from me, but his attempt feels feeble at best. There is nothing he can do to take the puppets back. I own them. The twenty-three rush him, piling on top of him and grabbing his arms and legs. And even though he howls and writhes and fights, there are too many of them.

They stretch him spread-eagled on the white tile, pinning him down, and I approach. He stares up at me, wide-eyed. I've never seen such a look on his face. He's always been so cold. But he's helpless now. Afraid.

I grasp the syringe and kneel by his head. Without hesitation, I plunge it into the flesh between his neck and shoulder and empty the contents of the vial into his blood. His black eyes light up, and he stops struggling. He's staring at the lights above us with an open mouth, and for several seconds, he remains in shock. But when his eyes roll back, my heart skips a beat . . .

He begins to shudder violently, his muscles spasming. His body contorts, and he arches his back, limbs flailing. Gurgling issues from his throat, and he starts foaming at the mouth with a locked jaw.

"No . . ."

I pull on his arm and turn him to his side. He continues to convulse. Saliva mixes with bile as he thrashes. And I'm caught in the horror, watching him choke on the fluid coming up his esophagus.

"NO!"

His body gives one last shudder, and he curls in on himself, motionless. I lean over him, and my fingers trace his neck to find his carotid artery. No pulse lies underneath. He's dead.

I sit there, stunned, staring at the needle sticking out of his skin. My stomach sinks, and realization hits me like poison. It was never a sedative . . .

I killed him.

Everything I had been working toward, the new world I wanted to build, the minds and hearts I hoped to win over with Camille's trial—all of it, gone. And the worst part: society will know I'm his assassin. Rage builds in my chest, and I throw my head back, yelling at the ceiling.

"EVANDRUM!"

I leap to my feet, pulling the puppets in my wake. Tingling reverberates through them, and I command them to lead me to the Testing Center's control room. We move together as one organism, twisting through halls and up the stairs until we reach the place where I can free myself. The thick steel doors still bar me from escaping, but not for long. My ability guides my selection, and I grab the man who knows the codes.

He lurches under my fingertips and rushes to a panel situated on the far wall. He taps on buttons and flips a switch. The earth-shaking groan of the doors rumbles through the entire building, and I turn on my heels, exiting the room.

The puppets flank me on either side, a warped entourage bolstering my wrath. We slink down the spiral steps and arrive in the lobby minutes later, where the glittering glass doors sit unobstructed. We exit the Testing Center, but as I emerge, grief replaces my rage, and I halt at the top of the steps.

Dawn is peaking over the horizon, and the cold morning air whistles through the silent city. It's as quiet as death, and the scene before me steals the breath from my lungs. The bloodied, broken bodies of the people Camille threw off of the roof are still here. Their dead eyes stare in every direction.

I choke back a sob, sinking to my knees. I clutch my chest, and even though every part of my spirit is telling me to look away, I don't. My gaze lands on my mother. I cry out, and it scorches my throat like smoldering sulfur. Then, I collapse onto the marble. The people under my command stagger, but even in my grief, I don't relinquish control.

Pain sears down to my soul. She's gone. I'll never get her back. She died in fear, obeying a regime that tossed her aside like garbage, and I was too late to save her. And the man responsible for her death—the man I hoped would stand trial to the world so they could finally learn the truth—is dead by my hand. Society has its martyr now, and Evandrum knew it would end like this . . .

I'm stranded in the city with no way back to the mountain, charged with keeping Area 19 under my ability until Arthur's people come. I lie on the steps, numb. And as the sun rises above the skyline, something stirs in my heart—a desire to lay my mother to rest. To honor her one last time. The beautiful, fragile woman who raised me.

My fingertips curl, and I direct the puppets to help me. They reach down with gentle hands and pull me to my feet. I turn away from the bodies on the steps and walk back through the glass doors of the Testing Center.

With a flick, I compel one of the nurses to my side.

"Go get some bed sheets," I whisper.

She leaves me, and after a few minutes, she returns with the sheets in hand. I turn to a man on my right, channeling the tingling into his chest.

"Find some shovels from the houses across the street."

He obeys, exiting through the doors and walking down the steps. With grief in my soul and pain in my heart, I pull the group of puppets with me. I step across the threshold of the Testing Center, crying tears that flow down my face like a stream.

My hands curve in a beautiful arc, and the people move together in sync.

"Wrap her in the sheets."

Tender hands pull my mother's body from the steps, and the puppets, under my flawless control, fold her into the white cloth. Every movement I force over them is gentle. Every motion deliberate. They are handling her like they knew and loved her too. She deserves nothing less.

"Follow me," I command.

The puppets carry her in my wake, and we walk down the steps into the empty street. The man I'd sent for shovels returns to my side with three in hand, and he falls in step with the others. I'm bleeding, and every part of my body is in agony, but I put one foot in front of another, pressing forward toward the outskirts of the city.

As I continue, people emerge from housing units. Some of them shriek at my presence, and others are silent. But it's the military men who stir my anger. There's a team of them at the end of the block. They raise their weapons, taking aim at my chest, but I pull them under my power with a slash of my palm, gagging them with my ability. They join the group carrying my mother.

One by one, I take more and more. Anyone in my way becomes my puppet. Hundreds of them collect under my power. We move as one, traveling to the edge of Area 19.

At the end of the sidewalk, cracked dirt protrudes into an expanse of open plain. Everyone marches in silence, and ten minutes later, I hold my hand up to stop them. We've arrived at the dried up pond. This is the last place I saw my mother alive— and the place that holds the most precious memories I have of her.

With a flick of my wrist, the man with the shovels passes two of them off to other men, and the three of them start to work.

Sadness seizes my chest in the rising sun. Light shimmers off the water, glittering in a beautiful pattern as the surface ripples in the breeze. My body feels like it's on fire. The deep slash mark on my calf still oozes with blood, and stars flicker in my vision, but I stand still, bearing the pain and crying bitter tears.

The men take half an hour to dig her grave.

With delicate care, they place my mother's body in the hole. I grab a fistful of dirt, and with a sob, I toss the dust over the white sheet. Then, my fingertips twitch, and the puppets cover her, shoveling the pile they'd created over her body until the sheet vanishes from view.

I kneel, kissing my palm and placing it over the packed earth. "I love you, mom. I will keep fighting for a better world. I promise."

Rising to my feet, I wipe my tears and turn back toward the city with scorn in my heart. The tingling prods me forward, so I listen, and the creature of my ability curls at my side, visible only to me. The puppets, forced to obey, follow me with quick steps, and we head back into the unfeeling arms of Area 19.

We travel block by block, everyone at my mercy. Besides the sound of shuffling feet, the streets are quiet. The morning is older now, and the sun glints sharper than a knife off of the reflective buildings. When we reach the Testing Center, I bring the brigade of puppets to a halt. I stand in the middle of the street, gazing up at the monument with hatred. It swelters beneath my skin at Arthur for how he fooled me.

I swear on my ability, Arthur Evandrum will pay . . .

Abruptly, a hair-raising noise echoes off of the surrounding buildings.

I spin on my heels, heart pounding. The screen on the nearest street transit stop flickers to life, and with it, every other screen in the city. Down the block as far as I can see, pixels burn bright, and what little stamina I have left snaps like a twig underfoot.

There, on the display right before me, Arthur Evandrum stands tall. He's in his office in the mountain, a haughty look chiseled across his flawless complexion. His crisp white suit is pressed to precision, and his gelled-back hair rests at the nape of his neck.

"Citizens." His voice booms over the street and across the entire globe. "Let me introduce myself. My name is Arthur Evandrum, Chief Overseer of the Area 7 Testing Center, and I am a Diseased One."

He pulls his shoulders back, fingering his sleek white tie.

"Today is a historic day. The Testing Centers of this world have fallen. We've infiltrated your most sacred institution to put an end to the Test and everything it stands for."

His voice swells, rising like an anthem to every ear on the planet.

"You have learned that the Diseased Ones are murderous and vile creatures—mistakes of evolution. You've been force-fed rhetoric that conjures images of slaughter and destruction. Even as you listen to my words, you may be thinking the worst—that now may be the hour of your death. But I tell you, do not be afraid. I speak to every man, woman, and child: we have not come to kill you. We do not want any blood on our hands. Though you may think me a liar, I am here to tell you that history is not what it appears to be."

He pauses to relish in the momentum of his speech.

"How long have we been striving for greatness? More than a lifetime! A hundred years of hate. Of blood. How many times have we been crushed, silenced, and beaten down? Too many times to recount. We were the people you deemed fit to discard. Because of our blood, we were persecuted. Murdered. But we bore the privilege of this fight with dignity, and now we've risen from the ashes, ready for a new world. Change is here. A revolution is upon you—and we did not come unprepared. For no revolution is worth anything unless it can defend itself."

Arthur breathes his words like fire, his eyes alight with power.

"History is happening right in front of your eyes; it takes all of us by the throat and forces a decision. And we have decided that we will hide no longer. It is our birthright to take back our place in society. Progress cannot be halted. Make no mistake. People with powers are here to stay. And to be our enemy is to be a soul marked for destruction, but to be our friend is to be a soul cleansed through repentance. You do not have to fear us if you do not plan to fight us."

Arthur turns to signal someone I can't see. Then, a second feed begins to play, displaying a view of the towering Capitol in all its grandeur. Trumpets sound, and over the side of the building, a giant white flag unfurls. At its center, a golden woman wears a lavish robe and holds her hands in front of her stomach, palms upward. And her eyes are closed.

I stare at the symbol, ice zipping through my veins. My whole body begins to tremble. It's happening, and all I can do is stand with the rest of the world and watch.

Arthur's voice surges over the city, and the feed changes from the Capitol back to him.

"Hear me, citizens, and listen well. We will no longer be known as the Diseased Ones, for we are not diseased. Our blood is more noble and precious than you could possibly imagine. From this day forward, you will call us the Pure Ones, and I, Arthur Evandrum, am your humble leader." He closes his eyes and holds his hands in front of his body, palms open to the sky. "Welcome to the new World Order."

ACKNOWLEDGEMENTS

Wow! This book was a long time coming. Since Book 2's release, I had a baby, resigned from my teaching job, and moved to a different state. Part of me felt like I would never finish The Pure Ones. It's been in my mind and on my heart for years. I came up with the scene at the end of chapter 31 back in 2017. That's how long of a journey it's been! But I did it. We're here. And there were so many wonderful people who helped me along the way.

First, to my husband: Steven, I'm so blessed to have you by my side, nerding it out with me and plotting all kinds of twists. You've read every draft of anything I've ever put in front of you. Honestly, you're a saint. You are my best friend, and I couldn't have done this without you. Thank you for being my number one fan and always encouraging me to pursue my writing dreams. This book wouldn't be as good as it is without you. We've spent years together working on this series, and I can't begin to express to you how grateful I am for everything you've done. I love you so much!

Next, to my critique partner: Josh! Excuse me, sir, but you're the best thing to have happened to this book. Your feedback was amazing! It allowed me to craft a clearer and more poignant story. I am forever thankful for your insight and your friendship. Thank you for all the video chats, emails, and DMs we exchanged during the drafting process. You're the real M.V.P.

To my editor: Miss Holly! I can honestly say that you're the reason why I'm a better writer. I've learned so much from you, it's crazy. Through this entire series, you've been there to guide my thoughts. Thank you for taking a chance on little newbie me back in 2019 and nurturing the storyteller in me. It's changed my life.

To my parents: You've always supported me in my endeavors, and that means a great deal to me. Thank you for praying for me, loving me, and being there for me through everything (for bookish stuff and for non-bookish stuff.) I love you!

To my siblings: Michelle, you've been the most tender-hearted and compassionate support. I treasure your kind words, and I'm so happy you've been a part of this process from the very start. And GIRL, chapter 25 was born from *your* suggestion that Hollis needed to have a "mom scene," and I am forever in your debt. I think it's the most impactful scene of the book. Luke, you've been the best at spit-balling ideas. You've helped me brainstorm some amazing twists along the way. And don't worry, you'll always get your "not for resale" copy of any book I release. Gabby, thank you for being a superfan of my series. Your comments make me feel so special. I'm happy you love the world I've created. Your support means so much.

To my beta readers: Molly, Jessica, and Sky. I love you ladies to death! I appreciate your time and your insight. You've helped me smooth out the rough patches. And I know I can always count on you for support and encouragement. Thank you for being such great friends.

To my proofreader: Tony, thank you for the amazing work you do. You're so good at catching mistakes. You've been with me since the start of this series, and I'm thankful for you!

To my savior: Jesus, thank you for giving me the passion for storytelling and giving me the drive to be studious and learn all that I can from those around me.

To my readers: You're the reason I do what I do. Thank you for trusting me to take you on this adventure. And thank you for making me an author! :) If you enjoyed this book, I'd love it if you'd consider leaving a review on any platform. Reviews help me reach more readers!